I0565510

Innocence

Murdered

By: GABRYEL KEVYN

Copyright © 2017

The Cassie Publishing House

ISBN: 0-9801432-3-3
ISBN: 978-0-9801432-3-2
First Edition

All rights reserved. No part of this book may be reproduced in any form or by any electronic or mechanical means, including information storage and retrieval systems, without permission in writing from the publisher and writer, except by a reviewer who may quote brief passages in a review.

The characters and events in this book are fictitious. Any similarity to real persons, living or dead, is coincidental and not intended by the author.

Gabryel is an accomplished novelist, songwriter, poet, lyricist, videographer, and music producer. He lives in Philadelphia, Pennsylvania.

Cover Design and Front Photo: Gabryel Kevyn
Back Photo: Kristine Di Grigoli (ArtChick Photography)
Editing: Gabryel Kevyn and Linda Foster

For more about Gabryel, including his music, please visit him at GabryelKevyn.com

Greed Motivates...

Revenge Kills...

(Philadelphia, City of Brotherly Love – 7:05 p.m.)

The Beginning ~

THE ICY BLADE CREPT DOWN her soft cheek. She shuddered. In an instant, the razor-sharp edge could easily slice her anywhere, like a butcher. Worse, it could simply slip under her chin for a quick and bloody death. The flat, cold steel froze on her jaw. The point pressed the bone. Closing her eyes, she prayed and prayed that it would not turn. Oh God, she thought. Oh, God, please don't—Mom, Mom!

"Good girl, good," he said. She remained still, not turning towards his strangely calm voice. The last blinding slap had taught her that. No breath came now. A suffocating feeling grew in her throat. She desperately tried to breathe but nothing came out. Suddenly, the cold blade was gone.

She slowly opened her eyes.

"This is for you, just for you," he leaned forward showing her the long knife. His hot, stale breath hit her face. She felt a light tug on the handcuff. She was too afraid to turn to look at the other girl attached to her. Not with him this close. Not with his smell. Not now.

Stephanie knew her mom was probably at the shopping mall, unaware of everything. She pictured her mom strolling along, smiling and window-shopping. When will her mom discover that she is gone?

She wanted to cry out. She wanted to call for her and not

stop until she came. Please, Mom, she thought, please hear me. Come and get me. Please *save* me! I'll never disobey you again. Please. Mommy!

"Oh, so pretty, so soft. Look!" he sang. He swung his arms like a dancer. He suddenly moved away. She knew her naked skin was being paraded. She felt flushed again with embarrassment. The men around her and her sister just kept staring and staring. Each had dried blood on their hands. Their eyes glared with lust.

"Please sir, oh please..." inadvertently came out of her mouth.

The blinding sting of the open hand slap was so fast that she blanked out for a moment. The intense pain brought her back. She prayed again. She begged to faint. His face was suddenly right in front of hers, filling her vision.

"Shut up, just shut up, okay," he shrieked. His eyes were bulging white in anger. He turned from her. "Gimme those damned cups," he demanded from one of the men.

"Okay, my two little girlies, I had enough. These are made special, just for each of you."

Stephanie looked up at him. She was amazed at his sudden soft voice. Why did he want them to drink anything? What was it? Why was she here? Why were they *both* here?

He was smiling broadly at them, baring his perfectly white teeth. For a moment, it was as if nothing dreadful was happening. The craze in his eyes told a different story. They mesmerized her.

"I just thought you may be a little thirsty, that's all. I mean, it's been a little bit of a trip here. Maybe you would like a little drink, a little sip. Maybe? Don't you think? Huh? Just a little sip, maybe?"

She dared not turn to her right. She felt the light tug again. She knew that the closest person in her life was sharing her horror. Her sister Tiffany was cuffed, wrist-to-wrist, next to her. They were standing naked, facing the men.

The little white cups were held in front of them. She knew they had no choice now.

No choice at all.

(Two Thousand Years Earlier, Ancient Israel - Midday)

Chapter 1 ~

DAIAFAR SAT IMPATIENTLY. His eyes wandered away from the small wooden stage. He had not wanted to come. However, Marius would not go to him, not to his home, and definitely not to the Temple.

He held his hood closely together with two ring-clad fingers. Secrecy was imperative. He thought to himself whether this was really worth it.

He smiled and decided it was. It really was.

Daiafar's thoughts suddenly went to his own son and daughter. He imagined them on that splintered stage. He pictured them attempting to cover their nakedness with arms and hands. A cold chill ran down his spine. He instinctively closed his eyes. He cursed quietly, trying to break the image. Suddenly, the cheering outside caught everyone's attention. He slowly opened his eyes. They were approaching.

Marius, large and fat, lumbered into the crowded room. He paused for breath. Sweat streamed through the dirt on his pudgy face. Droplets hung off his chin. He appeared exhausted.

All eyes turned towards him. An apprehensive silence fell. Following him was a slow-moving entourage. Daiafar saw none older than fourteen. Heavy iron chains bound them together by ankle, wrist, and neck. There were both boys and girls. They were all naked. None had their heads up. Bidders were discussing and pointing at their exposed genitals. Their young skin glistened with sweat. Meat for sale, Daiafar mused to himself. He felt no sympathy. Business was business.

Daiafar, High Priest of Israel, was truly happy in the age of Augustus Caesar. Augustus had just won over the *Triumvirate*, comprised of himself, Pompey, and Marc Antony. In bloody battles, Augustus had easily defeated Pompey. He then crushed both Antony and Cleopatra, who committed suicide rather than face capture. Finally, Daiafar thought, peace in Rome. Secretly, he knew Israel under Roman rule was to his advantage. But he would never admit it. At least the *Triumvirate* was gone. Rome had one all-powerful ruler. Daiafar recognized the value of that. He loved his own power.

Marius pulled the lead chain harder. The children lunged forward into each other. With one wave of his arm, they retreated backwards with little steps, like trained mules. Marius then paused in the silence. He looked around the throng. He saw Daiafar. Marius knew his identity and purpose. He made a nod so slight, no one saw but Daiafar. His own nod back was the same.

Marius turned to the unclothed children. He motioned to a guard to unchain them. Marius slowly walked down the line. He struck a boy's face when he covered his penis. A little girl in shame turned from the bidders. He seized her, making her face the men. For punishment, he ran his hand between her legs. Pressing upward, he smiled at the bidders. He then kissed her mouth. Men cheered.

With that, the murmuring in the room began to rise. The bidders were anxious to begin. Most had already picked out whom they wished to buy. They were eager. They knew the girl or boy they won had to submit to every wish. They were ready to collect their prize. Many just wanted sex. Some bought more than one to please them. Many men bought boys for their pleasures.

Daiafar's mind suddenly went back to his own son and daughter. He glanced at the bidders' faces. He controlled the rising disgust, forcing his feelings back. He had learned to do so as their spiritual guide, and more powerfully, their judge. The emotions he hid were very real. His control of them was a skill he had perfected.

Marius began his flesh proceedings without a word. He viciously pulled a pre-teen girl out of the line. Her tiny breasts were just developing. Her arms and legs were bony. She was shivering even in the extreme heat. When she stumbled, he violently dragged her up by her long hair, careful not to damage the goods. She cried out. Tears were flowing down her cheeks. Men in the room pushed towards her. Marius forcefully removed her hands from covering her vagina. He allowed men to caress her. One old man was licking the wetness off his white beard. The sight caused the High Priest quickly to turn away.

Marius enjoyed making him watch. He would pay Daiafar only when the last was sold. He also demanded the High Priest take payment himself. Marius refused to deal with servants. It was his protection.

Daiafar grinned with cold contempt. Go ahead, play your games, my cautious friend, he thought. I'll wait and play. Your days are soon numbered. His grin widened. The plan for complete control was ready.

The highest bidder dragged the crying girl away. Marius then seized the smallest boy for sale. Men flocked to fondle and cup him. Marius let each take their time with the boy. Fierce bidding began.

Daiafar had enough of the lust. He closed his hood. He shut out the images. He thought how much he loved his children. If this ever happened to them, he would hunt down and torture the slavers and buyers. Their deaths would be unimaginable. He was High Priest. His word was Law. Revenge was his, anytime he wished. Supreme power was his. Behind his hood, a covetous smile grew.

He ignored the yelling and bidding. He pictured his beautiful, handsome son on his lap. He would teach him the Scriptures. After long study, he would tickle him. The boy would laugh and squirm in his arms. In the end, his son would jump up and hug him. Daiafar would hold him tight. He would then send him off, feeling a deep, endless love.

It amazed him how, in an instant, someone else's child would be quietly stolen. They would take siblings, too. A father's child would become high-cost flesh for sale. He shrugged off the thought.

He resumed watching the bidding. In the end, he really didn't care. They were not his children. It was simply good business, very good business.

(Philadelphia — 7:14 p.m.)

Chapter 2 ~

IT SMELLED BAD, but she took the cup anyway. She just didn't want to be hit again. Just not again, please. The men stared and waited in their bloody clothes. It was only a matter of time. She turned to her right, seeing the absolute terror on her older sister's eyes.

"Wait," he said, as he motioned for the man who had given the cups to move back. "Wait a sec there."

He took an endlessly slow step forward. His face again surprised her. She knew she had seen him before.

"Both of you, sit. Now."

When they didn't move, his hand rose. They both quickly sat down, trying desperately not to spill the liquid. The sudden coldness of the metal floor felt like a million tiny, sharp daggers against their skin. Her whole body shivered. After the icy shock passed, she wondered why the floor was so freezing cold in the middle of summer.

The embarrassment of her nudity sharply rose again. She gazed down at her tiny breasts. She did everything in her power not to look up at the lustful eyes.

He leaned down and placed his hand on her shoulder. To Stephanie's surprise, it was very warm. She slowly looked up. As he stared into her eyes, he let his hand fall down, slowly, until it was right above her bare breast. She knew she couldn't move or complain. It was the first time in her life that she wished someone dead.

"Bet you would like it, huh? I mean, I do like girls, too. You know, we like all young people. Can I touch you?"

Her eyes glazed over. She couldn't speak.

"I'll take that as a big yes," he claimed with a wide grin. She saw the men chuckle, nudge each other, and nod in approval.

She closed her eyes and felt his warm hand cup her tiny breast with little squeezes. She was falling inside, drowning in fear, feeling she might throw up right there. She did everything in her will not to, not to move, not to do anything at all. Just accept. Just accept it.

"Okay, thanks," he said with no emotion, immediately removing his hand and standing up straight again. "You may drink now."

They both looked up at him in silence.

They glanced at the tiny white cups and then at each other. They shared the same helpless look. Without breaking their loving gaze, they slowly brought the cups to their lips and drank.

It tasted bittersweet. She felt the warm liquid hit her stomach.

"Aw, isn't that so cute," she could hear him say, as the men started to laugh louder.

All of a sudden, Stephanie saw surprise grow in her sister's eyes. She felt hard, wild tugging on the metal cuffs. She quickly looked at her empty cup. She then turned to see Tiffany convulsing, her eyes rolling back in her head.

She instinctively grabbed her sister and held her hard against her. The two naked girls melted together on the icy floor. Then, all Stephanie felt was limpness.

All she heard was laughter, loud continuous laughter.

In disbelief, she looked up from the dead girl attached to

her. She knew her drink hadn't been poisoned. In mixed emotions of sorrow and hope, her mind ran to possible freedom as the tears flowed down her cheeks. The world was circling all around her. Images faded in and out. Nothing was clear anymore. Nothing was real.

"That's right, we chose you," she heard him, far in the distance. She stared into her sister's vacant eyes.

"See?" she heard again, knowing he wanted her attention.

She looked up and saw, knowing she would be joining the other young children he was smiling and pointing at.

In horror, she finally fainted.

(Secluded Location, Miles Away — 8:22 p.m.)

Chapter 3 ~

SILENT AND STILL, the Figure sat. The only detection of movement came from the occasional blinking of its eyes. There was no one there to witness these solitary moments. They occurred more and more. As it sat unmoving in the center of the pitch-dark room, the Figure wheezed in and out, like a child who had just been reprimanded.

"Keep it together, keep it together," the mind warned itself repeatedly. "Always watch, always watch and see. They can't see it's me if I don't let them. Don't look at them; don't ever look at them. Keep the other pair of eyes for them. They can't see; they can't see me, ever."

This exhaustive mind-control had been an easy accomplishment. The sheer years of self-preservation had made it exceedingly simple to control its mind and every action. It wryly smiled. It felt that wonderful overwhelming rush of complete power. The smile widened with complete self-love. The absolute supremacy to fool everyone, every time, was its aphrodisiac. Seductions were easy, very easy—even simple. This was its gift, and it knew it.

The eyes closed and opened. It saw the same blackness each time. The Figure's gaze slowly shifted. It roamed the black-walled room. There was no furniture except its high-back, gothic chair. Nothing else existed. Even with the room temperature normal, it felt coldness. It felt emptiness, everywhere.

With malice, the Figure grinned at the creation of its hideaway. This was the only place it could be its true self. It raised its head as if to howl. The blackness of the room blended with the darkness it felt—the darkness of the pitch of night, of the deepest forest, of the dead thoughts that flowed constantly through it.

The eyes closed.

The mind became thoughtless.

Another skill. Another grin.

The emptiness resonated.

Only silence. Only darkness.

Silent darkness everywhere.

The wry smile came back.

(Central Police Headquarters – 9:02 a.m.)

Chapter 4 ~

THE TUMULT WAS INCREDIBLE. It was more deafening than Frankie Oswald could ever remember. No case was like this. No, not ever in his police career. If he could run away, he would. He did not want to start his morning this way.

Someone spied him approaching. The press and throng outside the station immediately crowded to him. They moved fast as one group. Only the quickly set-up police barriers stopped them.

People were yelling over each other. Microphones were everywhere. One pushed right into his face, hitting his mouth. He swung it away, glaring at the stunned reporter. His face remained stoic and hard. He tried to control his feelings. Everyone was calling his name. In his own frustration and knowing theirs, he spun around.

"Okay, okay, I'll answer what I can, and then I gotta go. Please be civil, or this interview is over, right now," he bellowed over the din.

The noise rose as people behind the press were screaming and chanting at him. Some reporters moved around the barrier, surrounding him. He waved his arms for them to calm down. He called on Janet Wright from the *Daily News*.

"Chief Oswald, is it true that two more kids are missing?"

Before he could answer, another yelled, "And Stuart

Martino's daughters at that? Both of them? Is that correct? Chief?"

"Alright, alright. Not enough time has passed to declare them missing. But I will let you know this, with everything that has happened in the last weeks, we are investigating every possible lead. We are assuming absolutely *nothing.*"

"What about the other missing kids? And the ones found murdered?"

A shiver went down his spine as he remembered what he had seen.

"Still investigating. Thank you."

The mob of reporters pressed up against him, asking questions so fast he couldn't decipher them all. The uniforms were trying to keep them back in a circle for Frankie. It was chaos. He nodded at one of the officers in thanks. The officer gave him a frantic look.

He looked over the microphones. He saw a mom behind the reporters, holding her little girl close to her. In his mind, they became his own wife and daughter. For a brief moment, he was home with them, playing, joking, and being the dad he loved to be. Suddenly, he saw the first young child lying dead in front of him. He had found her himself. He remembered looking into that frozen stare of horror. The victim's face suddenly turned into his daughter's face.

He no longer could hear the reporters or the crowd behind them. Everything was quiet and calm. He felt wetness in his eyes again. Then a shrieking reporter broke his trance. His attention returned. He realized his daughter was home safe.

"Josh Stein! *Times*! Chief! Chief!"

"Yes, one more, okay, please! You." he pointed at Josh.

"What about the passages, the ones from the Bible? What

do they mean?"

Frankie saw that the reporter was very young. However, the look in his eyes told Frankie he was hungry. He saw a person who would do anything for a story—especially the front lead.

"Sorry, don't know what you're talking about."

"Yes, yes, you do! I know all about them."

The rest of the reporters started in on it. Everyone was yelling again, wanting to know more, all writing frantically.

He turned to run up the stairs. As he did, his eyes suddenly caught the mom and little girl again. Both were staring at him. He glanced towards the entrance. As he turned back one more time, he froze. They were gone. He wondered if they had ever been there. Was everything just getting to him?

He quickly turned and ran up the steps. His heart was pounding through his chest.

(Suburban Supermarket – 1:31 p.m.)

Chapter 5 ~

AGAIN, MELANIE WAS PUSHED from behind. Okay, okay, one more time and she was going to turn and ... well, she didn't know what she would do. She felt there must be a reason why people can be so ignorant. Every time she was annoyed by someone and was going to press the point, something came over her. Her college psychology notes kicked in. She would reason herself out of striking back. Her college years had taught her much. With a growing empathy and a deep breath, she turned to her tormentor.

She had to hold back the giggle. She was staring at the smallest women she had ever seen. She had the whitest hair she had ever seen. The woman had to be somewhere between ninety and a hundred. Horribly bent over, she could barely lift her head. Melanie smiled as the woman accidentally pushed against her again.

She pulled her own grocery cart back and motioned for the old woman to go ahead of her. This would at least put her next in line to the register. She then saw what was in her cart. Melanie's heart went out even more to the old woman.

She saw three items: a pint of skim milk, cottage cheese, and a small but expensive New York strip steak. She shook her head in wonderment. She saw the old woman shake her head, too.

"Terrible, just terrible," the woman whispered.

Melanie followed her gaze. She saw the newspaper. It was among the many tabloids in front of the grocery checkout. She read the headline to herself with a mixture of awe and grave concern.

"THIRD TIME! STUART MARTINO'S DAUGHTERS!
NO CALLS, NO CLUES, POLICE HELPLESS!"

When she had first heard the story, it had hit her hard inside. How could anyone do these horrid things? It was one after the other. There was no remorse, no care about the young children they were hurting.

The new headline sent a sensation of fear through her. She started to read the article. She hadn't noticed that the old woman had moved forward. She heard someone clear their throat behind her.

She moved herself forward a little, still reading. Children. They're just kids, she thought with increasing anger. Finally, she had to continue forward. She picked up the newspaper and tossed it into her cart.

(Office Of The Chief Of Police — 2:58 p.m.)

Chapter 6 ~

HE TOYED WITH THE dangling cord of his desk lamp, pulling it on and off, again and again. He stopped and stared at it. He then flipped the cord out of his hand in disgust. Frankie opened his palms close to his face and saw the sweat. Not caring, he placed his chin in them, never taking his gaze from the closed door of his darkened office. Rage was swelling in him again.

He slowly read each letter of the backwards name that was etched on the other side of the frosted pane. He then read the title.

"Yeah 'Chief,' right. Sure. Yeah, me," he sarcastically muttered to the silence.

Covering his face with his hands, he felt the worst feeling of loss he had ever felt. He wondered how it all happened so fast. And now a third time. He knew one thing. He was responsible. He knew it was his fault—maybe not the first victim, but every child thereafter.

He could not sleep. The night before, in the early morning hours, he had stared at the ceiling in the quiet of the night. He heard his wife's slow breathing. That night, he had held back the tears. To his surprise, it all finally flowed out.

He had run to the bathroom. Quietly slipping the door closed, he heard it lightly latch. Sitting on the cold toilet seat, he cried more than he had ever cried before in his life. Even more than when his father had died suddenly the year before. In the silent darkness, a strange coldness crept over his skin. It was the dread of more to come. Another child, another child, another poor child—cruelly murdered, missing.

"Shit, stop crying, you fool!" he whispered between deep sobs. He wiped his eyes with the back of his hand and then suddenly slammed his fist on the sink. He slammed it again. Remembering where he was, he prayed his wife hadn't heard him, or worse, one of his kids. He caught his breath and stood up. He stared at the unfamiliar face staring back at him in the mirror. The teary eyes he saw no one ever saw. Nor would they, not even his family. He cared more than anyone knew. He felt so much, so deeply. Nevertheless, Frankie held it all in, never showing his true feelings, never allowing anyone in either. He knew he had to be the strong one, both at home and at the Force. It was his responsibility, always.

Staring at the name again on his door, he slipped the previous night's image away. Closing his eyes to hide the darkness of the office, he desperately tried to shut down his mind. The terrible images just kept appearing, like a worn movie clip, repeating forever in his mind. Anger began overtaking his personal feelings. He willingly let it in.

What was going on? Where were they? What did they find? Who did they find? He struck his desk so hard that his Twenty-five Year Award for Dedication to the Force bounced straight up off the desk. It crashed onto the floor. He looked over at it. He knew he did not deserve it, so he just let it stay where it fell.

"Please let this one be a hoax," he whispered, as he remembered the anonymous note he had passed to Fletcher.

He stood up and slowly stretched, reminding himself to get rid of that old rickety chair. He needed a plush executive seat, like Mike's. The aching ran down his legs as he walked around the desk. He had controlled himself in that chair for the last hour.

He was tired of waiting. He composed himself by inhaling deeply. The irrepressible fear kept trying to come back. He swore he would not cry, not here. Though he was tired and exhausted, he was mostly angry, angry with himself for failing to help innocent children.

The anger was good. He thought and concentrated on it, making himself furious. He wanted to build it into a frenzy. It covered the desperation he couldn't face.

"You've both had enough time," he seethed with such fury and annoyance that even he was surprised. He stormed out of the room, slamming the door behind him.

Chapter 7 ~

AS FRANKIE APPROACHED, the entrance to the squad room was open. He saw a couple detectives in close discussion. Some were on their computers. Others were quietly talking in whispers on the phone.

He burst in with a fury, not caring what he was interrupting.

"Okay, who's the Ein-fucking-stein who knows where they went? Has anyone heard from them? Did they call?" He stood in the middle of the room, hands on hips. His mind strangely wandered to how nuns used to stand in class in his Catholic school days.

All activity stopped in the room.

"Sorry Chief, not me."

"Not me."

"Nope."

"Who?"

Frankie stared at them. A silent moment passed.

"Oh, Danny Boy, oh Danny Boy, where the hell are you out there?" someone lightly sang. They all had their heads down suddenly. He heard muffled chuckling.

"Just shut it, all of you," he said, trying to be serious. He didn't want their humor to diminish any of the anger he had mustered. As he turned to leave, he just couldn't help it. A small smile grew on his face. He stopped at the door, grinning and shaking his head. He heard a couple more chuckles as he left. They may be crazy, but they were good cops.

"I shouldn't have given him that tip, real or not." He paced up and down the corridor, muttering to himself.

He couldn't believe how the case had gotten so quickly out of control. On top of the two murders, both victims' siblings were still missing. There were no leads. Now, two more children were missing. And Fletch was nowhere to be found. He was not answering his cell. That always pissed off Frankie. The Philadelphia Chief of Police knew his time was running out.

"Why do you have to be so goddamned independent all the time? Just once, Fletch, just once," he quietly spoke as he shook his head in his pacing, running all the facts through his mind for the hundredth time.

No apparent motive. No ransom calls about the missing kids. No contact at all—except that tiny piece of paper left behind on the second victim's body—and that didn't make any sense to him either. He was tired of being in the station, night and day, working on nothing and getting nowhere. He decided now to get personally involved in the case.

Fletcher told him the passage had to mean something. But even he couldn't figure it out. And it was a waste of time asking those priests. It actually had him so angry that he skipped the church collection that week, just for spite. Unless his old friend was hiding something from him, he knew he was going to get destroyed by the press and
public.

"And I'll be done," he whispered to himself. He suddenly stopped his pacing, right in the middle of the corridor. The image of himself in a uniform, again on the beat, in the depth of winter, freezing to death, made him cringe.

"Maybe we should have checked with the friggin' Pope," he had finally said, in exasperation, when he had first asked for

Fletcher's help. Now he wondered if bringing him on board had been the right thing.

He put his head down and started pacing again. He almost knocked over a passing uniformed officer. Another thought came.

He poked his head back into the squad room. "What's Danny's cell number?"

(Across Town, The Philadelphia Times — 2:58 p.m.)

Chapter 8 ~

JOSH STEIN KNEW THIS WAS IT. Finally, he found a superb story. Not being senior, he would investigate on his own. He had to find a way to capitalize on it. His sole goal was to advance quickly at the paper. He had planted his stake in Philadelphia and until now, he wasn't sure if it was the right decision. Now he knew it was right. The excitement was overwhelming.

He had done everything possible to meet locals to create a wide network for himself. He joined every discussion group he could find. In one, he actually found a cop whose confidence he had gained. The cop agreed to share information but never in person. It was a very valuable asset for any reporter. It had already paid off, too.

"Keep it together, my man," he spoke quietly to himself as he posted the two pictures of Stuart Martino's daughters on his corkboard. He sat back in his creaky old chair, in his tiny cubicle, and reviewed his work.

The board included clippings from every major paper from day one of the kidnappings. It also included pictures of the three pairs of teen victims, indicating the ones missing and the ones murdered. In a mosaic of colored sticky notes, he posted his own thoughts. He noted differences and commonalities. In the center of it all, was a white piece of paper. He had written on it with a large black marker: "Elijah's Wrath."

Everything was pointing to the ancient Jewish curse. He just knew it. How could he tie it together? His own knowledge of Jewish history was good, but not good enough. He knew what to do next, thinking of his cop friend who told him what they found. His excitement kept growing.

If only he could get his hands on one of those passages.

(The Main Line, the Martino Mansion – 3:17 p.m.)

Chapter 9 ~

STUART SAT STARING OUT the window. On the sill were the school pictures of two young girls. Tiffany and Stephanie were dressed in their white blouses and plaid skirts. His eyes went from the girls' smiling faces, to the bright summer scenery outside, and back again to the two happy faces.

He was never a man to cry, but there was no way he could hold it back.

"My girls, my girls," he whispered between silent sobs.

He told himself to get a grip. He wiped his wet face with his large hairy hands. He could not let his wife or servants see him like this.

He got up. He slowly walked around the big oaken desk in his home office. Stopping at the credenza, he switched on the police scanner. He had to know what was going on. It was mostly calls not related to the kidnappings. He didn't know what else to do.

He was beyond frantic. He had made a solemn vow that he would do nothing, no business, no pleasure, no friends, no nothing, until he got his daughters back safely.

He would eventually act. Once they returned home unharmed, he would immediately set his plans in motion. All the power behind his vast wealth, the power to spin the wheels of justice in his favor, would fall upon the perpetrators. It would fall so hard, they would wish that they had never been born. His penchant for utter revenge would be satisfied.

He turned up the scanner. He sat back listening through the noise and static. He had done this every day since his little girls were taken. He was on his own. His wife was useless. She refused to leave her private little room. She sat in complete darkness, day after day.

He had promised the DA, his good friend Mike, that he would keep a step back. Mike had repeatedly promised that he would find his little girls. What scared him the most, in his worst nightmares, was how the others were found.

He listened intently.

Finally, he couldn't hold it in any longer.

"C'mon you motherfuckers, find my babies or I will! I promise you. I promise you 'til my death."

(The Detective Squad Room — 3:24 p.m.)

Chapter 10 ~

"YO, BOSS!" DANNY EXCLAIMED. He squeezed quickly past him through the door. Frankie just froze. He gazed at him with disbelief. Danny strolled over to his desk. All the detectives looked up.

"Well?" Frankie asked, with his hands on his hips again.

"What?" Danny replied. He looked at him from across the room as if nothing was wrong.

"Um, Fletcher? Remember? Where is he? And, where were you? And why are you here? I told you to stay with him."

"I wanted to stay, but he told me to take off. I argued, but he said you wanted me back here."

"What the hell are you talking about?"

Frankie began to fume. The anger felt good again. He crossed the room. He leaned on the desk, looking down at Danny.

"What? No. He told me—"

"You idiot. I never said anything."

"Oh, well, sorry then, but I thought—"

"Stop thinking, okay? Please?"

"Yeah, boss, I will," he replied.

Frankie watched him pick up a stale soft pretzel from his desk. Danny jammed it in his mouth.

"Another Ein-fucking-stein!" Frankie declared with his

hands up in the air. He trudged towards the entrance. He suddenly stopped and turned. Danny just watched him, chewing the whole
time.

"Now what, boss?" he mumbled. A piece of pretzel fell out of the side of his mouth. Frankie tried not to laugh. He heard the other detectives chuckling.

"Um, where did you leave him at?"

"Oh, yeah, we were at the corner of 52nd, I think Rockland. He was reading that paper again. You know, the one you gave him. Then he picked up his cell. He was speaking to you. He told me to come back here. Funny, I didn't hear it ring."

Frankie just stared at him again in disbelief. After hearing more chortles, he huffed. He cursed at them and stormed out.

He knew he should have gone with them. Except he knew he couldn't, he just couldn't.

Not after what he had seen.

(Now, Vacant North Philadelphia Neighborhood — 3:27 p.m.)

Chapter 11 ~

HE TRIED THE PAINT CRUSTED KNOB. It turned easily enough. Thinking for a moment, he released his grip and raised his fist. Right before knocking, Fletcher glanced back to see if the detective was still gone. He hoped he had given him enough time not to have circled back. Fletcher turned back to the ugly green and red door. He lightly tapped it with his knuckles.

He waited. No answer.

He tried again, this time a bit louder.

Still no answer. He leaned forward letting his ear almost touch the door. He could hear no sound.

Looking around one more time, he grabbed the knob and turned it. Again, it turned easily. He slowly opened the door to a crack, just to peer in.

The smell hit him hard. He inadvertently took in a full breath. He quickly shut the door. He began to violently cough. Trying to stop the heaves, he turned away, taking a couple of steps back. Bending over, he stared down the landing. Finally, getting his breath back, he stood up. He stared at the closed door.

He knew that smell.

"Oh, my," was all that came out of his mouth.

He looked around. There was nothing usable. Finally, he brought the sleeve of his arm up to his face, covering his nose and mouth as best he could. Entering the room, he closed the door slowly behind him, hearing the latch close. He double-checked to make sure he could get out.

The room was dark. He had to stand in the smell and wait until his eyes adjusted a little. The stench was so great that he knew he could only stay a short while before he would start coughing again.

"Oh, my god, my god…" he kept repeating.

On the small bed in front of him lay a young girl, curled up in a fetal position. Her thumb was in her mouth. She was naked. Her skin's whiteness grew and grew as his eyes adjusted to the darkness. She looked like she was sleeping. He just stared at her in disbelief.

He broke his fixation from her, quickly looking around. There was nothing in the small room. The only window was painted over. There were no other doors. The apartment was just one room. It was apparent she did not belong there.

Instinctively, he knew the perp left her to decay just long enough to create an odor that was unbearable. The sweltering, summer heat made the stench of her rotting flesh even worse. He could not believe anyone would do this, especially to a young child.

His eyes started to water as he took careful steps around the cot. There was nothing on the floor but he knew it had to be there somewhere. He could only wait a little longer. He had to get out of there, both from the stench, and from the disturbing distress of her innocence.

He shook his head in complete disgust. As he was turning to leave, he glanced back a quick moment.

He saw it.

Chapter 12 ~

IT WAS FOLDED SO TINY and wedged in. Oh, my, he thought. He approached the unclothed victim on her little bed. He paused. He looked at her one more time. She looked so small, curled up there like a baby. Her breasts were so tiny, so young. Her other arm had fallen over the side, limp. Her legs were tightly pulled up. In the darkness, he could barely see under them.

Still mesmerized by her innocence, he summoned his courage and reached down. He gently separated her legs. He heard his own breath quickly inhale.

He began to think why he had decided to do this. All he wanted was to be left alone. He wished to be in his home, researching his favorite fine art, and planning how to purchase some. He had decided to be a loner, wanted to be a loner, had become a loner, and was happy being a loner. It was his life now, finally his alone. The only problem was that he still had friends, good friends. Frankie Oswald was one of them.

Now he was here.

When Frankie had called, he had heard an uncharacteristic desperation in his voice. His heart had gone out to him—not far out to him, but far enough to pull him back to the horrors of homicide he had left behind. Now he was back. Back to the Force he had come to despise. And they were dragging him right back to Hell. He could not remember how many times he had cursed and thought to call Frankie back and decline. Now he stood over a dead child. He was in a room so foul, it surpassed even his previous experiences. He knew it had been carefully set up to cause this exact effect. The murderer had waited just long enough.

Fletcher's police instinct kicked in. He swore under his breath. He blocked out everything but the job at hand.

"Oh, my, here I go," he whispered softly.

As gently as he could, he used his two fingers to separate her cold softness. Slipping them in slowly, he grabbed hold of the folded paper. It was jammed deep inside her vagina. Only a tiny bit of it had shown. It was so barely noticeable. Who would do this? Why would they do this? He never would have thought to look there, but his detective intuition told him to look everywhere.

And he had, to his dismay.

"Okay, okay, got it," he said a little too loud. Embarrassment and shame crept over him. "Sorry," he said to her. He wanted to be gentle, as if she were still alive, as if it would hurt her, or cause some kind of discomfort. She remained cold and motionless, asleep in death.

He examined it, turning it slowly around in the blackness.

It was a very fine, discolored paper. It looked like it came from an old, worn out Bible. He carefully unfolded it by the edges, trying not to tear the thin paper. He shook his head. It was another verse from Elijah, that Prophet—yeah, what did that priest say? From the Book of Kings. Why Kings? And at that, why this damned Elijah guy? He couldn't figure out the reasoning behind it all.

In desperation for information, he had decided to open it there. He was hoping it would lead to other clues in the room. If not, he wanted to get out. He was getting a little antsy, alone with her in that small space. The smell was beginning to overwhelm him.

Moreover, he knew by now Frankie would have figured out that he had sent Danny back. Soon, detectives and crime scene personnel would arrive. They would find nothing more than he had. He didn't care if Frankie got pissed at his initiative. He worked alone.

Well, he thought, their efforts had gotten them nowhere so far. He still just wished to go home and forget it all.

"Whatever," he said to himself, this time not caring how loud he was. "This nut is just playing you with this shit, Frankie, no matter what you think. It's gotta be some insane game. And you're losing."

Bible passages, encrypted anonymous tips, missing children, murdered children. This criminal was smart and probably well educated. Fletcher knew when he started analyzing, he was being drawn in.

Now the perp was messin' with him.

"I'll get you. If I could just figure out…"

He didn't finish.

He opened the passage and began to read it.

Chapter 13 ~

MELANIE TOSSED THE PAPER onto her couch as she passed it. She headed for the kitchen with her groceries. She wanted to read it in peace. She had to put everything neatly away first. It would bother her until she did. It would just eat at her if she started reading that story with things not in their right places.

She has always been that way. Put everything in its place, then play. Maybe this obsession was thanks to her mother. More probably, it was her sister. She had always looked up to Dana. They eventually found that fighting was even more fun. She smiled, remembering their spats. She finished placing the last yogurt container into the refrigerator.

She left the kitchen and froze in her tracks.

"Damn it," she said. She turned back. Something had caught her eye.

She went right to it. She fixed it. She couldn't have the towel hanging on the oven handle cockeyed like that. It had to be even in length. It had to be in the middle of the handle.

"There," she said, with a little pride. She went back to the living room. She did her best not to look back. She knew she could be there for an hour "fixing" things.

It was called OCD, Obsessive Compulsive Disorder. It fit her perfectly. She didn't care either. All had to feel right. When it did, things went right, she thought right, and everything was right.

She smiled as she jumped onto the couch with her usual big bounce, giggling as she landed. She still felt like she was nineteen. She loved it.

"Okay, let's see now."

She started reading the story. She was instantly captivated.

Chapter 14 ~

WHEN FRANKIE RETURNED TO HIS OFFICE, his phone was ringing.

"It's gonna be," he said as he leaned over the desk to see the caller ID, "I knew it," he cried. He closed the door before answering it.

"Oswald here," he calmly said, wondering why he was calling now, for the hundredth time.

"Frankie, man, c'mon, what's going on over there?"

"Listen, Mike, we're—"

"Don't give me 'We're doing everything we can shit!' I got big-ass Martino on my butt—for God's sake, it's his daughters! And the press is crucifying me—and you too by the way. And if one more parent calls, I'm gonna ... I don't know what. If we don't—"

"Mike, calm down. Look, I even got Saxtan—"

"Oh, no. Oh, no you don't!"

"Listen, Mike, we need everything we can. You know this is out of control. This psycho ain't leaving me any clues. No calls, no ransom demands, no motives, nothing. It's as if he doesn't give a flying you know what, just kidnap, murder, no talk, and gone. No trace. Almost as if he, she, or *they* – know our every move."

"That's why I put Fletcher to work on it. He's anonymous. Nobody remembers him or knows him out there anymore. He's been off the Force for years doing that PI thing. Or whatever he does. Who knows, it may work using him. Plus, he's smart and we need brains right now."

"Okay, okay, listen. I don't like it or him, but he's your friend and your responsibility. You do whatever you feel's right, okay Frankie?" the DA said in a calmer voice, which made Frankie ease a little. "But either catch this son-of-a-bitch or both our jobs will be toast. I mean fried."

"Sure, Mike. Sure."

"I'm holding Stu back as much as I can, but he's ready to blow and I'm not sure if ... well—"

"Will do, will do," Frankie replied, as he heard the phone hang up on the other side.

"Stuart Martino, big deal," he whispered. He sat down with a thump on the hard, wooden chair. It hurt again. "Man!"

He knew the DA and Martino were good friends. Mike fondly called him Stu, which always made Frankie sick to his stomach. He also knew that Martino was one of the wealthiest, most prominent men in the city. He had many close friends in City Hall, including the governor. When Martino screamed, even street-wise and politically tough Michael Parker, DA, got nervous.

He could understand that two of his kids were missing, too. Only *that* fact made him feel sorry for him. Otherwise, fuck'em, he thought, without remorse.

Nevertheless, it was always the same. He prayed this time it wasn't.

One teen murdered.

One missing.

Always siblings.

Always wealthy.

Always the same—no calls, no clues.

Only Elijah.

He slumped down and could only think one thing.

"Where the hell is Fletcher?"

Chapter 15 ~

"C'MON, JUST GIVE ME SOMETHING to go on," Josh pleaded. "I know you've gone too far, but have I let you down yet? No one will know. I may even be able to help you solve this. Wouldn't you look great?"

He heard a long silence on the other side.

"Great! Thanks detective. Can you fax—"

He had to take the phone away from the shout on the other end.

"Okay, okay, just read it to me."

He tried to write it but the pen had run out of ink.

"Damn it!" he whispered as he made frantic circles with no effect. "No, not at you. Hold a sec." He scrambled to find anything to write with. The excitement of the hunt was unbelievable. He wondered which he liked better, money or...

"Go, shoot!"

He quickly scribbled. He was amazed as he read what he wrote.

He had been right all along.

"Elijah!" he whispered with a wily smile. His inner glee was overflowing. "This has got to be part of..." he trailed off, as he started putting things together in his mind.

Chapter 16 ~

FLETCHER FINALLY LEFT the room and made his way down the stairwell. He was careful not to touch anything, especially the railing. It amazed him how many bullet holes were everywhere. It looked like multiple shootouts had occurred. Nice place, he thought, as he left as quickly as he could. He didn't want to be seen by anyone.

He walked down the broken steps leading to the sidewalk. Looking around only with his eyes, he casually strolled to his Jaguar around the corner. With each step, his heartbeat increased, knowing the killer might be nearby, watching.

He breathed easier as he got in. Driving slowly, he reviewed the neighborhood. After a couple blocks, he pulled out his cell phone.

"Frankie," he said when the phone picked up. "It's me."

"Fletch! Help me, please, what do you got? And where the hell are you?"

"She's dead, I'm sorry."

"Damn it," he heard on the other side. "Only one? You sure it's her?"

"Yeah, it's one of them. Got a clear look. I'll meet you at Maurice's around five or so, okay?"

"There again? Fletch, you're too preoccupied."

"No, I'm not," he lied and liked the lie.

Before he hung up, he told Frankie where she was so they can go get her. Fletcher closed his phone before he could be asked about anything else. He did not want to discuss anything until he could read the passage again. Maybe see those priests again, too. Maybe.

He placed the phone on the seat. It rang right back. He picked it up, saw the name, and carefully placed it back on the seat next to him. He wanted to help his friend Frankie, but knew he had nothing for him yet.

Martino's other daughter was still missing, like the others. He was glad he didn't have to tell him this daughter was dead.

His mind left the thought and went back to his investigative analysis.

No pattern except all young children, boys and girls alike. All were siblings. In addition, all were from very prominent and wealthy families.

He honestly didn't care about the wealthy families. Not wanting to admit it to himself, he really didn't care about the murders either. Murders were murders and that was it. Nothing more. He had enough of them. No matter how young or old, he just didn't care anymore. His life was now his and he was very happy with it. He had been away from all this mess, safe in the quiet world he had made. No one could come into it and no one was welcome.

He still did not remember how Frankie got him to do this. It just seemed to happen so easily. It pissed him off because he broke his own code. Simply stated, "I don't care anymore, and nothing and no one can make me care, ever again."

He paused a moment in thought. Yeah, something else does matter. Sex. He very much loved girls. He wanted as much as he could get, anywhere he could. Single, married, divorced, bi, lesbian, he didn't care. Playboy? Yeah, maybe. He thought fondly about the girls he'd had. He never had so much time on his hands before and now it was his time for fun and freedom, and lots of it. All for him, whenever he wanted.

He smiled to himself. Then his old friend Frankie came to mind again, causing his smile to vanish. Thinking how much trouble his longtime partner was in, he smiled again. This time it was sympathy.

"This is a good one, my friend," he said to the quiet phone on the seat as he drove off.

Chapter 17 ~

JOSH KNEW IT WAS RISKY. Wasn't that what his business was all about, anyway? How could any reporter make it big unless they risked *something*? Woodward and Bernstein did. He would too, every time.

He switched on his police scanner. At the same time, he tried to look up the number he knew he had to have. He tried the Internet. He used the phone book. He even called information, but to no avail. Being extraordinarily wealthy had its pluses. One of them was much protected privacy.

He was not concerned. He continually kept a positive attitude. It had never failed him. As he listened to the police chatter, he had a thought.

Finding the main office number, he decided to take the chance.

"Hi, this is George Kelly from National Cable. I've been sitting in front of Mr. Martino's house for over an hour now and can't get through for someone to open the gate. Sorry to call his office, but can you call the house and ask them to call my cell so I can explain who I am? I'm trying to answer their service call."

He crossed his fingers.

"Um well, sure, I guess," the young-sounding girl tentatively said on the other side.

"Great, here's my number." He read his cell to her. She repeated it and then hung up. He just hoped their unlisted number came through a cell phone okay.

He waited and waited. Finally, his cell rang. He looked

down.

"Yes!" he exclaimed. He was going to let it ring without answering, but curiosity got to him.

"Hello?"

"This is Stuart Martino. Who the hell is this? My secretary just called my home and said that you're here for some reason, for the cable. Our cable is fine. So who the fuck are you?"

Josh realized he was calling from his cell. That's why the number came through. A nice twist of fate he mused. He quickly thanked Fate. He also congratulated himself for his luck.

"Sorry, don't know what you're talking about. You got the wrong number. Sorry."

He hung up smiling.

Chapter 18 ~

MAURICE'S WAS ONE OF FLETCHER'S favorite strip places. It was nicely secluded in the middle of the off-beaten path. It was right outside the city and would do just fine. Nothing like good ole Essington to brighten up a person's day, he thought. Especially here, the filthiest and sleaziest sex joint in the area. He pulled onto Route 291 and started singing his favorite Beatles' song.

"Help! I need somebody! Help! Not just anybody!"

He smiled to himself at his new bad habit. He repeatedly sang the first two lines when deep in thought. Frankie hated it. He didn't care.

He needed to figure out how the teens were targeted. They had to nab this guy and find the other children. It was on him now. He didn't like it at all.

"Will you please, please, stop that! You're not even on key," Frankie had complained the very first time he had heard Fletcher sing. Frankie was beginning to think his old friend was going nutty on him.

"You want my help or not?" Fletcher had snapped back. It had immediately silenced Frankie with only a smirk. That's when he knew his friend really needed his help. No way would he have backed down that fast.

He also knew there was no easy answer with this crime. Whoever it was, they were perfect with their kidnappings. It was completely random. Somehow, they knew exactly where and when to do it. They left no trace, no evidence. Nothing until the one poor child's naked, decaying body showed up.

At least it was a fascinating case, Fletcher thought. He felt better about that. He was getting a little bored these days, outside of his girls. This was kind of an upbeat way to break the daily pattern. It was actually becoming interesting. He also knew the trap of caring too much.

The stench of cigarettes and hard liquor overwhelmed him as usual. A la Maurice's, he thought with a smile.

The bouncer at the door was a small but extremely wide bull-type. He had on greasy white cutoffs. Tattoos were everywhere. He sat on a stool that Fletcher could barely see because of the massive layers of fat. He lifted his bulging, bulldog face. The bloodshot eyes just glared at him with recognition and went back to the newspaper.

"G'day," Fletcher said in his best Aussie, walking by with a tip of his head. He was ignored.

"Hey, sweetie!" he heard from his right in the darkness.

"Hey, Mona, how you doin'?" he replied, walking right past her to the bar. She didn't follow. He was glad.

Under blue and red neon lights, he saw Frankie at the far end. He took his time going over.

"Got any ones? She looks nice," he asked Frankie with a grin.

"Aw, fuck you. Sit down," Frankie replied with a glare. He then grinned and shook his head. The lines on his face looked deeper, Fletcher thought.

After he sat, he ordered a rum and Coke. He looked up at the current dancer who, at that point, was completely nude. No panties and no pasties he fondly noticed, admiring her perky breasts.

"Nice," he said, nodding towards her.

"She's a slut."

"You would do her and you know it."

"Not a prayer, I'm happily married, remember?" Frankie said turning away from the stage, hoping Fletcher would, too. He did not.

"Yeah, yeah, of course, I forgot," he said as he motioned the girl over.

"Aw, stop wasting my time, Mr. Ein-fucking-stein! Whaddya got?" Frankie pressed straight-faced, grabbing his arm.

"Hey, that rhymed. Wait," he said giving Frankie the hand. "Let me first take a peek. That okay with you?"

"Go ahead, but you better have something good when you're done."

She came over. It was obvious to Frankie that she knew Fletcher. Maybe too intimately, he deduced from her wide grin. Fletcher took out a crisp twenty, showed it to her neatly folded, and waited.

Her eyes opened. She then pretended not to notice the amount, leaning down to him. She cupped her breasts together.

He pulled the money back a little. He motioned to her hips. Another method to break the boredom: murders, kidnappings, and strippers. He callously smiled to himself.

She understood immediately. She knelt down in front of him with her legs spread. Leaning back waiting, she looked at the ceiling smiling.

He noticed that the bartender was looking, too.

Fletcher purposely turned and glanced over. The bartender nodded his approval. Fletcher took the twenty and slowly slipped it between her lips. He held it there. After feeling it a while, she closed her legs to capture the twenty.

Suddenly, the same image of the dead, innocent girl

popped into his mind. He was again leaning over her.

"Thanks, baby!" the dancer blew him a kiss, breaking his trance.

"No problem," he said, still fighting his thoughts. He downed his drink. Turning to Frankie, he wanted to talk to get rid of the image.

"You're a pig, you know that?" Frankie said with a big smile. "Always a friggin' pig."

"Man, that's the nicest thing anyone has said in a long time."

"You that loaded to throw away a twenty?"

"I didn't throw away anything—just wetting her up for the ones she's gonna get from now on. And for, well, for other things when—"

"You're a slut, too," Frankie interrupted him with his best sounding reprimand. "And did you have to do that in front of me?"

"Did you like it?" he replied, starting to enjoy his friend's annoyance. Or was it embarrassment? He couldn't tell which and didn't care. He was just glad the dead girl vanished.

"Up yours," Frankie finally said with a growing smile.

"Well, hers. Actually, that's about where I found this," he said pulling out the rolled paper and holding it up.

"Shit, really?" Frankie replied.

Chapter 19 ~

MELANIE'S HEART WAS ABOUT TO BREAK. She put down the paper. Slumping low on the sofa, she let the images of the story sink in. She tried to picture each event.

It disturbed her so much that she decided to break the little spell she had put herself into and get back to some writing. After an hour of trying, still nothing came out. A sentence here, a phrase there, and not much more. Nothing worked. She had never experienced "writer's block" before. It was so annoying her that she threw her pen across the room. She flopped back into her chair. She had always loved writing with a pen, and not a computer. None of that mattered if nothing came out.

She opted to take a different break. She would watch some TV. She made her special drink of vodka and diet, caffeine-free iced tea. Jumping onto her sofa with a bounce, she held up her tall glass like a trophy. Not a drop spilled. She congratulated herself, tipping her head to her imaginary audience.

Grabbing the remote, she quickly ran through station after station. Bored, she went backwards through the same stations. She stopped suddenly on a national news network.

The images looked like pure mayhem. It reminded her of 1960's footage of college student protests. Except these were now parents. Many had picket signs with slogans reading: *"Save Our Children!" "Stop Murdering Our Children!" "Police Useless!" "Protect Us Now!"* and many other sayings. There was a man in the front with a big white mega-phone. He was screaming and chanting with his fist in the air. The crowd followed suit, pressing against the line of officers.

She watched in horror as a creeping fear began to grow deep within her. Images of a world gone mad formed. Constant upheaval and riots spread like wildfire. Parents in the streets trying to save their children. Police helpless and pushing them back to no avail. Growing murders went unsolved. All beginning here, here in Philadelphia, the named City of Brotherly Love. She took a fast and long sip of her drink to stop her imagination. Melanie cringed. The extra vodka she had a habit of adding hit her a little hard. She then froze. She stared at the screen.

"We're here once again at the entrance of Central Station where, every day, a steady crowd of parents have been demanding a stop to these hideous crimes, the murder and kidnapping of their dear loved ones."

The reporter actually seemed exasperated herself. Melanie wondered if she had children, too.

She went on about the megaphone character. As she mentioned his name, Melanie immediately recognized him. She had never actually seen Stuart Martino in the news looking like that, completely crazed and out of control. He was pumping his fist harder. His hair was wild.

She slumped back shocked. The reporter then went frantically through the sequence of events that had brought them to this very point. After each phrase, she raised her voice at the end to a high pitch. Melanie pictured a hyena in her place. She tried not to giggle. Deep inside she was feeling awful for those small children. But a small giggle was coming up inside her anyway. She hated this horrible habit of snickering, even laughing, when feeling terrible at the same time.

Even though she wasn't a mom, each murder had hit

deeply, as if it were her own child. Now helplessness and fear sliced right through her. She pictured the children begging for their lives. Tears started. She visualized with horror as they were killed. She saw their dead bodies.

She started to cry.

Chapter 20 ~

"YOU KNOW THIS IS GODDAMN evidence," Frankie exclaimed, looking down and shaking his head in disgust. He looked up at his friend's grinning face.

"So?" Fletcher replied. He took a long sip from his drink, appearing not to care at all, and actually not caring at all. He did not need a lecture. He will do what he wants or walk. He inwardly grinned at that.

"*So?* So, it means that you tampered with it again. Just like before."

"No, it means that it was there and I took it, and don't worry, I dusted it and nothing," he lied. He again thought of the dead girl and also where he had placed the twenty in the stripper. He closed his eyes, forcing the contrasting images to disappear.

"But the crime scene investigation! Gardner is going to kill me. He wants every scene pristine. Damn it Fletch! How am I going to explain this? Mike is going to flip if this goes against us in court when we catch this perp!"

"They can have it! He will find nothing more than before. The monster who's doing this is smart as shit. There's no evidence there, trust me. So, can we get to the point?"

"Yeah, yeah, go ahead, whatcha got?" Frankie replied, as he handed it back without reading it. He watched the grin slowly leave Fletcher's face. He tried not to think how Carl Gardner, Special CSU Investigator on the case, was going to crucify him for allowing his friend to operate independently. Fletcher never cared, even on the Force.

"Look, just remember, you asked me onto this whole thing, and if I can't do it my way, then find someone else."

"It's fine, just—"

"I mean it, find someone else. And after they fail, you'll be hanging from William Penn's statue, high above City Hall, after the fall-out."

"Okay, okay!" Frankie said as he motioned to the bartender.

"Drinking?" Fletcher asked with a genuine note of surprise. Not much really surprised him these days.

"Yeah, what the hell. I'm off duty now anyway, or at least I'm taking *myself* off duty." He looked at his watch and shook his head again. "Man, Fletch, it's not even five-thirty and you got me drinking."

"Sorry. Habit. Bad night and day, huh?"

"Got Mike so far up my butt it hurts. And Martino's up his even further, as well as the mayor, and the—"

"Okay, stop, enough. Get a drink."

They waited in silence as the bartender came over. Frankie ordered a scotch. He cursed at the crap they served. He took a long gulp before motioning to Fletcher, with his glass in hand, to continue.

Fletcher was now staring at the girl dancing.

"You really like her, huh?" Frankie finally asked, seriously.

Fletcher still said nothing. He looked as if he suddenly went into a deep coma.

"They must know the victims," he said matter-of-factly, not breaking his stare at the girl.

"Huh?"

Frankie downed the drink and motioned for another.

Fletcher glanced over, surprised again. Twice in one day, he mused.

"A real piss of a day, huh?" Fletcher asked, sounding sincere enough to Frankie.

"Just go on."

"Okay, they or whoever, has to know the victims or knows something close about them. That's why it's so easy and no trace. I should have figured."

"Aw c'mon, who knows all these kids, from the different neighborhoods, from different parts of town—and even Martino in the burbs?"

"I don't know yet, but they do. They have to. Or they know how to lead them on."

"Well, if they do somehow, you better act fast because after I tell Martino—or Mike tells him—the real shit, and I mean the real shit, is gonna be flying so fucking fast and hard, you may never see me again."

"Don't worry, I'll figure it out. There's some connection, somehow."

"By the way," Frankie said.

"What?"

"Do you have to look so scruffy all the time?"

"Scruffy? What do you mean?" He huffed, enjoying the question.

"I mean that worn out denim shirt from the Hard Rock and the corduroy pants that don't match at all. It's ninety friggin' degrees out. You've got idiotic penny loafers that no one wears anymore. No socks. And that stupid hat, with the one side up that makes you look like a nutty musketeer."

"Oh, that kind of scruffy," he replied, chuckling. "It's me and the way I like to look."

"You can't let Mike ever see you like that. No way."

"It's obviously your problem, and his. Definitely not mine."

He smirked, turning to the dancing girl who had inched over again. "Oh, and," he said without turning, "I never said I was ever going to talk with Mike anyway. He's yours."

Frankie ignored him for a second as the pretty, bare dancer came up close to him. He caught himself and turned back to Fletcher.

"What does the note say anyway?"

"Passage."

"Whatever."

"Read it yourself," Fletcher suggested.

"I will. But you know I think it's gibberish. I honestly want your take."

"I'm working on it, okay? I need to be alone."

"Yeah, the way you always like it, alone, self, you, you, and you again. Well, damn it! Hurry the you-know-what up."

Fletcher turned, seeing his smile. He cocked his head and gave Frankie a leer back, doing his best John Wayne.

"Read it anyway and just see if you can figure something out yourself, okay?"

Frankie took the paper, unrolled it carefully, and made a face as if he recognized something. He put it up to his nose.

He made a cringing look.

"Told you where it was."

"Aw, man."

He started to read it, holding it away from him.

Fletcher ignored him, taking another dollar bill from the bar. He slipped it between her butt cheeks. She wiggled them for him before skipping away with a smile.

Chapter 21 ~

MELANIE FINALLY STOPPED CRYING and started paging through the channels again. She needed a comedy. She gave up and inadvertently ended up on a local news channel. She threw the remote down in disgust. The pictures of Martino's two girls were everywhere. She stared at the screen, amazed at how innocent they appeared. She thought of her own two young nieces. In her mind, Martino's girls suddenly transformed into them. Her tears started again.

"Kelly. Kimberly. Kelly. Kimberly," she kept repeating quietly to herself. She looked down for a second, trying to clear her mind. Glancing back, the images were Martino's girls again. She stared at the two young, pretty faces.

A thought came to her. She quickly got up and ran to the phone.

She dialed and waited as it rang and rang. Her heart started to pound. Panic began to build. She knew they lived outside the city, in the far western suburbs, but still. She had to know they were okay. She had to know now. Finally, voice mail kicked in.

"Damn it," she whispered. She heard the line suddenly pick up on top of the recorded message.

"Hello? Hello? Who's this?"

"Dana! It's Mel.

"Hey, hi Sis!"

Chapter 22 ~

WHILE FRANKIE READ the passage, Fletcher was mulling over the locations of the three sets of victims. It started in Society Hill, then Old City. Martino's kids disappeared in Gladwyne, the suburbs. They also found similar child kidnappings farther west of Philadelphia, almost to Lancaster. Only the last three were double abductions, with one found cruelly murdered each time. Interesting perp, Fletcher thought.

All the other priors were just single kidnappings. Fletcher wondered why the difference. They were also working with the PA State Police to find any common or differentiating evidence. However, nothing developed. This guy is smart and all over the place, Fletcher thought.

"Means shit to me," Frankie said.

"You're Catholic, right?" he replied, still looking at the dancer who noticed his smile. Her body was smooth and luscious. As she inched over, he was trying to decide whether to start irritating his friend again.

"Yeah, Catholic, and I'm going to Heaven, not like you," Frankie retorted with a grin as he watched the girl slowly dance towards them. Fletcher instantly knew that sarcastic grin.

"Well, give it back and let me think about it. I'll get back to you."

"Make a copy or write it down. I need to get that to Gardner now. He's already gonna fry me." Fletcher rolled his eyes in contempt, almost causing Frankie to slam his fist on the bar.

Frankie was getting annoyed with his friend's aloofness while he took the heat. Fletcher's looked showed his apathy. Frankie sighed and continued. "So, what do you think it may mean? Any ideas at all?"

Fletcher could hear the desperation in Frankie's voice. He decided to show he was going to be nice and helpful. First the girl.

He slowly stuffed a five into her cleavage with his mouth. She stayed long enough to let him know he could go further. He thought Frankie could wait just a second more. He rubbed his mouth across both naked, sweaty breasts, enjoying the taste and feel. He knew that Frankie would kill him if he continued.

He turned back and saw the impatient look on his friend's face; he was clearly asking him to finish. Fletcher's heart went out to him and that irritated him. He did not like anyone touching his feelings.

"This killer likes his work," Fletcher suddenly became very serious, wiping his mouth. "He also likes suspense, or should I say *loves* suspense. Hence, the kidnapping and a murder of the sister or brother, and then no contact at all. Or any ransom note. He's enjoying the apprehension, even watching it. It's a game. It may mean more to him than the actual acts. That part's obvious."

"I see. Go on."

Frankie felt a growing relief as he realized Fletcher had just been playing with him. Years ago, he would have caught that, he thought. He knew the pressure was getting to him.

"Now, understand that you brought me into this whole thing after Martino's kids. I had no chance to see the other scenes. And you only found another passage at the second scene. There may have been one at the first scene. Since nothing was found in the autopsy, it's irrelevant now. So, I'm just right now working all this through with this new passage. Plus, we have the out of town kidnappings, too. Hopefully something breaks there."

"Yeah, yeah, stop making excuses, go on."

Fletcher saw he was making fun of him and not being serious, so he let it go.

"Well, without any contact about the ones kidnapped, he knows that the families and the city are not only going crazy about the murders, he also has everyone by the," he cupped between his legs, "with the ones he's holding. And nobody knows what he's going to do with them."

"If they're still alive."

"If they're still alive, yeah, but my bet is that they are and there's more to come. I'm just hoping he doesn't know me or that I'm on this. Because he'll adjust if an outsider is investigating. Which, mind you, I'll bet he's onto everything you're doing, on top of knowing the victims. It's all too safe for him. He's very smart. Perverted as hell, but smart. Possible insider, my friend."

"Shit, I was hoping not, but it did cross my mind. So, what's with this Elijah crap?"

"May be hints or something. May even mean absolutely nothing. But I think it's his 'line and sinker' for us to follow, seeing if we take the bait. It also may lead us away from him. Or what I really think, it's leading us to the next abduction. He's hoping we figure it out, and always a little too late. Playing it just like Moriarity leading on Sherlock Holmes. And his game and the passages cannot become public. It will scare him off."

"What if he *wants* it to become public, some kind of freak show or something," Frankie posed. "Publicity freak, ya know?

That probably would get his rocks off, too."

"Maybe, but I still think it's a game for us to play, not the public. This game is between him and us to see who's smarter. He's pretty brilliant."

"But what's the point of doing all this, what motive? It's horrible."

Fletcher paused.

"Frankie, I honestly don't know." This time he didn't lie.

"Well, maybe go see that priest again or something. If we can just anticipate his next move—"

"Let me think about it."

"Not too long. The heat is really hot. We gotta get these kids back." He didn't tell Fletcher that he himself was being torn apart inside.

He just smiled a weak smile.

Fletcher could see everything was wearing on him.

"No problem, friend. I'll get back to you."

"You're my best shot out there. Please don't forget, like you tend to when you drink. And do you have to drink this early all the time?"

Fletcher ignored him, motioning to the bartender. With the pen and paper he requested, he copied the passage and gave the original to Frankie. Fletcher then turned towards the girl, who had come over to him from the stage. Posing for him, she pressed her naked body up against his. Frankie knew it was time to leave.

"See ya, let me know." He slipped off the stool.

"Yeah, yeah, sure thing."

He saw Fletcher's arm reach around her and pull her closer.

Frankie turned and walked out the door, shaking his head

grinning.

He never saw Fletcher turn. With a deep feeling of friendship, Fletcher watched his friend leave.

Chapter 23 ~

SHE HEARD HER SISTER'S calm voice. It disturbed her, especially while she was upset over everything.

"So, you married yet?" her sister teased.

"No, and don't be cute," Melanie retorted back.

"Boyfriend?"

"No."

"Girlfriend?"

"No! Stop now, 'kay?"

"Sure. What's up girl?" Melanie could almost see her sister's smile.

Dana was constantly upbeat, and to Melanie, a little naïve about the world. She lived out in the far western suburbs. Melanie thought the air out there must be laced with something because nothing seemed to worry her or her neighbors.

"How are you and the girls?"

She tried not to sound alarmed or worried.

"Fine, we're all fine. Why?"

Dana's tone changed slightly to caution. Melanie knew her sister well. She smiled.

"Oh, nothing. Just checking in."

"What? A little strange, Sis, don't you think?"

"Why? You're my sister and—"

"Oh! Is this about those horrid murders of children?" Dana immediately cut her off.

"Well, a little. I just wanted to—"

"Well, Sis, thanks. That's so nice, but we're out here. I

don't think anyone cares about us out here, ya know."

Melanie thought it was a little cavalier of her sister, no matter where she was located. Things had always cut her deeper than her sister.

"Well, it *is* happening, now a third time, and you have two kids around the same age as all the victims. Kind of like likely targets, *ya know*," she mimicked her sister.

"Yeah, I guess so. But…"

"Not to worry. If everyone's fine, then I'm fine."

"Okay, Sis. How's everything else?" her sister asked in a cheerful voice.

After all she had seen on TV and in the news, Melanie just didn't feel like answering.

Chapter 24 ~

THINKING OF HIS FRIEND, Fletcher had enough playing around with naked girls. He graciously began saying his goodbyes to the beautiful unclothed girl, who was doing everything she could to get more bills out of him. He just wanted to leave, go home, relax a bit, and go over everything. This last passage had his attention. Like his friend, he also felt time was running out.

"Gotta go, honey," he said to her, doing his best to unhook her from him.

"Really? Can't you just stay a little bit longer? Pleeease?"

She cupped his crotch so softly, he paused. He glanced at her small milky white, pouting breasts. He started to think about it.

"No, gotta go, next time," he smiled at her.

"Okay, but I'll make you a deal right now. My place, for free, if you promise to come back and see me more?"

"Honey, really, would love to but gotta go," he heard himself say. The exact opposite was running through his head.

"Remember me," she said kissing him full on the mouth and stroking his cheek.

"Damn," he said breaking loose. He quickly walked out.

He got in his car, threw his hat on the seat, veered around the lot, and maneuvered fast out onto the road. For about ten minutes, he was convincing himself not to return to her.

He sped onto the Blue Route. He kicked it up to seventy-five. With his arm straight on the wheel, he leaned back to enjoy the ride.

When he got to Route 1, he turned south and headed towards his town of Media. It was a small but growing town, with a mix of new townhouses and old Victorian homes. Media was a quiet, pleasant place with many small pubs and restaurants. He felt at home there. It was his little Utopia.

He quickly pulled down State Street and on to Old Maple. It led to his home, a colorful Victorian manor he had purchased twenty-five years ago. Even though worth triple, he knew he would never sell it. It had that classic, warm feel he loved. Beautifully sculpted architecture characterized every room. Outside was a wide timber porch with large ornate wooden railings, painted white. The house truly had the touch of an age gone by, his private hideaway where he could forget his past.

He studied history. His expertise was war, from Periclean Athens, to the horrors of the Twentieth Century. It constantly amazed him what motivated nations to go to war. The insanity of what people called politics just fascinated him. His affinity for war mostly came from the strategies and the outmaneuvering of others. During his time on the Force, it was what had given him his feeling of power, and his fame.

It's probably, he mused, what had gotten him into police life. He later became a detective, solving criminals' real motivations. Each case was as if an individual puzzle was laid out before him. Later, when he had enough of the internal politics and restrictions, he retired at the ripe age of forty-five. He decided to pursue his desire to write poetry and maybe even try a novel. However, his real loves were rare antiques and fine art. Learning to paint in oils and acrylics was a dream of his.

He had never been married, nor had kids. That helped him save and invest most of his money. He also received a small inheritance, and coupled with a private investigation service from his home, he lived well.

Most of all, he cherished his privacy. He figured things out during his time alone. He worked solo, period. Another reason he left the Force. Too many know-it-alls who knew nothing. Like Frankie always said, "too many Ein-fucking-steins," always looking for a clue and never looking at what motivated the criminal mind.

Frankie understood it, too. Working together before, they found they naturally complemented each other. Becoming fast friends, they not only trusted each other, they also highly respected each other. Many had told Frankie to get rid of his relationship with Fletcher. "He's too weird, he's too cocky," they had said. Frankie knew better and knew who to turn to when that brick wall came rushing at him.

Fletcher made a rum and Coke in a tall glass. With a bottle of Jack, he strolled out to the porch. Putting it all onto a small table, he sat on his favorite wicker rocker. It creaked as he leaned back. He held it in place.

He took a deep, long gulp of Jack right from the bottle, chasing it with the rum and Coke. He leaned forward and shook his head from the alcohol rush. Fishing through his pocket, he pulled out the passage.

He hesitated, thinking of the nude girl's offer. He would never admit it, but in his deepest heart, he craved a companion, a female companion to share his life and passions. He thought of Desiree, a girl he had once so loved and adored. He had planned to be with her the rest of his life. She not only constantly lied and had other men all the time, she also feigned her love for him from the very beginning. He never had another love, vowing they would never get close to him again.

As he held up the little piece of paper, "Oh, fucking well," was all that came out of his mouth. He pushed back the memory of his Desiree.

He unfolded it, stared at it, and then read it aloud.

"And the ravens themselves were bringing him bread and meat in the morning and bread and meat in the evening, and from the torrent valley, he kept drinking."

He took another swig of Jack, hoping it would help.

Chapter 25 ~

HE HEARD HIS PHONE RING inside the house. He had forgotten to bring out the cordless.

"Damn it!" he said, as he put down the Jack he was about to swig again. He scrambled out of the rocker, running through to the kitchen. He grabbed the phone.

"Yo!" he answered, out of breath, feeling a little dizzy.

"Hey, it's me. What were you doing, playing with yourself after gawking at that girl?"

"What?"

"Um, like you're out of breath. Calm down."

"What the hell do you want?" he replied with a chuckle.

"You're invited to a cocktail party tonight," Frankie said, sounding suddenly serious.

"Me? Tonight?" he answered, still breathing hard.

"Yeah, you, tonight. Well, actually, I am and you're coming with me. You sound like you're having a heart attack. That's not allowed."

"Oh, yeah? Where?" Fletcher ignored Frankie's comment. He did not like being told he was doing something. Another reason he left the Force.

"Mike's wife Rosalyn is having it. It's going to be real upscale. I think they're trying to calm folks down, at least their own inner circle. Not a lot of people. But they all are rich to the hilt and political animals. I'm going to be bombarded. You're going to be there to fend them off me."

"I am?" he replied with apathy, but beginning to care about

meeting Rosalyn again. She always made him feel like ravishing her. Maybe he would go.

"Yes, you are," Frankie said matter-of-factly.

"Why do you really want me there?" Fletcher pressed, knowing Frankie had other reasons for everything. It's one of the things he loved about his friend. There was always a little mystery in Frankie's actions.

"Like you said, there's gotta be a connection. Every incident so far is always with the damned wealthy. Here's your chance to mingle with the pompous asses, to observe and ask, *and appropriately*, please."

"Oh, I see. Right. And they know something, huh? They are pompous asses, as you so well put it. Not my thing." He really didn't want to go. The picture of him and Rosalyn was fading fast.

"Listen, anything right now is worth it. Do it for me, as a friend, so they all can feel better and be off my back. Please?"

"Aw," he held back the expletive.

Frankie waited and then continued.

"Mike asked, too. As a favor."

So, the DA who hated him, wanted to meet with him at his plush home. Interesting, he thought. Mike must want something and is avoiding it formally.

"Fletch?"

"Damn it, Frankie. What time? Where?"

He could see Frankie's smile on the other end.

Chapter 26 ~

"BIG COCKTAIL PARTY? Tonight? Where? Really?" Josh replied, again grinning to himself. This was becoming too easy. He pictured himself accepting his new promotion, position, and of course, his Pulitzer.

He also knew he should repay his detective informant somehow. Josh figured he would worry about that later, after everything was over. He actually really didn't care. Cops sometimes used the press to help with investigations. Par for the course, he thought.

"Thanks!" he continued. "I promise I'm honestly trying every way to help you guys. Will let you know everything I find, too. I will. No problem. Total silence, yes. Yes, absolutely. I don't even know you, right?"

After another moment of promises, he was finally able to get off the phone. He knew the detective was seriously trying to help the case but Josh had other motives in mind.

"So awesome! Actually the DA's house. Yes!" he screamed at the top of his lungs. He did a little dance in the middle of his cube. No one was nearby so he didn't care.

There had to be many important folks attending, he thought. The talk itself would be great news all on its own. What an inside scoop!

He told himself to calm down and work out how to present the story. Maybe tag it as a "covert police meeting at DA's home," or along that line. Make the public yearn to know what they are talking about, better yet, planning—or better yet, scheming.

Smiling, he knew they couldn't do anything about his story either. On the other hand, they would have to reveal what they talked about or even better, look like they were secretly hiding something.

His glee kept building. He loved it. He so loved it.

"Perfect. Just perfect."

He had to find a way in somehow, but decided he would figure that out later. All in good time, he thought.

He packed his stuff, grabbed his tiny recorder, and ran out.

Chapter 27 ~

FRANKIE HUNG UP AFTER letting Fletcher know where to go and what time. He was tempted just to pick him up or meet him somewhere and go together. However, after today, he could use a break from him and that stupid hat. He smiled. He actually liked the hat but never told him.

He knew how good Fletcher was at investigating. It didn't matter to him what others thought. Frankie was a cop, first and foremost; his real job was not dealing with the political crap. He solved crimes and brought criminals to justice. If it meant getting Fletcher Saxtan involved when nobody else could think of a solution—even the State Police—that's what he was going to do, period. These were children, for God's sake. He would do anything to put an end to it and find them.

Moreover, he felt that sometimes it was only Fletch he could trust—trust to be honest, trust to be more dedicated than anyone, trust to be intelligent beyond anyone, and mostly, trust to see into things further than anyone he knew on the Force. He actually missed working with him. Except for his eccentricities and insatiable sexual appetite, Fletcher was brilliant. And these tendencies had gotten him into messes more than once. Trouble followed him on the job and with, well, sometimes victims. He had a magnetism that few could resist.

He always solved the case, though. Frankie reflected on that fact with an inner smile. Fletcher always won, no matter the odds.

He wanted him at Rosalyn's little cocktail party. First, the

DA could listen to him and gain trust that Frankie, with Fletcher, was doing everything possible. At the same time, he wanted his friend to dissect these upscale pompous asses. He wanted Fletcher to see into them, what they say, what they fear, and what they think. Maybe something will click. Not that they were suspects, at least not yet. They may have seen or knew something that was missed in their interrogations. From their inner circles, they all knew the victims or the victims' parents.

Frankie hated talking to any of them. Even with his apparent disgust, Fletcher still liked to talk with people and dig into their psyches. Many times just for fun. Somehow, he knew that Fletch, if anybody could, would find something, somewhere. That's why he knew his friend was partly playing about not wanting to go. Of course he wanted to go.

He mused how Fletcher did not know how well he knew him. Frankie prayed he would soon figure something out. He was going insane for the dead and missing young children. Every time he thought about them, it cut right through his soul.

He couldn't take the sleepless nights anymore. He needed a break in the case and a break in his life. The thought of the first murder crept back again. He saw himself standing in shock over the naked girl's rotting body. His heart sank as the tears welled up again from that image, and his own feeling of helplessness. He needed to shut his feelings down, and fast.

Damn, he thought.

He quickly dialed Fletcher's number.

He waited as it rang.

Waited.

Damn, he thought again.

He wasn't sure if Fletch had gone out, was taking a shower, or saw his name and wasn't answering.

He waited for the tone.

"Yo, forgot. Please dress right, or I mean appropriate for these people. You know what I mean. C'mon, for me, please, Fletch?"

He hung up.

He knew Fletcher Saxtan's little way of loving to shock people. When investigating, it was a great technique to get to them and catch them off guard.

But not at the DA's friggin' home.

Not tonight.

Damn, he thought again.

Chapter 28 ~

MELANIE DECIDED SHE had enough of the worrying and images. She needed a break. She made another drink and sat on her bed in silence.

Taking a very long sip, she allowed the strong drink to sink deep into her. She took a slow breath, silently putting the drink down.

"That's it. I'm out'a here," she declared to the empty room.

She got up. On her way to the bathroom to take a shower, she paused halfway. To anyone watching, she looked like a wax statue, caught in time.

She was trying to decide. Should she venture out or just go to bed? It went back and forth in her head. Then the images of dead children and those teen girls pasted across the TV reappeared.

In a blinding moment, she turned, grabbed her drink, and downed it. Her body shook from the vodka. She turned to her closet. She wildly swung the door open like a crazed woman. She frantically fumbled through hanging clothes until she found it.

She tossed the tiny red miniskirt and creamy white, waist-tied blouse onto her bed. Without turning back, she strutted into the bathroom.

She was going out on the town. She was going to party hard. She was going to look hot. She may even hook a man.

Chapter 29 ~

HE HAD NOT SEEN THE CALL. It wouldn't have mattered anyway. He would dress as he wished and that was it. Fletcher Saxtan didn't need to impress anyone. At the same time, he knew better than to embarrass Frankie. When in Rome, he finally thought. Moreover, these people were the types to open up to those they believed were like them.

He decided that the tie was too much for him. He did like the tweed jacket—formal but sporty at the same time. The jeans stayed. He did cancel the sneakers for a pair of casual brown shoes. At least nothing stood out that would cause any complaint from his friend.

He put the hat on and then took it off. He knew it would annoy Frankie. He made a wide smirk and then smiled. He even decided to shave. Looking in the mirror, he previewed the complete look.

"Mmmm," he hummed, "not too bad for an old fuck." He winked.

He wondered if there was a sex-starved wife he could hook up with. That would really piss off Frankie. His favorite ways to get information were sex and alcohol. Or both. He definitely preferred them together.

Pointing his finger as a gun to the mirror, he winked again. Finishing his rum and Coke, he strolled from the room. He ambled down the stairs and out the door. He paused in the evening air, taking a deep breath.

He was giving himself enough time to be late, not

fashionably late, just late.

Chapter 30 ~

IT NEEDED TO BE ALONE. Too many things were happening all at once. The Figure floated down the long corridor to the old door hidden under the stairs. It slowly turned the knob until it clicked open. Silently, it went in.

The chair remained where it had been. It knew no one had been there. The door closed quietly. The latch click echoed.

"This is our chance. We can find out everything and get back on course," seethed slowly out of its mouth.

It paused, as if waiting for a response that never came.

"We know exactly how, too. Then we can get back. We can't wait. Can't wait."

It let the silence fall again in the blackness. So dark, it thought. So wonderfully dark.

"We can't be seen. Never be seen. Never seen. Never seen."

Chapter 31 ~

AS FLETCHER DROVE ON, the passage completely occupied him. What could it mean? He kept repeating it. Was it where the next kidnapping will be? The next murder locale? Where the missing children were? Info about the killer? Nothing at all? Just to send them down a wrong path to avoid detection? What?

Mike lived in Center City in a beautiful home that encompassed two townhouse slots. His sexy, young wife Rosalyn was personally very wealthy. No one knew where she had obtained it. Even without Mike's salary, they could afford over a million-dollar home. It was located in one of the city's prime real estate areas, Rittenhouse Square and its popular park.

They had one child, Edward. If memory came back right to Fletcher, he was about sixteen years old. The kid was also a real brat. Hey, rich and a brat? Yeah, goes together, he thought and grinned. He also remembered everyone just called him Eddy.

Mike, though, was a straight shooter. Fletcher did like that. He was mostly on the cops' side, too. He would get pissed, however, when things weren't done by procedure. Nothing angered him more than being put on the spot with defense attorneys, the mayor, or the public.

Fletcher also mused that Mike always tried to impress his cronies. He catered to his wealthy circle of friends, sometimes at the expense of the very cops helping him. That is what Fletcher hated the most.

He made a mental note to tread carefully with him. He didn't want to lose the contract. He was not doing this for nothing. The payment was solely between him and Frankie. But if Mike pulled the plug on him being on the investigation, well, there goes the cash, too.

He turned onto Chestnut Street, starting the trick of weaving through crazy drivers on the three-lane road.

He crossed the Schuylkill River. He continued to the nearest parking garage. He reminded himself to get a receipt because he was definitely expensing everything. Sorry, Frankie.

After parking, he took the elevator down to the street and started walking towards their block. He arrived at the correct address, pressing the button to announce himself. He waited. He looked at the enormous wrought iron gate. It looked as if it was from a medieval castle. They may be rich, but they sure are scared folks.

"Yes?" he heard from the small speaker.

"Fletcher Saxtan here," he replied in as formal a voice as he could muster.

There was a long pause. He figured his name was being verified. He wondered if Frankie had remembered to inform them.

Chapter 32 ~

MELANIE FINALLY REACHED her favorite place in Center City. It was a quaint outdoor café near Rittenhouse Square, called the Luxury Café. They had a wonderful bar menu and served renowned flavored martinis. As she walked by the last designer shop on Walnut Street, she secretly eyed her reflection in the tall windows.

What she saw really pleased her. Her long bare legs looked sensual. From the high heels to her tiny mini skirt that moved slowly up and down on her exposed thighs, all looked perfect. She exercised constantly. This to her was the best pay-off.

She was now happy to be in town. She was going to make this *her* night. And she had no problem being alone. Actually, she preferred it. She knew that sometimes men got scared-off when the girl they wanted to talk to was surrounded by her girlfriends.

She also needed a male right now. It had been a long time since she had good, crazy sex. She was not inhibited at all. But she was picky. Whomever she met had to have certain qualities. One of which was intelligence. The other was confidence. Of course, he had to be so sexy it would make her squirm in her seat just being near him.

Not much to ask. She held back the giggle.

She confidently strolled into the café up to the bar. She gently placed her small red pocketbook down. The bartender saw her. He immediately came over.

Out of the corner of her eye, she could see the men

admiring. Some actually looked cute too, she thought.

The bartender came back with her martini.

"Thanks," she said with her best, demure smile. She didn't have to look around to know all the men saw it. "Please keep a tab for me, okay?" She cocked her head slightly, letting her hair fall into her face.

"Sure thing but this drink is on..." he said, as he pointed across the bar to a gorgeous young man. He had thick wavy hair, which appeared intentionally disheveled. He smiled at her, raising his martini.

She smiled at him and did the same.

He took that as his invitation.

Chapter 33 ~

AS FLETCHER WAITED, he decided to quickly check his voice mail. He pulled his cell out and opened it. Right as he did, he felt the hand on his shoulder. His mind jumped into full alert. He squarely turned to subdue his attacker.

"Whoa! Damn! Get off!" he heard, as he grabbed the man's wrist, turning it down and backwards.

"Who the hell are you?" he demanded. He started to relax a little when he looked eye to eye at him.

He saw a flush, young face. His dark curly hair was like a cropped mop. He was short in stature. Very schoolboy-ish, Fletcher thought.

"Ouch! Let me go, please," the young man politely demanded.

"Will do, once you tell me who you are and what you are doing here."

"I was just trying to get your attention. I didn't want to scare you."

"Scare me? Well, you succeeded," Fletcher said as he slowly released him, letting him up. "Well?"

"I'm Josh Stein, *Philly Times*," he promptly replied, as he rubbed his wrist and gave him a scornful glare.

"Shit, what do *you* want?" Then the buzzer rang.

"Sorry, gotta go," Fletcher quickly said, turning to the large iron door.

"Wait!"

Chapter 34 ~

FLETCHER IGNORED HIM. He honestly hated the press, especially young ones who wanted headlines at any cost. He just wasn't in the mood. Going to Mike's and mingling with rich snobs was actually now a better alternative.

"I got information for you. Please wait," Josh pleaded.

Fletcher didn't care. It had to be bullshit. He opened the door. He walked up the little flight of stairs, letting the iron door close behind him with a slam.

"Please Mr. Saxtan," Josh pleaded again through the gate.

Fletcher stopped still when he heard his name. This kid obviously does his homework. But that's not enough. He started back up the stairs.

"You're missing a big piece of the puzzle."

He stopped again.

"You got one second."

"I know about the passages. It's Elijah, right? From the Old Testament, right?"

"Don't know what you're talking about," he replied, still with his back to Josh.

"Yes, you do, but that's not important. What's important is…" He paused a second to keep control of the moment and because he was getting tired of what he thought was absolute arrogance.

"What's important?"

Josh could hear the tone of annoyance, but also read in it interest.

"What's important is *Elijah's Wrath*!"

Fletcher stayed still a second longer. Then without turning back, he went up the last step into the main door. He closed it silently behind him.

Josh stood there flabbergasted. Realizing his mouth was agape, he slowly closed it. Anger quickly rose in him. He did want the story but also wanted to help. He honestly did.

"You're missing it! You stupid fuck, you're missing it!"

That was it. He was going solo on this.

He already had his plans.

Chapter 35 ~

MELANIE WATCHED HIM casually stroll around the bar. She was quickly trying to decide on him. When he made it up close to her, he stopped, motioning to the bar spot next to her. He was asking if it was okay to join her. This she liked and nodded her approval. He smiled. He moved in next to her, carefully placing his martini next to hers.

His blue eyes immediately transfixed her. He also had a cute, boyish smile. She kept her composure.

"Hi, I'm Bryce," he softly said, flashing her with his fabulous smile again. His teeth were perfectly white.

"Melanie," she coyly replied, again cocking her head.

"Very nice to meet you," he said, never stopping his smiling.

"You, too. And thanks," she motioned to her drink.

"For a lady as beautiful as you, it's my pleasure."

Not bad, not bad at all, she thought.

"By yourself?" he asked as he took a sip of his martini. His eyes never left hers.

She shifted a little, allowing a better view of her breasts. They were half-bare from her slightly open blouse.

She was amazed how he noticed without really showing he did. She knew right away that he was very experienced with girls. A definite player, she thought. He probably scored with a high rate of success.

She was also very pleased she attracted this type of man. Getting older was definitely getting better, at least for her.

OK, playboy, let's see what you got, she mused. She nonchalantly ran her fingers up the side of her thigh.

Chapter 36 ~

IT ALWAYS ANNOYED FLETCHER when reporters ambushed him. As he made his way in, he was in conflict. He hated talking to the press, especially young brats. He also wanted to know what the hell Josh was talking about. He resolved he could research it himself. If all else failed, he could just contact him.

He first wanted to ask Frankie what he might know about this Elijah's Wrath thing.

His mind was interrupted by the home he had just stepped into. He stopped at the door. The decor was ultra modern, with a touch of exquisite baroque styling and statues. It appeared a museum to him, massive and immaculate. He could tell there was nothing, not even the grout in the glowing marble floor, that wasn't extraordinarily expensive.

He heard voices further down and walked casually along to where he found a small turn. It led into a very large, high ceilinged room.

His eyes were immediately struck by the sight of wood—lots of wood—dark, expensive wood. From the large desk area to the immense ornate framework that rose from each corner of the room. There were oversized beams across the ceiling. Below was a hardwood floor that was the most brilliant he had ever seen. There was not a scratch anywhere. A subtle aroma of very aged lacquer began to fill his sense of smell. Very Old English, he thought pleasantly. It agreed with his taste for a world-gone-by.

Everyone was dressed formally. The ladies were in long, exquisite gowns. The men wore dark suits. Each must have cost more than all the clothes he owned. The talk was low and even. He heard violins and cellos. The volume was perfectly unnoticeable. The flowing melody seemed to rise out of the walls. Again, all was to his taste.

His thoughts suddenly went back to the small apartment. He saw the still, dead girl lying there. He immediately blocked the image, wondering why it had appeared to him.

Damn, he thought, so this is the real rich, eh?

He began to feel a bit uneasy, just standing there alone. Nobody was looking his way. Wasn't someone supposed to announce people at these things? They were all engaged in hushed conversations in little groups. Most were holding champagne glasses. Some had martini or rocks glasses. No beer, obviously.

He felt a big slap on his back. He immediately turned, about to deck the hitter. People touching him from behind was getting very old.

"Hey Fletch! Glad you made it," Frankie said, in a loud, soft whisper.

"Yeah, I'm here," he replied, "and I almost decked you. You know better than to sneak—"

"Aw, get off it. Who here would be attacking you? Well, at least not physically," he said with a teasing smile.

"You really want me here?" Fletcher sincerely asked. He eyed Frankie up and down and wondered where he got such a nice black pinstripe, double-breasted suit. He couldn't tell if he looked good or stupid in it.

"Yes, I do want you here. It's important for these folks to know who's looking out for them. Trust me, they will judge harshly, so *be* good."

"Yeah, yeah, you keep telling me that. Where's the booze?"

"Oh, I didn't want to forget this. No abuse."

"What do you mean: no abu—oh, she wasn't—"

"Right. No semen, no penetration bruises, no nothing."

"Well, at least they're not perv's," he smiled a sinister smile.

"Yeah, not perv's, just coldblooded killers of children. Like that's any better," Frankie sneered back, sipping his scotch. Frankie did like the fact that they had excellent scotch. He really wanted to get drunk and was starting to feel the scotch's affect.

"Yeah, well, either way, it sucks. Need a drink, remember?"

"Be cool about getting sloshed, and listen, keep your hands off the wives!"

"*Booze, please?*"

"Over there, see the bartender?"

"La-dee-da! A bartender in a home, behind a bar bigger and nicer than my living room."

"*Fletch,*" Frankie pressed, grabbing his arm.

"I'll be good. Just messin' with ya."

"And refrain from your favorite words, too. Remember me and my position, okay?" he whispered out of the corner of his mouth as they started to walk towards the bar.

"Sure thing, friend. Should I just stand around and wait for the Spanish Inquisition?"

They both stopped as frozen statues, each smiling.

Frankie couldn't hold that one back.

"*Nobody EXPECTS the Spanish Inquisition!*"

He shared a love for Monty Python with Fletcher and started laughing a little too loud, drawing attention to them.

"Oops," Frankie whispered.

For a quick second, Fletcher thought Frankie just might be a little drunk. They continued to the bar. He hoped he was getting a little tipsy because he knew his friend could use a night of absolute inebriation.

"Oh, look, that little Eddy shit is here," Frankie motioned with his glass, which Fletcher thought was a little obvious.

"So? I ain't into kids. Just the moms."

"You idiot. He's someone you may wish to talk with. He's about the same age as——"

"Oh, yeah."

Chapter 37 ~

TO HIS DELIGHT, FLETCHER SAW Rosalyn coming over. He decided to ignore Frankie's request about the wives. Damned she looked good in that fire-red gown. It was delightfully tight against her ultra-slim, girlish body. She glided as she walked over. Fletcher imagined her not actually touching the floor, in her smooth stride.

"Well, well. Hi, Fletcher," she said with a shy smile that melted him. At the same time, she lightly touched him on the arm.

"Hey, Rosalyn, you're looking very fine this wonderful evening," Fletcher replied. He followed it with a slight cock and bow of his head, as a knight would to a lady. He suddenly wished he had his hat on.

Frankie gave him a quick glare, which Fletcher ignored.

His eyes never left Rosalyn. Her blonde, reddish hair was gently pulled up and back. Beautifully framing her petite face were long, exquisitely curled tresses. They hung just slightly forward. Her eyes shone like brilliant emeralds. They sparkled when the light hit them just right. The light blush on her cheeks highlighted her ruby lips, which Fletcher wanted to kiss.

Frankie stared at Fletcher. He knew he was enthralled. Frankie had not seen his friend charmed like this since his old flame. That seemed decades ago. It had devastated his friend. The sideway glance Fletcher gave him inadvertently confirmed that he was falling for Rosalyn's beauty. Frankie smiled, praying that his friend would be good. He finished his scotch and almost burped. Yep, getting drunk, definitely, he fondly thought to himself. It was helping keep the images away.

"Frankie here told me you were coming. So glad you're here," she said as she walked past Fletcher, not taking her hand off his arm until the very last moment. She gave him a tiny nod, which he took as an approval of some sort. She moved graciously towards a group of men. Fletcher stared at her petite hips as the scent of her perfume lingered.

"Do you *have* to be that way?" Frankie asked with a firm tone.

"What way? With her?" Fletcher replied a little surprised.

"Um, yeah!"

"Honestly, sometimes I think she's a whore, under all that trapping.

"*Fletch!*"

Fletcher heard a slight slur in Frankie's voice. He inwardly smiled.

"Look, you want me to talk to these people? Then let me do it how I want to, okay? Stop worrying. I did her before."

"What?"

"Kidding. But I wouldn't mind—"

"She does look wicked. But stop there or I will un-invite you right now. And by the way, here comes Mike. Ix-nay about the wife."

Frankie nudged him a little to make the point stick.

"Gentlemen," Mike said in his usual deep voice. Fletcher thought of Darth Vader.

"Mike."

"Hey, Mike, long time," Fletcher replied with his hand out.

They shook and Mike put a huge arm around each of them.

"Boys, I don't have to tell you. You know we have a

horrible situation here. Never been anything like this before and there's no end in sight. And I don't have to tell you the mayor is absolutely frantic. It's gotta stop and stop now. These people, my close friends and associates, are scared stiff of this maniac."

Frankie noted, to his dismay, that he didn't mention the rest of the public. As he spoke, he was leading them over to the bar.

Fletcher felt funny as he was being pulled. He wanted to run from under the big arm.

"Don't believe their apparent calmness and pleasantries," Mike continued. "They want answers and they want them now. And so do I. After Stu's daughter," he paused and looked down for a second to let it sink in, "and his dear little Stephanie who's still missing, these fine people don't even want their kids out of the house anymore. Some are even hiring bodyguards. This guy is crazy, killing boys and girls like that. You gotta stop him and now!" he demanded as he pulled them closer to his body, which was beginning to freak Fletcher. "Get those kids back safe. Hear me?"

When he got them to the bar, Mike released them. Fletcher felt uncomfortable the whole time. He was beginning to get angry. He didn't like being touched like that for that long. Being the DA gave him latitude with Fletcher, but only so far. Pompous ass, he sneered to himself.

"Charles, please give my boys here a drink," Mike said. He turned a second to talk to another guest who had come over to him. They walked a little away so that Frankie and Fletcher could not hear the conversation. That annoyed Fletcher, too. It appeared as if they weren't good enough. He suddenly felt very poor.

"Gentlemen?" Charles asked from behind the large bar. It

was not the portable type. It had a massive marble top. Shelved behind it were shining bottles of expensive liquor.

The upscale of everything was beginning to get to Fletcher, except for the charming Rosalyn. He caught her still surrounded by men.

"Scotch for me, rocks. Thanks," Frankie replied.

"Bacardi and Coke, very light on the Coke, thank you."

Another glare from Frankie. Fletcher eyed him back letting him know to let it be.

He had tossed a five for the bartender who promptly handed it back. Fletcher was told it was not necessary, nor allowed, thank you.

After they got their drinks, they moved further from the bar to get to a more open area to wait for Mike. Moreover, Fletcher just needed some room. He was just too irritated right now from being reprimanded.

"Look over there," Frankie said, as he was bringing his drink down from his lips. He wiped his mouth with the back of his hand.

"Where?"

"There, close to your girl Rosalyn. Little Eddy, remember him? Huh? Remember him?" Frankie sounded like a kid squealing on another kid.

"Yeah, I do," Fletcher replied, looking at his friend to make sure he was somewhat sober. Dude can't hold the scotch, he thought with a smile. "He's an arrogant shit and more stuck-up than most of these other conceited bastards in the room. He probably wipes his ass with more money than I have from my inheritance. Little snot."

"Got an opinion, I see," Frankie smiled, eyeing up Eddy himself. "Well, be nice. He knew some of the dead kids."

"Oh no, she's bringing him over here, I think," Fletcher noted.

"*Beeee* good, hear me?" Frankie pressed with a tight-lipped whisper.

Fletcher watched as the small bone-skinny teen walked over with his absolutely sensual mom. He tried ignoring the kid.

He was quickly trying to decide if it was worth talking with that little strange boy in order to get closer to his mom. Fletcher found himself desperately thinking how to get alone with her somehow.

Right before she got to them, she tilted her head back. She looked straight into Fletcher's eyes. A slow, captivating smile grew on her lips. Her eyes never left his. Her tresses lightly bounced back and forth with each soft step she took.

Too sexy, too sexy, was all he could think. Gotta have her. Just gotta have her once. He pictured her slowly taking that gown off.

Bring your kid on, girl, Fletcher finally decided. Maybe the little weird dude does know something. Maybe you and I can discuss later, alone, together, Rosalyn, my dear tempting lassie. He glanced from her slender waist and hips, back to her eyes. He smiled.

The hard nudge to his ribs woke him up. Frankie was reading his thoughts again. It meant to please stop fantasizing. It also meant to concentrate on the investigation and this strange, rich youth. Little girls' and boys' lives were at stake. It was all Frankie could think about. And the alcohol really wasn't working.

Rosalyn stepped up close. She touched Fletcher's arm again.

(Ancient Israel)

Chapter 38 ~

MARIUS HAD JUST TWO more to sell off. The best had already gone to the highest bidders. Daiafar could see his friend was getting weary in the heat. The closed-in room was making Marius sweat profusely down his pudgy, unshaven face. It kept dripping off his chin, disgusting Daiafar. He was glad it was almost over. He just wanted to complete the transaction and get out of this steamy hell-hole.

His plan was to wait until the last was sold and then confront Marius. As he adjusted himself on the hard bench, he saw Marius coming over to his section. All his inner alerts flared. He sat straight up and waited.

"You better not blow my cover, my dear friend, or your life will be lost before mine," Daiafar whispered behind his hood.

Even with his confidence of retaliation, he still didn't want exposure, especially not here.

He waited.

Marius came close to him. After a light nod, he leaned forward until his bulging, wet face was tight to the side of Daiafar's hood.

"I'm waiting. This better be good my friend," Daiafar spoke softly.

"My dear uncle," Marius whispered, using his code name,

"just wanted you to know that there is one more small batch of fine products I still must attend to, before we consummate our business. I apologize by all the gods."

His hot stale breath still reached Daiafar. He instinctively held his own to avoid breathing it in.

"I cannot wait any longer."

"Please, please bear with me uncle. It will only be a short moment, and I do not wish to interrupt these fine gentlemen's expectations."

Daiafar knew he meant the foul men nearby that so disgusted him. He knew he had no choice but to give in.

"How many more?"

"Not many, not many at all."

Chapter 39 ~

THE "LITTLE FUCK," as they both fondly referred to him, was dressed in a fine dark suit, with a deep crimson bowtie. Eddy was about five foot seven and appeared older than he was. He had a very round, fat face for a skinny kid. It looked like a pancake to Fletcher. What irritated him the most was his hair. Moreover, it was his actual haircut. It was in a perfect round shape, cleanly straight all around. Someone must have put a bowl over his head and cut away, Fletcher mused. He didn't think anyone actually did that.

"Kid's a freak, ya know," Fletcher whispered to Frankie, leaning over a little, without taking his eyes off Rosalyn.

Frankie leaned back towards him more, looking at the teen.

"Shut the you-know-what up!"

Fletcher grinned.

"Gentlemen, do you remember my Eddy?" Rosalyn asked, with a quick smile for Frankie and a beaming smile for Fletcher.

"Yes, ma'am we do," Frankie answered in an overly pleasant tone which somewhat annoyed Fletcher. He noticed Frankie's slight slur.

"Yep, what's up kid?"

"I remember you," Eddy said with a high-pitched girlie voice that further irritated Fletcher. Eddy completely ignored Frankie. At the same time, he stepped right in front of his mom. It appeared a very protective move to Fletcher, which he quickly noted.

"You're the old cop who couldn't take it anymore!"

"Eddy!" she softly reprimanded.

He looked up at her with what Fletcher could only determine as utter adoration. She warmly smiled back down at him and wrapped her arms around him. It was beginning to make him sick.

Fletcher could also see that her sweet reprimand had no affect on the kid at all. They appeared in love.

"I remember you, too," Fletcher rebuffed, but with a very agreeable tone. It nauseated Frankie because he knew what was coming next.

"Yeah, you do?" answered Eddy with a cock of his body, his hand landing firmly on his hip, looking very feminine.

Frankie could see that his friend might possibly deck him.

"Yeah, kid, you're the one who used to cry when mommy walked two feet away."

Frankie quickly gazed from him and then to Rosalyn. He saw that Fletcher had said it to Eddy, but had been smiling at Rosalyn. She said nothing. Frankie sighed in relief. But had he seen a fleeting moment of wickedness in her eyes? It was a quick moment but he was sure he saw something. He blinked and only saw her beautiful face again, curving softly from her smile. He shrugged it off. He felt better she hadn't taken offense to Fletch's comment about her boy.

"My father says that maybe you'll be able to keep us kids safe—and maybe not—being that you're old, not a cop anymore, and totally out of touch with reality." Eddy's high-pitched voice almost shrieked at the end.

Fletcher knew he didn't like this kid. He was fast thinking of a way to get out of it, before he punted him across the room. Rosalyn was still smiling at him. Her bright, emerald eyes never wavered. Obviously, this kid's behavior was normal to her or she just didn't care. He decided to play nice with little Eddy.

"I'm all you got, kid," he said in a firm whisper.

"Oh, that makes me feel better!" Eddy retorted with a huffing sneer.

"Eddy, be nice to Mr. Saxtan and Mr. Oswald. They want to talk with you about this whole mess, so be nice for mommy, okay?"

The child looked up at his mom with a rebellious glare. Fletcher then saw it become a big smile. It was one of the phoniest smiles he had ever seen. There's something seriously wrong with this kid, he thought.

Suddenly it hit him. They smiled exactly the same. They were like porcelain, inanimate toy dolls. A chill went through him.

"Yes, we would like to talk with you, wouldn't we Mr. Saxtan?" Frankie mimicked, again in his slurred, pleasant voice. His tone was really beginning to madden Fletcher.

"Huh? Well, maybe, yeah sure, let's, let's."

Chapter 40 ~

"I'LL BE BACK AFTER I MAKE my rounds," Eddy replied as if a doctor. "And I'd love to see your Elijah passages, too." He strolled off, leaving his slender, petite mom still smiling at them. Her lovely face lured Fletcher back into her mesmerizing, emerald eyes. He just couldn't look away. Her sparkling charm captivated him.

Suddenly she moved up close to him, too close for Frankie's taste.

Fletcher stood motionless as he felt her soft breath on his face.

Her perfectly sculptured, creamy hand rose to touch his chest. She was right up against him. As her fingers began to play with a shirt button, Fletcher instantly felt stunned and aroused. She was watching her fingers. He couldn't move. She lifted her head, slowly gazing into his eyes. Her expression was of a girl approaching sexual orgasm.

"Ya know," she whispered, "I'll be finished here a little later and would love to take a stroll with you. We can talk about this whole horrible thing and how you are going to solve it all. I know you can."

"Um, well, if you have time, I mean, fine, sure, just let me know," he whispered back, doing everything in his power not to stammer. He wasn't sure to jump for joy or run out as fast as he could, never looking back.

Frankie was also captivated. He couldn't believe what was happening.

"Now, you won't leave, will you?"

"Um, Rosalyn, not possible. Whatever you need. I mean it," Fletcher quickly replied, held by the depth of her half-closed eyes. He couldn't look away. His words had come out this time in a very even tone. But he was caught and knew it. He summoned all his strength and somehow gained back his confidence. He cocked his head at her.

This made her eyes fully open, dazzling him again. She pulled back from him. The aroma of her, her perfume and sweet smell of her hair was driving him crazy. He had to have her.

She still held his button. His shirt was slightly pulled forward by her grasp. He waited and didn't move. This heavenly young girl was now playing with him. With a wave of her hand, she released him. He wasn't sure if he saw a kiss form on her mouth. She quickly turned and just seemed to float away.

"Hel-*lo*?!" Frankie finally pressed.

"Oh, sorry, she's just so, so stunning, don't you think?"

He was still looking at her. He couldn't break the dreamlike feeling.

"Yeah, she is, and *not yours,* remember? So, what do we want to ask this kid?"

"Huh?"

Fletcher cut off his stare, turning to Frankie.

"You're not going to stay and meet her are you? You can't," Frankie pressed as he saw the entrancement in his friend's eyes.

"Um, I'm invited and absolutely will do. You told me to talk with everyone."

"Fletch, talk, not touch." Frankie looked very serious now.

"If she touches me like that, then——"

"Jesus, do what you want. Just don't let me know. Please?"

"Deal. Hey by the way, how does Eddy know about——"

"Fletch, his father is the DA, remember? And the kid is a bright pain-in-the-ass, but still bright. He's always stuck his nose into cases. That's why I avoid the crap out of him whenever he's around."

Fletcher's gaze had turned back to Rosalyn, who was now listening to some men who had corralled her. She had her hands clasped to her chest like a little girl. He wondered if her smile ever left.

Her head rose slightly as her tresses softly fell back across her rosy cheeks. As if in slow motion, her head tilted towards him. He found himself staring straight into her eyes. Her smile made him take a quick breath, and in an instant, she was talking with the men as if it never occurred. All he could think of was "witch."

"Hey Frankie, why am I here again?" he asked, still looking over at her.

"To help me show that we're on top of this to Mike and especially to some of these rich-y parents. Can't you remember anything?"

For a quiet cocktail party, things were happening fast and strangely to Fletcher. He was beginning to feel that haunting feeling when you're alone, watching everything happening to you from a distance.

Before he could answer, Mike was right with them again.

"Gentlemen, what do we got?"

Chapter 41 ~

MARTINO PRESSED THE PEDAL hard and felt the front of the Mercedes nearly lift off the ground. He didn't care as he weaved in and out of traffic. The car almost flipped over when a driver inadvertently swerved towards him.

"Fuck you," he muttered, ignoring the finger the woman gave him.

He was blind with fury and didn't care who was in his way. He glanced down at the speedometer. 65, 70, 75, 85, 95. Cars were flying past him so fast, he had to blink a couple of times to keep control.

He made it quickly over the bridge. In the hazy evening, he saw the skyline of Philadelphia. The lights of the tall buildings seemed like beacons to him. He pressed the pedal further. He didn't even care if a cop saw him. He would just outrun him.

"Someone's gonna pay! Someone's gonna pay! Someone's gonna fucking pay! My little girls, my little girls."

Tears rolled down his cheeks.

Chapter 42 ~

FRANKIE THOUGHT TO MOTION to Fletcher to be good, but decided to answer Mike first. Fletcher was surprised how quick Frankie's demeanor changed when Mike was there. He also noted no slurring.

"Mike, we have a full Task Force on this now. Every possible victim-type is being addressed from the pattern of very wealthy families to highly influential ones, politicians, etc."

Mike bowed his head a little. He was intently listening and nodding.

"The problem is that we can try to cover and protect everyone but where's the cut-off? What I mean is, we have an issue with manpower versus, how should I say, what level of wealth do we cover. There are so many places these kids frequent. We're covering most, so far."

Mike looked up at him, obviously waiting for the solution.

"We've created a Call Center within the Task Force. It's a quick-response group, like SWAT. Our goal is to get to a scene and handle it immediately when notified. This includes full chopper support. The State-ies are also providing similar actions and personnel outside the city proper. We're in constant communications with the burbs' forces, too. Everyone is very concerned, as you can expect, when children are being kidnapped and brutally murdered."

"We are also in contact with the Feds. Until we can prove crossing state lines, they are just advising."

Fletcher was now looking past Mike to one of the ladies

talking in the corner. Frankie noticed. He quickly ignored it and continued.

"Within the Task Force, which, by the way, we coined as SOC, for Save Our Children, we have distributed documents and information on how to best protect your children. Making sure the parents always know where they are, that they are never alone, and what to do if you think you are witnessing something. The hot-line number is distributed throughout the schools and activity centers."

"We are providing counseling services for those parents that are just plain scared out of their minds. And also for the children, if requested."

Mike looked down again, nodding his head.

Frankie paused.

Mike looked up and then at Fletcher.

"So, what are you doing?" he asked in a tone that meant Fletcher better have something for him.

Fletcher hadn't noticed he was being addressed.

"Fletch!" Frankie muttered.

"Oh, I'm so sorry, was lost in thought," Fletcher caught himself. "I'm sorry?" he asked smiling.

"Mike wants to know what you're—"

"Oh me, yeah, well, I'm looking into it all."

Fletcher was looking at Mike with an empty look. He was wondering if Mike actually made love to that beautiful thing. He brought himself back to the moment.

"Looking into what?" Mike snapped back.

Fletcher could tell from Frankie's eyes that he was getting very edgy, so he decided to play nice.

"Mike, as I told Frankie, I'm sure this perp is so into suspense and gets his, or her, rocks off knowing we're not only struggling to stop the murders, but also wanting to know what the hell is going on with those kids that are missing."

He paused and then continued.

"Now, this guy is smart and I believe knows your moves and strategies. I don't know how, but I believe it because there's absolutely no trace of any evidence that is even remotely useful. Nothing is significantly common between events or victims, except they are all kids from very wealthy families."

"The only clues are the passages from that Elijah, as you know," Frankie added.

Mike nodded. He gave a look to continue. Fletcher did.

"We found one at the second and third scene, but not at the first, though I'm guessing there was one. We checked the autopsy report but no mention. The second scene's passage was pinned to the body. They started the hiding trick with the third murder. I guess they felt it was more violating to the victim. Maybe to make us work more to find it..." Fletcher trailed off.

Mike nodded again meaning he knew what Fletcher meant.

"And the second passage wasn't understood either. I'm feeling we're probably frustrating the hell out of the perp because I believe it's part of his game and nobody has caught on yet. It's all really strange."

"What does it say?"

Frankie hoped Fletcher had it or a copy.

Fletcher pulled out a small Bible, which surprised Frankie. He opened it to a marker he had placed. He held it up, reading it formally like a priest would from the altar.

"And the ravens themselves were bringing him bread and meat in the morning and bread and meat in the evening, and from the torrent valley, he kept drinking."

When he finished, he closed the Bible with a snap and waited. Mike was still looking down digesting it. He finally looked up.

"What the hell does that mean?" he asked looking frustrated.

"I believe it's a reference for the next kidnapping. It may be in or near a restaurant that is probably open twenty-four hours, like a family place like Denny's. Or even some fast food joints. We're also checking all references to "ravens" in the city and burbs—any place that contains it in any way, like a catch phrase or something. Plus, we believe that the drinking part may mean simply a nearby bar."

"I see. Yes, it really doesn't sound like much," Mike pondered.

"Well, it's all we got right now," Frankie interjected, looking surprised that Fletcher had thought it through already and didn't tell him. He hated when his friend did that.

"Get on it ASAP and don't stop till you find this jack-ass. The press is having a field day with this one. It's Martino's kids! My ass is so far out there, and so is yours Frankie, and yours, *too*," he pointed directly at Fletcher. "And the next time you take anything from a crime scene before Gardner gets there, I'm going to prosecute the both of you. You hear me?"

He walked away.

Frankie breathed out heavily. He gave Fletcher a leering glance meaning to follow procedures and we need more to satisfy Mike.

Fletcher just stared for the moment, thinking.

"Let's go talk to that little monster," he said with a definitive tone. "Where did he go?"

They both looked around. They saw him at the same time.

"There."

"There. Let's go."

Chapter 43 ~

JOSH DID HIS BEST TO LISTEN as some sounds were a little muffled. He was so proud of himself at taking the chance of planting the tiny microphone into Saxtan's jacket pocket. He did it as Fletcher had abruptly turned on him. It's what he had hoped for so Saxtan would never feel the drop.

The volume was more than enough. He was taping it anyway. Later he could work around the muffled sounds and uneven recordings.

"Rosalyn. Wow. If you can get to her!" he said to himself, after listening to the intimate conversation.

He really didn't care if Saxtan found the microphone. It was his job to get information.

"What are you going to do about it anyway?" Josh whispered to himself with a wide grin, as if he was talking directly to Fletcher. He liked using the latest technology in his job. He especially prized the tiny cordless mike and receiver. It worked on specific, preset frequencies. And it's clear of prints. He made sure of that.

He sat on the steps, two townhomes down, and intently listened.

He so loved his job.

And even more, he loved winning.

Chapter 44 ~

AS THEY STARTED ACROSS THE ROOM towards the food table where Eddy had planted himself, three ladies intercepted them. The women blocked their way right in the middle of the room. Fletcher had no issue, as they were lovely ladies to him. He would never pass up such an opportunity. Frankie on the other hand thought differently.

"Hi!" said the blonde in the dark blue gown.

"Hi!" said the redhead in the satin black gown.

"Hello!" said the brunette in the teal gown.

Fletcher noted each swayed in a sensual motion as they stopped. It caused light ripples on each of their gowns. He suddenly had the image of meeting the alluring and deadly sirens of mythology that no mortal man can resist.

Frankie nudged him from the back. Fletcher ignored it and him.

"Hi, m'ladies," he replied with a slight bow. They all bowed very quickly in response and acceptance of his cordial reply.

"May we help you?" asked Frankie, a little too terse than Fletcher wanted. Now he wanted to nudge *him* but didn't.

"Yes," replied the redhead, "you sure can."

"Yes, if you will," replied the brunette.

"Well, first, I'm Fletcher Saxtan."

"Yes, we know who you are," replied the blonde.

"Well, I am—"

"We know you, too," replied the blonde again, this time to

Frankie. Fletcher thought Frankie looked a little embarrassed.

"And who are you, may I ask?" Fletcher took the lead.

"I am Rhonda," said the redhead.

"I am Julie," said the brunette.

"And I am Ellie," said the blonde.

"Ladies, how may we help you?" Fletcher nonchalantly asked in his best Cary Grant.

"Well, we were just wondering if you can tell us how Tiffany died," asked Ellie.

"Died?" Fletcher replied, being caught off guard. He immediately looked at Frankie with a look Frankie understood.

Frankie whispered in his ear that they meant Tiffany Martino. Fletcher nodded and turned back to them. In the moment, he had forgotten her name but remembered her twisted young body.

"Cyanide."

"Oh, my!"

"My, my!"

"Oh, dear!"

"Every time, every case in this investigation," Frankie noted very formally.

"Yes, ladies, it's the easiest method and can be by syringe or oral," Fletcher followed-up. "I can see why you would be concerned for your children."

"Oh, no! None of us have any children. We were just curious," interjected Julie, with a smile. It annoyed Frankie because it immediately appeared to him they were just gossips. He didn't have time for this wealthy chatterbox shit.

"No, not us, thank God!" said Rhonda, with a distasteful tone. Fletcher couldn't decide if that meant they were glad they didn't have kids who might get murdered, or they were glad they just didn't have kids. Or maybe that it was beneath them somehow. He lightly sighed and waited.

"Well, thanks gentlemen," Ellie said, with a big smile. They started to walk away, all turning at the same time.

When Ellie turned back, they all did, too. The image of a school of fish flooded Frankie's mind and he tried not to laugh.

"Mr. Saxtan?"

"Yes, Ellie?"

"May I call you Fletcher?"

"Yes, Ellie."

"Why do you dress like that?"

Frankie chuckled under his breath. Okay, Fletch, he thought, get out of this one.

"To impress you fine ladies, of course."

"Oh, I see," she answered back. Her small smile let Frankie know Fletcher had won.

"We hear you're a rebel. Are you a rebel, Mr. Saxtan?" asked Julie, with the curious look of a child.

"Are you married?" asked Rhonda, who now was beaming sweetly at him.

"Yes, it is said, and no, I am not. Are you ladies married?"

"Oh, yes, of course!"

"Yes!"

"Yes, definitely!"

"Good, and now, I must take my leave, m'ladies," Fletcher bowed and walked off. Frankie stood there by himself with three pretty, smiling females, all wealthy, all married, and all very arrogant and pompous.

He walked away with a bow, which he didn't want to do.

They were still smiling, like little girls, when he left.

Chapter 45 ~

MELANIE WAS TRYING to decide. Did she like him or not? Everything about him was absolutely right. He was a perfect gentleman, too. Thoughts of the children unexpectedly came back into her mind. For a second, she was back on her couch watching the terrible news.

"So, where do you live?" she asked, doing everything possible to block the invading thoughts. She felt her emotions swelling again and placed her hand on his. She willed herself to send the feeling back.

He looked down at her hand on his and smiled.

She saw it and knew it was being taken for more than it was. She didn't move it, as that would now be worse.

"Where do I live? Right nearby. See those condos? In there."

He was pointing across the park to a tall building with many levels.

As she pictured what his place must look like, and assumed it was as attractive as he was, the images of children vanished. She searched for something to say.

"They must be very nice," were the only words she could think of. She immediately knew what his response would be.

"Yes, they are. Would you like to see one of them?"

Chapter 46 ~

EDDY WAS STILL OVER AT THE food layout. When they approached it, they saw a wide spread of appetizers. There were things Fletcher had no idea what they were. He was hungry though; and it was clear that this was the food for the evening. There even was a chef behind it, explaining and serving. Fletcher toyed in his mind: Starve or eat this shit.

"Eddy, can we talk?" Frankie said, as he came up next to him.

"Oh, you finally want my advice, I see," he replied without looking at him. He pointed to various things for the chef to put on a plate for him.

Frankie saw Fletcher about to open his mouth and he quickly jumped in instead.

"Actually, yes, we would," he pleasantly said. At the same time, he eyed Fletcher to let him know to cool it.

Fletcher returned the look, slightly shaking his head in resignation.

"Yes, Eddy, please help us if you can," Fletcher agreed so nicely it sickened Frankie.

"Well, if you put it that way," Eddy answered with a corner-of-the-mouth smile.

Fletcher wanted to slap him upside his head so bad.

"Fletch, let's get some food. And Eddy, can we go over there to eat and talk?"

"Sure thing," Eddy answered. "I'll have some Cnidarians, too."

Fletcher watched as the chef scooped up this very thick noodle-like clear stuff onto a plate for Eddy.

"What's that?" he found himself forced to ask.

Eddy motioned towards the chef to explain as he prepared the plate.

"Sir, this here is a fresh jellyfish salad accompanied with cucumber, radish, soy, garlic, and vinegar. Very exquisite."

Frankie's mind immediately went to the washed up jellyfish on the beach. His stomach turned.

Fletcher couldn't believe the chef was telling the truth. He was getting annoyed that they seemed to be playing him a fool.

"What's that, then?" Fletcher tested him on another appetizer. It pissed him off seeing Eddy smile again, knowing he was enjoying it all.

"That is pate' and is a liver spread—"

"What's that?" Fletcher cut him off. He was not into liver and was beginning to believe he was going to starve.

"That, sir, is Kra-tong Tong..." he started.

Frankie laughed at the tong-tong sound.

"...and they are beautifully deep fried cups with chicken, potato, sweet peas, carrots, onions, and curry powder. Very nice indeed."

"Sure, some of that is fine."

"What's that?" Frankie asked, pointing at some sticks.

"Oh, it's Muf-Shal-Hen," he replied pronouncing each syllable with distinctive pride, confirming for Fletcher that he was just as stuck up as the rest in the room. "It is a very rare delicacy from China, near Nepal, a tender sweet meat sautéed in a hot sake extract, served wrapped on bamboo sticks with ginger and a heavy soy, with wine dipping sauce."

"I'll take some of that, if it tastes like chicken," Frankie chuckled.

Fletcher looked at him as if he was an idiot. The chef just looked at him with distaste and put two sticks on his plate with a cup of sauce.

"Yeah, give me some of that, too," Fletcher agreed.

"Try the Mee Krob," Eddy suggested.

Eddy motioned to the chef to explain.

"Mee Krob, crispy rice noodles sautéed with shrimp, chicken, tamarind sauce, bean sprouts, and egg nest."

The chef stood back appearing weary of it all. His look signaled that Fletcher and Frankie were heathens.

Fletcher again had the feeling that Eddy was playing with them. He noticed that Eddy had none on his plate. Must taste like shit, he thought.

"Nope, I'll pass. I'm okay; let's go," Fletcher said, with a mild tone of disgust.

"Here," said Eddy handing Fletcher and Frankie each a small sheet of paper from next to the chef. Fletcher saw it was a fancy little menu with each item and a description.

What the hell am I going to do with this, he thought. He stuffed it into his pocket and rolled his eyes. Frankie took it and nodded a thank you to Eddy and then the chef.

"Give me some more of that hen stuff," Frankie said with a smile. "It's good shit. Hey! Hen! Like chicken!"

Fletcher now looked at him as if he was a complete idiot.

The chef snorted and gave him more.

Chapter 47 ~

MELANIE LOOKED INTO his eyes and tried to see if he was a genuine nice guy or just wanted into her panties. All she could think was: *what a pair of gorgeous eyes.* She gave up trying to figure him out.

"So, where do you live?" he asked, as if he knew what she was thinking about him.

"Oh, out in the suburbs."

"So, where *out in the suburbs?*"

She smiled at his little wit.

"Pretty far."

His face told her he got the message that she wasn't going to tell him. He smiled back at her, letting her know he got the point.

In the little silence that followed, she looked out to the street and suddenly felt his arm go around her waist. It wasn't pulling her, just around her. She let it remain.

She came out for a man and here was one. She wasn't going to do anything to screw it up, not yet.

She continued in silence to view the street. Two parents walked by with a small child. Fear crept back in her. To avoid the rising images of dead children, she slipped her arm around him. It caused him to pull her closer. The images disappeared as he placed a kiss on her mouth.

She lightly kissed him back.

Chapter 48 ~

FLETCHER COULD TELL EDDY had enjoyed their ignorance of the food of the affluent. He was thinking this kid was extremely weird, weirder than he knew him to be before. May be a dead-end, he thought.

They walked over to a couple of chairs, near a small round table. Fletcher noticed how plush and ornate they were, with large purple cushions on the seat and back. It looked like expensive crushed velvet.

"Don't drop any sauce on these things," Fletcher noted to Frankie with a sarcastic smile.

"It's just a table and chairs," Eddy interjected, with a grin that meant they could easily afford more, and you can't.

"Eddy, is there anything you know or think that may be helpful to our investigations of these horrible crimes?" Frankie asked, as he munched on a Kra-tong Tong.

"Yes, it seems you may know something, have some ideas, or can add some light," Fletcher added, surprising Frankie once more with his civility and calm tone.

Eddy waited until he finished chewing and had swallowed, a mannerly point noticed by Fletcher.

"Well, I think our friend or friends are quite clever," Eddy started.

Fletcher thought he caught a slight British accent being added. He disliked teens and hoped this little egotist wasn't trying to play Sherlock Holmes with them.

"And I think, being a kid myself, that the perp, as you say, is smart enough to even hide himself from other kids' observations or knowledge."

"Go on," Frankie said, motioning with his hand. He leaned over his plate and chewed the meat.

"So, I think we can help," Eddy added, flipping his hair back. It fell right back into place.

"We?"

"We?"

"Yes, we—me and my friends, or should I say, associates," he replied with a quick, playful smile that sent a brief shiver down Fletcher's spine. His quick change to a soft-pitched voice also startled Fletcher.

"Well, I don't know about any kids getting involved."

"Hold on Frankie," Fletcher interrupted him. "Let's hear what this gentleman has to say first." He bowed slightly to Eddy to please go on.

Eddy did a slight bow back, gave a look towards Frankie, and then back at Fletcher.

"We have an organization that seeks to help people see the truth, the correct path to be and think. And we look for changes in the manner things are and try to implement them. Our parents fully support us. It's called the Fellowship of Hope and Change. We have an awesome website and a following that's growing, too. You should check it out."

And I'm sure it's totally a political, conservative viewpoint, Fletcher mused.

"I will," replied Fletcher. "But how can this help us?"

Frankie looked at Fletcher and then back at Eddy, appearing a little confused.

"Well, you see, it's mostly made up of kids our age and there are requirements to join, too."

"And they are?" Frankie asked, feeling his police instinct kick in.

"Income, status, politics, where you live, school you go to, stuff like that. We only want kids of the same mindset, though not necessarily wealthy like us. But definitely the same mindset."

Fletcher's glance to Frankie was so quick and back, he hoped the little conservative hadn't noticed. Well, at least he had been right about being a conservative shit, he thought.

"So? Your charter is to get votes or something?"

"Our charter is to change the world. But for this, we can become the underground watch team, right within the midst of the other kids. We can help monitor kids, be at places frequented by kids, be undercover sort of, or whatever you wish us to do. That's all. It seems you need all the help you can get. We're willing to help, even be targets. It really looks like you've stepped into the Lair of the Devil."

Frankie and Fletcher looked at each other, both thinking this kid may have something here. Fletcher didn't like how he said Lair of the Devil, as if little Eddy had been there before. He motioned for him to go on.

"I can introduce you to us; we're the four kids who started it all. Well we kind of picked up the idea from another who's only involved on the side now. And, listening to dad a lot, I've always wanted to be involved."

He ended with a pleading tone, as Frankie just stared at him.

Fletcher looked away, finishing his last hen thing. A noise from the far end of the room immediately drew all of their attention.

They looked over and saw Mike trying to calm down someone.

Both Fletcher and Frankie instinctively stood up and started to walk towards the commotion. Then they saw him.

It was Stuart Martino.

Chapter 49 ~

JOSH HAD SEEN HIM COMING from far off. He wasn't sure who the man was until too late. He stood up as the man approached his side of the street. He was coming right at him now. The man looked crazed and was just about to storm past him. Then Josh recognized him.

"Mr. Martino! Mr. Martino!" he had called and inadvertently stood in his path.

"Move out of my way kid or I'll—"

"Listen first, please, listen first."

"MOVE!"

He easily pushed Josh into the street, where he tripped on the curb and fell flat on his face. He tried to put his hands out to break the fall, but it happened too fast.

"Ouch! Shit!" was all that came out. He was getting tired of being beat up by everyone.

He turned and crawled to the sidewalk. He felt he was in a dream. He watched the wealthiest man he knew repeatedly bang on the iron gate, while wildly pressing the button.

"Yes, who is calling?" Josh heard from his crouched position.

"Open the goddamned door now. It's Martino! Now open!"

Josh watched him bang away, and finally, he heard the buzzer. Stuart Martino then disappeared.

He quickly got up, felt the pain in his knee, ignored it, and jumped back near to the door. He wanted the best reception he could get.

"Now, this is all getting so much better. So much better!"

Chapter 50 ~

"I DON'T GIVE A FUCK WHAT'S being done!" Stuart was yelling with his arms flailing. Mike was desperately holding him by the shoulders, but it was no use. Fletcher figured he just came on his own. He suspected that with his young daughter so recently found dead, Martino wasn't expected at the cocktail party. But he was here now, Fletcher thought, with a tentative smile.

"Stu! Stu!" Mike was pleading. "Calm down, let's talk, calm down, damn it!"

Fletcher and Frankie cautiously made it over to them.

"And YOU!" Stuart demanded of Frankie, pointing an uncontrolled, waving finger at him. "You fucked up, *you fucked up*! My little girl is dead and my little Steph's missing, and you better hope to your grave she's alive and we get her back unhurt!"

He was rambling so loud that everyone had silenced. They all moved as far away as they could. It appeared funny to Fletcher. Everyone looked like they were trying to become part of the furniture, completely quiet and motionless.

"Calm down!" pressed Mike, finally forcing him back facing him. Stuart was shaking and huffing heavily. He looked unshaven for days.

"Yeah, yeah," Stuart panted. He turned back to Frankie. Frankie could see a tear coming down his eye. His heart went out to him. Then the little room came back. He saw himself walking over to the bed. He tried not to look. The dead child was sitting up, looking at him. He desperately tried to turn away but couldn't.

"Please find her, please. Please find her," he begged, with a soft but beaten voice. The image slowly faded as Frankie saw his pleading face.

"I will, I promise," Frankie replied, trying to hold back his own tears. The dead child finally disappeared from his mind. He took a deep breath and looked over at Mike.

"Stu, let's get a drink and some food in you."

"Yeah, yeah, okay." He stopped for a second. "Mike, my wife won't leave her room. She won't speak at all. Please help. Please. Please…"

Mike had his arm around his friend. He led him to the bar.

"Shit, Fletch, we gotta find this psycho and find him fast."

They turned and there was Eddy. He was right there behind them the whole time. Fletcher was about to ask him why he was smiling, especially at a time like this. But the outburst had affected Fletcher.

He took a deep breath and said, "Listen, kid, we'll meet your friends." He had almost cried, too.

"Good. We are smart and we can find him or whoever," Eddy replied, still smiling a strange smile of victory. Fletcher wondered how such a young kid could get any pleasure out if this. Did affluent kids enjoy people suffering or not care at all, like the three insensitive ladies?

Frankie sighed and nodded in agreement to Eddy.

Fletcher turned. He went back to the bar. He was glad to see Stuart and Mike had left and gone to the food.

He ordered another Bacardi and Coke, plus Jack on the rocks. He downed the Jack, chasing it with the rum. He turned to see Eddy still standing there smiling at him. He quickly turned back to the bar.

All he could think was that this creepy kid knew something. He was toying with him. He was somehow setting him up to make him look like a fool. Did Eddy want to show them up and solve the case himself? Fletcher did want to solve the case fast. He just didn't want that freaky kid to get any credit at all.

None at all.

Chapter 51 ~

THE COCKTAIL PARTY was winding down. Most of the guests had formally said their thanks and goodbyes. Many also had come up to Frankie and Fletcher, wishing them the best in solving the crimes. Some did have grave concern on their faces, which relieved Frankie a bit that they did care.

"You going home?" asked Frankie.

"No, I think I'm gonna do as the lady wishes. Wanna come with us?"

"Me? Hell, no. Thanks. I'm out'a here, friend," he replied, sounding tired. "Fletch, please be good and keep your hands off. I know it will be difficult if she——"

"Frankie, my man, please leave it to me."

Frankie didn't like his friend's smile, but knew he could do nothing more. It really didn't matter, anyway, to him. The dead young girl was back filling his mind. His heart was aching. He couldn't take another child being found dead and vowed he wouldn't.

"Talk to you tomorrow about meeting with Eddy," Fletcher added.

"Sure thing, take care, Fletch. And thanks," Frankie said with a hand out.

"Yeah," he replied shaking it.

With his head down, Frankie started to walk slowly out.

"Yo, Frankie!" Fletcher quietly called back.

"Yo?"

He turned his head around. All Fletcher saw were vacant

eyes looking back at him.

"Think that little monster knows something we don't?" he called after him, smiling.

"Yeah, I do."

"Me, too."

"See ya."

"Yeah."

"Yo, Frankie!"

"Yes?" He didn't turn this time, sounding suddenly exhausted.

"I'm booking a room in the city, on the city."

Frankie paused, laughed, and walked away.

The moment touched Fletcher and he quietly wished his friend well. He took a deep breath and thought, time to get really drunk and laid.

He walked the other way, towards where Rosalyn was standing near the bar. One man remained who appeared to have the same idea as Fletcher.

"Not a chance, dude," was all that he said, as he saw her turn and smile so sweetly at him. He had to watch each step as his knees became weak.

Chapter 52 ~

JOSH COULDN'T BELIEVE what he was hearing. He was suddenly more interested in actually getting a recording of the DA's wife cheating on him. This was unbelievable to him. What a find was all he could think. Cocktail party, crazed Martino, adultery, and all surrounded by the kidnapping and murder of young children. He couldn't lose.

He moved his position from the DA's townhome, deciding across the street was better.

He quickly moved there, making sure his reception was still good. It was. He sat back in the darkness and listened.

His mind started to formulate how to present everything to his editor. So many ideas were flowing, but only one thought kept coming back to him.

He wanted front-page and wanted it now. He wanted it again and again and again. If there was ever a gold mine, it was his now, and it just kept delivering.

Chapter 53 ~

ROSALYN TURNED. She placed her hand on Fletcher's arm as he stopped next to her. Fletcher looked at the young man trying to woo the object of his intention. The man saw his look and slightly nodded.

Fletcher didn't know if it meant submission or war. They both turned to Rosalyn at the same time.

"Jonathan, will you please excuse us as we have important police business to discuss," she coyly said, touching his cheek. Fletcher saw him melt. Jonathan took her hand, she nodded, and he placed a long kiss on it.

"Till next time, my love," he replied, as he held up her hand.

She bowed, did a little curtsy, and smiled.

Jonathan's eyes glanced at Fletcher with a look that indicated that he had had her already and will have her again.

He watched the young man walk away. When he turned back, he found himself alone with a beauty he couldn't take his eyes off of anymore. With her lips lightly parted, her sparkling emerald eyes locked on his.

"Well, we find ourselves alone, now don't we?" she said matter-of-factly.

"Yes, I guess we do."

"Let's do shots, '*kay*?" she exclaimed, suddenly sounding like a little school girl.

"Fine, I can do one," he calmly said, trying to sound steady and firm.

"One?" she laughed, turning and swinging her long tresses.

She went behind the bar. Before he knew it, they had downed three shots of bourbon. He controlled the rising feeling of swaying as she came back from behind the bar.

She quietly led him from the room. They went down the corridor towards the entrance of the house. He followed without a word.

With this young girl attached to him, the warm summer night felt magical. He had no idea where they were going and didn't care.

She led and he followed. He stayed in step, enjoying her sweet perfume. She asked little questions about the case. Each question seemed to have obvious answers. Then she started asking in minute detail how they were conducting the investigation.

He answered everything he felt that wouldn't compromise the case. He couldn't help but try to impress her with his calm professionalism. At the same time, he wanted her to be proud of his investigative abilities. She kept smiling at him, making him feel honored.

They had just missed Josh. He had quickly hid from sight when the door opened. He smiled at his luck when he watched them go past him. He was really beginning to admire Fletcher.

She led him around the corner of the park. His heart jumped as she pulled him closer to her body. She began to lead him up steps that led to what looked like a building of very expensive condominiums.

He had to ask.

"Where we going?"

Without a break in stride, she answered him.

"To my place."

Chapter 54 ~

MELANIE DOWNED HER MARTINI and shivered. She was desperately trying to decide. She liked him. She needed sex. He looked gorgeous. He was very boyish and sensual. Now, she had the offer. She looked up at him and decided.

"Let's do it. I'd love to see your place," she beamed at him.

"Great! Let's go," he replied, obviously trying not to show his growing excitement.

She picked up her purse. After paying for everything, he led her out. Another great benefit, she thought, following him like a teen lover, hand in hand.

She felt all the men watch her leave. She loved how wearing a tiny miniskirt captivated men's attention so fast. She received lesbian attention at times, too. It all made her feel so appealing and alive.

When they got past one block, he stopped and turned to her. She almost ran into him, finding herself right up against him. Nice move, she thought.

He looked directly into her eyes. He then placed his mouth on hers. It was wonderful. She opened her mouth letting his tongue in.

An immediate sensation ran through her. She felt flush as his body tightly pressed against hers. His slow kissing was sensual and soft.

Wetness started in her crotch. So long, it's been so long, were her fading thoughts as she was swept up in his arms.

The next thing she knew she was being undressed in his

bedroom as he kissed every part of her body. When she was finally naked and dripping wet, he tore off his clothes and threw her onto the bed.

Suddenly the softness of his touch ended. He pounced after her, wildly throwing her legs apart. She instinctively pulled them back together. As he did it again, she turned over, away from him.

"What's the matter?" he huffed, looking a little ridiculous with his hard penis standing up.

She enjoyed rough play as much as the soft touch. Something stopped her. It was the quick change in him. He wasn't now what she had thought. This was a conquering, not a meeting of new lovers.

Suddenly, the picture of his bewildered look and rock hard-on just made her giggle. She couldn't help it. A little nervous laugh came out.

"What the fuck are you laughing at," he demanded.

She couldn't stop now. He looked even more ridiculous.

"I knew you were just a bitch! Fucking tease!"

She wanted to explain but she was laughing too hard. He just rolled off the bed and started putting his clothes back on.

"Just get out. Just get out!" he angrily said as he left the room, leaving her laughing naked on the bed.

"I'm sorry, really sorry," she giggled in huffs to no one in the room. She knew she had made him look foolish. She felt sorry.

Knowing it was over, she hoped he wasn't a lunatic with thoughts of beating her. She didn't want to wait. She got dressed and left in silence.

She decided a martini was in order. Especially after this failed attempt with a cute guy she thought was just right for her.

She settled on the same place. Why not, she thought.

As she entered, all the eyes followed her in again.

All she could think about was, here I go again. I know what you all are thinking. I'm feeling like a real slut and liking it.

It kept her mind off the children.

And that's what she needed.

Chapter 55 ~

THE MOTIF WAS PLUSH, SOFT, AND RED. It was fully furnished, as if it was someone's real apartment. The walls had a rosy hue, with the ceiling blood-red. The black couch looked more comfortable than a bed. Her taste in paintings and art amazed him. He wanted to examine some of the nude statuettes on the tables, but was afraid to touch them.

She acted as if she had always lived there. She excused herself and went into the bedroom. He stood in the middle of the living room not knowing what to do next. The bourbon shots were taking their toll on him. The room seemed to rotate slowly around him.

He finally decided to just sit and wait. But before he could, she suddenly appeared wearing just a small red, silk skirt. His mouth dropped. Her sudden nudity overwhelmed him. Her tiny, white breasts were pouting upward. His eyes couldn't help but follow down her slender, exposed waist to her perfectly shaped thighs. He stared as a schoolboy seeing his teacher naked.

She stood in the doorway with her arm leaning against the frame. Her eyes were half-closed, looking up at him. She said nothing at all.

He walked over and placed his mouth immediately on hers. He let his hand slip up her side to one of her breasts. He melted inside at the softness. His hand felt no panties as it slipped under her skirt.

She moaned at his gentle touch and walked backwards. He followed, still kissing her.

As he tossed off his jacket, he felt her hands at his belt. Before he knew it, his clothes were gone. He stood naked, with her on her knees.

His mind went unexpectedly to Frankie. He immediately told Frankie to get the hell out of his thoughts. As she increased her efforts, Frankie simply disappeared.

Her hands caressed him all over as she performed on him. All he could do was enjoy every second of her sweet, loving mouth.

She then stood, leaving him standing there. Her white body slowly slipped onto the bed, which had dark, scarlet satin sheets. In his dazed state, she suddenly appeared a demon-woman. As she slowly slid backwards with her thighs slightly spread, he saw the seductress of the devil.

With her legs fully open, he approached on his knees over her. He ran his fingers down the inside of her tightened thighs. A deep moan came out of her that was so low, he felt like he would melt into her.

The room began to spin all around him. He leaned down and ran his tongue down where his hands had left off. Her hips instinctively rose to his touches and kisses, pressing against his mouth.

The shots she had given him took greater effect. Then he felt more than alcohol. From his experience, he knew what it was. She had dropped acid somehow into one of those shots. He knew this feeling but it was too late. Everything melted away so fast he didn't care anymore. Every touch, every wet kiss, every moan expanded to the ecstasy of the stars, floating him past galaxies of pleasure he never imagined.

He knew he had found Heaven and never wanted to leave. Ever.

Chapter 56 ~

WHEN HE WOKE UP THE NEXT DAY, he turned and saw that the clock read 7:34 a.m. He could still smell Rosalyn's heavy perfume on him. He turned the other way. She was right next to him under the covers. He couldn't remember much through the wavering, thick haze of the acid and alcohol hangover. He wondered what had happened, other than sex. He hoped that had really happened.

"I wonder if she's feeling like me," he quietly muttered.

Something seemed wrong though. He went to the bathroom.

When he got back, she was leaning up on her elbows, looking directly at him.

He thought, nice round tits. But something was definitely wrong.

"Um, hi," he said. At the same time, he realized he was still naked.

"Hi," she replied.

"Um, how are you? And may I ask who you are?"

"Who am I?" she replied. She started to laugh.

He didn't know what to do, knowing full well his question was ridiculous. He didn't remember this girl or her name, and wasn't even sure what had happened. Something was very, very wrong.

She lifted the sheets and looked down at herself. She then put the sheets back on her tummy.

"Well, I think I'm doing fine, based on the fact that you fucked the crap out of me last night."

She was smiling, which made him feel better. He was quickly trying to search his mind for her name.

"My name is Melanie," she finally said, still smiling.

He had to smile at that.

"I'm—"

"Fletcher, yes, *I* remembered," she said with playful huff.

He looked at her for a moment. A light laugh escaped him. It was such a nervous sound. He desperately tried to remember what happened to Rosalyn. How did this Melanie get here? He looked around. It wasn't even Rosalyn's place. He hoped his experience with Rosalyn wasn't just a drunken dream.

"You're cool," was all he could think to say, knowing immediately it sounded stupid.

"Well, thanks. And you were very drunk," she replied. "Are you still drunk? And are you just going to stand there naked like that or are you joining me back under here?"

Again, he felt foolish. Somehow, he was beginning to like it. He muttered, "Oh, sorry. Yes, coming back there." He didn't want to tell her about the acid. He began to doubt that even happened.

She began giggling. She placed her hand over her mouth.

"Why are you laughing so much!" he cried. He unintentionally leaped onto the bed with a bounce that almost knocked her off the side. He hit his head on the headboard. He began to feel faint.

"Bet that hurt like hell!" she stammered, starting to really laugh.

"Why—why are you laughing?" he demanded with a smile.

"Be ... be ... cause ... be ... cause..."

She couldn't do it.

He folded his arms and waited.

She looked at him.

He pouted.

She laughed even more. She got up and went to the bathroom, still giggling. She was going to pee the bed.

He controlled his urge to say "BITCH!" knowing that probably would stop her from laughing at him.

She strolled back, still naked. She looked very nice to him. She stood there at the foot of the bed. He continued to lay there with his arms folded. She was completely clean-shaven. He didn't remember that at all. It looked very smooth.

She finally lay at the foot of the bed, smiling up at him.

"WHAT?" he cried at the ceiling.

"Sorry, baby, but you have the funniest look when you have a hangover. It was funnier when you couldn't remember my name. Which I saw bothered you. And even *more* funny when you pout like the little boy you look like right now."

"I am not pouting!"

She covered her mouth.

"BITCH!" he cried and immediately wished that he hadn't. He turned from her.

She dropped her hand. She stood up and eyed him.

He turned back at her.

Her face was contorting. Short huffs of air filled her mouth. He waited for the verbal attack he knew was coming.

Her mouth tightened. She shook her head. She looked down. He heard a snort. She broke down giggling. She bounced back onto the bed. She playfully looked up at him.

He couldn't believe it.

How could she?

After what he just said?

She slithered up to him, positioning her body next to his on top of the sheets. She wrapped her arm over him.

"You know you're quite out of your mind, little girl!" he said with a big smile, feeling very relaxed now.

"Well, thanks!" she replied, hugging him. "And you're cute."

"Melanie, huh?"

"Yep, that's me, a little girl!" she looked up at him with a smile that warmed him. "By the way, I'm older than you."

"No you're not!"

"Um, I'm the one who remembers things, remember?"

"Age?"

"Forty-nine."

"Me, too, so there!"

"I'm an Aries, you're a Libra. I'm older. Na na na na!"

He couldn't believe she just na-na'd him.

"Na na na *na?*" he said looking at her a little shocked.

"Yeah, and to you!"

A smile grew on his face. He instantly knew she was something special.

As she cuddled up to him, he just wished he could remember.

For the first time in his life, he cuddled back. Something about her closeness made him do it.

Then as he relaxed, the thought suddenly came back.

What happened to Rosalyn?

Chapter 57 ~

THE CHILDREN WERE PLAYING outside. The boys seemed to be playing a game of "Army" with each other. One suddenly ran out from behind a tree. Pretending to have a machine gun, he mowed down the other boys. They all play-acted as if they were really shot. The girls were on the lawn tossing a big ball around.

He first smiled at the boys' play. Then something hit him. He remembered playing with toy guns as a child. He had loved it. Now, as he looked on, sipping his coffee, he had a realization.

If we let such things go with our children's play, or even worse, actually promote it by buying toy guns, what does it do to them? How much of this play actually settles into their minds and hearts as they grow and eventually become adults?

The images of people he had personally seen shot to death or bloodily knifed appeared as he watched the boys play. He remembered one mom was shot in the head, as her kids watched. A deep-seated uneasiness rose in him again. He never had sympathy for killers, but now he began to wonder if society actually had a part in creating them.

All of a sudden, he wanted to go outside and try to get the boys to play another game.

Instead, Frankie took another sip of his cold coffee.

Chapter 58 ~

AFTER A WILD SESSION of sex, he would never forget again, they lay exhausted. She suggested they shower, dress, and grab a bite. His head was still spinning though. Not just from the drinks the night before, but now from this girl. It was hard enough for anyone to strike up a conversation with him. Now, he's having brunch with a girl he normally would have run out on and chalked up to another one-night-stand.

He told himself to stop thinking.

"Ready?"

"Yep, let's go," Fletcher replied with a smile.

He didn't know why, but he felt like he knew this girl from somewhere. More strangely, she acted as if she knew him, too. He figured he'd play it out for now. He let Rosalyn fade from his thoughts.

"Hold on a minute," he stopped her at the open hotel room door.

"What? Anything wrong?" she answered with a button-cute smile and big blue eyes that shined up at him.

He slightly shook his head to clear that little girl image of her so he could say what he wanted to say.

"Yes, there is. Where did you come from? Do I know you?"

"Um, no, not that I know of," she replied, still smiling up close to him. She realized he didn't remember how they met.

"Do you know me from somewhere?" he asked.

She started to giggle a little.

"I knew it!" he cried.

She started to lightly laugh that wonderful laugh he had no defense against and he knew it.

"What?" he pressed.

"You are so cute and funny when you get like this!"

"Like what?"

"Like playing detective or something. Like, you got to know everything. Just live the moment," she said. This time she just grinned, pressing a little up against him. A bit of an evil grin at that he thought.

"Well, I *am* a detective, well a PI actually, but I work with the police and—"

"Well, cool! I'm an aspiring mystery writer. We fit," she said. After kissing him on the cheek, she started walking down the corridor.

He stood there in the open door.

Finally he went after her.

"Wait a minute. Wait for me."

Chapter 59 ~

THEY WENT TO A COZY LITTLE restaurant on Chestnut Street. They sat outside in the warm air. They talked about their lives. Both were surprised how they ended up with small inheritances, allowing them to break out of the everyday working world.

Melanie had been employed as an antiques salesperson in one of the many fine shops in Philly. She brushed up against prominent people in her every day dealings. Many were from all around the world.

Fletcher found this to be fascinating. He expressed his own love of fine art and antiques. He admitted though, he didn't have anything as expensive or rare as she had sold.

They both shared a taste for literature, too. They discussed their common love of English literature, from *Beowulf* through Chaucer through the Renaissance and even through modern times.

They talked for hours. Taking a stroll through Rittenhouse Park, they stopped at the Luxury Café. She noted, with a laugh, it was where they had met. He playfully pouted again, admitting not remembering.

They continued to discuss everything about themselves over drinks. As they watched the people in the park pass by, they lost track of time.

"This is a lovely place, isn't it?" Melanie posed as she took a sip of her Sauvignon Blanc.

"Yes, it is, lovely," Fletcher agreed with a smile. He felt

light.

He also took a sip of wine. He decided he was going to buy a couple of bottles of this stuff.

The curiosity finally got to her. "You don't know how we met, do you?"

"Sure, I do."

"No, you don't. I can tell."

"Um, well, maybe I was a little drunk and—"

"Not good enough, sorry," she smiled and waited.

"Fine, no I do not. *Okay?*"

She suddenly felt for him. "It's not a big deal, honestly. I'm sorry."

"Well, you have every right. I do remember this bar and us talking. Just not sure how I got here."

He started laughing, not remembering anything he said either.

"You almost appeared drugged, ya know," she laughed back. She didn't discuss how he had clung all over her, slurring every word.

He ignored the drug comment. Suddenly he felt his cell vibrate. He looked down at the notice of a new text message.

"Will you help be a resource for me?" she asked with a slight tip of her head. She added a cute, shy smile to the question.

He heard her but opened his phone to see who it was. It read:

"had a wonderful time last night. let's do it again sometime. call me. R! :)"

"Hello?" Melanie tentatively asked. She cocked her head

forward.

He heard her again, but his mind was still trying to connect everything. He remembered the cocktail party. He remembered the bourbon shots. He remembered being at Rosalyn's secret place. And he remembered the sex. Yes, he definitely remembered the sex. Then it clicked. He suddenly saw Rosalyn's pretty face at the door telling him he had to go. As he argued to stay, her lips kissed him goodbye. He then stumbled out of her place. That was it. He must have gone to the nearest bar and met Melanie. Nothing else clicked, except the next morning. And here he was. Then he remembered her question.

"Well, of course, just not real stuff I'm working on, ya know."

"Oh, of course. I mean help review plots and ideas. Maybe co-write with me. It would be fun!"

"Absolutely, I would love to."

She smiled, looking out past him into the world.

As he was thinking about Rosalyn, he found himself staring at Melanie. He observed her bright blue eyes. He watched her short brown hair softly lift in the light breeze. He gazed at her Celtic face and light skin. He pictured a princess in a meadow, in flowing garb, with a beautiful crown of flowers.

She glanced back at him, catching him staring in his daydream. She smiled inside.

He broke his gaze. The mysterious, distant vision faded.

"You back?" she asked with a light, little chuckle.

"Oh, yes, sorry. I was just—"

"Daydreaming about me as your princess."

"How did you know that?"

He looked at her with a perplexing but curious eye.

"I'm a writer, remember?"

"Yeah, but—"

"It was in your eyes. I didn't want to interrupt. Honestly, I could feel something from you. And being a natural empath," she said with a pausing grin, "I sometimes can put two and two together and get nine."

He quizzically looked at her. He then grinned, as he understood.

"So, what else do you do with your spare time outside of antiques, mystery writing, and drinking wine?" he asked, toasting his wine glass to her.

She looked at him. She took a moment to think.

He thought he had stumped her.

"Sex!"

"Huh?!"

"I love sex!"

"That I know," he smiled, as she laughed at herself. "What else?"

"I cook."

"You cook."

"I cook."

"Like what?"

"Like food."

"Like what food?"

"Like the food you eat."

"What food ... *I* eat?"

"Chef-type food you eat."

"You're a chef?"

"No."

"No, what?"

"No, not a chef."

"But you said you cook chef-type food."

"Yes."

"Yes, what?"

"Yes, I did."

"Did what?"

"Did what, what?"

"Stop that!"

"Stop what?"

"That!"

"What?"

She just looked at him.

"THAT!" he cried. "Fucking Abbott and Costello shit!"

She couldn't hold it. He knew he had been led again like a fool. She had her hand over her mouth. She was lightly giggling to herself. He shook his head.

Somehow, she could get to him. She simply led him down a path. She could obviously see right through him. In his whole life, nobody was ever able to do that. Not even his old flame Desiree. The feeling was completely different than being with Desiree, too.

Melanie made him feel like a silly, little boy. All he could think of was how this lovely girl made him giddy. Her mirth was contagious.

"I'm so sorry," she coyly said. She blew him a kiss. It was a cute motion that made him shake his head more.

He had only known her less than twenty-four hours. It felt like years. Either it must be a dream or it's some set-up, he thought.

He decided it was a dream. Now he was facing two girls and two dreams. It began to feel pretty good to him. He definitely decided to stay in these dreams and not wake up.

Not if he could help it either.

He felt his phone buzz again.

Chapter 60 ~

"WHO THE HELL IS MELANIE?" was all Josh could think when he played back the tape the next day. It had gotten too late the night before. He had put a new tape in after he realized that Fletcher and Rosalyn were just going to continue ravishing each other for a while.

He really began to admire Fletcher for both his luck and especially his stamina.

"Dude, you're all over the place. Pretty cool. Definitely jealous," Josh said as he kept moving the tape forward and back to different spots.

After he was satisfied that Melanie was just a picked-up girl and not relevant, he went to his computer and started noting everything.

He put it all in chronological order, adding his side notes next to each event or relevant fact.

He was sure this had to be related somehow to Elijah's Wrath, the ancient fear of children suddenly found missing in Israel. The children never returned.

Somehow, it got coined Elijah's Wrath. It was a warning to children to be good or the wrath of Elijah the prophet would get them. Josh smiled at the similar idea of the boogieman that parents use today to scare their children into being good. It also helped teach them not to talk to strangers.

Elijah's Wrath, he had researched further, had partially originated from the kidnapping of the children of Israel by slave traders. Any child who resisted was simply killed. Any found not worthy were slain, too. The dead bodies were left by the roadside.

The remaining children were sold away. They never returned, leaving the parents insane with fear and loss.

"None ever returned," he wrote.

He looked at what he wrote and thought:

Ever.

Chapter 61 ~

IT WAS AN INCOMING CALL. He saw who it was and was glad it wasn't Rosalyn calling him. It was Frankie. He didn't want to be interrupted but knew Frankie would keep trying to track him down.

Damn it, he thought, looking over at Melanie. Just once, when he was working with him, could Frankie simply get the point that if he didn't immediately answer his call, maybe he was busy?

"Who's calling you? I noticed someone also texted you."

"It's Frankie, my boss, both times," he lied. "I gotta take it. Will you please excuse me?" he asked.

"Of course, go ahead," she replied with a motion of her hand towards him. "I'm going to freshen up and check my messages, too."

"Cool."

"Be right back," she said standing up. She came over to him faster than he could imagine. She gently placed a warm, wet kiss on his unsuspecting mouth.

Before he could kiss back, she had walked away, disappearing into the restaurant.

"Where the hell are you?"

"Frankie, please, I'm with someone."

"Oh, no! Please don't tell me you hooked up with Rosalyn or one of those girls! Not someone's wife last night! Who is it? That blonde? Rosalyn? No, no, you're with the—"

"Whoa, whoa, big boy! Neither and no!"

"No?"

"No! I'm with someone I met."

"Last night? In the city?"

"No, from Mars."

"Oh really? Is she pretty?"

Frankie always had a way of changing moods and thoughts faster than Fletcher could catch up.

"Uh, yeah, she's pretty."

"I bet hot, too!"

"Watch what you say. You haven't even met her."

There was a long pause on the other end.

"Excuse me," Frankie eventually said, in a whisper.

"What?"

"You just met a girl. I assume slept with her, and spent the day with her. And are now defending her honor?"

"Whatever, well, yes, I am."

Another long pause.

"Now, listen, whoever you are, can you please put Fletcher Saxtan, horn-toad of the century, Ein-fucking-stein of the criminal mind, king of the one-night-stands, winner of more trophies of broken hearts—"

"Aw, shut the fuck up!"

Frankie was laughing. Fletcher was beginning to wonder why everyone found him so goddamned hilarious lately! He retaliated.

"I did Rosalyn, too."

Silence.

"Frankie?"

"Um, you said it was—"

"Both."

Silence.

"I honestly don't know how you do it. I'm not sure to congratulate you or fire you." Frankie sounded a bit exhausted now.

"Listen, it's all okay. She led me on and I had no choice. Neither would have you. And I'm still trying to figure out how I ended up with the other girl, and in a different place. Working on that one."

He was smiling at his own words.

"Enough, enough. We'll discuss this later," Frankie said through his chuckles. He decided to let it go. "We need to get a hold of that kid and fast. I really think time's running out on this shit. We gotta find Stephanie and the other kids. Mike just beat my brain again. I got practically every detective on this now."

"Yeah, understood, I'll be done here soon. I'd like to first check his site in detail before meeting him. And tomorrow, I'll see that stupid priest again or maybe try another church or something. You call the mom and set up something for tomorrow afternoon, like after school or whenever those little kiddies are free."

"Mom? Not Rosalyn? Man, who is this girl you met?"

"Just shut up, please. I kind of like both. Nevermind."

"We'll talk about *that* later. I do agree about doing the site thing and checking with priests or whoever may know something about these senseless passages. Try a university or something. Maybe another Rabbi. I'll call Rosalyn. Answer your phone, got it?"

"Just leave me a message. I'll get right back to you."

"Okay, you better. Don't fucking lie to me."

"I will. I promise."

"Good," Frankie said. "By the way, what's her name?"

"Melanie."

"Melanie?"

"Yeah, why?"

"That's my wife's name."

"Yeah, I know."

Chapter 62 ~

MELANIE AND HE PARTED, making plans to meet again soon. He intended to review the kid's site for Fellowship of Hope and Change. He asked her to do so, too. They would regroup and compare. He didn't tell her why, nor who created it, nor how it was part of an investigation. Her untainted view would be a check of his own potential bias with the kid.

Fletcher had expected a very conservative site. It was far from it. Instead, he felt like he was all of a sudden in a far-left liberal world. It shocked him, being a site created by very wealthy teens.

The site opened with a quick dynamic presentation. Then an animation began that had an acronym logo of "FHC." The letters flew in from the sides, hung for a moment, and then formed the final logo.

The site promoted peaceful change in the world through the youth of the world. They were to bring equality to everyone.

Very interesting, he thought as he looked around.

He saw there was a membership sign-up section. Then there were links to additional pages. Some described how Man had completely become self-centered. It was the most ever since the beginning of recorded time. The website also said that unless there was widespread and sweeping change, the world would ultimately plummet into a *1984* or *Brave New World* society. Each situation would be horrible to contemplate. A very powerful, hidden few would rule. The population wouldn't even know.

He went further.

Another page bitterly disclaimed the rich. He found this extraordinary. Or possibly, he thought, the wealthy teens were rebelling against their parents. Maybe that's why little Eddy was such a freak. Could be a defense mechanism, too, he thought. He wondered how defiant ideas went over with other kids in Eddy's circle. Very sixties-ish, he thought. He remembered that many of the rebellious sixties kids were very rich.

It kept going on and on about level-loading the wealth of the world. Even if capitalism remained, it had to be changed to *cap out* how much riches one could accumulate. Now here Fletcher began to agree.

No one in the world could be worth more than two hundred million dollars and no company could exceed ten billion dollars. If you took the remaining money, in trillions, and spread it out across the world, poverty would disappear. Slums would become ideal places to live. Third world countries would be fed and would flourish on their own.

A rolling banner read, "Stop the greed and jump start the world!" He thought it was an interesting saying from them.

There was a reverse side. It did not allow for lazy, non-contributing people. They could not leech off the re-alignment and re-distribution of wealth. No work, no money—period. Not even welfare. Have children? You still have to contribute. Childcare would be provided until they were in school. This balance of responsibility would be attractive to gaining wealthier individuals' buy-in, he thought.

It claimed that competition would remain to allow enterprising people to grow and excel. It simply eliminated the extremes. No *extreme* wealth or *extreme* poverty, nor the laziness and apathy that accompany both.

"Interesting theory," he mused. Eddy was creative in his luring.

It was obvious to Fletcher that the site targeted the youth of society. Only they could cause the change. The site catered to them. It made it easy for them to sign up. It showed how to create meetings in their own town. All the necessary literature was free. Very cultish, he mused.

They could attend local meetings, too. Fletcher figured Eddy led these.

He thought to maybe sign up himself and see where it took him. He decided no. It would be better first to meet these kids. He could then get a sense of their goals and feelings in person. Then he would compare that information with what they are presenting online. He would look for inconsistencies. Everything was motivated.

Something wasn't sitting right with him, though. He could not pinpoint it. Was it Eddy himself? His huge ego? His obnoxiousness? Was it that he targeted young people? Was it because it was so radical? Was it that wealthy kids seem to be rebelling? Why should they? Would they actually give up their wealth for the benefit of the world? Alternatively, is that why there were the two hundred million and ten billion dollar allowances? Be a crusader and still stay rich.

He smirked. He wondered what Melanie's thoughts were.

There were also particularly contrasting pictures throughout the site. Photos of yachts, enormous mansions, and seclusions of the extremely wealthy were shown alongside horrid scenes of poverty and want.

Overall, Fletcher was impressed. It truly showed the current human state of the world. How incredible greed existed, with the full knowledge of extreme neediness and sorrow. Eddy had made his point very well.

He felt a little sick to his stomach. It really showed Man as a being of heartless, uncaring selfishness.

"No wonder," he quietly said. "No wonder."

He sat back thinking as he put his hands in his jacket pockets.

"What the fuck is this?" he asked suddenly, as he pulled out the tiny microphone.

Chapter 63 ~

JOSH HAD PRESSED THE NUMBER into his cell phone and just couldn't get himself to press SEND. He had gotten up early to clear his head, get some coffee in him, and get his courage up.

"Damn it!" he muttered.

He wanted desperately to call Martino. He hesitated as he kept repeating different opening statements so Martino wouldn't hang up on him. Every line made him sound like an opportunist reporter prying into his little girls' case.

After preparing ten different opening lines, none seemed right. He decided to wing it.

He pressed SEND.

After it rang and rang, it jumped into voice mail. He had no idea if Martino saw a number he didn't know and didn't answer. Maybe the phone was off. He didn't care. He was now faced with what to say on a recording he couldn't take back.

"Um, hi. Mr. Martino. Please listen to my message. It's about your daughters. I have information about them. Call me back."

He decided to leave it at that.

No call came back. Nothing at all.

He slumped in his chair. After a half-hour passed, he thought to call back to go into further detail.

Before he could pick up his phone, he fell off his chair from the tremendously heavy banging on his door.

"Open up! Open up! This is the police!"

Chapter 64 ~

THE FIGURE WAS SITTING STOICALLY. The glee it felt was so deep, it couldn't find a reason not to smile.

"Perfect, it's all now perfect."

As it kept whispering it over and over again, the wry smile in the dark never left.

"Just a couple more things to take care of. Close the gap, hide again from them, from them all. Then my plans are back. Plans are back, plans are back, are back, are back, are back."

It closed its eyes. An immense feeling of power surged inside. Its hatred surged right with it.

"Mine is the kingdom, the power, and the glory, forever and ever, and ever."

It never moved.

"Mine is the kingdom, the power, and the glory, forever and ever, and ever."

The smile never left.

"Mine is the kingdom, the power, and the glory, forever and ever, and ever."

It kept repeating the Catholic prayer ending.

Chapter 65 ~

THE CELL PHONE RINGING woke her. Melanie wildly tossed the sheets. She couldn't find it. She wondered who was calling her this early in the morning. She found it and rolled over. The clock read 10:15 a.m. She had slept late. Looking back at the calling number, she smiled.

"Well, good morning!" she said, rubbing her eyes.

"Did you get a chance—"

"Oh, yeah, I did."

She knew what he meant.

"Unbelievable, huh?" He didn't tell her about the microphone.

"What a site! Who did this?" she asked with surprise in her voice.

"First, tell me what do you think? I need an unbiased opinion."

"Okay, well, it was shocking. At the same time, their solution was interesting. It was somewhat refreshing seeing that someone cared and possibly found a method to make the world work for everyone."

"Go on."

"Who created this?" she pressed again.

"Just go on. I will tell you."

He hoped she would just go on.

"Okay, okay," he heard her surrendering tone. "Well, it's also a little disturbing because it's like playing God. I mean, they have the whole thing figured out. It's funny. They don't provide the means to get there. It's almost as if God is handing down the solution and saying, here it is, now figure a path to get there. Know what I mean?"

"Yes, I do."

"But that may not be that bad, anyway, either. So, who's the target audience?"

"Who does it appear to be?"

"Mmmm, I would say teenagers, first. It all points to them. They have open minds. And then college students, and then liberals, and then the poor, and then after that, I don't know."

"Yes, I agree."

"Fletcher, please tell me everything."

He proceeded to tell her the whole thing. He told her that he was on the case. They had met with priests and rabbis. He mentioned Eddy and his friends. It was their site and they wanted to help.

He also swore her to confidentiality. He knew he was taking a risk. He just felt trust with her. It was his call. She happily agreed.

"Well, I'm glad you're on the case," she added to his story.

"Why? You really don't know me at all."

"Yes, I do. And it's good you're on it."

He didn't challenge her back. He could tell she meant what she said. He sensed she did know him, even after a very short time. He had heard about relationships starting like this but never thought it would happen to him.

A thought came to him.

"Mel, how would you like to help me?"

"*Me?!* On a murder kidnapping case? Are you kidding?"

"I guess that's a big yes?"

"Uh, the biggest!"

"Now remember, I work hand-in-hand with Frankie Oswald. He is personally running the whole investigation. It's that big."

"Yes, the chief-guy, right?"

"Yeah, the chief-guy," he repeated with a chuckle. From what he had seen so far, plus what his instinct told him, she had innate insight into people. She reminded him of him. She could play the role of an outside, unbiased analyst. She also had desire and drive. She was valuable.

He knew it might be a tough sell to Frankie. He was also betting on her charm to win him. He chuckled inside that he was selling her cuteness. And, if he wanted an assistant, that was his business. At this point, they could use all the brains they could get. Somehow, he trusted her. If she didn't work out, he could always drop her, too.

"So, what's the next move, Sherlock?"

He liked her reference.

"Well, my dear Watson, I believe it would behoove us to take a jolly ride and meet up with a priest or two, and then some lovely children."

They both laughed.

"Hold a sec, okay?" he asked.

"Yep."

He quickly got his cell, turned it on, and of course, there was a message from Frankie already.

They were to meet with Eddy and his three friends after school. They would all meet downtown at Eddy's home again. Fletcher still wanted to see the priests beforehand.

He saved the message and got back to Melanie.

"You free today?"

"For you, baby?"

"Are you free?" he laughed.

"Yes, I am. Where we going?"

"First to Heaven and then probably to Hell."

Chapter 66 ~

JOSH STOOD UP SO ABRUPTLY from the banging on his door, he severely hit his thigh on the underside of his desk. He cringed at the pain. He rubbed his leg as he attempted to pull his chair out more. As he struggled, he realized it was appearing that he wasn't going to answer the door.

"Open up or we will break it down!"

"Coming! Coming ... ouch! Damn it!" His foot caught a box of paper on the rug. Rather than slip, he ended up twisting his ankle.

He got to the door, almost falling into it. He opened it and mayhem broke loose. The SWAT team grabbed him and threw him to the floor. One of them had his knee buried deep into the small of his back as the others quickly handcuffed him.

"What the hell are you doing?" instinctively came out of his mouth.

"Shut up!" was all he heard. He stopped moving when the point of the assault rifle was at his eyes.

"Anyone else in here?"

"No, just me," he said as calmly as he could. He really didn't want to get shot.

The rest of the team ran through his place. They came back saying all was clear to the commander.

"Get up, punk! You have the right to remain silent..."

"Are you arresting me?" he asked. He realized how stupid that was to say.

The officer ignored him and finished his rights. They then

pushed him out the door. As he turned back, he saw them unplugging his computer.

"Please, please be careful with that. It has everything on it I need."

"Yes, we know. And now it's ours."

"Shit!" he said as they dragged him down the stairs and out the door. People were now gathered around, all whispering to each other. He knew some and felt like a fool. He still didn't know what was going on.

After jamming him into the SWAT van, they sped away. Approaching the station, there were reporters everywhere. As they pulled him out, he suddenly knew what it was like to be on the other side of the press. He didn't like it at all.

They dragged him up the steps and into the station. Walking past some detectives, Josh noticed a man who was quietly sitting nearby suddenly stand up.

"You! You bastard! I know you! Where's my daughter, you son-of-a-bitch!"

Detectives immediately moved between them, shielding Josh. Another detective tried to subdue Martino, but he broke free and came after Josh. Two uniformed policemen stopped him.

"C'mon, get him out of here," one of the detectives yelled, grabbing Martino again. As they hurriedly left the room, Josh could hear Martino screaming wildly.

They proceeded to a security room and pushed him in. As he turned, he saw the door securely slam. There was no way out.

He couldn't believe how fast it all happened. Suddenly, the door opened. A man in a loosened tie and disheveled shirt walked in.

"Please sit, young man. I am Frankie Oswald."

"Yes, yes, I know who you are."

"Wait a minute. Why do I know you?"

"I'm Josh Stein, *Philly Times.*"

"Oh, yeah, the young reporter. Funny being here, huh?"

He saw a grin on Frankie's face that wasn't very pleasant.

"Sir, please, why am I here?"

"You really don't know?"

"Um, no…" Then it hit him. "Are you kidding me? Because I left that message for Martino?"

"Well, when someone directly calls a father about his missing child, well you either gotta be very stupid or in on it. Sounded a bit like a ransom call, don't you think?" Frankie sat back with his arms folded.

"Honestly, I was just trying to get him to talk with me. I know absolutely nothing! And you gotta protect me from him. He's crazy."

Frankie ignored his concern.

"We are taking no chances. Why did you say to him—"

"Because I believe I know the possible motive."

"Motive? How? Why? Why would *you?*"

"It's Elijah, right?"

Frankie appeared not wanting to answer but finally said "Go on."

"Well, I'm Jewish and know something about our history."

Frankie appeared a little more interested, but Josh could tell he had an excellent poker face. "Go on," he repeated.

"Have you ever heard of Elijah's Wrath?"

"Elijah's what?"

"Wrath. It's an ancient fact that the children of Israel were sold into slavery and the practice might still be going on. I think it has been for centuries."

Frankie could only stare at him. He asked him to explain. Josh did.

"So this is what you meant by—"

"Yes, yes, yes," Josh replied. "Can I get these off please, sir?"

"Oh, yeah, sorry." Frankie took the cuffs off and tossed them on the table as Josh rubbed his wrists.

After a couple more questions, Frankie was convinced the kid was innocent. He warned him to stay in town and out of his way.

"Can I get my computer back?"

"Yeah, sure, no problem, after we dissect it first. Okay with you?" Frankie gave a look like there was no option or the cuffs were going back on.

"Yeah, sure, I see. Just be careful, okay?"

"No problem, kid."

"And is he gone?"

"Yes, I had him removed. We don't know how he slipped in. He's very determined as you may appreciate. He is gone, now."

"Thanks for telling me. I kept thinking he was—"

"No, he won't, and I will personally explain to him you're innocent, so far," again Frankie gave him the grin that wasn't pleasant.

Josh turned to leave as Frankie opened the door for him.

"By the way, kid."

"Yes," he replied turning back to Frankie.

"You find anything, you call me."

Josh knew this also wasn't an option.

"Absolutely sir. I really want to help. That's why I tried to tell Mr. Saxtan."

"You did?"

Chapter 67 ~

FLETCHER PICKED MELANIE UP at her home. He felt a little awkward. It was uncharacteristic for him to remain with a girl this long, moreover liking it, too. He didn't know why he was feeling like this with someone he had just met. He had sworn never to get involved again. Somehow, she was different.

To complicate things more, after reviewing Eddy's site, he had spent the rest of the evening with his beautiful mom at her secret place. He had bowed to her request. He couldn't turn her down. He was so mixed with emotion. Two girls were the last thing he had expected to happen to him. He forced away the thought that being with Rosalyn was running from Melanie. So much for wanting to be alone all the time, he accused himself. But Eddy's mom was so appealing, so sensual and soft, so aggressive and passive. Every time he was with her, he was enthralled, never wanting to leave.

She had laughed when he accused her of dropping acid on him and asked him what the problem was. She reacted so seductively and coy. He didn't know how to respond. When she slowly reached for him to lie down next to her soft, creamy nakedness, he forgot all about the acid.

When he arrived, Melanie was excited to see him. It made him feel guilty. He tried to push it aside but it remained. They started heading downtown again.

She lived in a charming secluded home with a lot of ground, out in the Chadds Ford area. It wasn't far from his place either. She told him she needed her privacy and quiet time to write. He began to think she wanted him for his work more than him.

"I know you only want me for my work, so you can steal it all and write a bestseller."

"You got that right!"

He looked over at her, surprised. Then seeing the caring look in her eyes, he knew he was completely wrong even to think that. He also couldn't believe how the guilt kept growing. He just couldn't tell her about his other love.

She slipped her hand onto his thigh and then between his legs and he jumped a little.

"I'm here for *that*, my man!" she laughed.

"Get off, girl! Gotta drive," he snorted back.

"Babe, I'm here because I truly like you and everything about you, including your work. And if it helps me, would that be bad?"

He paused.

"No, not at all, I would love it," he heard himself saying and couldn't believe his words.

"And you are benefiting more than me being such a wonderful girl!"

"Oh, yeah? How my dear?"

"You get my criminal-thinking mind. As a writer, I create and know characters and how they work. I know what motivates people. You need, and get," she smiled, "my analysis and outsider point of view."

"Yes, I guess I do."

It sounded like he didn't care and he was about to rephrase.

"You'll see."

He hoped so. He didn't answer and decided to let it go.

They were almost at the church.

After another mile, the thoughts running through his head spilled out.

"I was thinking about something."

"Yes?"

"About that website and all."

"Yes?"

"Does anything about it trouble you?"

"Outside of what I already said?"

"Yeah."

There was a little pause as she seemed to mull it all over again.

"Well, it just seems surreal, actually. Like why? Why would they do this and promote this? It's very admirable. But, yes, to tell you the truth, there is something bothering me. I would like very much to speak to these kids."

"Me, too. Frankie, too. So, you're coming with me when we do, okay?" He wanted to confirm her desire to help.

"I'm in, definitely."

"You'll be coined my assistant."

"Yep, I can assist in many ways, too!"

He glanced over at her. He smiled and continued.

"Actually, there's something about how they try so hard on every page and every link to draw kids in, don't you think? And they promote it both online, and in person."

"Did you sign up?" she asked.

"No, I was going to wait till we talked with them. Plus, if they caught us, it could spook them."

"You should have."

"Why?"

"Now that you're mentioning all of this suspicion, something just occurred to me."

"And?"

"Well, I tried the sign-up path and didn't go through it all, but it's like a questionnaire. Part of it was asking what kind of family you came from, your estimated income and money stuff like that. In addition, it was embedded within many other questions. It struck me as a little strange. I had shrugged it off as just information they wanted in order to know where their new recruits were coming from."

"You mean, if they were rich, they may be less willing to agree with all their theories and all, right?"

"Yeah, that was my thought at the time but now, I'm thinking maybe there's another reason."

He looked over at her and then pulled the car over, stopping on the side of the road.

He sat looking forward in thought. She waited. He finally spoke, still gazing forward.

"You mean to say that you think that these kids may have something to do with the crimes?"

"I've seen worse."

"Yeah, me, too," he replied, still looking forward.

"Well? What do you think?"

"Okay, yeah, there could be a connection, but why? Why would they care to do this? What's the motivation?"

"I don't know; that's the constant loop and problem with it."

"I wonder," he mused.

"Revenge maybe?"

"For what?" he quickly replied back, looking over at her. He realized how much he liked being with her, analyzing everything. And she was really pretty, too.

"I don't know."

"They seem awfully interested in helping, too. That had kind of disturbed me. I mean, this is dangerous shit."

"Yeah, yeah," she looked down, thinking she may be falling for him.

They sat in silence for another moment, both in their own thoughts.

"Okay, let's log it as a possibility that they may be wanting to help just to keep tabs on us," he said breaking the silence.

"It has happened before, both in real life, in books, and TV shows; the perpetrator befriends the cops," she posed, glad to get away from her thoughts and her growing feelings for him.

"Yeah, I know."

"Yeah."

He started the car and before continuing to the church, he pulled out the microphone.

"Ever seen anything like this?"

"What the hell is that? Looks like one of those lapel things, those little microphones you see on TV," she said taking it from him carefully.

"It is a microphone and has been in my pocket since I don't know when. See the antenna on it?"

"Who do you think?" she said holding it up, turning it around slowly.

"I'm betting my little reporter friend. Pretty smart kid."

"Yeah, I'd say." She handed it back to him. "Maybe you should have a little talk with him, at least to shut him up if you can."

"Yeah, I will. Was planning on it," he said with a commanding voice that increased her curiosity about him.

He suddenly felt her hand on his shoulder. She was lightly rubbing it.

Though he was having emotions he never had before, he was really glad she was with him. His quiet thoughts and feelings were quickly interrupted by his phone vibrating.

He didn't want to open it.

He glanced over at her. She was looking forward with a warm smile. He turned, quietly opening the phone.

"hi my lovely sexy man! do you know what I want to do to you right now? your girl, your slave, R! :)"

He quickly closed it.

Chapter 68 ~

AFTER HIS RUN-IN WITH the police and Martino trying to kill him, Josh still decided to take the chance. He really wanted to get in with Martino. More now, since the cops just didn't seem to care. He had to know what he was planning with all his influence and wealth. Especially since Martino was throwing himself directly at the media and the cops to find his daughter *and* find whoever did this to his little girls.

He sat at his computer at home just staring at the screen. He had no idea why Martino would ever talk with him. At the same time, he was a little scared of the guy.

"You've gone nuts, ya know," he said to himself.

He kept thinking there's gotta be a way. Somehow, he's gotta get in his confidence.

He looked over at his bed and all the scrambled papers and notes strewn all over it. It looked worse than his board in his cube at work. The clutter of information made him smile.

Count your blessings, my boy, he thought happily to himself.

He knew he was already ahead of the game. Even though he felt for the children, he still had to look out for himself, didn't he?

"Of course, I do," he continued talking to himself, still staring at the screen. It was his job.

Suddenly, the computer screen gave him an idea. Actually, it gave him two ideas.

He frantically looked for a pen and piece of paper. He

always seemed to have a hard time finding a damned pen. He finally found one, but all the papers had notes all over them.

He took the pen and leaning forward, he wrote on his wall next to the screen.

Chapter 69 ~

SAINT JOHN'S ROMAN CATHOLIC CHURCH appeared on their right. It was a colossal, old church built with massive protruding stones. Very impressive, they both thought at the same time. At the top of the church stood a large, sculpted stone crucifix.

"Nice church," she said, as she stared at the many steps that rose from both the front and side entrances.

"Yeah, not bad," he agreed.

"Who we meeting?"

"This is a different priest from the last one I spoke with at another church. I had also spoken with a Rabbi but again nothing seemed to click with it. I figured to mix it up again. This is Father Michael Brandon."

"I see."

He thought he heard a familiar tone in her voice.

"Why, you know him?"

"Nope, I'm not Catholic either."

"Me neither."

"You anything?" she asked.

"Not at this time. You?"

"Nope, not at this time."

Her casualness amused him.

"Well, let's go see the Padre then, okay?"

"Let's," she said and leaned over, planting a warm kiss on his cheek.

He thought to kiss her back and start something. He

refrained since they were parked in front of a church. He had some scruples, he smiled.

They got out and started up the long steps.

"Hey, are we meeting him in the actual church or in that place where they live, the—"

"The rectory, you mean?" he posed, giving her a glance.

"Yeah, that thing," she beamed back at him because he knew it.

"No, meeting in the church."

"I guess, whatever," she replied with a shrug.

When they got to the top, they were confronted by immense wooden doors, with iron framework and two big round knockers.

"Wanna get married?" she asked before he could reach for the handles.

"What?!"

"We're at a church. There's a priest inside."

"Are you kidding?"

"Yes, I am kidding, you idiot!"

He looked at her, again knowing she was messin' with him. He kept falling for it and loving it, every time.

He pulled hard on the ring. The big door opened with a creak that reminded him of old horror movies where the characters fearfully entered the evil castle and everybody died.

"After you, madam," he bowed extremely low with an outstretched arm and hand.

"Thank you, sir knight," she replied with a quick bow and curtsy.

He could see from his low vantage that she hadn't moved at all. He was still bowing low.

She started to giggle.

"Well!" he demanded.

"If you come a little closer, you can place your tongue right between my—"

He quickly moved forward and did exactly that. She had on short tan, hot-pants and his face pressed against her naked thighs as he slipped his tongue where she had wanted it.

She jumped back so high, he broke out in laughter.

"You dick!"

He stood back up, still laughing. She was smiling with one hand on her hip.

"So, there!" he declared.

"I didn't think you were going to ... in front of a church ... the door ... the priest..."

"Now you know something more about me!"

He reached out his arm again, but remained standing and smiling.

She didn't move, giving him a look of suspicion that was so endearing he wanted to kiss her.

He decided to just wait and play.

She slowly inched in front of him, walking sideways, never moving her front from facing him.

He grinned and waited.

She smiled and attempted to run, crying, "Yipe!"

He grabbed her ass, right at that moment, anticipating her move. He definitely liked her small, cute butt.

She jumped again and broke free, making it past the intimidating door.

He couldn't help but laugh even more. He got her twice and enjoyed it. He couldn't remember ever having this much fun with a girl.

He wondered how he could have found such a wonderful

lassie, his own age, with such a youthful outlook as he had. They had a great deal of chemistry growing in such a short period of time. And what legs! He felt like a kid with her.

He decided to say a thank you prayer when he got inside.

He followed her into the dim church, closing the door behind them.

It echoed like distant thunder.

Chapter 70 ~

FATHER MICHAEL BRANDON WAS not to be found. In contrast to the bright sunshine, the church had a very dark, eerie feel to it. Little red candles in the coves caused sinister shapes against the walls. Every step strangely echoed. A shadowy, haunted castle image crept back into Fletcher's mind. Demons appeared everywhere. He imagined Hell opening up in front of him, dragging him down screaming.

He turned to see that Melanie was still with him. As they walked slowly up the main aisle, he was relieved she was there. She was walking right behind him, almost up against him.

"Quiet in here, huh?" she mentioned.

"Yeah, a bit ghostly too, don't ya think?"

"Uh, huh," she whispered.

They kept creeping up the main aisle. They noticed an old woman, sitting quietly, in the third pew from the altar.

Fletcher wondered if spending his old age in church would erase all sin from his life and guarantee Heaven, no matter what he did now.

He figured it might just be better to live well, love well, and let Heaven and Hell worry about it. He clasped Melanie's hand.

She looked up at him, a little surprised. Then she smiled and didn't care. It was nice to hold hands.

They walked up to the large altar and stopped. Neither knew what to do next.

Should they go up, and if so, where? They spotted a slightly lighted opening to the left that led down a corridor. Fletcher supposed that's where the priest and company must come out for the Mass.

"Should we wait?" Melanie asked, still very quietly, with what sounded like a little fear to him.

"I don't know. Maybe go through there?"

"Are we allowed?"

He chuckled.

"Allowed by who?"

"I don't know," she giggled. "God, maybe?" She just loved how he challenged everything.

She was now close beside him. He looked over at her and shook his head with a smile. He looked down at her bare legs, wondering if that was allowed in here, too. He decided he really didn't care.

"Let's just go," he said, starting up the altar towards the opening.

He felt right away that they were intruding, committing some sacrilege. He had to pull Melanie by the hand. She didn't want to go.

From the side below, a door opened. A man came in dressed in all black, except for the white square in his collar.

"Excuse me," he loudly whispered.

"Oh, sorry, we were looking for Father Michael Brandon," Fletcher answered in the same volume.

"That would be me. I assume you're Fletcher."

He was on the other side of the rail separating the altar from the rest of the church. He waited, giving a little look to them that appeared a sneer to Melanie. Fletcher also noticed the Father had quickly eyed his girl up and down.

He had a handsome face with salt and pepper hair. To

Melanie, he appeared young and old, at the same time. His hair was perfectly in place like a helmet. His horn-rimmed glasses gave that studious look. But his eyes said something else to her.

"Oh, sorry, we didn't mean to come up here," Melanie said after noticing what he meant.

She quickly pulled Fletcher back down and around to the Father. She immediately felt better.

"Thank you. And you are?"

"Hi, I'm Melanie Sanders."

She reached out her hand, which he firmly took hold of. This time he didn't take his eyes off her.

"Nice to meet you both. Please, follow me."

He went up the altar where they had been. Fletcher looked at him, then at Melanie, who shrugged, and then back at him.

They followed through the opening they had seen. The priest went down a small hall, making a left into a small room. It had wall-to-wall wooden cabinets. In the middle was an opening with a desk-like shelf. Gold objects on it looked foreboding and very altar-y to Fletcher.

He saw some robes on a stand and figured this is where they got dressed for Mass.

The wood looked very expensive and ancient. The room smelled musky, but not the damp type, more the aged type. It reminded him of Rosalyn's home, her real home.

It all made Fletcher feel uncomfortable, like a lost sinner. Melanie looked funny, being half-nude with what she was wearing.

"So, I understand you have some questions about the Bible to help with your investigation."

"Yes, we do," replied Melanie.

Fletcher looked over at her and then figured to let it go.

"Okay, go ahead," Father Brandon said.

"We need some help in understanding some passages from a guy called Elijah," Fletcher said as he fished through his pocket for the passage.

"The *guy* named Elijah," Father Brandon said, with a slight tone of reprimand, "was a prophet of the Old Testament. I know it well."

Fletcher almost gave him a look at that last comment, but immediately hid it.

"And that means?" Fletcher replied back, a little annoyed that he was being reprimanded and didn't know why.

"He was a very prominent prophet of the Israelites from the Book of Kings."

"Right, and this Kings' thing?"

"Yes, Kings. You know, Saul, David, Solomon, etc."

"Oh, *those* guys," Melanie said, with a smile, suppressing the giggle.

Fletcher gave her a glance, almost laughing himself.

Before the Father could begin again, Fletcher handed him the passage. He just wanted answers and not this Catholic grade school attitude.

He read it quickly and handed it back. He took a Bible from the desk drawer and fished through until he stopped. He was silent, reading something.

They waited.

"You see, Elijah was favored by God, and his purpose, if you may put it that way, was to warn the Israelites to change their lives and follow the truth. This reference is about how God fed him with bread and meat, sent by Him, in the form of a raven."

"I see," said Fletcher.

He waited for more information.

"That's it?" he felt forced to ask.

"Well, yes, that's it. I don't see why anyone would use this for a crime or something. I would just think they are playing with you."

Melanie looked at Fletcher and him back at her. Their eyes both said he was lying and trying to mislead.

"No other hidden meaning or message?" Melanie asked, this time being serious.

"Actually, not that I can see."

"Help, I need somebody, not just anybody," Fletcher lightly sang, which caused a glare from the priest.

"Can I assist you with anything else? I'm very busy."

Fletcher and Melanie looked at each other again, both wondering why the man seemed to be getting nervous and wishing them to leave.

"Thanks, Father. We may be back for additional questions, if that's okay with you," Fletcher posed, never taking his eyes off the priest.

The Father stared back at him. With a thin smile, he finally agreed. Then he looked down and up, like someone being caught in the act. It concerned Fletcher immensely. His police instincts were flying high right now with this guy. He made a point to see him again to find out why.

He looked at Melanie. Her face confirmed his thoughts. He turned to the priest and thanked him. They were about to leave when something clicked in Fletcher.

"By the way, have you ever heard of Elijah's Wrath?"

Melanie gave him a strange, quizzical look. Father Brandon gave just a blank stare and said, "Nope, never did."

"Again, thanks for your time, Father." The priest nodded

and they left.

"That was awfully strange, don't you think?"

"Yeah, I think he didn't like us at all," Melanie replied, feeling very glad to leave the place. "What's Elijah's Wrath?"

"Something someone had said to me. Not really sure."

"Did you look it up online?"

"Nope, not yet." He was still pissed at the kid reporter.

She gave him a reproachful look. She figured she'll just do it herself.

Outside they stopped midway down the steps. Fletcher continued.

"It seems our friend, the killer, may just be playing with us. And this Father Brandon is hiding something, no doubt."

"Yes, I saw that. Why would the killer just be playing with us? You think the passages are nothing more than false leads?" she asked, looking down, with her fingers lightly touching her chin.

"I honestly don't know," Fletcher replied. "I was expecting something hidden, an encrypted clue given for the next attack, something that would point us to the missing kids. Or something like that."

"Yeah, but it's only about a warning and food and a raven."

Fletcher walked down a couple more steps.

He stopped.

"Do ravens eat meat?" he questioned.

"I believe they do."

"Interesting."

"What? What are you thinking?" she pressed.

He just stood there looking out into space.

She knew to wait.

"A warning, huh?"

"Yeah, why?" she pressed again, coming up close to him.

"Not sure. Not sure."

He walked down the rest of the steps, not even looking at her.

She followed in silence.

Chapter 71 ~

HE STARED AT THE STAINED-GLASS window to the side of the church. He just wasn't sure. He kept thinking he had to do something. He didn't want to put anyone in a position of denial, especially within his own order. He was caught with deep, opposing feelings in his heart.

He thought of God. He thought of his peers. He thought of his calling. He thought of his own responsibilities in every way. It was the thought of the children that made him do it.

"Hey," he said as he opened the big church doors at the top of the steps. He said it too low. They didn't hear him.

"Excuse me, hey, pssst."

Melanie heard something and turned. She nudged Fletcher, who turned towards her motioning look.

"Interesting," was all that came out of his mouth.

At the top of the steps to the church was a young man dressed in a black robe, like the priest. Except he had no white square. His brilliant blonde hair and boyish face appeared like an angel to Melanie.

"What do we do?" she quietly asked.

"What do we *do*? We listen to him."

They waited. The young man realized he was to come to them, so he quickly jumped down the steps. He motioned for them to start walking. Fletcher nodded to Melanie.

They all walked quickly away from the church. Fletcher had noticed the young man eyeing up Melanie's bare legs. He smiled inside. Being in the clergy didn't stop making you a man, he mused to himself.

"So?" Fletcher finally said.

"I know why you came. I overheard you. I want to try to help."

He sounded sincere to Fletcher.

"Fine, that's great, but who are you?"

The young man smiled. "I'm Deacon Wellington. I'm part of this church and order. I really shouldn't be talking with you."

"Shouldn't? Then why are you?" Melanie asked.

He paused. Fletcher stopped. They all did and just looked at each other. The deacon started slowly walking again. They followed.

"Well, Father Brandon wouldn't want me to. I know you want to know why, but it's best left at that, if you want my help..." he trailed off.

"Depends on the help, I guess," Fletcher finished it.

"Fair enough."

"Go ahead."

"Elijah's Wrath. It's real."

"That's great! It's just that we don't know what the hell it is."

"Sorry. It's child slavery and I believe it's real."

"What do you mean real?" Melanie felt exasperated all of a sudden. She really didn't want to know.

"The public is naïve. Parents are naïve. So are the police. So naïve, everyone." He sounded in despair. He ran his fingers through his hair.

"Go on," Fletcher said, touching him on his shoulder.

He proceeded to explain where the term came from and how, back in ancient Israel, no matter how parents tried to protect their children, if slavers wanted them, they got them.

"But didn't the authorities—"

He laughed and then apologized for it.

"The authority in Israel was in on it."

That stopped Fletcher and Melanie in their tracks.

Chapter 72 ~

"BOSS, LOOK WHAT I FOUND!" Danny burst in, blurting a bit of flying spit. Frankie looked up, still feeling tired from another sleepless night and nightmarish morning. He was controlling his emotions, day to day, as best he could. He hoped this had to do with the case and not some wild thing Danny tended to follow-up on all the time.

"Yes, Danny, what is it?"

His low tone didn't deflate Danny's enthusiasm.

"Remember you told me to keep researching perps with the same MO, right?"

"Yep, so? Whatcha got?" He was getting more interested. So far, every MO-lead led nowhere. The recent incident with that young reporter just made things worse. He was really tired.

"Guess who's back in town?"

"Just tell me."

"Merrie!"

It took a second.

"Whoa! Really?"

"Yep, he's been back for a while and no one knew. He slipped under the Megan's Law radar." Danny was beaming with pride.

"Let me see," Frankie perked up, holding his hand out.

He read the report and the address. Merrie "The PP" Watson was definitely back in town. Knowing "PP" stood for "Ped Perp," he didn't like it at all.

The MO was considerably close, too. All his "alleged"

activities were with both boys and girls. All were between the ages of 10 and 14. But there was only enough evidence to convict him once. That didn't stop Frankie.

"Danny, pick our 'PP' up. Let's have a little chat with him."

"Right boss, it'd be my pleasure!"

Chapter 73 ~

FLETCHER AND MELANIE grilled the deacon. They did it with respect, but still pressed him. After hearing the whole story, they weren't convinced.

"So, why do you think this has anything to do with this case?" asked Melanie.

"The similarities are too much, don't you see?" the deacon insisted.

"Yes, children are missing. Right. And some were discarded, too," Fletcher said.

"Murdered," the young deacon corrected.

"I was being nice. But who—why would anyone be doing this now, two thousand years later?"

"You're not listening. Child slavery exists today, in this world, in this country, here in this city! From what I've seen, I honestly feel it's true."

Both Fletcher and Melanie stared at him in disbelief. Melanie broke the moment.

"So, you're saying that there are slavers out there, modern day slavers, who are randomly kidnapping children in broad daylight, and selling them on some secret block?"

"Yes."

"To people who buy them and use them as slaves, in their homes?"

"Yes."

"Are you crazy?" was all that could come out of her mouth.

"No. I'm not. I can get proof. But if I get caught—"

"So, you're not sure. Tell us why and we'll believe you."

"Try to believe you," Fletcher corrected her. She gave him a little glare back.

"Can't. Too risky. You'll have to just trust me and find out for yourselves. I can try to get proof but I must remain anonymous."

Fletcher wasn't in the mood for more games. "Not good enough, Padre. Sorry," he said in a firm, unwavering tone the deacon could not miss.

The young man paused. He knew he was losing this battle. He made a decision.

"Okay, I'll give you this. My own life could be at stake."

They both stared at him again.

"Your life at stake? Are you kidding?"

"All I'll say is that when the Roman Empire became the Holy Roman Empire and the church started its journey to ultimate power, through the bishops and clergy in the early church, the practice didn't stop. It was too lucrative and sad to say, the same authorities were involved."

"The same as the High Priests did!" Melanie exclaimed.

"Exactly."

She nodded to Fletcher, indicating she knew something about Israel.

"And you're implying that this practice has been going on for two thousand years, 'til this very day, and the church is fully involved?"

"Well, Miss, not the church, but a select sect of clergy. I can say no more. No more about that."

"Listen, I'm with the police," Fletcher jumped in.

"I know and that's why."

"I can—"

"Do what you will. I must leave you now. I'll be in touch."

He suddenly looked frantic with fear. It immediately reminded Fletcher of the movie *The Exorcist*. He saw the same fear in this man's eyes. He still didn't care.

"Listen you," he demanded.

Melanie never saw such fright grow on a man's face so fast. She watched him quickly depart back to the church, like a terrified little mouse.

"What?" she whispered.

"Um, look." Fletcher's head motioned.

"Oh, I see!"

At the top of the steps stood a man, stoically still. His face was grim and hard. His arms tightly folded.

It was Father Michael Brandon.

Chapter 74 ~

IT WAS GETTING CLOSE TO the time they had to meet Frankie back downtown. They were to meet at the park and then to the kids. Fletcher wanted a drink first before entering that home. He left a message letting Frankie know he was heading for the Luxury Café.

"Wanna drink?" he asked Melanie.

"Um, sure, if we *must*," she replied with a smile.

"I knew I liked you," he turned, returning the smile. "It's the one nice thing about not being a cop and still being able to investigate."

"Yes, I see. And that's why you quit the Force? Alcoholism?"

"Well, no. I'm really not that shallow. But thanks for the compliment. I quit because I had the money to quit and I didn't like playing within all the rules."

"Oh, I see; you're just a rebel at heart."

He knew she was messin'.

"I'm a rebel all the time!"

"I know. It's what I like."

He drove into the parking garage. After they parked, they strolled to the café.

She slipped her arm around him. He felt her pull him closer.

He did the same to her.

When they arrived at the café, Frankie was already there. The look on his face was one of complete shock. His mouth was agape, too.

Fletcher saw it, immediately realizing why. He had not met Melanie. And more so, he would never have expected to see Fletcher smiling with a girl on his arm. It must also be her sexy legs, Fletcher mused.

"Hey, Frankie!" he said with an upbeat tone.

"Uh, yeah, Fletch, um, how ya doin'?" Frankie replied, lightly stuttering at the sight of her.

"Like you to meet Ms. Melanie Sanders," Fletcher said, grinning from knowing the shock he was creating.

"Hi!" Melanie said releasing herself from Fletcher to go over to Frankie to shake his hand.

Frankie was still sitting when he realized his loss of manners. He stood up abruptly, knocking over his chair. He knew he appeared shaky as he turned to pick it up. Then he realized she had her hand out. He quickly turned towards her, paused for a deep sigh, and took her hand.

Melanie grimaced a little. He was squeezing too hard. He released it, finally planting a smile on his face. She smiled cutely back.

He looked at Fletcher for a moment, saw his wide grin, and then he turned back to Melanie.

"Very glad to meet you!" he blurted out. He couldn't believe how wholesome and lovely she looked.

"Glad to finally meet you, too. Fletcher speaks very highly of you."

At that, she could see him compose himself and relax more.

"Him? Of me? Yeah, right."

They all chuckled.

Frankie heard the nervousness in his own laugh.

"Let's sit and talk before we go to meet these little folks, okay?" Frankie posed as he caught himself staring at her. He just couldn't take his eyes off her. And he wasn't sure why she was there.

"Sure boss," Fletcher said, still noticing Frankie's attention to his girl.

"Yep," Melanie replied and graciously sat down. Fletcher moved her chair for her.

Frankie's mouth opened again.

"Will you sit down!" Fletcher said to him. "And close your mouth!"

"Yeah, yeah, sorry."

She beamed back. Frankie had to catch himself again from staring at her. He also wasn't sure how far he should continue about the case with someone he just met. He didn't want to compromise anything and glanced over at Fletcher. His raised eyebrows told Fletcher his concern.

Fletcher caught his look and understood. "It's ok, I'll vouch for her," he said, giving Frankie a sincere look and nod. Frankie just stared at him, ignoring Melanie, who began to feel uneasy. Fletcher nodded again, this time more forcibly, meaning it was on him. Frankie continued looking at him and then grinned, letting him know that it was on him. He could use all the help he could get and if Fletch vouched, then ok.

"You understand," Frankie turned to her, "that anything discussed is completely confidential and that you are fully his responsibility, not mine, okay?" She nodded. "I'm okay if he wants an assistant but follow all orders—got it?" She nodded again, trying to look serious.

"I will follow all rules. Trust me. I just want to help Fletcher, and everyone, help solve this. If you feel I'm not, then tell me to go."

"She's good Frankie. I wouldn't include her if I didn't think so. It's on me. Please?" He kept searching for the waitress.

Frankie looked at both of them and then smirked. "Sure, ok. You're his assistant from this point forward. You're not a cop. Remember that."

"Ok!" She smiled. Frankie shook his head, trying to ignore the cuteness. He knew his friend could incorporate an assistant if he wanted. And he had enlisted him. He didn't want to lose Fletch now.

Fletcher had enough of the interrogation, motioning to the waitress.

After she came over and they got their drinks, Frankie leaned forward to them. He was clutching his Diet Coke.

"Tell me about the priest."

Suddenly, Melanie saw him as the Chief of Police.

"No use, just mostly told us that Elijah was some kind of prophet and gave these warnings to the Jews. And the rest is just what it says about bread and meat and all."

"So, no idea on what it means. Shit. Was hoping—"

"Yeah, me, too. But we had a nice run in with this other priest guy."

"Deacon," Melanie corrected him.

"Yeah, Deacon guy. Get this, he claimed that there is child slavery still going on, and get this too, that the church is actually involved."

"A secret sect of the church," Melanie corrected him again.

"Yeah, what she says," Fletcher smiled at her.

"You're fucking kidding, right?" Frankie glanced over at them. He had not really believed Josh. Now it has come up a second time. This time the idea came directly from a member of the clergy.

"Nope. Whether true or not, it's at least something," Fletcher posed.

Frankie leaned back and went silent.

Fletcher glanced at Melanie. She shrugged, waiting.

Frankie turned and quickly said to her, "Any ideas on your end?"

She took a deep breath. "Well, I'm thinking about something, but if you will, I'd rather wait till we talk to the kids."

Frankie was taken aback by her confidence, which appealed to him.

"That's fine, I'll wait. Not long. I do want to know today," he said firmly, but with a smile.

She smiled back and it melted him.

"Yes, yes, I will. Trust me, I will."

"So, Melanie, I've never seen this man so happy. What's your secret?" Frankie asked, trying not to show his growing discomfort at meeting this amazing girl.

"Ya know, he does seem happy, doesn't he?"

"Yeah, a little too happy, I would say," Frankie followed.

"Maybe he's in love? What do you think Frankie? Is he the type to just fall in love?"

Fletcher decided to let them have their fun. He had his drink now and was in deep thought.

"I didn't think so, but looking at that crazy happy grin when you guys came over, I may have been wrong all these years."

"Well, I think you may have been!"

"So, what you're saying is that: Fletcher's in loooovvve! Fletcher's in loooovvve!" Frankie felt more relaxed with her now and felt like having some fun at his friend's expense.

That woke Fletcher up from his deep thoughts, and after an

apparent startle, he gave them both a long sneer.

They both snickered. He just stared at them.

Frankie decided he liked this girl. And he couldn't get himself to take his gaze away from her smile and her wonderful, sparkling eyes.

"So, tell me about you," he asked her, ignoring Fletcher again.

Chapter 75 ~

MELANIE GAVE SOME OF HER background to Frankie. They talked a little until Fletcher finished his drink. They paid up and started towards the Parker residence. The hot sun shone through the interlocking trees. They naturally seemed to take their time, enjoying the warm day.

"Beautiful out, isn't it?" Melanie declared, not looking for an answer.

Neither Fletcher nor Frankie replied. Frankie did add in his mind: and more beautiful with you. He still couldn't understand his attraction.

When they reached the home, Frankie took the lead, pressing the button. He identified himself to what sounded like a servant. After hearing the buzzer, he opened the door. They quietly entered.

Fletcher vividly remembered the place. Even without the guests, he felt uncomfortable again with all the splendor and elegant décor. He feared unknowingly walking into something and breaking it. He would probably have to pay for it, unless he could run out fast enough.

A young girl in uniform greeted them. She asked them to follow her. She was very timid and spoke so low, they could barely understand her. They followed her, more because she just walked away.

Suddenly, Fletcher realized he might see Rosalyn. Thinking about the case, it hadn't occurred to him. He felt a small panic growing in him.

They climbed up a flight of steps. They weren't the main stairs, but a staircase behind a tucked-away door.

The stunning furnishings even here were exquisite. Everything was obviously expensive, from delicate cherry wood tables to elaborate, gold candelabras.

Fletcher heard Melanie mutter a whispered, "Wow!" a couple times.

When they reached the top of the stairs, they followed the girl down a short hall. She stopped at a closed door on their right. It was a sculptured door like the rest in the house. It surprised Fletcher though because it was painted flat black. It looked incredibly gothic. In contrast, there was a large, colorful "FHC" logo on it.

Fletcher instinctively looked down the hall, past the girl. Rosalyn was standing there. She appeared out of nowhere. She was motionless, frozen. She wore a white, silky negligee that clung to her slender form. Her firm legs were exposed. She was barefooted. Her hair was down covering part of her face. Her gaze was solely and intently on him.

He was instantly captivated. The hypnotic moment disappeared immediately, when suddenly she smiled, causing Fletcher to blink out of the spell. He turned to Melanie and Frankie to see if they saw her, too. They were still staring at the large logo on the door.

Fletcher glanced back. She was gone.

In a daze, his arms suddenly felt weak. His heart began to race. Was it a spell? Was it just his surprise at seeing her again, in all her loveliness? Her cold, frozen loveliness, he suddenly thought. He wanted to get into that room. He wanted to get away from her—and her away from Melanie.

The servant never said another word. She just motioned to

the door. She left them in the same direction where Rosalyn had stood.

They quietly paused, looking at each other. They didn't know whether to wait, knock, or just enter because she motioned to it. Fletcher didn't want to say anything about Rosalyn's appearance. He decided to wait and see what was behind the door.

"Well?" Frankie posed to them.

They both shrugged.

"Are you going to come in or not?" was yelled from behind the door.

"I guess we got our answer," Fletcher said, in an obvious tone of annoyance at being yelled at.

"Be nice," Melanie said to him, touching his arm.

"Yeah, big boy, be nice, like the lady says," Frankie repeated with a parental look.

"I'll surely try but if that little monster—"

"Let him be whatever he wants. It's better that way. So, we can see it as it is. Got it?" Frankie pressed.

"Sure Frankie, we'll do it your way—for now."

Fletcher took hold of the handle, turned it, and opened the door.

What they saw stopped them instantly.

Chapter 76 ~

FATHER BRANDON QUIETLY SAT in his private room. He appeared in deep thought, almost meditation. But he was seething. He couldn't believe anything about child slavery and secret sects was brought forward. The police probably would start to investigate. Nobody would ever understand their mission, he thought.

He had severely chastised Deacon Wellington. The young man would never say another word and promised Confession. Father Brandon knew how much he could put fear into underlings. He knew from the young Deacon's eyes that this would never happen again.

Now he had to figure out damage-control.

He leaned forward to his desk drawer. Pulling a small key out from his frock pocket, he unlocked the drawer. He opened it slowly. He could smell the cedar aroma pour out.

The only item in the drawer was a large, ornate, rope-bound book. Deeply inscribed on the cover were the letters, "FHC." He pulled it out. Under the letters was an etched inscription. It read: "Faith – Hope – Charity."

He sighed. He looked at the gold ornate ring on his finger. It also had the same lettering as the book.

He carefully opened the book he had perused so many times before. He knew the book was much older than the inscription which was added recently. He remembered the day Cardinal Meneditia had secretly met with him. He was to safeguard the book. It could no longer remain in Rome. The

Cardinal placed the ring on his finger as he swore the oath. He was now the entrusted bearer. He answered only to Rome.

Father Brandon was a proud man. He felt complete loyalty to both his order and now to "The Order of Faith, Hope, and Charity." The anger slowly left him as he read.

The entries dated back to Augustus Caesar. Each section had hand-written descriptive personal notes, dates, and meticulous accounting notations. Under each section were names: names of Roman senators, names of high priests, names of bishops, names of popes, and then many, many other names listed below each of them. Sections were in Latin, Aramaic, Hebrew, Greek, Medieval English, Italian, and Modern English. The only common factor was a small symbol next to most of the names.

The list went on and on.

Chapter 77 ~

"WELL, ARE YOU GOING TO COME IN or not?" Eddy asked. They slowly entered. The room was dark. The contrasting colors against black reminded Fletcher of hippie era head-shops. It appeared to him a cross between dark psychedelics and Rambo. Posters of revolutionary figures pasted the walls, from Lenin to Castro to Gandhi to Timothy Leary to John Lennon.

The lighting was bounced and angled in various dark hues, so that nothing was glaring. An eerie, dim glow permeated from the black lights and lava lamps. The furnishings were like a 1960's coffeehouse with large and small pillows of fluorescent colors. One large black ornate chair was in the center of the longest wall. It appeared a throne. Skinny Eddy was sitting under a poster of Lenin, smiling.

There was a computer area with a laptop opened to their homepage with the "FHC" logo. The same logo and design was on a huge tapestry that hung next to Eddy's throne.

Three others were in the room. Fletcher noticed they were somewhere around Eddy's age, all dressed in a combination of hippie clothing and fatigues. Two had on Army paratrooper high jump-boots. The other had on sandals.

In contrast, Eddy was dressed in a black fine-pinstripe suit. His bright white shirt had the collar open. He wore dark sunglasses, reminding Fletcher of Jim Jones in the Guyana cult.

They stopped just inside the door; it took a while to take it all in.

"Hello! Please, please come in," said a pigtailed, hippie-looking girl who bounced up to greet them. She had painted hearts on her face.

At least she smiled at them, Fletcher thought.

They crept in, like children, not wanting to enter. She then closed the door behind them. With the hall light gone, the room glowed even more. There were no windows for any outside light. More likely, Fletcher presumed, so that no one could look in.

"Mr. Saxtan, so nice to see you again," Eddy spoke up but stayed on his throne. "Mr. Oswald, too, I see."

They both nodded in acknowledgement.

"And who, may I ask, is this lovely angel with you?" Eddy asked in a knightly manner. It had a very suggestive tone, too, as he gazed at her bare legs. He slowly took off his sunglasses.

Melanie looked at him as Fletcher read her mind. She must have been thinking who is this little fuck of a kid to talk to me with that tone. Well, at least now she had a taste of it, he mused.

"Sir, my name is Melanie Sanders and it's a pleasure to meet you and your friends," she formally, but pleasantly, replied.

Fletcher couldn't help himself from turning and staring at her for that answer. He noticed Frankie did so, too.

"Miss Sanders, you are welcome," Eddy said and nodded a little, glancing again at her legs and then back at her face.

"Please sit down," said a very chubby girl with a half-shaved head and dressed like a little Rambo-girl. Her voice cracked like a small child. Melanie couldn't believe that voice came from someone dressed like that.

She rose when she spoke and moved her arm around the

room pointing out all the pillows.

They looked at each other and shrugged as if to say, "When in Rome."

Fletcher propped a large pillow up against the wall, leaning on it so he had back support. He immediately felt uneasy sitting on the floor.

He noticed a small table that had some candles lit and what looked like a Bible, lying wide open. He wanted to see where it was opened to but decided to wait.

He did another glance around the room and saw another tapestry with the saying: "Courage, Honor, Friends." He realized right away that it was a reverse acronym for "FHC." All strange, he thought to himself.

He leaned over to Melanie, motioning to it.

"There's a lot of game playing here, isn't there," he said matter-of-factly and very quietly.

She motioned with a nod of her head towards a corner that had a stack of computer games. She couldn't see exactly which ones. Fletcher nodded, seeing it. Lots and lots of game playing, he thought.

They noticed the other boy in the room stand up, look at Eddy, and walk over to them.

"Please, no secrets in here!" said the boy, in a firm whisper.

Fletcher wondered how long he was going to put up with this mad charade.

He felt a nudge from Melanie. She was again reading his thoughts and for him to be cool.

He nudged her back to let her know it wasn't going to take long before he had enough.

She just smiled, staring forward.

Chapter 78 ~

JOSH GOT OUT OF HIS CAR. He slowly walked up the street. Trees and tall bushes hid most of the homes. He approached his planned destination. His heart started to pound so hard, he hesitated for a moment to gather his courage.

He decided there were only two ways to get to Martino. The first was to stalk his home. Which as a reporter, he felt he had the right, as long as he remained on public property.

The second option was a little envelope he pulled out addressed to Mr. Stuart Martino. He had placed a stamp on the envelope. He did not intend to mail it. He had carefully drawn little wavy lines so the stamp appeared cancelled by the U.S. Postal Service.

If Martino wouldn't talk with him directly, his fallback was the letter. It described his ideas, his purpose, and willingness to help him. Of course, it would help Josh, too.

He found a spot close to the massive gate. It was near a large elm tree. He decided just to wait. His heart was still heavily pounding. He felt lightheaded. When he saw the large Mercedes turn the corner, he almost fainted from the adrenaline rush.

Chapter 79 ~

FLETCHER NOTICED MELANIE and Frankie acting comfortable, obviously playing the role of happy, respectful guests. He was trying to play, too, but he couldn't. It was burning inside him to get up and smack that skinny, bowl-shaped haired kid right off that pretend-throne of his.

He was a little concerned too about Frankie. He knew behind his façade, Frankie could actually be very uncomfortable. He also looked like he was ready to pull his gun at any moment. Must be the cop thing, Fletcher thought.

"So, glad you all could stop by to our consortium room," Eddy softly spoke up again. "This is our control center for our Movement and our website." He stood up now. With his hands clasped behind his back, he slowly began to stroll around the room like a professor.

"Here is where we push our ideas and thoughts out to the world. We help others of our Movement do the same, in their areas of influence."

Yeah, and your teen-brainwashing, Fletcher thought.

"All I ask is that you please respect us and our place, when here."

He sounded like such an adult and looked like such a boy, Fletcher thought. What made this kid tick? And why was such a Movement created by these weird kids? His cop instinct went into full alert.

"Now, let me introduce to you our primary members and associates. This is Stacy. This is Marcy. And this here is Stanley."

Each rose when their name was mentioned and remained standing. It was particularly strange with all of them standing and each of them sitting. When Eddy sat back down on his throne, they all sat back down in unison. Images of Charles Manson's family flashed in Fletcher's mind.

After a long pause that seemed to go on forever, Eddy began again.

"What we'd like to do, all of us in this room and any willing member out there, is to help and assist you in your quest to find and punish this criminal."

Frankie was about to speak but Eddy continued.

"We have discussed it and have a plan. We would like to implement it as soon as possible."

Frankie looked over at Fletcher. Fletcher gave a tiny nod, meaning let him finish. Frankie nodded in return.

There was another uncomfortable long pause in the eerie darkness.

"Would you like to hear our plan?" Eddy finally asked. Melanie could tell he was annoyed that no one asked.

"Yes, we would," answered Fletcher for all of them.

"Good," he curtly replied. He seemed to rest back in his throne as if he was finished.

Marcy, the chubby girl, then stood up.

"We would like to provide targets for this criminal."

She promptly sat down.

Fletcher paused to make sure no one else would start talking if he started. No one did.

"If I may?"

Eddy nodded.

"Thank you for wishing to help. I have some questions."

Eddy nodded.

"How would you provide targets? I mean, where?"

Stanley stood up.

"We know where they were when they were abducted. It has been, each time, after school and on their way home."

He sat down.

Fletcher looked at Frankie. Frankie nodded.

"There are a lot of places many kids go to. It seems impossible to know which route, which school, etc."

Stacy stood up.

"Not as hard as you think. Has it not always been wealthy kids?"

They nodded.

"Therefore, we target the wealthy areas and their schools. There aren't that many around."

Frankie looked over at Fletcher, nodding again.

"Still, there's only four of you," Fletcher added.

"Three," Stacy said.

Fletcher got the point that Eddy would not be involved. He figured it was a benefit of being the leader.

"Okay, three. Even more so."

Stanley then stood up as Stacy sat down.

"We will monitor only. You forget we have many members and—"

"Wait, hold a second," Frankie hurriedly spoke up. "We cannot just allow any given minor to be a target. We would need parental approval, and even so, I don't think this is a good plan or if any parent in their right mind would allow it."

Stanley looked at Eddy. Eddy nodded. Stanley sat down. Eddy stood up.

Fletcher felt like he was on a friggin' seesaw.

"Not to worry," he began. "We will provide written

approval from the parents of the appropriate members and you may check it out."

"But—"

"Mr. Oswald, do you really have any other plan that could work?"

Fletcher and Melanie were looking at Frankie.

He looked at them and then back at Eddy.

"Assuming the parents agreed, how many do you think you could get? We would have to cover each one, every time, everywhere. This doesn't mean I'm giving my approval."

"There're really only three to four main schools of the age group and MO. So how many do you think?" Eddy posed, appearing to be helpful.

"Well, we could use maybe ten kids," Fletcher interjected.

Eddy nodded.

"Ten? Why ten?" Frankie asked back, directly to Fletcher.

"Because, they must be in pairs. Remember, they have to be siblings," Melanie whispered to him.

"Yeah, right," Frankie nodded. "But doesn't the perp know they are siblings, I mean we couldn't just use any two combinations, could we?"

"They will be siblings," Eddy said, as if it was apparent.

"You're telling me you can find five families that would allow not just one but two of their kids to be placed in the highest danger, for this? Knowing the consequences?"

"We will only use absolutely willing members with parental written approval, too. We're sure we can find them and have already started. You must guarantee that you can without doubt protect them and us. That is your job. We would only proceed with the assurance that you can do that. Can you?"

Silence came to the room with Eddy's question.

For a moment, Fletcher saw a man talking, not a boy. It concerned him a lot. He knew there were prodigies out there, but this was ridiculous.

Frankie was thinking and then spoke up.

"Of course, we would guarantee protection, with your father's permission, and will have undercover everywhere. Not an issue. By the way, he should be here. I just can't, nor will authorize—"

"Then we're all set, I see," Eddy finished, ignoring the note about his father. He calmly sat back down on his throne.

Fletcher saw that he had waited for Frankie to make his claim, and then he made Frankie accept, based on his own claim. Too shrewd for a kid, he thought again. Too shrewd.

Chapter 80 ~

THE BLACK MERCEDES PULLED up slowly. Josh heard the gate automatically open. He froze, not knowing what to do next. He had planned so many things. Everything escaped him now. He slipped back to hide his presence behind the elm tree.

Martino approached the open gate. Josh could see his eyes staring straight ahead, guiding the car through it. Suddenly, the slow-moving car stopped. Josh's heart jumped. He seriously felt a heart attack coming on. He couldn't believe what happened next.

The passenger side door opened by itself.

He couldn't move. His knees were so weak and shaking, it wouldn't have mattered anyway.

"Well?" he heard in a very deep voice.

Josh tried but couldn't speak.

"Are you going to get in or not?"

At that, he suddenly found the will to peak out from behind the tree. Martino's face was staring at him through the open door. He had a look of impatience but his eyes told Josh he was in a calm mood.

Slowly and carefully, Josh moved from the tree towards the big car. He reached the open door. He leaned down slowly, hoping in his soul this wasn't a trap.

"Get in or I'm driving off."

"Okay, okay."

He slipped in and immediately felt the thick lushness of the seat.

"Stuart Martino. We haven't formally met." He held out his hand. Josh saw a small smile creep at the corners of his mouth and then it disappeared.

He took his hand. The grip almost crushed his smaller hand.

"Nice to meet you. I'm—"

"I know who you are and don't worry, I'm not going to kill you, not yet at least."

"Oh, good, that makes me feel so much better."

Martino gave him a quick glance that reminded Josh of John Wayne. Josh also noticed the deep lines of sleeplessness behind his façade.

"Listen kid, I may be out of my mind for my little girls, but I'm not stupid. And Oswald told me everything, especially how really stupid you can be."

"Yep, that's me," Josh replied with annoyance in his voice. Again he got the John Wayne look. He assumed he wasn't getting an apology for the police station. He nervously ran his fingers through his hair.

"Let's talk. My place okay?"

"Yes, yes, sure, I was going to—"

"Yes, I figured you'd never give up, so let's go."

He drove on as the car door closed by itself. It was beginning to freak Josh out. He decided to ignore it. He wanted to get to business because again, he just couldn't believe his luck.

Chapter 81 ~

FLETCHER WAS GETTING ANTSY. He wanted to end this discussion. He wanted to ask some real questions he had about them and their so-called Movement. He looked at Frankie to let him take the lead. Frankie nodded.

"Eddy, may I ask some other questions?" Fletcher asked in a pleasant tone.

"About what?"

"About your Movement."

Eddy paused. He was looking at him, as if processing something in his head like a robot.

"Sure, you can."

"Fine. How long has your Movement been going on?"

"That information is on our website."

Fletcher looked annoyed but continued.

"Okay, I see. Well, then, how many members do you have?"

"That is confidential, I am sorry."

"Then, it appears you target young people. Any reason?"

"They have fresh open minds; plus, we are young people."

"Why not older people?"

"They can join, if they wish."

"How can you put down the wealthy when you yourselves are wealthy?"

"My colleagues are somewhat on the wealthy side, but not as much as I am."

"Okay, then, how can *you*?"

"Sometimes wealth is necessary in order to operate. We do not charge any fees, if you have not noticed. Somebody has to pay for the flyers, the site, and all our materials and travel."

"Travel?"

Fletcher felt he had just found out something.

Melanie looked over at him. Frankie didn't budge.

Eddy paused.

"Yes, travel. We do go places."

"I see. Where?"

He thought this might shake the kid a little; but there was absolutely no change at all in his demeanor, his posture, or his expression. Fletcher did note he kept occasionally staring at Melanie's breasts and bare legs. Guess he's going through puberty, Fletcher mused.

"We go wherever our Movement takes us."

"Like?"

"Like to help support others not in our area."

"So, you travel to other parts of this state?"

"Yes, and other states, too."

"Do you just show up?"

"Sometimes."

"How do you know when, where?"

"All meetings must be scheduled on the website."

"Oh, I see."

Silence.

"One last question, if I may?"

"One last."

"Do you help these other places sign up new members?"

Another short pause.

"If requested, of course."

"Well, then—"

Marcy stood up and spoke.

"That was the last question, Mr. Saxtan, as you said. All other information is on our site. Please feel free to go visit. There's a FAQ section and a place to contact us with any other questions. We would like to thank you for your time, as we must continue our own meeting. We hope you have a nice day."

Her arm was out indicating it was time to leave.

"How will we contact you to—" Frankie asked as he stood up.

She interrupted.

"We will contact you."

Frankie was about to continue, until he saw Fletcher's look.

They got up, said their thanks, and left.

The door closed slowly and firmly behind them, with a sound of completeness.

Chapter 82 ~

FATHER BRANDON FINALLY put the ancient book down. After thinking a moment, he picked up his phone and dialed the number. He waited and waited. It went to voice mail.

"Hello, you have reached the rectory of St. Stephen's, to leave a message for Father Quincy, please press one, for Father Harris, press…"

He looked at the phone, pressed one, and waited.

"Hi, you have reached Father Quincy, pastor. I am unavailable at this moment; please leave a message at the beep. Thank you."

He waited for the beep and started.

"Quincy, Brandon here. I need to speak with you as soon as you can. Call me on my cell, and call me when you get this, no matter what time it is."

He hung up and sat back. Suddenly his cell rang.

"Brandon, what's the matter?"

He took a deep breath. "I wouldn't normally call, but I think we need to meet, and soon. Possible problem."

There was silence on the other end.

"I see. Meet here, but we cannot stop it now.'

"Yes, I know, I know."

Chapter 83 ~

THEY WERE ALL SURPRISED TO SEE the young servant standing there for them, ready to lead them out of the house. Fletcher looked over at Frankie. He didn't like his expression. He had seen this before. He knew that his friend was not satisfied with what had just happened.

He also knew the cop in him would not allow him to lose control of a situation. More so with kids involved, regardless of how wealthy or confident they may seem or actually be.

"Frankie?" Melanie asked, as she stopped following the girl. "You okay?"

Frankie was just standing there staring at the floor. He was obviously in thinking mode. Or as Fletcher thought, he was in police analytical mode. He figured he was deciding what to do next.

It didn't take long for him to find out.

In a swift motion, Frankie turned and without a word, grabbed the doorknob. He turned it in a flash and was gone, back into the room.

He left the door open. Either because he didn't care or left it open for them to follow. It didn't matter. They followed.

Melanie instinctively grabbed Fletcher's hand, holding it tightly.

The room was pretty much the same as when they left. The only difference being that all three kids were sitting on the floor. They were up front and around Eddy. He was pointing his finger, saying something to them. He stopped when he saw

Frankie and them reenter.

Fletcher was a little amused to see Eddy's look of surprise. He had never seen that on his face before. There was also a look of indignation.

"Please stop right there," Eddy stated, firmly and loudly.

Frankie didn't stop but walked right over to him in his chair.

"I said to stop. You are in my home and my room."

He finally looked and sounded like a child to Melanie.

"I believe this is your parents' home and I work for one of them, *your father.*"

Eddy's look was turning to anger, but then all of a sudden, it returned to his normal casual tranquility. With a touch of craziness, Melanie thought, watching with amazement. The child was gone again.

Fletcher saw that he relaxed and slowly sat back. He appeared to accept the intrusion. The other kids suddenly stood.

Frankie was standing right in front of Eddy. The two girls on one side and the boy on the other flanked him. He looked surrounded. Fletcher wondered if they might actually attack him. Who knows, he suddenly thought, what weapons may be concealed in here.

"Mr. Oswald, I apologize for my inhospitality. I am sorry, but your entry had taken me off guard. I do hope you accept my sincere wishes to speak with you again."

Fletcher saw he was smiling from ear to ear. There was no way, nor would there be a way, that he would ever trust *that* smile.

He looked at Melanie. She was frozen behind him, still grasping his hand. Then he looked over at Frankie. He appeared not to even have heard Eddy. His taut face was getting redder and redder.

"Listen, you," he started, pointing his finger at the kid. "I don't believe you understand the gravity of this situation. Expecting parents to willfully put their kids in danger is absurd, no matter how much you think they will."

He was still pointing his finger and it was getting very close to Eddy's serene face, his bowl-shaped hair, and frozen smile.

"I am letting you know that we will not be needing your assistance in this matter, and furthermore, I would like to know if your father knows what you do in here and with that website."

It wasn't a question at all, Fletcher noticed.

There was a long pause. Finally, Frankie lowered his finger and arm.

Eddy looked at him with a blank stare. The other kids were motionless.

His high-pitched voice was monotone, never taking his eyes off Frankie.

"Mr. Oswald, I and we appreciate your concern, but we are very capable of handling this and taking care of ourselves. Moreover, I am sure our parents will be fine. We will give you proof, too."

"And what if we don't need your help, being targets and all!" Frankie was almost yelling.

"Mr. Oswald, if you do not wish our help, that's fine. We will do it anyway, and neither you nor anyone else can stop us."

Eddy looked over at Fletcher and Melanie when he said that.

Fletcher thought Frankie would blow up. He didn't. He actually seemed to relax a little.

"You see," Eddy continued, "this is our fight, too, and if we wish to be targets to capture or eliminate this menace, we will with or without your help, Mr. Oswald."

Fletcher could see that it was a no-win situation. At least for now, he hoped Frankie would concede and allow them to regroup before acting again.

"Listen, kid," he began with a much lower volume, but still firmly, "I will be speaking with your father. We will discuss this again."

"Be my guest. I already have."

Frankie appeared a little shocked at that.

"You see, I'm very close with Daddy and we talk a lot. We're investigating both passages. I know, as well as you do, that if this criminal isn't stopped now, the heat from both the parents and the press will be on all your heads. You see, there's no other option. And as you said, you can protect us. When the criminal tries something, you get him. He doesn't hurt anyone in the open anyway. Aren't all the dead kids found in secluded rooms well after abduction?"

"Well, yes—"

"And therefore, it's actually safer than you think at time of abduction. It will be fine. But go ahead. Talk, talk, talk. We'll still plan and we'll wait, not long, for you to look at our plan and work with us. It could very well be one of our own friends, or even one of us, who may be kidnapped or murdered next. We not only want to help, we *need* to help. *Please.*"

Fletcher could only think: brilliant. This kid is brilliant.

Frankie stood still thinking for a moment. In the dark, fluorescent room, under the glow of the lava lamps and black lights, he turned to Fletcher and Melanie. Fletcher could see his questioning
glance.

Fletcher motioned him over.

"Frankie, listen, if Mike is going to let his kid and their friends do this out of frustration, and if you can guarantee their safety, like with a plan of surveillance and undercover personnel, what the hell. Why not? Hey, you don't even like these kids. So? Any loss?"

And how Fletcher felt about these kids, he felt fine about it.

Frankie looked at him as if he was crazy making that kind of remark to a cop. But Fletcher also knew he was a human being, too, and that was what he was going after.

Melanie touched Frankie's arm. He turned to her. Her blue eyes and smile melted him again.

"Let's regroup and talk. Make peace and let's leave, okay?"

He couldn't take his eyes away, but finally nodded. Fletcher wondered why a woman's advice seemed to carry more weight than his. He allowed himself to think it was the combination of both of them and leaned closer to Frankie.

"It's okay, for this once," Fletcher whispered.

"Eddy, I will speak with your father and we will see."

"Thank you, Mr. Oswald."

Eddy did a little bow to Fletcher and Melanie, in acknowledgement.

They all turned and left again.

Chapter 84 ~

AFTER BEING ENTIRELY HUMBLED by Martino's spacious home, Josh just wanted to get to work. They arrived at another set of towering white doors. Martino opened them. He waited for Josh to enter.

"Wow," instinctively came out of his mouth. The whole wall facing the outside was glass—ceiling to floor, corner to corner, and side to side. On a massive, dark-oaken desk lay stacks of papers, a keyboard with a huge flat-screen monitor, a laser printer, and a headset phone. On the credenza, he immediately spied the multiple police scanners.

"Take a seat," Martino commanded. Josh found a chair and did as he was told. He then fumbled for his recorder. When Martino saw it, he told Josh to give it to him. He removed the tape and put the recorder on his desk. He tossed him a pad of paper and a pen.

"Use this and only this."

Josh nodded.

"Now, tell me what you know. And I want to know everything."

Josh looked up at the big man standing behind the enormous desk. He felt the room closing in on him. He summoned all his courage. More importantly, he summoned all his goals and dreams. Suddenly, he felt at ease.

"Here's what I believe."

Chapter 85 ~

THEY WERE ALL SURPRISED TO SEE the young girl still standing there, again waiting to lead them out. How did she know? Fletcher wondered. She couldn't have been standing there the whole time. She led them the same way they came in. The contrast of that room and the brightly lit house that reeked of wealth was amazing to them all. He also noticed that Rosalyn was nowhere to be seen. The image of her still troubled him. He wanted to get out before she...

"Shit!" he abruptly said.

"What is it, honey?" Melanie asked, slipping her arm in his.

"I wanted to ask about that Bible! Shit!"

"Yeah, I saw it too, on the table," Melanie noted.

"Yeah, me, too. And I forgot to ask, too," agreed Frankie. He tried not to look at her arm in his.

"Or at least ask what they may have found tied to either passage," Fletcher added.

"Yeah."

"Yeah."

After outside, the thought was pressing to her. "Do you think they may be involved?" she asked them.

"Wouldn't really be the first time. They are definitely fucking freaky! They remind me of Columbine High School, sorry to say."

"Yeah, I can see that," she replied, nodding her head.

"Yeah, but probably worse. They have access to who *knows* how many kids and other people," Fletcher added.

They walked a block in silence.

"Damn it! Fucking games," Frankie froze and said. Fletcher stopped, causing Melanie to trip forward because they were arm in arm.

"What do you mean?" Fletcher asked, looking over at him.

"Can't tell if that damned Bible was there as part of a game or just how they are doing their own investigation from the two passages. I also want to confiscate that computer but can't explain that to Mike yet."

Fletcher stood there and nodded.

So did Melanie.

Then Fletcher looked up with a strange look.

"Assuming Eddy only got his information from Mike and not some other informant, and we only discussed the second passage with Mike, when did we disclose the *first* passage to anyone else?"

Frankie quickly looked at him.

Melanie's eyes opened wide.

Fletcher cocked his head, seeing their recognition.

Frankie looked down, then glanced up, answering him.

"Never."

"That's what I thought."

Chapter 86 ~

THEY CHOSE TO GO BACK TO the café to recap. It was late so they all decided to get a drink. Fletcher knew they all needed one. He also needed a shot. These kids were amazing—out of character with their wealth, and yet, they kept a high and mighty attitude.

Fletcher put his arm around Frankie. He pulled him to him.

"Listen, my friend, it'll be fine. If Mike is okay with it, I say let's use them. We really need to solve this and solve it fast. If they want to be potential targets and you can protect them, then I will be ready to look at their plan. Let's dissect the shit out of it, so we're all comfortable with it, especially you. Okay?"

Frankie just nodded as he walked.

"What about me?" Melanie asked, with a childlike tone.

Fletcher grabbed her with his other arm. He had them both walking in unison with him.

"You're with *me*, babe," he playfully replied. "I will need all the help and unbiased views I can get."

"I was coming along anyway!" she answered back, snuggling under his arm.

Frankie noticed and gently broke free.

"Let's go get a drink or ten," he said, not looking at them. He picked up his pace ahead of them.

They followed, smiling, knowing Frankie was back from his little hell.

"You're buying, Fletch, for opening your big mouth," Frankie said as he went faster.

"Oh, yeah?"

"Yeah!"

Fletcher felt a nudge and knew better.

"Okay, this one time, it's on me."

"Good, because it was anyway. I'm ordering a twenty-five-year-old scotch that will blow your fucking mind!"

Fletcher just grinned. He walked with Melanie, fast losing ground with Frankie, who was almost there.

Chapter 87 ~

ALONE, IT WAITED. NOTHING MORE TO DO. Had to let it play out. Had to be watchful. Watchful always. Always.

Lifting its head back, it took short little breaths and thought and thought. It knew its only weapon was thought and controlling thoughts.

The plan was good. Wait a little longer. May have to shut it down. May have to. Don't want to. No. Can't want to. May need to.

Keep going. Right path. Let it go for a little longer and see. Promises are promises. Police are useless. Stupid. Only me.

Remember. Remember it all. It's all mine. Mine to have and do and be free. Revenge to anyone in the way.

Maybe allow one more time. Maybe.

Maybe allow two more times. Maybe.

No more. Unless they are that stupid. Then more. Get more, do more, have more.

It's our money to use. Our money. Mine, too.

It put the Bible down.

Money is power. Revenge mine.

Money is power. Revenge mine.

Chapter 88 ~

THE LITTLE CAFÉ WAS CROWDED but Frankie found a lone table outside in the corner. He wanted isolation, Fletcher knew, so they could quietly talk and get drunk. He inwardly smiled.

"So, Fletch, what's the plan?" Frankie asked, leaning forward on the small white table.

"Easy. Rum and Coke, and a shot of Jack. Chilled this time."

Frankie grinned. Fletcher got a playful smack on the hand from his girl.

The server eventually saw them and came over. They ordered. Then they all sat back to relax and release the moment.

Frankie was just waiting, looking at him. Fletcher noticed.

"You have no plan yourself?" Fletcher posed back, with a tilt of his head.

"Um, I'm the protection, as you so warmly offered."

"Yeah, I guess you are."

"I have something," Melanie said.

Fletcher turned a little towards her and nodded for her to continue.

"Well, these kids obviously have thought this out. They were prepared. Agreed?"

"Yep."

"Yes, they were."

"Okay, let's think about this. I believe they will place a set of siblings together, daily, at or near one of the schools, or at one of the close local hangouts."

"Yeah," Frankie agreed.

"If you know where they are and instruct them, you can easily watch them and keep them safe. Correct?"

"Yep. No issue."

"And I suppose that any other sibling pair who's not a planned target must be watched, too. Or keep them in close ties, with the parents nearby or driving them or whatever, just in case. Correct?"

"Yes, of course."

"And when this maniac makes a decision and tries to take a pair, you will swoop down and nab him."

"Or them, Mel. It probably is more than one. How can one grab two and go unnoticed?"

"Exactly my point. It cannot be one person. And kids disappear right out in the open. So, it all seems so easy, right?"

"Yep, it does. They have a good plan," Frankie noted, with a little distasteful tone in his voice. He tried again not to stare at Melanie. He knew he couldn't feel like this. He took another long sip of his scotch.

"Mel, what's up?" Fletcher asked after downing his Jack.

"It's all too easy. Don't you see? You could easily find out all kids with brothers and sisters of around the same age and also stake out all the known places and situations where these acts seem to occur. We could do that."

"Okay, and?" Frankie posed.

"Well, then *why* do *you* need them to be targets?"

There was a long silence.

"Well, because, they will not be so suspecting," Frankie answered but like a question.

"Yeah, well, maybe, but I see your point, Mel," Fletcher interjected, as he leaned forward onto the table as if making a dramatic point. She continued.

"See? It's too easy on their side. It's as if they are interposing themselves into the crime scene. I just don't know why. I guess they have more contacts and may be more trusted. Then again, we never said we were going to inform any other kids of their involvement. They are putting themselves into everything and there appears to be no real reason."

"So, why do we really need them at all?" Frankie said to himself, as he leaned back. He appeared to go back into deep thought again.

"No, Frankie, that's not the point. It's—"

Fletcher interrupted her and finished her thought.

"It's *why* do *they* need us?"

"Exactly!"

Chapter 89 ~

MARTINO SAT AND LISTENED without a sound. When Josh was finished, he remained unmoved. Josh knew better than to break the silence. He sat quietly drawing little doodles.

"Here's what you're going to do," Martino ordered.

"Me?"

"Yes, you. Got a problem with it?"

"Well, depends on—"

"Listen kid, I want my daughter and you want the big story, right?"

"Um, well, yes."

"Then shut the fuck up and listen."

Josh nodded, seeing the desperation in his eyes.

"You will befriend this Fletcher person and offer your help. I'll clear it privately with Oswald and Parker," he lied. "Find out what he knows and make sure he understands exactly what you told me—"

"I tried."

"Don't interrupt me. Just do it and get it done. Befriend him and get his confidence. I don't care how you do it. I need to know what he's thinking and where he's going. He's the key. You obviously have my cell. I expect constant updates. And if you want to know what you get out of this, well a nice check. And I will personally speak with the owner of the *Times*, who I know. Good enough?"

Josh stared at him in disbelief. He felt a warm feeling of victory rising in him. I was the same feeling he got from the start of all of this craziness. He nodded and smiled.

"Don't fail me, kid. My wife has gone insane. Your first mission is to get our daughter back. Everything else will be yours, including the front-page. This is so well known, every paper in the world will want you."

Josh looked at his face. He knew he had the power. The only thing that was concerning him was the shaking in Martino's left hand. It hadn't stopped since they had arrived. Josh felt that he must be holding in such anger and fear that he is still liable to explode at any time.

"Sir, I will do more than my best and will keep you always informed."

"Good." He leaned forward. He pressed a button on his large phone pad, almost missing it from the shaking. Suddenly the door opened. A man in a silver suit entered. "Samuel will escort you out."

"Thank you, Mr. Martino," Josh said standing up. For some reason, he gave Martino a slight bow. To his surprise, he did the same. Martino turned away from him as Josh followed Samuel out the door. They quietly left the mansion.

Samuel drove him to the gate in a BMW 740i, which surprised Josh. He guessed every car here was expensive, with a BMW for a utility car.

When outside and past the gate, he slowly walked down the street. He waited until he was out of sight of the gate. He stood still for a long moment. Then he jumped so high in the air with both arms outstretched.

"Fucking-A! Fucking-A!"

Chapter 90 ~

THEY WERE SILENT FOR A LONG while. Each finished their drinks and ordered more. They individually stared off into space, allowing each other to muse quietly over everything. It was a sign of friendship to Fletcher. He smiled inside, and more so, when he looked at Melanie. It honestly pleased him to feel like this, especially after just meeting. They were becoming fast friends. There was something to chemistry, he decided, as his fear of another Desiree was vanishing.

Suddenly he felt his phone vibrate. A wave of fear and anticipation ran right through his chest. He excused himself and went in the direction of the men's room. He stopped halfway. Knowing he was out of sight, he opened his cell.

"love, want to see you. need to see you. can you come over now? ill wait. can't wait to touch you. your wet slave, R!"

He typed a quick reply, closed it, slipped it back, and went into the men's room. He waited a little and then came back out.

"Well?" Frankie broke the silence.

"It just doesn't connect," Melanie added.

"Yeah, you're right. Why does our little Mr. Eddy want to be involved?" Frankie said, looking away from her.

"I got it!"

"Mel, why?" Frankie turned back to her as Fletcher sat down listening.

She leaned forward this time.

"To keep tabs on *us*!"

"Yes, interesting," was all Fletcher said as he leaned back in his chair far enough so that the front legs were in the air. His hand was on his chin. It reminded Frankie of Basil Rathbone as Sherlock Holmes.

"Yes, that could very well be true," Frankie added, "but why? Do you think they are the perps? And if so, why the hell would they ever do such a thing? *How* could they?"

"I don't know but it's really, really fishy. In fact," she looked at both of them, "if I may, it fucking reeks."

"Yeah, I agree," Fletcher replied, smiling at her expletive. He leaned forward, letting his chair fall back to the ground. "They are up to something. That's why Eddy so easily placated himself. He didn't want anything to mess up his plans, whatever they are."

"Yeah, well listen! How could they be the perps if they are acting undercover?" Frankie questioned.

"I think we need to watch these kids with as much vigor as we will be looking for the criminals. They may either be the criminals or part of a whole, larger plot."

"Fletch, it's insane but I agree totally. Watching them closely makes me feel a whole lot better. I didn't want to rely on them, especially that weird Eddy nut. And fuck that he's Mike's kid."

"Agreed, Frankie, and I think you or we need to talk with Mike ASAP!"

"I'll set it up for tomorrow morning, okay?"

"Yeah, definitely," Fletcher replied.

"And if I may?" Melanie posed.

"Yes, dear?"

Fletcher smiled as he said it. Frankie also smiled, thinking what lovebirds they were becoming. He felt a bit of jealousy rising in him.

"Meet with him in his office, not his home. Stay off their turf," she said.

Frankie nodded his approval and downed his scotch. He began to feel admiration for this girl for her insight, as well as a desire to be around her. He could see why she captured Fletcher.

"It's funny," Fletcher added.

"Yeah?" Melanie asked.

"Yeah, what?" Frankie followed.

"We see that home as Eddy's turf, not Mike's."

"You're right. That is a little funny, I guess," Frankie said with a hint of apathy.

"No, he's right," Melanie added. "Plus, Eddy's so confident he will get his father's approval too, or already has it, which to me would be normally improbable if not impossible."

"Exactly, babe."

"I see," was all Frankie could say, trying to get her out of his mind.

They ordered another round.

Chapter 91 ~

"WILL YOU EXCUSE US?" Fletcher asked Melanie. He looked to Frankie. She nodded with a smile, sipping her drink. Not knowing why he was being summoned, Frankie's eyes went from Fletcher to Melanie and then back to Fletcher, giving him a quick quizzical look.

"Ready?" Fletcher said, with a slight nod towards the inside of the café, meaning just to go along.

Frankie got it.

"Thanks, Mel."

"No problem, Frankie," she said. As she cocked her pretty face towards him, some of her hair naturally fell across her cheek. It melted him inside.

When they got inside, Frankie grabbed Fletcher's arm.

"What's up?"

"You gotta do me a favor."

"What do ya need?" Frankie asked.

"I have to go see Rosalyn."

"Excuse me?"

"Yeah, just shut up. It's fine, she needs me."

"Uh, yeah, we know."

"Listen, she said it's important and may be something with Eddy. I don't know, but can you drive Mel home for me? I know it's out of your way." Frankie just stared at him for a moment.

"Yeah, sure can, no worry," he replied, trying desperately to sort out that fact that he was actually going to have time alone with her.

"Thanks, bud, thought I'd have a fight with you about me seeing—"

"Man, I know you're banging her and it's your thing. Just keep me out of it and it out of the case. Got it?" Frankie tried to sound serious.

Fletcher paused, and just for a moment, couldn't understand why he was being so reasonable when he expected a complete onslaught of "don't do it," "be good," etc.

"Sure, Frankie, it won't interfere with anything, I promise."

"Good. Now let's go outside. You tell her."

"I will," Fletcher said turning slowly, still looking at his friend with a little wonderment.

They went back outside. Fletcher said to her that he had to meet Rosalyn, at her request, and he didn't know why. He figured to keep as close to the truth as possible because he didn't know yet how smart Melanie just may be. He was surprised at how easy she took it that he wasn't driving her home.

"Okay, you ready Mel?" Frankie asked with a smile.

"Yep!" She jumped up and seemed to bounce. "See ya, honey," she said to Fletcher, kissing him on the cheek. He looked at her and only three words came out.

"Yeah, sure, okay."

Chapter 92 ~

HIS HANDS WENT UPWARD as he cupped her hanging breasts. He pulled them to his mouth and tongue. She writhed more and more on top of him. Leaning down, she smothered his face with them. The whole while, she was forcing him in and out of her. She was so soft and strong at the same time. It was driving him crazy.

"Ohhhh, Fletcher, honey, baby, yes."

He couldn't speak, as he heard a small moan escape his own lips.

"Some kind of afternoon delight, huh, baby? Uh!"

"Yeeaah," he heard himself say. He didn't care anymore as his waist instinctively rose to her body as her small sculptured thighs pounded him over and over again, each time coming down harder and harder on him. Finally, he felt it coming so deep, so much further down than he had ever felt. He knew he had lost all control. His body seemed to rise by itself. Holding her up in the air, crotch to crotch, he came harder and longer than ever in his life. She screamed at the same time. He knew, he just knew, there was no other woman in the world like her. No other.

They fell together, both limp, except for their heaving breaths. His heart was pounding in his chest. She just lay on him like a dead body, breathing in and out so fast he thought she might pass out.

"You're good," she panted.

"Yeah, so are ... are you."

"Wanna go again?"

"Huh?"

"You know, again," she leaned up on him, her sparkling, emerald eyes staring down at him. Her disheveled hair caressed his cheeks.

He looked up at her and just had to kiss her moist lips.

"I think I'll take a rest," he smiled, tickling her sides. She wiggled, laughed, and rolled over. Her soft body was unbelievable to him, so smooth, so creamy, so perfect, so girl. She suddenly appeared a child to him.

"So, if we can't do it again, let's talk about how your case is going. I'm always so fascinated. Mike tells me some things but you seem to be right in the middle. So exciting! So, tell me, 'kay?" she asked, kissing his side. As her smile grew, her eyes seem to dim and brighten all at once.

"Well, if you care, I mean, if you're interested." He was just too enthralled to say no as she ran her fingers over her small breasts.

"I am," she replied, cocky like Scarlett O'Hara.

"Well, then my dear, I DO give a damn," in his best Rhett Butler.

"Well, then go on, sir gentleman." She tickled him back.

"I do see that I will," he then bowed from where he lay.

She giggled and flopped back onto him with a little "Yelp." Her hair flew back and then forward. She was so girlie; he just adored it. He felt himself getting hard again from her close, silky nakedness touching him.

He proceeded to tell her everything. He figured she could find out from Mike anyway. After he talked about the priests and the deacon, she stopped him right there.

"It's gotta be them!" she exclaimed.

"Huh? I see they may be—"

"No, no. It's them. Trust me. I know people."

"But there's no direct evidence."

"Shush, my love. It's the only logical conclusion. Slavery," she said softly, "I can believe it." She stroked his chest as her long hair fell over her face like a lion's mane, lightly touching his cheeks again. He gazed up at her beautifully draped face.

"Well, maybe."

"Tell me you will look into it more. For me?" She stroked his neck.

"Sure, I will." He took a deep breath as she cocked her head, still stroking his neck.

"And you will look after my boy? I think all the excitement may be too much for him. That's all I really want, for him to be safe. Please?" She stroked his tummy.

"Yeah, yeah."

"You know, I love you."

He looked up at her. The candle behind her made a halo affect all around and through her hair. He saw an angel again as she smiled down at him. His words were an echo in his mind.

"I really do love you, Rosalyn. I really do, my love."

Chapter 93 ~

FRANKIE DROVE UNCHARACTERISTICALLY slower than he normally would. He was thrilled to have this adorable girl sitting next to him. He liked how she closely examined all the police gadgets from the radio to the computer to the large shotgun in the middle.

"Did you ever shoot this thing?" she asked, sounding like a little child to him.

"Well, yes, I have," he quickly glanced at her and saw her running her fingers down the barrel. He quickly looked back to the road.

"Kill anyone with it?"

"Yes, why are you asking?" he smiled, still looking forward. His heart was jumping strangely.

"No reason."

"You can ask anything. It's okay," he felt as if he had to explain.

"Okay, why is Fletcher with Rosalyn?"

The question went right past his mind and then slammed right back in. He didn't know what to say. He knew he'd better say something right away. She was a smart girl.

"She requested to talk with him, that's all."

"Why not you or both of you?"

"It's weird. She likes to talk with him. She opens up to him, so I let it go. Sometimes one-on-one is better, ya know."

"Yeah, I think I know."

He wanted so bad out of this conversation but he

continued.

"She's pretty strange herself. Very young for Mike. She has many circles of friends. Very popular girl."

"Yes, I can see that. I would like to meet her."

"You probably will."

"Good."

It sounded final to him and yet not. He wanted to open up to her, but didn't know what to say.

"So, sorry about sometimes, ya know, looking at you." It wasn't what he wanted to say. He wasn't sure where he was going with it, but he felt she had noticed it, every time.

She laughed, seeming to snap out of her desire to know more about Rosalyn.

"It's nice. I do enjoy it."

He was a little shocked, but liked it. He wasn't sure what to say next.

"You are a very pretty … I mean nice … well, pretty girl."

"Well, thanks, Frankie," she replied genuinely, touching his arm.

He felt a warmth run through his chest. He took his other hand and placed it on top of hers. As he turned to her, she was smiling her curvy, cute smile at him. He wasn't sure if he even smiled back.

"Frankie, it's okay. I understand," she continued.

Her hand turned upward into his. His heart skipped.

"Understand what?" he stuttered, having no control over it.

"You kind of like me a little," she closed her hand around his.

"Um, well, yeah, as new friends."

"Well, maybe a little more."

He didn't know what to say. Again, he wanted to say so

much.

"It's okay," she repeated with a smile, "I do like you and—"

"'Mel, I've never met..." he trailed off.

She squeezed his hand again.

"I know. I'm still shocked at meeting your friend. And now meeting you. He's wonderful and so are you. Any other time..."

He squeezed her hand and she squeezed back.

"Well, okay then," was all that came out of his mouth.

"I know this sounds so cliché-ish, but let's be the best of friends and let the future go where it goes. I would like that."

"I would like that, too."

She leaned over and kissed him on his cheek. He turned suddenly. He was right up to her face and her sparkling eyes and her pouting mouth and her soft breath.

He quickly turned back and laughed. He felt like a schoolboy.

"What?" she coyly asked.

"You're gonna get us killed," he laughed again as he took her hand, kissing the back of it. "Best of friends we are!" He felt so relieved and happy at the same time.

She took his hand, kissing the back of his, too. He never had a girl do that before.

"Yep, we are! I do adore you, Frankie. You are such a strong man, and I can tell behind all that rough hardness, you're just a doll."

"I'll never tell," he laughed again.

She nudged his side. He pretended it hurt.

They sat in silence watching the road go by.

"So, honestly, what's your take on Eddy?" she quietly asked.

He could tell she was really interested.

"I think he's a highly intelligent brat, likes to play games, wants to be king of the world—or at least his own world—and has nothing to do with these murders at all. He's playing."

"Nothing? Nothing at all?" she asked, a little surprised.

"Nope. I think he's gonna end up wasting our time. I don't like them being targets, it complicates everything and is very, very dangerous."

"I see. Then who do you think? The priests? The church?"

"Too easy." Frankie paused a second. "And all this stuff about slavery is silly. Maybe in the Middle East, but not here in America."

She thought he may be a little naïve on this one but didn't want to upset the pleasant time they were having.

"Well, maybe," she replied. "Then who?"

"I'm actually betting on someone else."

"Yeah, who," she said, nudging him again and laughing.

"Stop that!" he yelled as he laughed.

"Then tell," she giggled. The giggle went right through him. He so wanted to kiss her, knowing he couldn't and wouldn't.

"There's this perp, in fact his name is Merrie 'The PP' Watson, who was convicted once, served, and is loose. There've been many arrests since, but only one conviction. Most of the kids backed off prosecuting, probably because of the parents' shame or fear of exposing their child."

"That's silly."

"Yeah, but it happens and the MO really fits him. He's had multiple children with him at times, and one of my detectives found he's been in town—and long enough for all the kidnappings and murders. I didn't tell Fletcher yet that he's back in town."

"So, what do you do with him now?" She sounded extremely interested. He liked that.

"Bring him in. Question the shit out of him. Then get a search warrant and go to his place. In the meantime, we'll play Eddy's game. But Mike has to be onboard with it. I think it's crazy. What do you think?"

"Honestly, I think it's totally Eddy."

"Really?"

"Yes, really."

Chapter 94 ~

THAT EVENING AT FLETCHER'S HOME, he and Melanie sat out on his porch in the warm night air. They let the starry sky quietly pass by in peace. He had light music playing in the house. It mingled wonderfully with the countless chirping crickets. He heard Melanie humming along with the song. He breathed a sigh of contentment.

"You sound peaceful," he whispered.

"I am."

They sat for a while.

"What are you thinking?" she playfully asked.

"Nothing really, just how nice it is we met. And how amazing it is when we're together—like we've known each other forever."

"And you call that nothing?"

He turned. She was smiling that wonderful warm smile he loved. Her blue eyes gleamed at him. He pushed back the guilt. He didn't want it. He kept trying to tell himself it was fine to be with anyone he wanted. And more than one, if he wanted.

"Well, you know what I mean!" he taunted back.

"Yes, I actually do," she said. He heard her breathe a long sigh. He still couldn't shake the growing guilt that kept creeping in. As he usually did, he finally blocked it out and made himself enjoy the moment.

"Mike, tomorrow."

"Yep, Mike. You sure you want me there?" she whispered, feeling a little out of place.

"Mel, of course. I know I've always worked alone. But I want you there," he said. He knew he could use her insight in a case out of control. He wanted her to feel comfortable about it, too. "We're a team now. We're not cops, so we answer to ourselves first. If they want my help, they get yours, too. Plus, I need you."

"You do?"

He turned and touched her arm. She didn't turn. She smiled, leaning her head back. Her Celtic cheeks glowed in the moonlight.

"Yes, I do," Fletcher continued. "You see things that I don't. I see things you don't. Together, hopefully we see everything."

She giggled a little.

"What?" he pressed with a smile.

"You should have been a poet."

"Well, maybe I am!"

"Well then, show me some of your poetry," she challenged.

She had turned to him, cocking her head. Her hair fell to the side.

"Okay, follow me," he said with a mischievous grin.

He got up, opened the screen door, and went into the house.

She wasn't sure if she should go or not. The suspense was too much, as he had hoped. She followed him with a playful grunt when she stood up.

He was nowhere to be found.

"Honey, where are you?"

"Up here, in my study."

"Hold on," she said, shaking her head.

She climbed the stairs, turning down the hall to where his

voice had come from.

All of a sudden, she was pulled into the room she was passing.

"Whoa!"

He was laughing as he pulled her in. He immediately pulled her to him, face to face, body to body.

She let herself be tight up against his chest, feeling a warmth rise inside her.

Her soft breath touched his face. He kissed her softly.

"You call this poetry?"

"Nice opening verse, huh?"

Chapter 95 ~

FATHER BRANDON KEPT DEBATING. Every day that went by, his fear grew. It was his responsibility and no one else's. When you're promised to be a Bishop, and in his heart eventually a Cardinal and maybe even further, you don't lay back and just do nothing.

He made his decision.

He picked up the phone. From memory, he pressed the intricate sequence of numbers that were not an actual phone number.

He waited as he heard the buzzing in the earpiece. He knew what he had to do. It didn't bother him at all. Even though his call probably would ignite a sequence of panic, he felt he had no choice. No one was going to take away his path to the Vatican.

He thought of his parents, their goals for him, and how proud they were of him. He could never disappoint them, ever.

Finally, the buzzing stopped. A high-pitched chime rang. He proceeded to enter the seven-digit code and waited.

"This is Gabriel. Who is this?" The voice meant business.

"This is Lucifer."

"Talk."

Chapter 96 ~

MELANIE AWOKE TO THE SMELL of coffee and bacon. Fletcher wasn't in bed or in the room. She stretched widely for a long time. She looked around the room. It was the first time she had seen his bedroom in the daylight. She got up and looked around.

Everything looked country-ish, very tastefully rustic. Some things looked like antiques. Nevertheless, she could tell that he wasn't into whether it was expensive or not. It appeared he liked what it actually was and how it gave off a feeling to the room and the observer.

Everything seemed informally arranged. She felt he was creating a mood. It was all nicely planned to feel casual.

She looked in the mirror at her own nakedness. She cupped her breasts upward, smiled nicely at them, and walked out of the room. She slowly stepped down the stairs. She followed the smell of breakfast. She also loved creating suspense.

She turned the corner into the kitchen, strolling in as demurely and sexy as she could. The anticipation caused a thrill to run down her nudity, from her breasts through her thighs.

"WHOOPS!" she cried.

"Good morning, dear," Fletcher said with a broad smile.

"Good morning, dear," Frankie mimicked him, with an even broader smile.

"Oh, shit, you two!" she cried as she covered her breasts with one arm and her crotch with her other.

She walked out with her head held high.

"Nice butt, Melanie!" Frankie mentioned and then wished he hadn't.

"Eat me!"

"Don't answer that," Fletcher immediately replied to Frankie who was sitting there munching on a piece of bacon, smiling from ear to ear.

Fletcher knew it made Frankie's day no matter what else happened.

"You know you got a helluva girl, there, my man."

"Yeah, I know. She's amazing in every way."

"Yep, she is," Frankie said suggestively, hating to agree.

"Shut up! How do you want your eggs?"

Fletcher tossed a towel at him, which Frankie immediately caught in mid-air from instinct. Their friendship shone in their faces.

"Easy, baby," Frankie grinned.

"How do you want—" Fletcher pressed again.

Frankie laughed.

"Easy! Over easy. Okay?"

"Oh, sorry."

Melanie returned in Fletcher's bathrobe. Frankie assumed she was still naked under it. His imagination followed suit with the real image he had a moment earlier. As she sat down, he mulled over the conversation they had together.

"Did you have fun?" she teasingly asked Frankie, giving him a knowing look.

"Um, honestly? Um, yeah!"

"Smells good, honey," she said, ignoring Frankie with a smile.

"Thanks. Want some?"

"Yep, two please, over easy."

"Easy, just the way I like it."

"Frankie!" She reprimanded him with a mischievous grin.

"Sorry," he laughed.

"We got a lot to cover before we see Mike," Fletcher mentioned, still facing the stove. Over the frying crackling, he didn't notice their playfulness.

"Yeah, and first," Frankie interposed, "if I may, let me take the lead with him. I know how he's been these days. He's been on edge a lot. Not sure, but there seems something more than just the crimes."

"What do you mean?" she asked, grabbing the bacon out of his hand before he could eat another piece.

"Mike's a cool guy. I mean, he's *cool*. Nothing ever bothers him. It's one of the traits that makes him such a great DA."

"So?" she followed up.

"So, ever since this shit started, he's been on edge about everything, even things not related to this case."

Fletcher was tired of Frankie babying Mike. He took a different take.

"Maybe Eddy sees that. And being the manipulative maniac he appears to be, he's taking advantage of his father's current weakness to get what he wants, whatever that is."

"Maybe Fletch, but for now, just listen and let me lead. Interject, but carefully. We are talking about his boy."

"You make Eddy sound like an angel!" Fletcher said as he walked over with Frankie's breakfast. "Even so, I still think the priests are the best bet. They are seriously hiding something. I know it."

"Well, I have my own theories," Frankie said, looking at Melanie. "Anyway, Mike probably thinks he's an angel. The kid is brilliant. He's always talking about the honor roll his son is on, and this and that."

"I know his mom thinks he is."

Melanie looked up at Fletcher and decided to ignore it.

"Dads will be dads," she dryly added.

"Very *proud* dad!" Frankie noted.

"Well, let's see if he's into this charade of Eddy's," Fletcher raised. "I'd also like to know what he thinks about his site 'FHC.'"

"I'll bet he's into it," Frankie replied as he dove into his food.

"Why would you say that?" she asked, stealing another piece of bacon.

"Hey! Get off!"

She smiled. "Well, answer, or I'll take another."

"Fletcher!" Frankie cried, sounding like a little boy complaining about his big sister.

"Now, now, kiddies, play nice!" Fletcher playfully reprimanded.

"Well?" she again asked, feigning trying to steal another piece.

He slapped her hand lightly.

She pouted. Then smiled. He melted inside.

"Okay, if you have to look like that."

She shook her shoulders in approval, acting the little girl. Her short hair was now draped wildly over her face. Her sexiness was driving him crazy. He pushed it out of his mind and continued.

"Because Eddy is almost like a brother to him. Mike talked to him about everything since he was old enough to understand. Eddy's unbelievable intelligence shone right through. Who better to discuss things with than your own kin? He has a son who is willing to listen, and who understands. He's a very proud dad."

"What about the wife, the mom?" she asked seriously now.

"Her?"

"Her?"

She was surprised they both answered like that.

"Well, yeah, her."

"Um, Frankie?" Fletcher posed back to him, hoping nothing between him and Rosalyn was showing through.

"Um, Fletch?" he answered back, trying not to smile.

"Okay, you two, what's up?"

She looked back and forth to both. Each shrugged.

"Fine," Frankie gave in. "I never said this, got that?"

"Sure," she replied, leaning forward waiting.

"Fletch, how do I put this?"

"Um, it's all yours."

Fletcher was smiling broadly, not wanting to answer. He hoped Frankie would come up with something to satisfy Melanie's interest.

"Well, um, you see," Frankie started, trying not to smile, "she's an absolutely gorgeous dimwit. Like, I mean totally gorgeous, *and* totally a dimwit."

"Dimwit?"

"Yeah, that kid has her wrapped around his finger; he can do no wrong. Nothing. I think they're in love."

"And?" Fletcher egged him on, liking the line Frankie was taking.

"And ... she's so goddamned loaded that it will spin your head."

"Loaded? You mean?" She placed her hands onto her breasts.

"No! Not that!" Frankie exclaimed. "I mean she's loaded: cash, money, wealth, millions upon millions! Actually, we're not sure if she inherited it or what."

"Oh, that loaded. What about him?"

"He's your basic DA, makes great money. But he married the real money," Fletcher forcibly noted with his interjection to stay on that thought.

"Yep," Frankie said, leaning back, as he grabbed Fletcher's hat from the counter. He placed it cockeyed onto his head and smirked at him. Fletcher gave him a wink back. She noticed.

"So, what we have here," she stated slowly, "is a fucked-up, egotistical kid who may be a psycho, a mom and wife who has no idea what kind of kid this is possibly, but has more money than fuck, excuse my French again, which he probably uses freely, and a husband and father who's the top lawyer guy and believes in his kid because it's his son. The son is highly intelligent, and ironically, he may be a criminal under his own father's DA nose. He probably is manipulating both of them and has been since he could breathe. Correct?"

They both looked at her, then at each other, and then back at her.

"Yep. Fletch, she's a real Ein-fucking-stein!"

"Yep. She is at that!"

She sighed, flopping back in her chair. The robe opened. Frankie caught a full glimpse. His heart jumped. He closed his eyes, trying not to look. He opened them. The robe was closed again.

That was it. He shook his head and looked down hoping no one could tell how uncomfortable he was. His emotions were brimming over with finding the missing kids. The frantic parents and the unrelenting press were hounding him. His personal feelings were running wild about little children being murdered. Now he found himself staring at his best friend's girl's breasts. Plus, she had let him know how much she cared for him and how much they were alike. Now her cute sexiness was completely driving him crazy. And, he had seen her totally naked! All his passion suddenly built up in one instant. It all finally overwhelmed him.

He got up to go to the bathroom.

He had to escape the feelings.

Chapter 97 ~

FATHER BRANDON KNEW the voice. A rush of anticipating adrenalin ran through him. He composed himself quickly.

"We may have a problem."

"Problem? Speak."

"Well, more a leak."

"Leak? Speak."

"'FHC' may have been compromised."

"Speak."

"Police involved now. I closed one leak. They may be pressing more. They know about The Wrath."

There was silence on the other end that seemed an eternity.

"How much?" the voice finally firmly asked.

"Not much. I've diverted them. My informants tell me that their trail is leading them away from 'FHC.' They seem to be involved with some crazy kids, one of them the DA's."

"Good or bad?"

"Good. As long as they follow that path and we shut down for a while—"

"No. No shut down. Will not go over well."

"Okay, okay, but it may be necessary—"

"Never. Never necessary."

Father Brandon waited to make sure the next thing he said wouldn't cause any more reprimands, which if continued, he knew would cause the trust in him to be eliminated faster than he could stop it. All his plans would be gone, totally gone.

"I will ensure all will be fine."

Another pause on the line.

"Good. Do whatever you need to do."

"I will."

"I know you will, Lucifer."

"Thank you, Gabriel."

The line went dead.

Chapter 98 ~

THEIR MEETING WITH MIKE WAS AT 10:00 a.m. Fletcher drove Melanie. Frankie followed in his undercover car. The one thing that Fletcher missed about being a detective was all the new technologies in the car. Absolutely amazing, he had told Frankie when he had looked at them recently. Frankie had laughed and just said, "Too fucking bad."

They had decided to take I-95. It would take them past the airport, the stadiums, and over the bridges. It was a bit longer, but all highway until they got to the Center City exit.

As they approached the airport area, Fletcher had the radio blasting. They were both singing an oldies song.

All of a sudden, Fletcher stopped singing and stared out the front window. Melanie was still singing until she saw what he saw.

He hit the brakes and pulled towards the shoulder, weaving through cars until he came to a screeching halt. A cloud of black and gray dust blew up around the car.

He saw in his rearview mirror that Frankie had done the same, following him. His car created his own massive fog of road dust as he screeched in behind him, barely missing him.

"Turn that thing off, please," Fletcher cried to Melanie.

She turned off the radio. They both stared out.

Frankie was up next to his window yelling something.

Fletcher hit the switch to lower his window. Hot air immediately gushed in, as did Frankie's screams.

"What the HELL are you doing?"

"Huh?" was all he could answer.

"I said WHAT THE FUCK are you doing! Lucky I'm a cop and can drive through insane traffic and not get killed. And you pulling that idiot stunt, I want to know what the —"

"Frankie. Frankie," Melanie had leaned over Fletcher and was looking up at him, pleading with him.

"What?!"

She saw that his face was all red.

"Look," she said and pointed.

"Look at what?"

He turned, following her finger.

"Holy shit!"

Chapter 99 ~

THEY JUST STARED OUT at the road. Off to the left was a billboard sign. All it had against its white backdrop was black lettering in italics. They just kept looking at it and reading it.

It read:

"To this he said: 'I have not brought ostracism upon Israel, but you and the house of your fathers have, because you men have left the commandments of Jehovah, and you went following the Ba'als."

"What the hell does it mean?" Frankie loudly asked, above the noise of the traffic flying by.

"I don't know but I'll bet any amount of money, it's a passage from Elijah, from that Book of Kings," Fletcher yelled back out his window as a semi screamed by.

"Shit!" Frankie muttered as the wind almost knocked him over.

"How did they get that there?" Melanie yelled to be heard.

Another tractor-trailer flew right by them. Melanie felt the car tilt from the powerful sweeping gust. She fell back on top of Fletcher's lap.

"Shit!" I'm gonna get killed. "Unlock! I'm getting in."

"Okay, go ahead."

After he got in, Fletcher closed the window. The sound from the highway subsided. Still the car rocked with each car and truck zooming by in the lane next to them.

"In there," Fletcher said to Melanie, pointing to the glove

compartment.

"What?" she asked as she went to open it.

"My Bible, get it out."

She opened it. Seeing the Bible, she took it out and handed it to him.

Frankie leaned up between the seats from the back to see.

Fletcher opened it at the strand that he had placed to mark the Book of Kings. He scanned up and down the pages.

"Okay, there! Here it is!"

He read it aloud, as both Melanie and Frankie read it on the billboard.

It matched perfectly.

"Well, our little critter has gotten one up on us," Frankie said with exasperation in his voice.

"Yeah, I would think so," Fletcher added.

"What do you think it means?" Melanie asked, still staring at it.

"I think it's saying it's not his or their fault," Fletcher immediately answered her. "I think they're saying that we have brought this on ourselves. They are just the executioners, if you will."

"Goddamned bastards! It's innocent children they're killing and taking!" Frankie cried out. His feelings for the kids quickly started rising.

"Yeah, I would think so," Fletcher added.

"Well, it does do one thing."

"What's that, Mel?"

"It may lead to motive."

"Oh, yeah, I see," said Frankie in a low whisper.

"Kind of points back to our little friends and their motivation to change the world, now doesn't it," Fletcher added.

"Yes, it does," Melanie followed, "but if it is them, why would they just expose themselves like this, having something point to them?"

"Some criminals love the exposure and game playing. It doesn't prove a damned thing, ya know," Frankie added.

"It's a tease, that's what it is. A fucking tease!"

"Honey, calm down," she said evenly with a small smile.

"Yeah, yeah, I'll calm down when I see that little shit's smiling face when they inject him!" He let his emotions play it up, though he still kept most of his bets on the slavery angle. Eddy could be guilty or playing, but the priests made a lot more sense to him.

"Well, we don't know that. We have to keep an open mind," she said with a motherly tone, lightly touching his arm.

"You're right." Fletcher smiled at her; again, glad she was there. "But it does point to motive. They're letting us know that they have their reasoning for it all. It's almost like saying they're innocent and just acting in God's name." He did wonder why priests might expose themselves like this. Part of some cover-up or redirect plan maybe, he mulled.

"You sound like a friggin' priest yourself, Fletch."

"Maybe we should start thinking like one."

"Maybe we should," Frankie agreed.

"You know," Melanie spoke up, "they may just be trying to mislead us, too. Put out this crap about doing God's work, when all the time it's just about money or something."

"But if it was money, why no ransom and no contact at all? Who the hell knows where these poor children are right now? I have practically every detective on it," Frankie said exasperated.

Hearing that, Melanie sat quietly, as her heart went out to

the children again. She realized how hard she had been holding everything deep inside. The tears started to come. To stop them, she continued.

"There is the note of 'fathers' in it. It may be a reference to the clergy. Or maybe someone else we haven't considered is trying to tell us something about these secret priests and their societies. Maybe this time, the passage is not from the criminal. Maybe it's from someone who doesn't want us to know who they are but are trying to help."

They all sat quietly and digested it.

Fletcher thought of the Deacon who had attempted to warn them.

"Babe, that's actually a very good point. Or it may be a reference to Mike if this is actually Eddy and his crew."

"I think it's time to get talking with Mike, don't you?" Frankie interrupted, thinking how much he wanted to get his hands on "The PP."

"Frankie, man, you read my mind!" Fletcher agreed.

"Honey, it seems like we all can," she mused. She kissed his cheek.

"Oh, God," Frankie said. "I better get out before I start a video of you two!"

"Then get out!" Fletcher laughed as Melanie grinned over at him.

Chapter 100 ~

WHEN THEY ARRIVED, they went in together. Frankie asked them to wait in his office until he came back. He wanted to check the situation first with his team. Then he wanted to feel out Mike before they went in to discuss his son's idea.

"Just don't be long or discuss anything in detail, unless we're there," Fletcher pressed with an air of authority.

"Um, I'm the Chief of Police, not you, mister!" Frankie rebuffed, with a big smile.

"Just don't," Fletcher rebuffed back, smiling, too.

He knew Frankie wouldn't. He also liked to play with him. It kept the tension down and things light. It was the best way he learned to investigate anything.

Keep cool. Breathe. Let the shit flow out. When your mind and emotions are gone, think like the criminal: cold, hard, unfeeling.

It always worked for him.

They sat in Frankie's office. Melanie was surprised how small it actually was.

"Kind of small for a Chief of Police."

"Yeah, but he's hardly in here. Relative to other city offices, it's actually pretty large," Fletcher noted.

"If you say so," she replied and walked around, looking at the things in the office. She decided to sit in Frankie's chair.

"What's up with you?"

"Oh, nothing."

"Oh, I think something."

"That sign disturbed me," she said, toying with the dangling lamp cord. "This nut is playing with us and playing with young kids' lives. It just bothers me that someone could not only be a killer and kidnapper, but also an arrogant, self-absorbed one at that."

Fletcher smiled.

"What?" she asked, seeing his smile.

"Welcome to the world of criminals!"

"Yeah, yeah. At least it's all good material stuff and ideas."

"For your next novel?"

"Everything in life is for my novels, just depends how it comes out."

"You don't plan them?"

"Only a sketchy outline. Most just flows out. Things take different directions and still stay in the framework. It's great that way. I get surprised a lot myself."

She smiled a thin smile. Fletcher knew it was all troubling her still. He wondered if she could handle the actual realities, rather than just the fantasy world of fiction. He started to worry about her.

She looked at him.

"Listen, don't you worry about me. I know what you're starting to think!"

"What, me? Think what?"

"Fletcher, my love, remember? I can read your mind."

"Read this then!" he immediately retorted, with a playful straight face.

"You want a blowjob, right here, in Frankie's office?"

"Bitch!"

She laughed.

At that moment, the door opened.

Melanie's mouth dropped.

Chapter 101 ~

STUMBLING IN AS IF HE TRIPPED, Melanie watched a crusty, bent over man come through Frankie's door. He appeared in his mid-sixties, with straggly gray hair that looked like he had stuck his finger in a live socket. The white stubble on his wrinkled, sun-streaked face made him look like a cross between Albert Einstein and Ernest Hemingway. His torn clothes appeared as rags soaked in oil. When his body stench hit her nose, Melanie knew she didn't want to go anywhere near him.

He grabbed hold of the nearest chair. Right behind him was a detective bringing him into Frankie's office. The old man stopped for a moment. He labored in a wheezing breath. He looked around. She saw recognition come to his alert eyes, which seemed the only thing alive about him. His smell was beginning to overwhelm her.

"Well, well," he said between hacking coughs, "Fletcher Sax'an. Nev'r t'ought I'd ever t'ee you 'gain." Spittle blew out of his mouth.

"Merrie, how you doing you old pervert?" Fletcher answered right back. Melanie was shocked by him using the direct word, "pervert."

"Well, as you say, d'at's me alright-y, but I gots nottin' to do with d'ese kids t'ing. I mean, well, I may like da' little ones, well boys, and um girls, and..." he trailed off in a drooling babble, looking down. He slowly wiped his mouth with his slimy sleeve.

"Listen, enough of that," snorted the detective with a shoulder push.

Melanie couldn't believe what she was seeing. The man just looked up from his chair at the detective and smiled a smile of two black teeth.

"Thought the Chief was here. Sorry to interrupt. I'll just take him——"

"No, wait," Fletcher stopped him. "I'd like to talk with him."

"Fine, but I'll stay, just in case."

"Thanks."

Fletcher paused. He walked to the front of the chair. Merrie was slouched. His chest heaved. He seemed struggling to breathe.

"Okay, first things. Merrie 'The PP' Watson, Melanie Sanders."

"Hello, missy." His eyes looked up at her. She just nodded back, fearful to say anything at all. Fletcher noticed and decided to continue.

He asked him where he was on different occasions, what he'd been up to, where he's living, and has he seen any of his old buddies.

Merrie seemed agreeable. It was obvious he wanted out as fast as he could. He had no alibi on any of the occasions, except that he was home alone. Finally, Melanie had had enough.

"Are you telling me that you like little boys and girls?"

"Well, yes, missy. Don't you?"

She shuddered but continued.

"Ever murder anyone?"

He slowly smiled the most horrid broken smile, with the most rotted two teeth she had ever seen. The gray stubble on his

cheeks seemed to jump out at her. His dark face blanked. He seemed to go into another world. Then she saw the wetness appear in his pants. She couldn't believe he just peed himself right there, in front
of her.

"Um, no, why would I ev'r? I like d'em, know what I mean?"

"You disgust me!" flew out of her mouth before she could stop it.

"Sorry, not in'rested in you, missy." He got another push from the detective. This time, he looked up angrily. Melanie shifted in her chair. Fletcher took a step forward, somewhat between them. Merrie saw it all. He calmed down with a wide, wrinkled grin and a couple hacking coughs. Spittle again spewed out in all directions.

"One more question," Melanie decided to ask, ignoring the white drool starting at the corner of his mouth. "Are you a religious man?"

That paused Merrie into thinking. They all caught it immediately as suspicious. He looked up at her.

"Why d' you ask?"

"Just answer."

"Why d' you want to know?"

"Are you a religious man? Are you Catholic? Jewish?"

"Jewishhh? Wit' name like 'Watson?' You stupid or som'thing?" Another push was delivered but he never took his alert eyes off her.

She just stared back and waited. Time seemed to stop for the moment.

"Ok'ie, I tell you d'is."

"What?"

"D'at's it."

"What's it?"

"It."

"It what?" she asked frustrated. She just wanted to get away from him.

He was now laughing between coughs. She instinctively leaned back to avoid the spit.

"Can I leave now?"

"Answer her!" the detective firmly demanded.

"Not unless I hav' lawyer here. And if you have not'ing on me…" He stopped. She saw fear in his eyes.

Frankie walked in. He instantly stopped next to Merrie.

"Well, well, my old friend is here."

Melanie got up to allow Frankie to sit, but he didn't move from the side of Merrie's chair.

Fletcher pulled him aside. For some time, they were whispering back and forth. In the end, Frankie warned Fletcher Eddy's mom was with Mike. Fletcher stared at him. Finally, Frankie put his face right down to Merrie's. Melanie felt she was going to puke. Merrie froze.

"Do you know anyone named Father Brandon? Deacon Wellington?" At his tone, Merrie flinched. Fear increased in his eyes. Obviously, he was terrified of Frankie.

"Chief, no, don't know d'em. And I ver' religious." He quivered, avoiding Frankie's gaze. His now glazed eyes found Melanie.

"Get him out of here," Frankie demanded.

As the detective pulled him up by his greasy shirt, Frankie spun around. Merrie almost fell back into the detective to keep away from him.

"Don't fucking leave town or, like before, I'll—"

"No worry, Chief, no worry, no worry..." he kept repeating as the detective dragged him out.

Fletcher saw Melanie looking petrified. "Well?" he asked matter-of-factly, hoping to snap her out of it.

"Um, yeah, what?" she stuttered.

"What do you think of our friend 'The Ped Perp?'" Fletcher asked as if it was understood. She weakly smiled, knowing Merrie had unexpectedly disarmed her. Then her strength came back.

"Honestly," she started, "I can totally see him doing these things. Definitely the kidnappings and he may be part of something more. And behind all that filth, he's a very smart man." She moved to the chair farthest from the chair Merrie had sat in.

"I agree," replied Frankie. "It just throws more shit-heads into the mix of confusion. Priests, perv's, maniac kids, crap and more crap."

"Eddy might be our only real hope right now," Fletcher added.

"Yeah, I know. I know," was all that came out of Frankie's mouth.

Melanie just stared blankly into space, wondering where and when it was ever going to end.

Chapter 102 ~

"NO LUCK ON THE BILLBOARD COMPANY," Frankie informed them. He went to his desk, sighed, and sat down with a loud bump.

"Figured that," Fletcher followed, "no way that shit would give himself away *that* easily."

"They, or whoever, posted it on a lot of billboards. Cost a small fortune to make a small point! I guess they really wanted someone to see it."

"Yeah, and also to make sure we saw it in time," Fletcher added.

"Huh?"

"Frankie, so that we are in the 'game' and don't miss the play."

"Yeah, yeah, I see. Sorry, missed that with all this crap."

"What did you find?" Melanie asked, leaning forward on the desk, trying to forget "The PP."

Frankie started to look a little pale.

"The detectives are bringing in something that was left with the advertising company. They were told to give it to whomever came asking about the billboard. It's being fingerprinted and analyzed."

"And?" Fletcher asked with a slight inflection.

"A torn piece from a Bible."

"No fucking way!" Melanie whispered under her breath.

Fletcher heard her, turning sharply at her.

"Um, I can say that if I want," she coyly said, noticing his surprise.

"I know, but it's totally sexy."

"Will you two—"

"Sorry, Frankie," she said, hitting Fletcher on the arm.

"Yeah, sorry," he said, returning the hit.

"Kiddies, let's focus on this, please?"

"What does it say?"

"Hold a sec," Frankie said, putting up a hand.

He opened the file and pulled out a white piece of paper. Fletcher could see that it had handwriting on the other side. He assumed they called it in and either Frankie or someone wrote it down for them to read immediately.

"Ready?"

"Yep."

"Yes."

He read it out loud:

"Choose for yourselves one bull and dress it first, because you are the majority; and call upon the name of your God."

"Interesting," Fletcher finally said, after a long pause. "A new twist."

"What do you mean?" Frankie asked.

"A boy or boys this time," Melanie interposed.

"Yeah, exactly. Maybe brothers."

"We should concentrate on that, but I don't think we should go overboard with it," Frankie posed.

"Yes, I agree," Fletcher said. "It may or may not be a trick, so we should cover all bases, regardless of this. Does 'bull' or 'majority' ring any bells with you guys?"

"And 'dress it first?'" Melanie added.

"Who 'calls upon the name of their god?'" Frankie asked.

"A priest does!" Fletcher spurted out.

"Yes, a priest, but that's crazy."

"Mel, nothing's crazy. Frankie, make a note to have all personnel keep an eye out for any clergy, suspicious or not, in the vicinity of our coverage area." Fletcher really began to feel that this was it. It was going down very soon. Father Brandon, he thought, I know you're involved somehow.

"Will do."

"I think we should also be aware of any schools or areas where there are more kids than others," Melanie added.

"Why?" Frankie turned and asked.

"Because of the word 'majority.' Just in case."

"Yeah, right."

"It's a good idea because we'll need more undercover in larger areas anyway," Fletcher added as he stood up to stretch. "I honestly think this is going down soon."

At that moment, a detective knocked on the door.

"Yeah," Frankie said as he leaned to the side to see who it was. Fletcher was blocking his view.

"Hey, boss, no go on that billboard place. It was a cash deal and was mailed in. Nothing else."

"Fine, thanks." Frankie turned away.

"Yep."

The detective nodded and left.

"Dead-end again," Frankie said exasperated. He tossed his pencil onto the desk. "All a game. Probably misleading us again."

"We ready for Mike?" Fletcher changed the subject, trying to brace himself to face Rosalyn with Melanie in the same room.

"Yeah, Fletch, let's do it."

"I think we have our plan, and everything possible from all

of this scant stuff," Fletcher confidently said, but was shaking his head.

"What's up, babe?"

He turned to Melanie and then to Frankie.

"I want this guy and want him bad—or whoever it is. I don't like these games and the crazy carrots he keeps dangling in front of us. It's like a puzzle with no ending. And young kids' lives are at stake. I don't like people like Stuart Martino, but it's the children."

"Babe, we'll get them."

She smiled up at him, cupping his hands in hers.

"Thanks for being here," Fletcher whispered.

"I'm with you all the way."

They both turned to Frankie.

Frankie picked up his phone, pressed the extension, talked a minute and hung up.

"Okay, let's go."

Chapter 103 ~

WHEN THEY ARRIVED AT THE DA'S OFFICE, Frankie held up his hand for them to stop and wait a sec. The door was ajar. Frankie knocked and walked in a bit. They heard him talk with who they presumed was Mike. Then Frankie opened the door wide, walking completely in. They knew it was their invitation to enter.

They both felt impressed by being *in* the room. The office was much larger than Frankie's. Law books covered the walls in what looked like very expensive cherry wood cabinets. The furniture was all sculptured dark wood. It truly looked like a law office from a TV show. Fletcher saw Melanie raise her eyebrows. It had an old, sweet musky smell that fine wood gives off.

Mike was standing behind his desk with his cell phone in hand. He was quietly talking to someone. He was a big man with large hands and a look that appeared to Melanie always stern. His body was remarkably athletic in shape. His chest was broad; his waist was slim. His jet-black hair was slicked back and perfectly trim-lined, almost looking unnatural. His eyes had a darkness to them that unnerved Melanie. He reminded her of gangster movies. He raised a finger to them meaning to wait.

To the right of him, Melanie got her first glance at Rosalyn. She was standing there looking up at her husband, smiling. Conflicting thoughts and feelings immediately ran through her mind and heart. She viewed her absolute, perfect beauty. She had to look away.

They all just waited, standing there, looking around.

Finally, Mike flipped the phone to hang it up and turned directly towards them.

"Please, everyone, take a seat," he said as he slowly swept his arm at the chairs in front of his desk.

They all sat, except for Rosalyn. Fletcher avoided her eyes, shifting in his chair. He hoped Melanie wouldn't notice.

Mike just stared at them for a second. Fletcher thought he was going to blurt out something. The DA closed his eyes for a second. Then he picked up a newspaper that was on his desk, turned it towards them, and threw it back down on his desk at them. It almost fell
off.

They all were startled for a moment. Each inched forward, as if afraid of being hit.

"Look at this crap! It's gone national!" Mike bellowed, waving his arms over the paper. Melanie almost jumped out of her chair. After "The PP," her nerves were just frayed. Everything was getting to her.

They all read the large bold heading:

CHILDREN STILL MISSING! PARENTS IN TERROR!
NO CLUES, NO LEADS! POLICE, DA HELPLESS!

Fletcher sighed. Melanie just shook her head.

"Ah, damn," was all Frankie could say.

There was a long pause as each of them leaned slowly back into their seats. Mike just stared at them. The tension was unbelievable. Melanie now wasn't sure she really wanted to be there.

Mike let out a long, loud breath that sounded like a sigh.

Fletcher wasn't sure if it was just a huff of frustration or intense anger.

"I'll deal with this shit and the press and parents," Mike calmly said, as if his outburst had never occurred. He took the paper back, sitting down in his high-back, red leather chair. He swiveled it a little. He looked up at his wife who beamed back at him. Fletcher shifted again in his chair.

Mike abruptly turned, saying to all of them, "Water over the bridge. Let's move on. And let's move on FAST!"

Nobody moved or said anything. The tension hung heavy. Mike smiled a small smile, as if he knew what they were all feeling. He let out a heavy breath again.

"Okay, Frankie, man, what do you guys have? What's the plan now?" Frankie immediately jumped on it, which made Fletcher and Melanie relax.

"Well, we're using all our undercover cops, as well as being supplied by the State-ies, too. We have outlined a detailed grid of the anticipated attack areas, mostly near schools and kid hangouts."

"We have informed all parents, through the schools and the administrators, not to let their kids out of their sights if the kids are not in school or in a crowded public place. We also firmly asked that parents instruct their kids to go only to known hangout places, if they have to go at all. We are trying desperately to have parents keep their kids inside 'til this is all over."

Mike was nodding. Rosalyn was smiling at him. Frankie just kept his gaze on Mike.

"We are covering all areas. We also have received another passage."

He went on to explain the billboard. He continued with

their analysis of it, including their feeling that something was imminent. He also explained about Merrie and him being a possible suspect or accomplice, with his appetite for children. He finished noting Merrie had no alibi for any of the occurrences.

Mike continued to be silent. He just nodded with his hands folded under his chin.

Frankie paused and looked at Fletcher and Melanie.

Mike finally spoke up.

"Hi, we haven't met," he said standing up, walking around to Melanie.

"I'm Melanie Sanders. I'm with Fletcher." She was caught off guard and felt awkward with her response. She shrank next to his physique.

"Nice to meet you," he replied, giving a look towards Frankie.

"Um, she's part of Fletcher's investigative team and has experience in the psychology of criminals, both their minds and motivations."

"Yes, I see," Mike said as he turned and went back around his desk, sitting down. His hand was back on his chin. It appeared he was thinking.

Fletcher's glance to Frankie told him he had made up a great reason.

Frankie nodded.

"Well then, Melanie, from your experience, what's your take on all of this?" Mike asked in a very monotone voice. His unwavering gaze went right through her.

She hesitated, quickly looking at Frankie and then at Fletcher. Both their looks back told her she was on her own. She gave them a quick glare.

"Well, the perpetrator is an egomaniac for sure."

"Why would you say that?" Mike interrupted her, but nicely.

"Because he believes that he cannot get caught, ever, and is absolutely taunting us ... well, you ... well, all the cops ... all of us, by playing these billboard games and passages."

Mike leaned back and nodded. She continued.

"Like *these* passages. I mean, the Old Testament of the Bible is worded almost poetically. A lot of these passages could mean anything. It's like someone gave you a puzzle and the last pieces you need to fill it in aren't even part of the puzzle they gave you."

"That's a very good way of putting it."

She smiled a small victory smile.

"Gentlemen, she's on board and okay with me."

Frankie nodded.

Fletcher followed suit.

Melanie looked at all of them with a slight look of surprise. She made a mental note to slap both of them for not informing her that this was also an interview of her skills. They were looking for Mike's approval of her being on the team.

She could tell Frankie and Fletcher had planned it. It started to irritate her. She decided to play along, for now.

"Let's get moving on it!" Mike loudly said, sounding like an army commander. Putting both palms on the table, he pushed himself up.

They all stood but didn't leave.

Mike gave a wondering look.

"Well, Mike, we have another thing to discuss with you."

"It's okay. I'm fine with Eddy and his team assisting. I'm sure you will keep him and them very safe. He's very insightful and brilliant, too."

"But——" Frankie tried to interject.

"Frankie, I'm fine with it and so is Rosalyn," who only nodded. Her smile never left her face. "We have also personally talked to some other friends ... um, parents ... who have children with siblings of the right age, and of course, from the right families. The more aware the kids are the better."

"They gave us their blessing with my absolute guarantee of safety. In addition, all kids will be in the open for our constant surveillance. They'll just do what they normally do but being more aware. Only one parent didn't agree, but we pressed the point that we must be proactive, all of us—even parents. We cannot afford to have another child killed and another one kidnapped. I trust my son."

Fletcher saw that Mike's look and demeanor meant this was *not* up for discussion. He wondered how much was directly fed by Eddy to him.

"Right, Mike," was all Frankie could think to say.

Fletcher knew Mike as a person and a DA. His word was final. He just didn't understand how he could be so nonchalant about his own son's safety. Eddy had obviously done a great sell job on his father and their friends. Maybe also since the police seem to be getting nowhere.

They all turned to leave.

"Hey, Frankie!" Mike called, as they passed the doorway.

"Yeah?"

"Find those other kids, will you?"

"Been on it."

"Get *on* it *more*."

Chapter 104 ~

"WHAT THE HELL WAS THAT ALL ABOUT?" Melanie heatedly asked when they were clear and walking down the corridor. Fletcher looked at her. Her face looked distorted to him. He thought, now there's a look I haven't seen before.

"Oh, it's just the enormous pressure on him to not only catch this perp, but to bring those other kids home safely to their parents," Frankie replied.

"No, you damned guys!"

"What?" Fletcher stopped and asked.

"What the hell was that whole crap about *me?!*"

"Pretty good, huh?" Fletcher answered, smiling.

She saw it was genuine, but didn't care. She hit him on his arm, hard.

"What!" he said, grabbing his arm.

"Tell me NEXT TIME!"

"Oh, we just thought it up, right before going in," Frankie said. He stepped back in anticipation of being hit, too.

"When did you two idiots have time to talk about this?"

"Um, in the men's room?" Fletcher answered again, also stepping back.

She now stood a little alone. She got more annoyed.

"We just knew Mike would not allow someone from the outside in on the investigation, if he didn't know why and the benefit."

"Babe, but still let me know," she pressed. "You made me out to be a psychologist or something."

"You *are*," Frankie answered back, still covering his arms as protection from being hit.

"Actually, honey, you are. Being a writer and knowing characters and creating them, you study humans and human nature and behavior and all."

"Yeah, so?"

"Well, it's invaluable. Plus, we posed it as you work for me. He will feel I'm responsible for you and your actions. You earned it, too."

"Work for you? Ha! Never," she retorted and then started chuckling.

Frankie looked questioningly at Fletcher. Fletcher knew he didn't know how she could go from anger to laughter so fast.

"She does that at times. Just ignore her."

That generated another hard slap, causing them all to laugh.

"Okay, let's go and get this sting a' rolling."

"Fletch, I'm with ya," Frankie said, turning to go.

"You coming?" Frankie asked Melanie sweetly.

Her face made a strange look. Frankie moved a little further away.

"Aw, what the frig'!" she said. She walked right past both of them, chuckling again.

They glanced at each other, shrugged, and followed her.

"Bet she's good in bed," Frankie whispered.

"She is," he whispered back.

She stopped and turned. They halted in their tracks.

"I am GREAT in bed!"

She swiftly turned, walking away with a strut they both made an approving look at.

They continued after her, until they heard a voice behind them.

"Um, Fletcher?"

Chapter 105 ~

THEY ALL TURNED. ROSALYN was leaning up against the frame of Mike's door. She was smiling widely at them, just waiting there. Her tiny, sky-blue miniskirt exposing her bare thighs seemed pulled up higher. Frankie thought he glimpsed something. It wasn't panties. Fletcher felt so uncomfortable, a quiver went through his knees. Frankie just stared and waited. Melanie didn't know what to do.

"Yes, Rosalyn?" came out of Fletcher's lips.

She slowly shifted her weight, looking just as mesmerizing to Frankie standing the other way. It confirmed what he had thought. No panties. Melanie couldn't see Fletcher's expression as his back was to her. She was intent on Rosalyn, seeing the same thing as Frankie.

"Can I speak with you, please? Privately, please?" she softly asked. Her hair crossed her pretty face as she slightly cocked her head. She gazed at him with sparkling, emerald eyes that were begging with desire. Frankie glanced at his friend, who just stood there.

Fletcher didn't know what to say. He could feel Melanie's stare burning through him. He could taste Rosalyn in front of him.

"Well, we were just leaving..."

The look on her face was like a ripe plum, instantly becoming a distorted prune at the possibility of being pushed off by him. Suddenly her instant-smile was back, as if nothing happened. From behind him, Melanie saw Fletcher flinch.

"Frankie?" Fletcher turned and asked, trying not to look at Melanie.

"Sure, Rosalyn, Fletcher has time," Frankie interjected. Melanie wanted to kick him.

"Just for a moment," Fletcher said, walking towards her. Rosalyn's face lit up. Melanie couldn't tell if it was because of the victory, because she really liked Fletcher, or both.

Frankie turned to Melanie. He walked right past her. She stood still for a moment. Realizing it was a lost cause, she turned to follow Frankie. She had a million questions for him. She wanted straight answers and straight answers now.

Chapter 106 ~

ROSALYN SEEMED TO JUMP like a little girl. She flipped her hair back, took his hand into hers and led him the other way down the corridor. Fletcher felt so strange with his hand in hers. He removed it only to have her arm slip into his. He knew he couldn't win this. He could only hope where they were going wasn't far. He prayed Mike remained in his office.

He tried not to look down at her gorgeous legs. He was already getting crazed from her perfume. No panties, came back to him.

"Where—"

Before he could finish, in one motion she pushed open the door to her left. She pulled him in. As he passed the open door, he realized it was the men's room.

"Rosalyn!"

"Shush, boy. I'm sure no one's in here. I need to…"

She didn't finish. She led him into the handicap stall, closing the door. All other stall doors were wide open. Fletcher had seen no one in the room. He wondered how she'd known that.

"Listen—"

"Shush," she said kissing him hard on his lips. She had wrapped her arms hard around his neck. He struggled a little but couldn't help himself. With the excitement of being caught and the excitement of being with her this close again, he pressed his mouth onto hers.

She broke loose. Still up close to his face, she smiled. He

didn't know what to do next. He immediately felt himself hard from her crotch and bare legs caressing up against him.

"So, how's the case going?" she asked whimsically, still slowly rubbing her legs up and down on his.

"Huh?"

"Are you protecting my boy like you said? And going to keep him safe as he helps you?"

Her warm breath so close to his face felt magical. Her eyes shined.

"Um, well, yeah, of course, I told you so—"

"Good! Now, who are the suspects now?" she asked, kissing him full on the mouth again. He kissed her back until she broke away again. He knew she wanted an answer.

"Well, I still believe the priests have a big thing in all of this and ... and we are also looking at some pedophiles."

"Yes, yes! I told you those priests are involved. I knew it! I mean how many times have they touched little boys? You've read about it."

"No, it's about slavery—"

"Yeah, yeah, yeah, and probably touching them, too, like you said, you know, the pedophiles. I just know there's something bad about them, somehow." Her smile never left. Her soft breath against his face kept driving him crazy. He knew she was getting a little confused, too. He tried to ignore her wonderful body perfume that filled the stall.

"Well, yeah, between the priests and Merrie 'The PP'..."

"Who?"

"Our prime pedophile."

She paused a second.

"They could be working together, ya know," she said, giving him a peck on the lips. He had actually thought that, but was still betting on the clergy and their secret sect. He just had that feeling.

"I agree with you. We're looking into all of them for sure."

This seemed to satisfy her.

"But remember you promised."

"Yes, to keep Eddy safe no matter what. Even though Mel is worried about maybe…" he stopped, catching himself.

"Huh? She thinks what? My son? Are you kidding?"

"Well, she's new and doesn't know——"

"Then straighten her out! I want no one accusing my boy about anything!" He could tell she was seriously getting angry. He actually believed she was completely sincere about her boy.

"Listen, I don't think anything. I will protect him, even from any hint of anything, okay?"

He saw her thinking. She smiled again, appearing to come back from somewhere.

"Oh, thank you so much! You know I love you!" Her hands clutched up his chest. She kissed his cheek like a little girl kissing her daddy.

"Listen, let's get out of here before——" He couldn't finish.

Suddenly her face was gone. He felt his belt buckle being toyed with. Oh, no, he thought, but it was too late. She had instantly undone his pants and was starting on him.

That's when he heard the men's room door open and what he figured were three detectives walking in, talking among themselves.

Chapter 107 ~

MELANIE WAS LOOKING BACK AS Frankie led the other direction. She suddenly didn't want her man to be with that woman. She turned to Frankie.

"What does she have on him?" she lightly pleaded.

"Oh, it's nothing," Frankie lied. "She just wants her son protected."

"Well, why isn't she talking with *you*?"

"Because I think he appears to be a rebel to her and she likes that. Plus, I think she believes anything she tells him won't get back to her husband. Maybe she thinks I'll tell on her or something. She is childish, ya know," He was making it all up as he went. He only cared about spending this little time with Melanie.

"Oh, okay," she replied in a tone of uncertainty that Frankie caught.

"Let's get some coffee. You in?" he asked with a smile.

"That will be good," she said as she followed him.

When they got to the little cafeteria, he got them both little cups of coffee from the machine. He led her to a table, knowing that Fletcher might be a while.

"So, a coffee for your thoughts," he joked. She weakly smiled back. He could see the stress in her, from both the day and Rosalyn.

He just wanted to hug her.

"I don't like her. Something about her."

Frankie figured it was her beauty.

"You're more beautiful, ya know."

"Aw, Frankie, thanks," she replied. Her wonderful smile lit up her face. He smiled back with his own uncertainty.

"Well, I honestly feel Merrie has something to do with all of this or some ped. Just a feeling. I'm not too sure about all those priests like Fletcher thinks." He waited for her reply.

"Mmmm, well, I still think Eddy's in this somehow. I just don't trust him."

"But why, Mel? What does he have to gain? At least the peds know what they want. And if not them, I'm with Fletcher on the Church folks."

She smiled at his use of "folks" and it melted him.

"I can see your point. I guess we have to watch them all. You *know* Fletcher wants to investigate that Father Brandon. And he thinks you're hemming on it."

"Yep, I am," Frankie agreed.

"You are?" she asked, with a wide smile at the intrigue.

"Yes, because the last time I went down that path, I got so burned by the press and the Church itself. Needless to say, we were wrong about this one priest and I paid the price."

"Then just let Fletcher—"

"It won't matter. I'll pay, not him."

"Yeah, I guess so."

"But I'm not discarding it. I just want to see first about Merrie. He is being watched all the time. I know the priests aren't going anywhere."

"Logical," was all she said as she stared out the window. He knew she was thinking about Rosalyn being with her man.

"And sorry about Merrie. I know he's pretty disgusting."

"To say the least. I was totally grossed out, ya know. Even though he's not my top choice, just so you know, I can easily see him doing these things."

A silence fell as she continued to stare out the window.

"Tell me about your book," he broke the silence.

"Huh?"

"The book you're writing," he smiled, sipping his coffee.

A small, cute grin grew on her face. She couldn't help but love how Frankie, the cop, could so easily and obviously read her mind.

They sat for a while just talking about her book. He was enthralled listening to her. She was happy for his intended diversion by asking.

After about fifteen minutes of the fun talk, she saw Fletcher come into the room seeming a little frantic.

"You okay?" Frankie asked, looking up at him.

"Oh, yeah, just didn't know where you guys went to. I checked your office and then asked a detective and, well, you're here."

He could feel Melanie's eyes on him, evaluating his every move and word. He finally smiled down at her.

Frankie heard the venom.

"Did you have fun?" slipped out of her mouth.

Chapter 108 ~

WHEN THEY GOT BACK TO FRANKIE'S office, they were all shocked at what they saw.

In his office sat Eddy. Behind him, Stacy, Stanley, and Marcy were standing. It appeared set up to show Eddy's prominence. He was grinning. His eyes shined victory.

"Well, look what the wind brought in," Frankie said with an intended tone of apathy. He walked right past them, not looking at them until he ended up behind his desk.

Melanie was shaking her head a little. Fletcher just stood at the door watching Frankie, waiting.

"Make yourselves comfortable," Frankie sarcastically said.

"We have, thank you for your hospitality," Eddy returned. He flipped his bowl-shaped hair back. It fell perfectly back. He looked like a teenager again.

Frankie shot Fletcher a look and sighed.

"How did you know we were here?" Melanie asked, which caused raised eyebrows from both Frankie and Fletcher at the quick and direct question.

Eddy still sat facing Frankie's desk. He answered her without moving or turning. She just wanted to slap him.

"The DA called and asked our presence here to coordinate with you."

They all looked at each other, then back at them. It hit all of them at once who was on the cell phone when they had entered Mike's office.

Fletcher could only think that it was all just weird,

wondering how they got here so fast. They must have been waiting or prompted earlier. He couldn't wait to get Melanie alone to talk it all through again. He also wanted to make sure she was fine about Rosalyn. Her body language told him she was thinking about it.

"Now, Eddy, what's your plan?" Frankie asked, with clear disgust in his voice.

Fletcher saw him eyeing Eddy with suspicion. He knew Frankie was going to weigh every word out of that little maniac's mouth.

"Mr. Oswald, as we said before, we will be planned targets with the hope that one of our pairs will be approached. You will know our every move and then come to our rescue and capture this criminal." To Fletcher, he sounded like a damsel planning her own distress.

"Without following you directly, how will we know—"

"Mr. Saxtan, you will know because we will be in constant touch with you."

They all looked at each other again, then back at him.

He saw it and continued.

"We will use micro-processing communicators that will be live constantly. Each target pair will talk quietly, at designated moments, to let you know where they are. These are concealed either behind the ear or on the upper clothing and are very, very powerful."

"I see. I never heard of anything—"

"Mr. Oswald, no you have not. We have modified tiny PA microphones and their transmission frequencies, developing them ourselves."

Again, they all looked at each other and then back at Eddy.

Fletcher noticed the others were just standing around him

motionless. They couldn't have just developed these. Fletcher knew they must have had a prior purpose for them. This really concerned him.

"You have. I see. And do we also get some to communicate—"

"No, Mr. Oswald. We will give you our private frequency and you may tune in through your own communications channels. We will be live, all the time, and talking among ourselves. You will get the information of our locations and what we observe."

"I see you follow in your father's footsteps," Melanie stated, with slight contempt in her voice. Eddy was showing off his intellect.

"Ms. Sanders, why ever would you say that?"

Eddy actually turned this time to look at her. Fletcher caught an ever-so-slight slip in his eye at being caught off guard. Then it was gone.

"Well, Mr. Parker, it seems you have it totally planned out. You are very confident about winning."

Eddy let that absorb in and just looked at her. It reminded Fletcher of a computer while it processed information.

He answered after a long moment.

"Ms. Sanders, even though I do not see the connection, I do agree with your assessment. And I thank you."

He turned back to Frankie in one motion, exactly one point to one point. As a robot would, Fletcher thought. His bowl hair spun in the motion. It settled right back down where it originally was, perfect around his head. Even his hair was robotic, Fletcher mused.

He made an important mental note never to forget how smart this kid really was, no matter how much he disgusted him.

A man/boy: all-in-one. He still agreed with Rosalyn. But this kid was entertaining.

"Now listen," Frankie began, "I will assign a senior detective to each pair. They will be in complete control of the situation. With that, I mean, if they pull you, you are pulled. Absolutely no argument."

Eddy looked at him. He spoke.

"Yes."

"If they tell you to do something, you are to do it—absolutely no argument."

"Yes."

"If they tell you not to move, you do it—absolutely no argument."

"Yes."

"If they tell you anything at all, you do it—absolutely no argument."

"Yes."

There was a pause. Fletcher saw that Frankie was a little surprised with Eddy's agreements. He appeared prepared for arguments. Fletcher now saw Eddy had read that and instead agreed to everything.

Of course, Eddy may tell his people to do whatever he wants. He'll have access to all conversations, with his little homemade telephones or whatever they were. He could use different frequencies for privacy, too.

"Where will you be?" Melanie asked him.

Eddy again turned to her. This time Fletcher did not like his expression at all. It reminded him of a crazed animal trapped in a corner. He was getting tired of Eddy's attitude.

In an instant, the expression was gone. Serenity returned to his face.

"Ms. Sanders, that I believe, is none of your business, as I am not a target in this affair."

"I see," she returned. Fletcher could see the white knuckles of her clasped hands.

Hold back, babe, he thought, hold back.

Melanie must have read his mind again. She turned from Eddy. She just looked up at Frankie with her lips pressing together. Frankie tried to hide his fondness of how cute she was with her growing anger.

Eddy was still looking at her. Fletcher unwaveringly watched him. Eddy then turned back to Frankie and waited.

A long, annoying, uncomfortable pause hung in the air.

"Wait here and I will bring in your counterparts."

No answer or movement.

Frankie got up with a quiet huff and walked out. He gave Fletcher an eye when he did.

Yeah, friend, I agree, he thought, this is all insane but what else can we do?

Chapter 109 ~

FRANKIE BROUGHT IN THE DETECTIVES. Each appeared ready to kill someone, Fletcher thought. He knew Frankie had handpicked them. He was sure Frankie had also prompted them about the attitude they would encounter with these kids.

"Gentlemen," Frankie began. It was a firm and professional voice. "These are our little helpers. They will attempt to draw out our perp."

Fletcher noticed a slight twinge in Eddy at the sound of "little helpers." It disappeared very fast. He just sat there smiling at them.

Fletcher wondered for an instant what Father Brandon was up to. It again worried him that they weren't applying as much investigation to him. He was going to do it himself, with or without Frankie's agreement. He made a mental note to contact that reporter.

They all introduced themselves. Fletcher saw that Detective Danny Castle had the greater air of superiority than the other three. At the same time, he appeared nervous for some reason. Fletcher could tell Eddy noticed it, too.

They worked out the stakeouts. The kids were told the plan. It amazed Fletcher how cooperative Eddy and the kids were. For a second, the thought of them being involved evaporated from his mind. He cautioned himself not to go that far, but to be ready for anything.

After all was said and done, the detectives left. Eddy took his bow. They were alone again in Frankie's office.

"So?" Frankie asked.

"I just don't know anymore," replied Melanie.

"Me, neither," agreed Fletcher as he scratched his head. "Shouldn't we be tracking Father Brandon, too?"

"Yeah, yeah, but we're still back to square one again with these weird kids, eh?" he asked, ignoring his comment.

Fletcher didn't like being shrugged off. He knew however, it was still Frankie's show.

"Well, maybe not exactly square one," Melanie began.

Fletcher noticed she said it while staring into space. She was thinking.

They waited.

"Well, my *mind* is telling me that maybe they are okay. I mean did you see how cooperative they were? Seemed just like normal kids again."

They both nodded and waited. Frankie was looking at her intently and patiently, keeping his feelings for her at bay. He just wanted to get up, hug her, and kiss her mouth. Instead, he just looked down.

"But my heart says different. I just still believe there's something there."

"Yeah, but what? They are so deceptive—"

"That's it!" she exclaimed. "It's the feeling of being constantly deceived that hits me right here."

She made a fist, hitting her chest.

"You know something, that's exactly it. It's not evidence of anything except there's a deception going on. Who knows, they may even be involved in that slavery thing. But definitely a deception. Definitely."

"Yeah, Fletch, I feel it too. Constantly with them. Maybe they can hide all other things, but they forget that it's our line of business. We can tell when someone's lying all the time."

"Yep, and they *are* lying," Melanie agreed. "I just don't know why."

"The question is definitely why?" Fletcher added, nodding his head.

"Well, hopefully, we'll soon figure that out. Let's just get started, tomorrow," Frankie added, knowing the only thing to do now was to follow through and watch and wait.

"We'll be here bright and early. You can decide then where you want us, okay?"

"Yeah, sure, thanks Fletch."

They got up to leave his office.

"Fletch?"

"Yeah, Frankie," he stopped and turned back.

"Thanks."

Fletcher immediately saw the look of distress in his eyes. He fully understood the magnitude of it all and what was at stake.

Young kids are missing. No idea where, or even if still alive. No contact or ransoms calls. Way too much time has passed. Three kids are dead. The perp is teasing, testing, and giving up nothing, except that it will happen again. This maniac kid Eddy is trying to run the show *and* with the apparent blessing of his father, the DA. Too much ground to cover. Not enough personnel. Kids are being put at stake as friggin' targets. Parents don't seem to mind. Biblical notes that appear to be clues. Nothing ties them together. So they mean nothing. Child slavery may actually be happening. The clergy are obviously hiding something. Merrie is loose out there somewhere.

And everything is falling on this man's shoulders. Fletcher saw the mounting pressure in the lines on his face. His heart went out to Frankie again.

"Friend, I'm there for ya. Always will be."

"Me, too," said Melanie, with a friendly smile and a soft touch on his arm.

"Thanks, guys."

He looked down, paused, and then looked up at them. He was suddenly clear-eyed and determined, as Fletcher always knew him.

He slammed the desk.

"Let's get this goddamned psycho!"

Chapter 110 ~

FLETCHER AND MELANIE DECIDED to spend the night. They could then go back together to the police station first thing in the morning. They both knew otherwise, too. All the rushing, thinking, and pressure made them both want to hide for a while. Plus, getting close alone was on both their minds. Except Melanie needed some answers first.

They drove home in silence on I-95.

After passing the airport, Melanie abruptly shifted in her seat in an unusual manner.

Fletcher immediately noticed. She noticed he did.

She knew something was going on between him and Rosalyn. For her, it wasn't hard to figure out. She guessed there was sex, too. For now, she had resolved to let it go. She wanted him to be with her willingly, not because of any pressure. Knowing she could lose him, she had patience. Nevertheless, there was one thing that had to be said.

"You okay?" he tentatively asked.

"Yes and no," she replied a little coldly. He could feel the ice.

"What's wrong?" he asked, not wanting to know the answer.

The pause seemed forever to him.

"I'll ask once. I just need to know."

He looked over at her. She knew his silence meant "Go on."

"Do you care about me?"

"Honey, I—"

"Just say 'yes' or 'no.'"

"Yes."

"Would you ever hurt me?"

"No."

"Do you want me to stay?"

"Absolutely."

She looked at him.

"Sorry. Yes."

"Just so you know, I'm fine with anything you ever do. Anything. Just don't hurt me, okay?"

"Yes."

Another long pause from her got him anxious. Guilt was running all through him.

Finally, a warm smile appeared on her face and she turned to him.

"And just be careful."

He didn't answer. Holding firmly on the wheel with one hand, he pulled her close to him with the other. Quickly turning, he planted the softest kiss he could on her lips. She suddenly felt so warm, tightly throwing her arms around him. She did have a nice part of him.

After a moment, they broke loose. He playfully pushed her back to her side. She bounced like a little girl and then suddenly stared off into space.

"Now what's up?"

She laughed. His insight into her was getting better.

"What?" he pressed again.

"You're getting to know me as much and as well as I know you."

They both smiled.

"Shoot," he said, pointing his finger at her.

"Well, ya know all those passages?"

"Yeah?"

"Do you have them on you?"

"Yeah, copies are in my pocket."

He leaned, showing the left pocket of his pants. She glanced at him with both an aggressive and coy smile.

"Well?" he said.

"You're a pig!" she replied, starting to giggle.

"If you want it, well, you gotta get it," he teased.

She waited and thought and decided.

"Okay, you asked for it."

She leaned over his waist with her arm. She had to reach completely across to get her hand into the left pocket. She did it fine, which surprised Fletcher. She kept her hand in the pocket. She let her arm lay on his crotch and started moving it a little, then a little more. She was determined to let him know who owned it.

"See, I knew you'd find it," he said with a mischievous chuckle.

"Yeah, guess I did. Just not sure which 'thing' I really want."

"Well, decide then."

"I will."

She paused and then took the passages out. She noticed his playful disappointment.

She leaned over fast and grabbed his crotch, which had gotten bigger.

He swerved to the right. Overcompensating, he swerved to the left. He quickly made it back to the center of the lane.

"Oh my god! You almost got us killed!"

"I wanted both," she giggled again, ignored him, and sat back to read the passages.

(Ancient Israel)

Chapter 111 ~

MARIUS HAD RETURNED to the platform. He was surrounded by a few men. It appeared they were transacting something. Daiafar couldn't figure it out nor did he care. He only cared about why he had to wait.

He took a deep breath, slowly hissing it out. His anger quickly grew. Part of him wanted to kill Marius, take whatever he could, and be over with it all.

He knew though, at this point, Marius had the upper hand. Daiafar still couldn't risk being found out, especially not here.

His mind wandered. He thought of his son and daughter. An inner smile grew that slowly quieted his anger. He saw his boy playing with the small sword he had given him. He again smiled inside, remembering how he had tried to get him seriously to practice the correct technique. But his son just wanted to play.

Suddenly, he heard a horn blare. He almost jumped off the bench. He composed himself. He watched as the men around Marius stepped back, allowing Marius to move to the opening of the room. He grabbed something.

In an instant, Daiafar saw the most horrible thing he had ever seen.

Chapter 112 ~

FLETCHER WAITED A LITTLE BEFORE his curiosity became too much for him. He made some grunting ahems, followed by a couple coughs. She still didn't budge but kept going back and forth between the passages. They went off the Media exit of I-476. He had enough.

"Okay, lady, what's up?"

"Oh, nothing, except I think I figured it out," she said so nonchalantly that it didn't immediately register in Fletcher's brain. Then it did.

He screeched to a halt on the shoulder of the off-ramp.

"You what?"

"I think I *got it,* at least these passages. Well, maybe."

She kept shuffling them and reading them.

He waited a moment.

"Do you or don't you?"

"Umm, I do."

He looked at her. His excitement didn't match her calmness.

"Well, are you going to tell me?"

"I want a kiss first."

"A what?"

"A kiss."

"C'mon, just tell me."

She didn't answer and only smiled at him.

"Oh, crap!"

He leaned over, kissing her cheek.

"Mouth."

"Damn!"

He leaned over again, kissing her mouth. She kissed him back.

"Well?"

"Say I'm good."

"What? C'mon Mel."

She waited.

"Okay, I'm good."

She looked at him and saw his smile. She gave him a scornful look, turning away.

"Fine, FINE! You're good. You're fucking great!"

"Now that's better. Thanks babe! Don't forget."

He instinctively knew what she really meant.

"Now, what do you have?"

"Follow me on this."

"Go!"

"Each passage by itself means nothing. They go together. Each has a piece of the whole picture. It tells where the next kidnapping will be, at least the type of place and event. It's a cumulative pattern."

"Very cool. Well?"

"Do you have a pen and something to write on?"

"Yeah, yeah."

He pulled out his little pocket notebook and pen he always carried.

"Shoot."

"From the first passage of the last victim, write down: Bread, Meat, Morning, Evening, Drinking, okay?"

"Yep. Go ahead."

"Now, from the second one, hold on ... now, write down:

Israel, House of Fathers, Ba'al—and put the apostrophe between the a's like the passage does."

"And?"

"And for the third … write down: Bull, Dress it first, Call upon the name of your God. Got it?"

"Umm, yep."

"There."

"There what?"

"It's plain as day, or maybe only for a genius like me."

She tossed her hair, cocked her head at him, and started her cute giggles again.

"Hold on a moment, let me read and think it through."

"I'll give you a hint."

"What?"

"It's an event and fits perfectly into the whole MO."

"Okay, hold a sec."

She waited. Cars passed by. Finally, a PA State Trooper pulled in behind them. In the side mirror she saw his lights on. She knew he was doing it because they stopped on the shoulder of an off-ramp on a major highway. She saw Fletcher didn't see the cop. He was intent on reading what he had written. It was hard for her to hold back her giggles.

The cop got out. She noticed he put on his trooper hat low to the brow. He closed his door and proceeded up to Fletcher's door.

She now couldn't stop the snickering. The giggles followed, as she put her hand to her mouth.

A smile came to Fletcher's face. Then he noticed her giggles. Getting annoyed, he turned to her with an irritated, pissed look.

"What is your problem?" he almost shouted.

"Oh, nothing. Nothing at all."

She saw his annoyance disappear. He went back to reading.

He smiled even broader. She knew.

"I GOT IT!" he shouted.

She couldn't keep it in. He turned to her, wanting to know what the hell she was giggling at. All she could do was point.

He turned and saw the State Trooper glaring down at him through the closed window. He was now tapping the window with his stick.

He heard her bellow with laughter.

"And he's got you, honey!"

Chapter 113 ~

HE GAVE HER A QUICK DIRTY LOOK, turning back to roll down his window.

"Hi, Officer," Fletcher said as calmly as he could.

"Um, is there a reason you're stopped on this off-ramp?"

He could tell the officer was not in a good mood, or maybe, he thought, no PA State Trooper was ever in a good mood.

"Um, we are investigating the murder/kidnappings in Philly. We just got a breakthrough."

"Here? On an off-ramp?"

They could tell he was not believing them.

"Officer, I'm sorry to have stopped. But honestly, we did."

"Who the hell are you two?"

"Fletcher Saxtan and Melanie Sanders."

The officer's face changed a little. Then it went back to rock hard.

"Yes, I've heard of you Mr. Saxtan. Not you, ma'am. ID please, both of you."

They got their ID's out. Fletcher passed them to him.

He went back to his patrol car. Fletcher could see him calling it in.

After a short moment, he returned.

"Mr. Saxtan and Ms. Sanders, you check out. Please get off this off-ramp and go somewhere where you're not causing a public safety issue."

"Thank you, Officer. We'll move right away."

Fletcher heard a short gasp of a giggle come from the passenger seat. He lightly smacked her leg.

"Do you always have to laugh?"

"Only when it's funny. You're so cute!"

"Let's get out of here."

"Yeah, good idea. Stop stopping on highways."

He gave her a quick glance. She blew him a kiss.

About a few seconds after they pulled out, the Trooper turned on his lights and siren again behind them.

"Now what?" Fletcher moaned.

"I know."

"Oh, you do?"

"Yep."

"What?" he said as he rolled down his window. The hot air came in again.

Right when the Trooper got to the window, she whispered to him.

"He wants to know what you discovered. Remember, he's a cop, too, and probably already informed of the case."

"Yes, Officer?"

"By the way, what was it you discovered?"

The officer was smiling this time.

Fletcher glanced at Melanie, looking for permission to tell him.

Melanie shrugged.

He shrugged back and turned to the open window.

"Well, we'd like to keep it confidential, for now, so that we don't blow the cover."

The officer's smile faded. Fletcher didn't offer any more information and just sat there. The officer gave a small smirk.

"I do understand. And to tell you, I would have been

surprised had you told me."

"Well, thanks."

The officer left. Melanie clapped lightly.

"You did good!" she finally said.

"Yep, no reason to blow this, even to a State-ie."

"So? Tell me what you think," she asked.

"Give me that kiss."

She did, with an open mouth, and another grab at his crotch.

"Yo! I give!"

She smiled. With her mouth right up against his, she whispered, "Tell me, babe, and prove to me we're equals."

He lightly kissed her, whispering back, "Babe, we're equals in all ways!"

Her eyes sparkled at that. She gave a cute tilt of her head, with a small endearing smile meaning: Tell me.

"Babe, you're good. They happen on Saturdays for the most part, correct?"

"Yep, you got it."

They said it together.

"A Bar Mitzvah!"

Chapter 114 ~

WHEN HE GOT HOME, HE IMMEDIATELY called Frankie. He could tell he was elated and impressed at the same time. He told Fletcher he would investigate all Bar Mitzvahs scheduled for Saturday, especially in Bala Cynwyd. He had told him that the Ba'al god name switched around spelled Bala.

Frankie would have it all ready to review for tomorrow, Friday. He thanked him again and hung up.

"Ya know, I was thinking."

"Yeah, babe," Fletcher answered as he put his arm around her on the couch.

"Should we have any of our little targets for any of the Bar Mitzvahs? I mean if they are involved, they would know about the events. If we place them there, wouldn't we be tipping them off that we know?"

"Good point. I don't know. At the same time, Frankie is not going to tell Mike, to eliminate any possible leaks to maniac Eddy and his crew."

"Yeah, but what do you think?"

She snuggled under his arm against him.

"I think I wanna make love to you, if you keep doing that," he said pulling her closely.

"Let's, right now."

"I would love to but let's first figure this out and then fuck our brains out, okay?"

"Ooookay."

She jabbed him lightly.

"Thanks!"

"Welcome!"

"My dear," she continued, "I say we don't mention it at all. It's a Saturday. We were only covering the typical meeting joints, like fast food, libraries, local parks in the city, stuff like that. They can be at those. We'll be at the Bar Mitzvah's. Hopefully, there aren't many."

"At the same time, what if it's just a diversion and they figured we'd figure it out. We'd stake out the Bar Mitzvahs, leaving the real targets less protected?"

"Well, shit, we can't cover everything. It's been and still is a crap shoot and you know it," he shrugged.

"Yeah, I know it is. We just have to play the odds."

They sat in silence for a while. Each was thinking it through, playing the criminal role in their minds. They had to try to see it as criminals in order to anticipate their moves.

"Hold on a sec."

"Yes, babe," Melanie replied.

Fletcher got his cell and placed a call.

He waited.

"Yo, Frankie! Yeah, we've been mulling something over. Before we meet tomorrow, we wanted to discuss it now and hopefully decide so we have more time to plan."

He proceeded to tell Frankie their thoughts and ideas. He then waited as Frankie was obviously thinking it through.

"Okay, fine, I see."

He hung up.

"What did he say?"

"Stay the course. He agrees. We go alone—you, me, and him. No leak to anyone at all, except a select couple of detectives. I trust who he picked. He's confident that they have as much covered as physically possible already, with parents informed. We will take care of the Bar Mitzvahs, or should I say Bar Mitzvah? There's only one."

"Really?"

"Guess where?"

They both whispered it in unison.

"Bala Cynwyd."

Chapter 115 ~

THEY ARRIVED EARLY AT FRANKIE'S office the next day. They reviewed the area. They noted the times of the ceremony and the celebration. Both were at different places. The ceremony was early in the day; the celebration later in the day, as the clues indicated.

"Good job, guys," Frankie applauded after they finished mapping out everything. "Our special detectives are ready and would never leak anything, even to the DA. They will be covering the grounds from different angles."

"For us, we'll be watching the whole scene from the start to the end. Hopefully, we'll hit gold."

"Yeah, I hope so," Fletcher followed. He seemed deep in thought.

"What's the matter, honey?" Melanie asked, sensing an issue.

"Yeah, Fletch, you've been awfully quiet so far, quite unlike you."

That sarcastic remark made him look up with a sneer at Frankie. A small smile then replaced it.

"I don't know. If it's these kids and that Eddy, too, somehow, I just feel we're being led down a false path. Or we missed it totally."

"I know what you mean," Melanie replied. "Even though it appears to be this event, it's still suspect. We may be missing the picture totally with the clues, or maybe they're really not clues at all. Still very cryptic."

"Thanks, guys!" Frankie interrupted them. "You made me feel great that this is it. And now, not just one of you, but both of you are second guessing the whole thing, which you *both* came up with!"

"Calm down, Frankie," Fletcher said. "I'm just playing all sides. It does appear this is it. It's just that, do we actually think they'd do it at a Bar Mitzvah, in the total open?"

"Well, I think Eddy has the balls to do anything, if it's them," Melanie added. "And if it's not, then whoever it is already has shown they have the balls. I also don't think that's Merrie's style. I do think Father Brandon has the balls, though."

Both Frankie and Fletcher looked over at Melanie, with open mouths. Again, they were shocked with her choice of words.

She noticed.

"C'mon guys, I know these words. Balls! Fuck! Shit! Pussy!"

She started to giggle. They both smiled and shook their heads.

"Hey, she's your girl, buddy," Frankie said, wishing she were his, even for just one time.

"Yeah, but I accept her anyway."

That immediately prompted a smack on the arm, which he smiled at.

"Well, regardless, it's a go for tomorrow. We still have all else covered as best we can, too."

They all agreed.

Outside, Melanie stopped Fletcher with a touch on his arm.

"I know, I know," he said. "I'm still concerned about it all. Somehow, I just have a feeling that we're being duped, even with this analysis."

"Yeah, I have that feeling, too. I felt so up yesterday. I honestly believe it's probably Eddy and crew, or people like him. And if so, I believe he's the kind to plant false clues to either watch us waste time or divert us. So, we may have figured it out right, but not the real thing."

"Well, I also think our suspected clergy-slavers are capable of it, too. A la Father Brandon and crew," Fletcher added.

"And Merrie acts stupid, but isn't, and may be an integral part of it all or a diversion himself. I still can so see him involved," she added back.

"Yeah, well, let's hope we have it right."

"Yeah, let's."

Chapter 116 ~

THE FIGURE PICKED UP THE CHAIR in the middle of the room and crashed it against the wall. Then in the darkness, it picked up the chair again and threw it against the other wall.

"No! No! No!" it screamed as it kept throwing the pieces of the broken chair all around the room. Finally, it fell onto the floor exhausted.

In a voice garbled with dripping saliva, it quivered on the floor saying over and over again, "No, no, no, no…"

Then, as if a brilliant light blinded it in the pitch blackness, all motion stopped. It slowly sat up. In the eerie silence, it spat on the floor in front of it.

"This is for you, for you. I promise for you."

It stood up with the new thought it had found in its crazed mind.

"Now you will see. Now you will. No one does this without me."

It bowed its head in its cold conviction. For an hour that seemed an eternity, it stood in the middle of the silent room and repeated:

"No one."

"No one."

"No one."

Chapter 117 ~

JOSH LEANED BACK IN HIS CUBICLE chair. He raised his interlocked fingers over his head, cracking his knuckles. He couldn't stop thinking about Martino and what he wanted him to do. Knowing Martino had the power to get him the dream he wanted, he wasn't sure how to proceed.

Fletcher Saxtan wasn't an easy man to befriend. After his first encounter with him, he really didn't think he could just walk up to him and say "Hi," asking him if he could buy him a beer.

He shook his head and tried to put himself into Fletcher's shoes. After an hour of mulling over every possibility, he just came up short. He would never get close enough again for the microphone trick either. In disgust, he threw his pencil down. It bounced wildly off the desk.

"Damned arrogant bastard," was all he could say.

He stood up. Staring out into the newsroom, he vowed he'd find a way to get to him. Then he closed his eyes and said a small prayer that maybe Saxtan would come to him. After all, everything kept going his way. Why should it stop now? He smiled as he pictured the front-page headline with his story. He walked out of the building with high hopes again.

Chapter 118 ~

THE BAR MITZVAH WAS SCHEDULED for 10:00 a.m. They arrived in Frankie's undercover car at exactly 9:00 a.m. Frankie had his men in position at all key points by 7:00 a.m.

They watched and waited. All the guests arrived on time, strolling into the synagogue. They watched as the last entered and the doors closed.

A couple of pedestrians had walked by but nothing out of the ordinary. Some cars had stopped near them, but soon drove on.

All the time, Frankie was on the communications link with his officers. Melanie could hear the light chatter. Nothing seemed to be of any alarm. Fletcher just stared out the side window.

After a while, the ceremony ended. The guests flooded out. Everyone was mingling.

They took careful watch of any kids, especially ones together who appeared to be brothers and sisters.

Nothing happened.

Eventually, they all proceeded to their cars and left without incident.

They sat in Frankie's car for a while, just making sure all had left. They saw an undercover detective walk up to the synagogue and check inside.

The sheer excitement that had grown in Melanie disappeared. She heard the police chatter and from Frankie's face, all was clear.

"Well," he said motionless, "it appears this wasn't anything."

"Yeah, well, we got the banquet thing still," Fletcher added.

"Yep, let's grab a bite and wait the time out."

"I could use a drink, too."

"Okay, Fletch, a drink it is, but only one. You're on duty."

"Frankie, I'm on *my* time always, but fine, only one."

He picked up his hat from the floor and put it on.

Melanie tipped it off his head.

Frankie laughed, shook his head, and drove away.

Chapter 119 ~

THE BANQUET WASN'T FAR. They stopped for a bite. Fletcher got his drink. All they could do was sit and wait. Frankie spent most of his time with his back to them. On the radio and his cell, he checked each local checkpoint, including all the other key points in and around town.

After he was satisfied that all was calm, he turned back to them.

"We seem quiet enough," he said with a huff.

"You okay?" Melanie asked.

"Yeah, yeah, yeah."

"Just checking. You seem very apprehensive," she followed with.

"I just got this strange feeling that this is it. Something's going to go down. It's today."

"Really?" she answered, as her excitement grew again from his apprehension.

"Yeah, really, Melanie."

"So, why?" Fletcher asked after downing his rum and Coke. He was in his apathetic mood again.

"I don't know. I just feel something's going to happen. I just got that feeling. Maybe because it's so damned calm out there. Like a storm coming."

"Police instinct and jitters," Fletcher noted with a smile. He called the waiter over.

Frankie ignored the second drink request. That made Fletcher know he was upset.

"Frankie, we've done everything possible. Scant as they are, the clues point here."

"Yeah, I just know something's going down."

He turned away again to answer his cell. Then he was back on the radio. While talking, all he could feel was a deep combination of fear, apprehension, and absolute hatred of whoever was doing this. When he finally got them, which he unrelentingly vowed he would, it would take all his cop discipline not to unload his clip into them, right then and there.

Fletcher shrugged to Melanie. She lightly shrugged back.

"Let's go," Frankie continued. "I want to get there earlier than we said."

Fletcher knew not to argue when Frankie got like this. Usually, his hunches were right on. He immediately downed his drink. Melanie watched in a bit of amazement. It was just delivered and full. She smiled, shaking her head. She knew he could handle it. Moreover, she was not his judge and never wished to be either.

They left in a hurry. Fletcher threw a couple of twenties on the table, hoping it covered it. He still felt no sentiment, at all, about anything. He felt he should, but just couldn't. Suddenly his cell phone vibrated. He ignored it.

When they got in the car, Frankie drove off like a maniac. Melanie was glad that he was a cop. First, he was *allowed* to drive like a maniac, and second, he knew *how* to drive like a maniac.

They arrived at the banquet hall. It was a popular mainline restaurant, so there were many people inside and out waiting for tables. They sat in the car for a while waiting for the guests to arrive.

After about an hour, they began to recognize people from the ceremony. There was a separate door for the banquet. It was right next to the door for the restaurant. Frankie was frantic on the radio because of the other people mingling around who had nothing to do with the Bar Mitzvah. Any one of them could be the perp or perps. It made it hard to spot anyone and keep an eye on all guests.

Eventually, all the guests disappeared inside. Quiet ensued.

They patiently waited in the car. Frankie was still going back and forth on the radio and his cell.

After some time passed, people started to come outside to smoke cigarettes. Occasionally, kids came out. The children seemed to be bored with the events inside. They were laughing and playing outside. Some had parents with them. Some had no parents, but were in plain sight of the adults. Continual activity went on for about an hour. Adults and children kept coming out and going back in.

Melanie couldn't believe anyone would do this in broad daylight. She started to question her own analysis and instincts. They were all now getting a little antsy in the car.

Fletcher was staring out the side window when someone caught his eye. It was a police officer in uniform. He was walking up the street. He watched him get closer to the hall. He then stopped, looking around.

Fletcher's heart started to beat faster. Something didn't seem right. He felt his chest tighten. For a moment, he was frozen in a fearful state. It was like when all of a sudden, a dangerous, imminent thing is about to happen and you can't move, even though you clearly see it coming. He took a deep breath.

He watched the officer start walking again. He was still heading towards the restaurant.

He nudged Melanie. She looked and saw him, too. He was

almost at the restaurant. Right before Fletcher was about to say something to Frankie, the officer turned right. He walked away in the opposite direction across the street.

Fletcher breathed a sigh of relief, looking back at the hall. He couldn't believe he had suspected a cop.

There were still kids playing in front. They were running all around the parking lot. He eyed them all and then saw two boys leaning against a parked car. He watched as they fumbled with something between them. Then they walked around the car and down a couple more cars, away from the hall.

They stopped, after another ten feet, and looked around. Then one put the cigarette to his mouth. He lit it, handing it to the other boy. Fletcher shook his head, thinking they must be about twelve years old. Then the first boy lit another. They strolled a little further. They headed towards the street. They looked back at the hall, paused, and then crossed the street. It seemed they wanted to distance themselves from the folks mingling outside.

Fletcher's eyes followed their path. He looked ahead. His eyes fell back on the police officer who was just standing on the other side of the street.

The boys saw the cop and froze. He thought, okay, here it goes, they got caught and the officer is going to make a scene about their underage smoking.

He was right. The officer perked up, motioning to the boys to come to him. They both looked at each other and then back at the cop. For Christ sake, he thought, leave them alone.

The cop started to walk towards them. He made another motion for them to walk to him. They looked at each other. They then started towards the cop. Fletcher saw them flick their cigarettes behind them.

The cop pointed to the butts on the sidewalk. He was obviously scolding them.

Fletcher suddenly realized the cop had a full beard. It appeared incorrect and foreign. He couldn't understand why it bothered him. The illogic of it caused the moment to freeze in time to him. Then he heard it.

"Who the FUCK is that?" Frankie yelled.

Fletcher turned to him with his mouth open wide. Melanie instinctively jumped back.

"Charlie-1, Charlie-1. Who the hell is that cop?"

He was yelling right into his radio.

"Get over there! NOW!"

"What's up?" Fletcher yelled back.

Frankie's face was fairly distorted when he said, "There are *no uniforms in this area!*"

"Oh, shit!" Fletcher bellowed. He looked back.

The kids were struggling against the strong arms of the cop. He had both by the collar. In an instant, a black sedan pulled up. The back door opened right next to the cop.

"Damn it!" was all Fletcher heard. Their car reeled from the turn Frankie just made through the parking lot.

All appeared in slow motion to Melanie as Frankie did his best to veer past parked and slow-moving cars in the lot. The expressions on the people he nearly hit, and the constant swaying of the car, made it all seem like a wild movie scene.

He quickly turned back towards the street. The sedan was peeling out up the street. It already disappeared past the store buildings.

Melanie, holding onto the top of the front seat, was amazed at how Frankie could drive through everything, still on the radio, and yelling commands to his detectives.

He finally made the street. They almost toppled over at the sharp turn he made. They were well behind the speeding black car. It appeared to be about a half-mile ahead of them.

The sedan wildly banked a turn, disappearing down a side street. Frankie did the same. He was yelling the street name into the radio. He was demanding a cut-off move.

"Damn it!" he cried again, as he saw the sedan cut back down the opposite street they had come up. He tried to do the same but a passing car almost hit him. He had to slow for a second and then sped right back up.

He reached down, tossing the red light to Fletcher, who immediately placed it on the top of the roof with one move. Melanie could see the cop in Fletcher all of a sudden. It made her proud. Then Frankie veered again. She toppled over in the back seat.

He flipped the siren on. It was deafening.

The sedan had gained distance. After she managed to get up, Melanie could see another detective car appear behind them.

The sedan made another swerve onto City Line Avenue. It was now headed south, away from Bala Cynwyd. It made another crazy turn onto a small side street that jutted out. The oncoming traffic caused Frankie to screech to a halt and inch into traffic. It took some drivers awhile to figure out which way he wanted to go.

Finally, the traffic stopped. He pushed it hard. They made the turn with a loud screech. It was a quiet, residential street. About two blocks down, the black sedan was silently parked on the right side of the road. It had partially jumped the curb.

Frankie careened in front of it, jumping the curb himself. The motion threw Melanie backwards and then down onto the floor again. He blocked it diagonally.

"Stay down!" he yelled to Melanie. She ignored him, watching as he jumped out with his gun pulled. He pointed it at the sedan from his side, using the car to protect his body.

Fletcher had dove onto the front seat. He crawled out Frankie's side. Melanie did the same from the passenger door.

She heard them both, and herself, breathing heavily. It seemed in complete unison.

She crept up a little to peer through Frankie's car's windows, back at the sedan.

All she heard next from Frankie was:

"OH, WHAT THE FUCK!"

Chapter 120 ~

ALL OF A SUDDEN, THEY WERE COMPLETELY surrounded by police cruisers. Both detectives and uniformed vehicles arrived, all with sirens blasting. Melanie's heart was beating through her chest. She tried her best, but just couldn't catch her breath. She felt like she had just run a marathon.

"Goddamn it! Goddamn it!" Fletcher kept repeating.

Both he and Frankie carefully rose up from behind the car, looking into the sedan. Melanie followed suit.

She saw no one in the driver's seat. The cop imitator who had jumped into the front passenger seat also had disappeared.

In the back seat were the two boys huddled together. She could see tears flowing from their eyes. They were shaking uncontrollably.

"Mutherfucker! *MUTHER*-fucker!" Frankie cried. He went around the back of his car with his gun pointing directly into the sedan. He inched up to the driver door, peeked in very fast, and then back.

"Damn it!" he said under his breath this time. Fletcher had come around, too. Melanie just watched from where she was. She felt a whole lot better there.

Frankie holstered his weapon, casually opening the front driver door. He lifted the handle with his pen.

Melanie heard Fletcher mumble something as he looked in. Then she saw Frankie turn his back and lean against the sedan. She wondered if the boys were okay. Two detectives were already opening the back doors, checking in on them.

The boys came out. Both were still shaking terribly. A weird thought came to her mind about offering them a cigarette, but she blanked it out as fast as it came in.

She decided it was safe to walk over and see what they were looking at. Her heart wouldn't stop pounding. Her chest felt like it was going to explode at any moment, with her heart flying out.

She got there. Fletcher moved out of the way for her. He also leaned his back against the sedan.

She peered in and gasped.

On the driver's seat was a large Bible.

It was opened to the Prophet Elijah, Book of Kings.

Chapter 121 ~

"DO YOU BELIEVE THIS SHIT?" Frankie said. He slammed the car door with the butt of his weapon. Fletcher knew it was both in frustration and to preserve any prints. Frankie walked away to his car. He was right back on the radio and cell, demanding a combing of the area. Fletcher looked over at Melanie. She looked back, almost in tears.

"You okay?" Fletcher asked as he walked up to her.

"Yeah, I guess, so," she weakly answered. "It's just that I'm not normally in high-speed chases, in heavy traffic, ending with guns pulled."

Fletcher smiled, hugging her.

She hugged him back, holding on for a bit. He didn't stop her.

Frankie came back.

"…in absolute broad daylight, too!" Frankie picked up where he left off, putting the radio down. "Playing with our fucking, goddamn minds!"

Melanie couldn't believe the words coming out of Frankie's mouth. Then suddenly, she pushed Fletcher back, realizing that, in the heat of the moment, they missed something.

"Hey, then it's an obvious diversion!"

Fletcher and Frankie both simultaneously looked at her.

"Fucking-A, Mel!" Frankie blurted.

"Yo, get on the horn, Frankie."

"On it, Fletch," Frankie said, as he disappeared back into his car. They could hear him barking orders, demanding where people were. His face was grim when he came back to them. He then disposed of most of the officers back to their preplanned coverage areas.

He discussed the scene with the remaining detectives and told them to dust everything, saying they'd better be thorough or he will hang each from the highest rafter.

"Let's head out," Frankie ordered Fletcher and Melanie.

They got back in his car. He sped off, just as fast as he had arrived.

Melanie began to think about taking a bus.

Chapter 122 ~

ARRIVING AT THE STATION, they were bombarded by reporters, cameras, microphones, questions yelled, bystanders jeering, and police barricades. The barriers had apparently been quickly set up to make a path to the steps. Melanie had seen this on TV, but was never at one. Moreover, she had never been part of the focus and attention.

Frankie huffed loudly at it all. He quickly ran up the steps. They hurried behind him. Fletcher was feeling an uncomfortable sweat under his arms. When they got inside his office, Frankie was right back on the radio and phone. They both sat opposite him, catching their breaths.

"So, what do you think?" Fletcher asked her, in a low tone, so as not to disturb Frankie. It sounded as one would speak at a funeral.

"I think they really fooled us and somehow knew. But how? How?" she replied in the same low tone but firmer. He sensed anger.

"I don't know. I just don't know. Maybe they knew we'd eventually figure out the clues or knew there were only so many possible ways to figure them out."

"Wait a minute!"

"What, Mel?"

"Where are the passages?"

He pulled them out of his pocket again and gave them to her. Another piece of paper fell on the floor. She saw it and picked it up. After looking at it, she held it out to him with a quizzical look.

"Oh, that's just an idiot list of food from one of Mike's cocktail parties," he said offhandedly.

She looked it over and made a face of recognition.

"Kind of cool recipes. May I?" she asked, meaning to keep it.

"You're the so-called chef, go ahead. It was all crap anyway."

She stuffed it in her purse with a smile of thanks. She quickly went back to scanning the passages again.

A feeling of pride fell over him as he watched her, his girl, go right back to analyzing things. She was tenacious and dedicated. He loved that. He planted a thought to make passionate love to her when this was all over.

"Shit," she muttered.

"What?"

"Can't see anything more. You?"

She handed them back to him.

"I don't know. What else could it all mean? It really did point to where we were. I mean it's obviously about a bull and house of fathers and—"

"Hold on a sec," she interrupted.

"Yeah?"

"House of fathers? Priests? Maybe you were right about that."

He looked at her.

"Give me them back," she demanded.

He immediately gave them.

She perused back and forth, using her finger.

He waited and watched.

She mumbled, "Majority, call your god, commandments,

bread, bull." She kept repeating the words and phrases.

He couldn't take it. Frankie's constant commands were getting to him, too.

"Give me anything!" he firmly whispered.

"Maybe not Jewish. Maybe Catholic."

"Oh, yeah." Thoughts of child slavery filled his head again.

"And if that were a diversion, they'd be doing something today or——"

"Why have a diversion," Fletcher finished it for her. "It could just be a nasty trick, too. Back to the fucking games."

"Yeah, but I don't think so. I think he, they, whatever, wants us to play and figure it out. You know, they were probably watching the whole time, still hoping we're figuring more of it out now."

"You know, babe, this is really perverted."

"You think?" she innocently posed.

"Mel, these are perverted people. It's not just the crimes. It's the game. It's the ego."

"Like the Eddy kind…" she trailed off.

"Exactly like Eddy, or the Brandon kind: superiority complex and the constant need to prove it. If it's Eddy, he's probably been upset we've been so slow to figure things out. You can almost feel the joy when we meet with him, as if he's egging us on." He finished with a smirk.

"I know exactly how you feel and you put that perfectly. Who knows, if it is Brandon, the Jewish rite *would* be a diversion. Or maybe just trying to implicate away from himself."

"What the hell are you two talking about?" Frankie interjected, as he hung up his cell. It was obvious from his face he was tired.

They explained and caught him up to where they were.

"So, you think something's going down as we speak?"

"Or already did or will."

"Well, Frankie," Fletcher stated as he stood up, "why go through all that trouble?"

"Well, they would get the greatest thrill if they succeeded in duping us, still pulling off what they intended in the first place," Melanie added.

"While we were foolishly taking the bait," Frankie followed with.

"If anything, I believe they would do something, still *today,* after this incident."

"Why Fletch?"

"Because it's even a bigger rush of superiority, don't you think? They would know we knew we were duped, right?"

Frankie and Melanie nodded. He continued.

"So, they would then think, and hope, we were doing exactly what we are doing. They would pull it off, as we're in confusion—"

"Showing just how stupid we really are!"

"Thanks Mel, but speak for yourself," Fletcher said and laughed. He knew the hit was coming. It did.

"Well, here's another thing," she said after hitting him and giving him a nasty, but fun look. Her face twisted with a smile and then a wink.

"What?" Fletcher asked, faking a big wink back.

"Doesn't it seem odd to you guys that, instead of us coming at them, they're coming at us?"

"What do you mean?" asked Frankie, leaning forward with his hand on his chin, ignoring her cuteness.

"I see," said Fletcher.

"Yeah," she continued glancing at Fletcher. "They come at

us, not the other way around, almost as if they know exactly what we're doing. They planned for it. It's not the other way around where we're going after them. See what I mean?"

"Yeah, *yeah*," replied Frankie nodding. "I see. You're absolutely right. It's almost as if they are lying in wait for us. Psychotic shits."

Melanie laughed at that. She hadn't expected it and it tickled her.

Frankie looked at her with a questioning look. After seeing Fletcher shrug his shoulders at him, he realized it was just her cute way.

"Leak?" Fletcher asked, glancing over.

"Sounds like it, but who? Where?" Frankie replied raising his hands.

"Mike?" Melanie asked.

"No, no way. He doesn't know anything, unless one of my folks told him, but why would they? What motivation? And if so, then we're saying Mike's involved?"

"Well, maybe not knowingly," Fletcher answered with a cock of his head at his implied hint.

"Eddy!"

"Yeah, Eddy, using him," Fletcher confirmed back to him.

"But that would mean he'd have to be in constant contact with his dad to keep up with us. At the same time, Mike doesn't have every detail of our moves either," Melanie added.

"True. Not very feasible," Frankie followed with.

"Well, if it is that little monster, he has some technique of knowing ahead of us," Fletcher posed.

"I fucking hate Ein-fucking-steins. Especially little Ein-fucking-steins!"

Melanie giggled again, which made Frankie smile. She kept

charming him.

"Well, let's just keep it in mind," Fletcher said, giving her a smirk, and grinning when she giggled more. "Ya know you're really out of your mind, don't you?"

"Yep, I know, sorry," she replied, giggling again, this time trying to control it, but still failing.

Frankie shook his head and began again.

"Okay, then, what do you got on those passages. A Catholic thing or something?"

They all paused. The room fell into silent thought.

Melanie composed herself. When things went so ridiculous, she couldn't help herself. It was just that sometimes, life was so absurd, it seemed like a comedy play or insane satire to her.

"Well, what I was going to say was, what occurs on Saturdays with Catholics?" she continued her previous thought. She held back a tickling feeling. She felt like a kid.

"CONFESSION!" Frankie blurted.

"Figures you'd know," Fletcher smirked again.

"Well, hey, gotta tell God what I keep wanting to do but never get a chance to," he said, this time laughing at himself a little.

Fletcher was glad to see him loosen up. He was getting a little worried with all the pressure, the chasing, and the "cat and mouse" games. He didn't want to see one of his best friends in his life keel over with a heart attack.

"Confession, eh?" Fletcher quizzed, with tentative tone in his voice.

"But it does fit!" Melanie agreed.

She went through the passages again.

"Fathers. That's gotta be priests. Bull could mean boy or

maybe a name or possibly a street, like where a church is located?"

Frankie immediately went on the intercom, barking more orders to locate all churches that may be on any street or corner with the letters "b-u-l-l" in them.

He finished, giving his attention back.

"Then the commandments would be the Ten Commandments. That's what someone goes through when they confess. It's gotta be!"

"Mel, hope you're right. Sounds right, or at least enough to go after," Frankie said.

He got back on the intercom. He was asking if any news came in about anybody reporting anybody missing. If it did, he must be notified immediately, no matter how innocent the call may seem.

"Majority must be, or may be in reference to the fact that Catholics, or Christians in general, are in the majority in this country. A stretch, I know," Melanie said, rubbing her chin.

"I'm still betting this all has to do with our friend, Brandon," Fletcher posed again. Melanie nodded at that real possibility now of slavery.

All of a sudden, Frankie's phone rang. They all looked over and froze. He went to pick it up. He listened.

He slammed the phone down, jumped up, and ran right past them.

Melanie jumped up.

"What?" Fletcher loudly asked as they both followed him out the office door.

"We got one!"

Chapter 123 ~

MELANIE FELT LIKE SHE WAS in a whirlwind. She again found herself in the fast pursuit of an insane criminal. Between the tremendous excitement being back in the car with a maniac driver, and the frustration of being duped, she knew she'd psychologically crash hard. She couldn't wait until this creep was found, tried, and executed.

She held on for dear life. With the siren blasting, Frankie was quickly weaving in and out of traffic. The car tilted a couple times. She noticed more police cars in line behind them.

Frankie was so intent on driving, that he forgot to tell them what happened and where they were going.

"Frankie?" Fletcher cautiously asked.

"Yeah, yeah, what?" He never took his eyes off the road.

"What's up?"

"Um, oh, shit, sorry guys. We just got a call from a woman, a mom, and it was just a missing person call, but when asked, it was her twin little boys…"

He trailed off as he swerved to miss some pedestrians crossing the street. Their wide eyes reminded Melanie of cornered animals.

Fletcher waited.

"…and guess where they were supposed to have been going?"

"Confession?" Melanie and Fletcher asked, in unison. They both knew it was true.

"Con-*fucking*-fession!" Frankie bellowed. He hit the gas

harder.

Melanie actually began to get scared. She didn't want to die in this damned car. She prayed Frankie's years on the Force—

They made such a hard turn she lost her thought. She flung into the door from the turn.

"Sorry, guys, but we gotta get there and try to find—"

"You mean you think they are already abducted?"

"Oh, yeah! Oh, yeah! The mom waited an extra *two fucking hours* from the time they normally returned from church. How many times have we told and educated these damned people. It's their goddamn kids! Half hour to an hour max. Then call us. A false alarm is better than this shit!"

Melanie said a silent prayer.

Chapter 124 ~

FRANKIE FINISHED THE INFORMATION about where they were going. Melanie had positioned herself up behind the gap between their seats. She locked her body there. She watched intently where they were going. It was definitely Bala Cynwyd.

So, the Ba'al part appeared still to be part of the clue and game, she thought.

Frankie was making turns so fast and then speeding up that it was hard to catch street names.

He was on the radio again. She could hear the others speaking. Without a trained police ear to the static of radio replies, it was hard to determine what they were saying.

She did get that there were detectives on the scene already. It appeared to be at a church.

So, the "house of fathers" also appeared to be right. Damn! Why hadn't she figured it out like that? Damned perp, she thought, playing the clues different ways. Smart. Too smart. They must have had both locales watched. They knew where we were. Either would have worked. Brilliant, she thought.

She vowed that, between them, they were going to catch this guy and find those missing kids.

Frankie began to slow down. He made another turn. This time Fletcher and Melanie saw the street name: Bullock Avenue.

"Okay, there's one 'bull,'" Fletcher muttered, with a little distaste.

"Yep," Frankie replied, still intently watching where he was going.

Melanie saw many police cruisers with lights on up ahead. Then she saw the church.

There was already police tape up. Uniformed officers and detectives surrounded the area. That wasn't what caught her eye.

"Holy shit," she muttered.

Frankie and Fletcher mumbled similar expletives.

Frankie suddenly screeched to a halt. They just stared.

Everywhere they looked, there were small papers strewn all over the scene – on bushes, lawns, cars, steps, everywhere. They appeared to be pages. A light breeze was blowing them around. They flew down the street like scampering little mice, directly towards them. It was the eeriest site she ever saw. A blanket of prophetic passages covered everything, as if it had rained Bibles.

Melanie still couldn't believe this was occurring in broad daylight and right out in public.

"Unbelievable balls," she muttered to herself. "Look at that!"

That caused Frankie's attention to return. He went right back to pulling up to the scene. He came to a slow halt. He jumped out. Fletcher had already left the car.

Melanie opened her door. She followed them as their stride picked up speed to the church steps. All the passages were fluttering around their feet and up into the air like autumn leaves.

There were priests being interrogated. A couple of older men and women were waiting around. Melanie figured they must have been in the church for confession, too.

The sun was beaming down. Even with the wind, it was still very hot.

She looked up at the church. It was a very large church, all in exquisitely sculptured stone. The bright sunlight glistened off the stained-glass windows. Various points of reflections occasionally blinded her. A gold crucifix shown brilliantly like a beacon at the apex.

In her writer's mind, it was a perfect contrast and irony. The dark crime of an abduction leading to a possible murder occurred on a sunny day at a church. And clergy were there for slavery and prayers.

She blanked it out. She followed them to the steps where the priests stood.

"Parents here?" Frankie immediately asked.

"No boss. On their way," replied Danny, the strong-looking young detective.

"Okay, I want to see them A-SAP!"

Frankie went over to the priests. Their faces appeared calm and ready to cooperate. But to Fletcher, that kind of false calmness was just irritating to him. They gotta be freaked or in on it, he thought.

"Okay, what do we got?" Frankie began. He posed the question to the two detectives who had been talking to the priests.

"I am Father Quincy, the pastor here at St. Stephen's."

Fletcher could see Frankie's annoyance. He wasn't talking to the pastor.

"Yeah, Padre, be with you in a sec," was the curt answer back.

Melanie almost giggled at the term "Padre." There was nothing funny except the fact that the Chief of Police just told a Catholic priest and pastor to basically shut the fuck up and speak when spoken to. The laughter was seeping out.

She turned and cupped her mouth.

Fletcher noticed, smiled, and shook his head. He loved her. This was one of the best things about her.

The pastor made a grimace and waited.

"Chief, there were two boys ... um ... twins ... age thirteen each," one of the detectives rattled off.

"Joe, they're twins. They would be the same age."

Melanie almost lost it. She walked away.

"Oh, yeah, sorry. Well, the parents said they always go to confession on Saturdays, at 3:00 p.m., and are home no later than 3:30 or 4:00 p.m. They didn't return and so they called."

"And waited way too long," Frankie said, in disgust.

He looked around and noticed an officer with a bucket.

"What is that? Bring that fucking thing over here," he demanded.

The two priests made a shocking face. One of them coughed.

"Oh, sorry you guys, just normal police talk," Fletcher put in, smiling.

Melanie had come back, and hearing that, just walked away again.

Fletcher smiled, seeing her holding it in.

"They're all just Bible pages," the other detective nonchalantly said. "We've been picking them up."

"Um, well obviously Bible pages. Get it over here! Anybody see where it all came from? And who? Anything?"

The detectives looked at each other.

"When we got here, this whole area was already littered with these." The detective swept his arm around from the steps to the street.

Frankie took out his plastic gloves and put one on. He

picked one up and then another and then another.

"Mutherfucker," he mumbled.

Fletcher grabbed his other glove, put it on, and fished through the bucket.

"So many!" Fletcher exclaimed. He glanced around the street and houses.

"Yeah, I mean, it looks like a trash dump," Frankie noted. "Someone had taken care to place and toss them everywhere. They're even on car windshields. Look, they took the time to put them under the wiper blades. It's really intense."

"Son of a bitch," Fletcher said, as he examined each one in the bucket.

Melanie saw all of this happening and returned. She looked at the ones he held. She didn't touch any, for sake of lab analysis.

"Kings, Kings, Kings, Kings, Kings," Fletcher kept saying.

"Yeah, and all pages from Elijah, from Kings," she added.

"Guy is so playing with us," Frankie said. "Any pattern?"

"Looks like every page of Elijah that exists. There must be a lot of Bibles with missing pages around."

"Yeah, babe, sure does," Melanie agreed, exasperated.

"You two," Frankie said, now turning towards the two priests.

They almost stood at attention at Frankie's tone.

"What happened and what did you see?"

"Well, actually nothing," the pastor said. The other nodded. "I guess Johnny and Justin were here. I think I had one of them in confession, but it's hard to tell."

"And I think I had one, too, from the voice," the other priest said.

They were both nodding. It reminded Melanie of bobble-heads. She held it in again, turning back to the passages.

"And then what?"

"Nothing. I mean, we remained in the confessional for other people. And it was only when the police arrived that we knew there may be a problem."

"You got their full statements?" Frankie asked Danny.

"Yep."

"Okay, free to go. What about other people, in the church or outside?"

"Honestly, nobody saw anything. No abduction, no passing cars or the boys being pulled in."

"Huh? Nothing? Then how—"

"Chief, I know. I was actually in the church."

"What? What do you mean in the church?"

"I was going to confession with Father Brandon and—"

"With who?" Fletcher immediately interrupted. At the same time, he stepped up close to Danny. He looked eye-to-eye to Danny with a stern, questioning look.

"You were here when the crime occurred and didn't do anything? Hey, Padres, hold it there a sec," Frankie called at them.

The two priests stopped, turning back.

"Boss, I said I was *in* confession the whole time. And when I came out—"

"Is that Father Brandon in there now?" Fletcher interrupted Danny.

Frankie stared at him. He then looked back at Danny.

Danny glanced over to the other two priests. He and the priests all nodded. Melanie tried hard not to laugh at the triple bobble-heads.

"Can one of you go get him, please?" Fletcher asked. His suspicions were running high. He wanted to talk to this priest, who for some reason was at this church.

"Frankie," Fletcher moved over to him.

"Hold that thought," Frankie said to Danny. "Everyone stay right here." He and Fletcher slowly walked aside.

"What's up?"

"Maybe they weren't abducted," Fletcher said in a whisper.

Frankie saw Melanie was nodding her head.

A questioning look came to his face. Fletcher knew to continue.

"Well, if there was no scene made and no apparent struggle—in broad daylight, on a sunny summer afternoon, with people coming and going, and cars, too—maybe they weren't abducted at all."

"You trying to say two thirteen-year-old boys, twin boys, ran away from home?"

Fletcher smiled.

"No, not that. But did we ever consider that they went with someone willingly?"

Chapter 125 ~

AFTER A COUPLE OF MOMENTS, Father Brandon appeared through the large church doors, strolling down to them. Melanie noticed the pompous air in his stride down the steps. It soon disappeared when he saw Frankie's scowl.

"Hello, again, Mr. Saxtan," he said pleasantly. At the same time, he nodded to Melanie in recognition. Frankie motioned to Fletcher that it was Fletcher's show.

"Um, Father Brandon," Fletcher began with his hand on his chin, "may I ask why you are here at this church today?"

There was a short pause.

Fletcher and Melanie saw him glance at Danny and then quickly back at them. Fletcher turned towards Danny, as did Frankie now.

Danny looked down.

Fletcher quickly turned back to the Father and waited.

The Father shook his head slightly. Then he looked like he was thinking something through.

"I help with confessions here, at times, as it is of my same order," he finally said.

"You mean to say that we had talked to you before about these passages, you seemed not to care at all, and then all of a sudden, you appear at this church the day of another kidnapping of children? And, look around."

Frankie looked at Fletcher with surprise at his hard pressing. He liked the pressure he was applying.

Again there was a quick glance from the priest to Danny

and gone again.

"Mr. Saxtan, that is correct, but are you saying I have something to do with these heinous crimes?" He slowly folded his arms across his chest as he raised his chin in apparent defiance.

Melanie almost laughed at the word "heinous" and the pompous manner he said it.

"Um, maybe, yes, in some way, yes I do," Fletcher didn't hesitate to reply. He knew he had at least something to do with children possibly being sold into slavery, continuing the ancient practice, or knowing that it existed.

"Fletch!" Frankie whispered firmly.

"That's okay," the Father interjected. "I can see his point, but I promise you that I know nothing about these crimes, nothing at all." The Father smiled a smile that actually scared Melanie.

Fletcher stared at him. Feeling the priest was hiding something, his mind raced that maybe they were chasing the wrong people. Maybe Eddy was innocent, weird but innocent. And a bit egotistical, he sarcastically thought. But, maybe after all, he was right about Brandon.

And this priest rubs him the wrong way. He vowed to find his connection, especially after all the many years it took to discover that a few priests commonly molested children and who knows what else.

"Fletcher?" Melanie posed.

"Okay, Padre," he said, mimicking Frankie, "you don't go anywhere anytime soon. I'll be back, either here or at your church."

"That would be fine," the Father replied, with a thin grin. He turned and walked back up the steps, about to disappear into the church.

The arrogant grin got under Fletcher's skin. He just stared at him in disbelief as he went up. Frankie broke his stare.

"Um, Father?" called out Frankie.

"Yes, Mr. Oswald?" he stopped at the very top, turning. Fletcher got the image of God looking down.

"May I see your ring, if you will," Frankie said in more of a command than a question.

Melanie felt a chill when she saw the recognition appear on the priest's face. It then disappeared just as fast. He stood still for a moment.

"Sure," he replied, not moving.

Fletcher looked at Frankie, seeing no emotion at all.

"Down here, Father," Frankie again commanded.

The priest still didn't move. Then he started taking slow steps down. It seemed forever. Melanie watched the confrontation grow.

When he got to Frankie, Fletcher watched him step right up to Frankie, face-to-face, like two boxers in a ring, right before the fight begins.

Frankie waited and finally, eye-to-eye, the priest lifted his hand to Frankie's face.

"FHC?" Frankie posed to him. "You have 'FHC' on your ring, correct Father?"

"Yes, why? Is that a crime, Officer?" His arrogance made Melanie want to just walk over and slap him hard across his confident face.

"I think you know something," Frankie shot off.

"Mr. Oswald, this is part of my order."

"Order? What order?"

"As well as being a member of the Franciscans, I am also

one of a select few who also belong to the Vatican Order of Faith, Hope, and Charity." He said it so matter-of-fact that anyone else would have shrugged it off. Fletcher saw how good this priest was and it only increased his suspicions dramatically. "Seriously?" he thought.

Frankie just gave him a look of contemptible disbelief.

"Mr. Oswald, it is *our* sacred *tenets*, our way."

Frankie deliberately held his glare. He knew the man knew his thoughts. At the same time, he didn't know what to say. His Catholic upbringing flooded back to him. He felt like a child, suddenly, in front of this priest. He tried to control the mounting anger.

"Order of Faith, Hope, Charity?" Fletcher snidely interjected, echoing Frankie's bristling mistrust. It seemed much too common a phrase to him to be just a "*select few*."

"Yes, Mr. Saxtan," Father Brandon replied, never taking his gaze off Frankie. Fletcher pulled Frankie aside. Frankie's head turned but his gaze never left the priest.

"Good catch but we have nothing. We both know there's something very wrong with this whole charade, and with him, but we can't charge him with anything, yet. He's arrogant as balls and real slick, even prepared. We need to get more info on this 'FHC' that keeps popping up. I suggest we leave and we continue with Eddy's group. I'm sure we'll find a connection, somehow, somewhere."

Frankie was still staring at the priest, who remained fixed on him, too.

"Frankie?" Melanie posed, which broke off his stare.

"Yeah, yeah, you're right Fletch," he said as he turned back to the priest.

"Listen, Mr. Brandon, I don't like you, I don't trust you,

and I will find out what you're up to. And if it has anything to do with children, in any way, I will have your ass hanging from that cross up there."

The priest's face distorted for a quick moment and then became serene again. His eyes glared through his small, round glasses.

"It's 'Father,' Mr. Oswald."

"It's whatever I want it to be. Got it?"

The priest looked at him and then at Fletcher and Melanie. He knew it was fruitless to continue. He just turned and walked back up the steps.

"Remember what I said. Don't leave town or I'll have the Feds—"

The priest raised his hand, as he kept his back to Frankie. He disappeared into the church. The large doors slammed shut.

"Fuck 'em," was all that came out of Frankie's mouth. He wanted now just to get these boys back. He went back to the detectives.

"Something's up," Fletcher whispered to Melanie.

"I don't know," she replied, still looking at the closed church doors. "Definitely weird, though."

"Something's fucking up," he fumed and walked away.

Chapter 126 ~

AFTER PUTTING OUT AN "All-Points Bulletin" and the immediate combing of all neighborhoods, Frankie felt exhausted. He was so fed up with cocky people, from Eddy to this priest. He did his best to keep his feelings for the kids as far back as possible. He knew it would only cloud his intuitive police mind. He really just wanted to hide somewhere and let it all out: all the frustration, all the fear, all the pain, and all the tears.

The crime scene investigators arrived. Frankie spent a moment with them. He realized Fletcher's point about kids going willingly was a possibility that they just hadn't taken into consideration. Posing it to the investigators, he wondered why children would ever go. And obviously, they would not knowingly go to their deaths. There's gotta be a reason, if this were true. It was the only thing that made sense, a lot of sense.

After they left the scene, they proceeded back to the station to regroup. They were all exhausted. Not just from running around but mostly from the emotional stress. Fletcher was dying for a rum and Coke, but held off until they could talk about everything.

Frankie drove normally. It made Melanie feel a whole lot better. When they arrived, they walked through the yelling reporters and crowd with complete apathy. They made it to his office. They all flopped, slumping on the chairs. No one spoke. The exhaustion level needed to come down with a little quiet thinking and soul searching.

After about ten minutes, Fletcher noticed that Melanie was in deep thought. She had grabbed a pad of paper and was writing.

"Okay, what's up?" he asked in a quiet monotone, as if in a church.

"Have a thought," she replied. She looked up, putting the pad on her lap.

This got Frankie's attention. He and Fletcher waited for her to begin. Anything, at this point, would be great.

"If we feel that the culprits may be Eddy and his crew, and if we think that maybe these kids went somewhere, at least initially on their own volition, maybe it has something to do with 'FHC.' Not sure why Brandon has it though. Maybe he's part of it too or in cahoots, each getting something out of it."

They both just looked at her, digesting the thought for a moment.

"So, what you're saying is that they may be using 'FHC' as a front or something?" Fletcher posed.

"Yes, possibly. We also have two meanings for it. Doesn't that concern you?" she asked.

"But what's the motivation?" Frankie interjected. "Why would they do this? They're just kids."

Fletcher answered.

"I don't know but their assistance obviously didn't help. At this point, anything is worth investigating and following up on, don't you think? And that pompous ass of a priest we need to look closer at."

"Yeah, you're right. Mel?" Frankie asked.

She knew he was asking her what she thought the next move was. She suddenly felt a very warm camaraderie with him. She smiled. So did he back at her.

"Let me think about it. Don't want to scare them away. Then we would be done."

"Fine," Frankie said, "you take the 'FHC' angle, and Fletch, we'll go headstrong into finding these two boys, A-SAP! They can't be far. If we ever needed an Ein-fucking-stein, it's now!"

"Okay, let's get on it. The witnesses need to be first, and anyone who knew these two boys," Fletcher added in agreement.

"Good, let's go!"

"Hold a sec," Fletcher stopped. Frankie waited.

He opened his phone, called information, got the number and keyed it into his phone. Frankie looked at him questioningly.

"I'm gonna call that young reporter and find out what he knows." Melanie now looked at him, skeptically.

"Sometimes reporters are ahead of the police in investigations," he answered her unasked question. Frankie nodded in agreement.

Fletcher gave Melanie a cheek kiss. He told her a uniform would drive her home. They quickly left.

She sat alone in the office in silence. She took a deep breath and looked back at what she had written.

It was the website address. She had circled it about a hundred times.

Something about it troubled her. She just couldn't pinpoint it. She made her decision and knew what she needed to do.

"I'm gonna get you Eddy. I know it's you. Fletcher thinks it's Brandon. Frankie thinks it's still the peds or some combination."

She smiled.

"But I know it's you."

Chapter 127 ~

FLETCHER AND FRANKIE DECIDED the best use of their time was to split up the effort. He assigned Danny to Fletcher. He wanted at least one detective with him to get him through any bureaucracy. Fletcher was ok with this. He was going to ask for Danny anyway to try to find what the connection was with Brandon.

Danny seemed fine with him, too. Fletcher didn't suspect him, but he knew there was something there. Frankie wasn't sure. He knew Fletch wanted to press him a bit, though.

It was getting late so they decided to meet as soon as possible. Fletcher thought the strip joint was the best place. It was secluded, in case there was a leak and someone was trying to keep a trail on them.

He arrived at 7:00 p.m. Danny was already there, in his undercover car. Fletcher thought it was unnecessary, but decided to ignore it.

He pulled into a spot opposite of Danny and got out. Danny saw and waited. Good, Fletcher thought, don't tie us together.

He entered the place. The bouncer glanced up, nodded, and returned to his magazine. Fletcher noticed as he passed that it was a *Hustler*. He peeked and smiled. She was pretty hot.

He went through the next door. He was immediately greeted by a dancer. She only had on a G-string, with a sheer short robe. Her breasts were small and perky, showing right through.

So much for pasties, Fletcher thought, smiling.

"Hi, honey!" she began. She came up close to him.

He fished for a dollar. He showed it to her. She smiled a wishful smile, opening her robe. She posed, with one leg forward. Her nipples stood firm. Her skin shimmered with the red rotating lights. He could smell a tinge of sweaty musk. There was only one place to put it, he thought. Looking down at her, he felt his bulge

start.

Okay, he thought, you just earned this.

He stepped up close. With the folded dollar, he pulled her G-string back, looking down into it. Her pubic hair was sculptured in a tiny heart shape. His crotch now was extremely tight and getting tighter.

She leaned up to him. He slipped it in with the back of his hand rubbing against the hair. He loved these places.

"Mmmm, baby, don't take it out," she moaned, smiling up at him.

He grinned and then noticed a big thing next to him.

He turned to see, his hand still in her crotch.

"Oh, hi, Danny," he said grinning more.

Danny's look was one of shock. His face went straight with no smile.

For a second, Fletcher thought Danny might arrest him. Or at least that's the feeling he got.

"Yo, Danny, um, meet..." he said as he leaned towards her, since he didn't know her name.

"Sky," she said with a cute smile. Fletcher's hand was still down her crotch.

"Hi," Danny answered. He walked past them. He stood inside, obviously waiting for Fletcher to finish.

"Looks like I gotta go," Fletcher said, after watching him go in.

"Do you?" she pleaded.

"Yeah, maybe later?" he said up close to her. He slowly pulled his hand out, leaving the money.

"Sure thing," she said, smiling. She bounced away.

He went in to see what was up with Danny. He had thought he was happy about going there. But one never knows how certain men act in a strip joint, especially with Maurice's girls.

Chapter 128 ~

MELANIE WENT HOME AND FLOPPED on her couch. She was exhausted. But not enough to stop thinking about Eddy. She took a deep breath, letting it out slowly. After doing that for long moments, she got up and took out a bottle of Riesling. In a tall wine glass, she poured the wine right to the rim. She took a long, slow sip, letting it hang in her mouth and then drank it.

"Mmmm ... love this wine," she said to herself as she went back to the couch.

She grabbed the stereo remote, clicking on the CD player. The room immediately filled with classical music. She kept it at a nice low but full volume. Need to hear the bass, but not kill the ears, was her motto.

She kicked off her shoes and slowly got undressed. After a minute or two, she was sitting with her wine glass and just panties on.

She stretched out, reviewing herself. Her breasts were still standing tall and pouting, which every man she ever had always loved. She ran her fingers down over one, down her tummy, and then over her panties.

Sensations immediately filled her. She took a sip of wine and then another and then put the glass down on the end table.

She got up, found a pack of matches, and went around the room lighting her candles. Some were tea lights and others were full-length tapers.

She then turned off all the lights. She was ready to unwind.

"There!" she whispered to herself, as she slowly got back on the couch.

She looked around a bit. The glowing candles made the best shadows, moving with the music; it was dreamy.

She took another two sips of wine and sighed deeply. She was relaxed now. She felt all her muscles start to loosen. She closed her eyes and dreamed of floating on air. To release the day and clear her mind, she knew she needed to let go, both physically and

mentally.

She had to be ready to analyze this kid. There was no way she'd be able to with any stress or thoughts of the chaotic day she had just spent. A day full of screaming sirens, running from one place to another, and almost being killed each time. And forget the craziness of the constant press and public attention.

She started humming to the music. She looked down at herself again. She was in great shape and liked what she saw.

For some reason, the female body always turned her on. She had even made love to women at times. She kept it as an option for herself. Somehow, the feeling of another girl up against her just drove her crazy. It was different than the feeling of a man, which was her preference. But there was a special feeling when making same-sex love. She knew this was true with guys, too. Such a big deal made about something so precious and good for both sexes, she always thought.

She felt the growing feeling between her thighs. When she again touched and cupped her breasts, the feeling ran quickly and violently down her legs.

She took a very deep breath, letting her fingers run up and down over her breasts, and up and down her tummy, each time just brushing her tiny hump and panties.

Her waist started to writhe. She spread her legs a little

more and then let her fingers find their way over her panties and down over her hidden lips.

A small moan escaped from her mouth. She pressed lightly against her wet lips under the small panties. She moaned again, bringing her fingers back up to her tummy. And then both hands went to her breasts.

She heard her own breathing deepen and quicken each time she found that spot. Then it was becoming too much. She quickly pulled off her panties and laid there naked, feeling the moistness on her thighs as she lightly squeezed her legs.

Her fingers spread her lips, feeling her full wetness. It was a lot already and surprised her. She knew a release was almost there and decided to go for it.

She began to caress her lips, each time slipping her finger through them into herself and then back up to her clitoris and then back in, and then back, and then back in. With her other hand she caressed her breasts and body. When it found her upper thighs, the blissful sensations flowed so strong through her that her finger stayed on her clitoris. She couldn't stop herself.

She brought her finger up to her mouth and tasted herself. That made the ecstasy grow even greater. She kept tasting and tasting herself, each time. Then with her open palm, she cupped herself. Her whole palm was soaked. She brought it to her mouth and licked it, like licking a pussy. The wetness and taste drove her crazy.

She did it again and found no loss of wetness. She rammed three fingers into herself and then palmed it again. It was beginning. She moaned wildly, arching her back.

With a titanic flow of pleasure right through her, her waist lifted even higher and held and held and held, and then the enormous blinding climax ripped through her whole body. She screamed and panted and screamed again.

She couldn't believe how long it was going. Her waist lifted again and she screamed louder, and then with a final deep moan that felt like it went down to her deepest soul, her body collapsed. She closed her eyes as every part of her body tingled wildly away with the pleasure that slowly subsided into short spasms. She was panting uncontrollably. Her breath finally slowed and she was able to return to almost normal breathing. Almost.

She couldn't move, and didn't want to, as the whole day simply disappeared. She smiled. It worked.

She started to think about what she looked like slumped on the couch. Her head was bent forward from being down so low. She had slipped off the couch a little. Her legs were still spread eagle. She was pretty much horizontal to the floor, dripping wet.

The image started to make her giggle. Within a moment, she was just plain laughing. With that, she unintentionally slipped right off the couch and onto the floor.

She paused from the thump but that couldn't stop the laughter.

After another couple of minutes, she calmed down and curled up. She took a deep breath and got up to get her wine.

She finished it and went back to the kitchen, still naked.

After pouring another glass and taking a sip, she stood leaning against the kitchen counter.

She took another deep breath, letting it out slowly.

"Okay, Eddy, it's time for you," she whispered. Still naked, she went upstairs to her office.

She put her glass down and typed in the website address.

After a moment, the animated logo "FHC" came up.

She smiled and cocked her head, speaking to the logo. "Let's rock 'n roll."

Chapter 129 ~

FLETCHER WENT PAST DANNY. He didn't bother to motion him to follow. Danny had just been standing there, by himself. Fletcher figured he wouldn't want to continue just standing there. He went to his normal spot at the bar. He saw his girl up dancing again. She was the same one when he and Frankie had been there.

She recognized him, smiling widely. He nodded back and sat down. Danny soon sat next to him.

"What'll ya have?" Fletcher asked.

Danny hesitated.

"It's okay, it's late, and aren't you off duty?"

"Um, yeah, but here? In this place?" Danny answered with apprehension in his voice.

Fletcher made a discerning look. He couldn't decide what that meant. He had figured that Danny was the rough and ready type, like a Marine, and could handle anything. So, what was all this shit?

"Yeah, here, it's a little getaway we go to, Frankie and I, to escape and hide, especially from anyone who might be trying to locate us or follow us."

"I see," Danny replied, but not with much enthusiasm.

Fletcher thought this would have been the perfect place for this guy. Apparently, he was wrong. Danny was acting like a little high school boy. He appeared as if he was just caught with his father's Playboy or something. Then he noticed the tiny gold pin on the lapel of his jacket.

"Danny, check out..." he turned so Danny wouldn't notice he saw it. He was pointing and nodding towards the girl dancing. She was inching over to them. For the life of him, he couldn't remember her name.

Danny looked up at her. She was smiling at him. He then started to look around the place. Fletcher glanced again at his pin. He controlled a gasp.

It was three letters that formed a circle like a high school ring. They were hard to read. But he got it. "CHF" were the letters. The pin had not been there before or he hadn't noticed it.

Danny was still ignoring the girl, who Fletcher would have jumped right then and there. Oh, boy, Fletcher thought, this guy's a really cool dude. Oh, well, not gonna ruin my time.

"Rum and Coke, please," he said to the bartender, who had just arrived and was waiting.

"Water, please," Danny said.

The bartender gave him a questioning look. Danny looked over at Fletcher.

"You better order something with alcohol or something that at least costs something," he loudly whispered over the pounding music.

"Oh. Well, um, I'll have a beer, light, thanks."

"Good, now after I take care of what's-her-name, we can talk," Fletcher said. He motioned to the dancer. She started kneeling spread-eagle in front of him, bending backwards at the same time.

Danny watched and looked down. He played with his beer bottle.

Fletcher pulled out a one and a five and held them in his hand.

She noticed and leaned forward. He placed the one between her big breasts. She cupped them together, capturing it.

Fletcher didn't let go. She then opened up again. He moved the back of his hand from one breast to the other, and then back to the middle where she again captured it. She pulled back smiling.

"Not bad," he said, nudging Danny lightly. He almost jumped. Fletcher figured he was somehow getting to this guy, like with Frankie.

He decided not to continue. With Melanie now, and trying to resolve Rosalyn's advances and his want of her, he really didn't want to go too much further with more girls. He had to try to keep himself sane.

"Wanna get a table?" he asked him politely.

"Yeah, that would be good, thanks," Danny said with a weak smile.

Maybe he's married and this is not his thing, Fletcher thought. Anyway, he really didn't care. He got up. They looked for a table.

They found one in the corner. Danny seemed much more relaxed.

"So, Danny, what are your thoughts on all of this?" Fletcher said as he downed his rum and Coke. He motioned to a waitress, who came over with almost nothing on. He slipped the five down the back of her G-string thong, putting it right into her crack. She wiggled a little and kissed him on the cheek. She whisked away to get him another drink.

"It's really not my kind of place," Danny answered, "but okay if you like it."

Fletcher laughed. Danny looked at him quizzically.

"I meant the crimes we're investigating," Fletcher said. He smiled.

"Oh, sorry, sorry about that," Danny replied. He cautiously sipped his beer.

Fletcher lightly shook his head. He made a mental note to ask Frankie about this detective. He could appear ready to kill somebody and then another time act like a little boy. In fact, he decided to ask Frankie now. But before he got up to call him, he had to ask.

"Um, Danny, I happened to notice your gold lapel pin. Very nice! What does it mean? I mean, does that say 'CHF?'"

"Oh, yes, it does. Thanks!"

Fletcher waited with a look that asked him to continue.

"Oh, it means Courage, Honor, Friendship. It's a great discussion group I belong to, that's all. We exchange social ideas and comments."

Fletcher nodded. He let it go, which appeared fine with Danny. Fletcher noticed that he seemed to get a little antsy at the questioning. He remembered where he had seen this before, too. He couldn't wait to tell Melanie.

"By the way," Fletcher continued, "do you know Father Brandon?" He went right for the jugular. He smiled inside.

"Um, Father Brandon? Um, yes, I do."

"So, what's your relationship with—"

"It's kind of private, though..." Danny trailed off, looking away.

Fletcher could see he wasn't going to get much from this. He pushed one more time.

"Do you confess to him or something?" he decided to press.

"I'm honestly uncomfortable with this, okay? I will tell you one thing ... and that is ... he's my uncle ... I mean my mom's older brother," Danny stuttered a little.

Fletcher nodded. He knew to stop. He knew that could be true about the uncle thing, since Danny's name would not be the same, being on his mother's side. Easy to check, too.

But he did know the Father was up to something. He was directly related to a young, seemingly impressionable cop. Brandon had quickly brushed them off when asked about the passages. However, he seemed very familiar with them. He was around too much for Fletcher's liking. He was with Danny in a church at the same time of a committed crime. He had on a ring with "FHC" on it. Danny was wearing a pin with "CHF" on it!

It was all too much to be coincidence. All he could think of was that Danny has his hand in too many places. With that pin and being his nephew, he must know that this priest is involved somehow. He was probably protecting him. Or worse, he was feeding him information, being a detective.

His mind began to hurt.

One thing was for sure. The priest *was* involved in something. He was convinced of that. He just needed to connect him with evidence. And Danny may just have that pin because he wants to be part of something good. He may actually believe in it.

Why would he wear it publicly? Unless he didn't know what Fletcher knew. There was no evidence either way. He may still be completely innocent. But that cocky priest *wasn't* innocent. Slavery crept back into his mind.

"Will you excuse me for a sec?"

"Sure thing, I'll be right here."

"I'll be right back."

He got up. He decided to pee first. When he was finished, he stepped outside to quickly call Frankie.

He was also glad to get the smell of that urine-ridden thing they called a bathroom away from him.

Chapter 130 ~

"YO, FRANKIE!" HE BEGAN INTO HIS CELL. He was trying not to yell into it as cars and trucks passed by.

"Hey, Fletch, how's it goin'?"

He seemed upbeat to Fletcher. It sounded good after everything his friend had gone through in the last days and weeks.

"Your guy, Danny—"

"Yeah, Danny, good man."

"Yeah, well, maybe a good cop, but I don't know if I should have come here."

"Now why would you say—wait, are you at Maurice's?"

"Bada BING!"

"Well, he's a little like, not that way I think."

Fletcher lightly hit his forehead with his palm.

"Oh, now I understand. Why didn't you tell me he's not into girls? Didn't want to embarrass anyone. I feel bad, now."

"Um, first you didn't ask. Second, I would not have thought you would have taken anyone to Maurice's, though I wish I were there."

Frankie broke into little chuckles.

"Okay, well, I'm glad I called."

"Don't worry about it. And Fletch?"

"Yo."

"It's not widely known he's gay. Ya know, with the other detectives. He's really shy behind that hard exterior. He had told me in confidence."

"No problem."

"Gotta go," Frankie said. "Let me know what you guys work out."

Before he went back in, a thought came to him. He pulled out his phone again, searched for the number, and called it.

"Hello? Josh Stein, *Times* here."

"Stein, Fletcher Saxtan, you got a moment?"

There was silence for a moment on the other end.

"Yes, Mr. Saxtan, I have a moment," Josh replied, holding back his excitement. He couldn't believe how things just kept falling into his lap.

"Need to talk. Would like to discuss what you had mentioned the other day to me at the Parkers', if you will."

Josh waited. He swallowed the remark he wanted to make, after he had been completely blown off. But he knew this was too unbelievable of an opportunity. Saxtan was just the man he wanted to talk to.

"Sure thing, anytime—"

"Thanks. Gotta go; I'll call you very soon."

"I'll be here."

Fletcher closed the phone. He thought for a moment about it all and decided it was still a good move. They needed anything and everything they could get. The heat was rising very, very fast. He went back in.

Danny was still at the table playing with his beer.

Fletcher sat down, taking a sip of his new rum and Coke.

"Okay, let's get down to business, detective."

That business-y type of talk went well with Danny. He turned, looking ready to go at it. Fletcher smiled inside.

"We need to talk A-SAP to the witnesses that were anywhere near that church and/or inside it. I'd also like to talk with those two priests and anyone else in that place where they live. And if there's a nun place, whatever you call that, too, let's see if they know anything."

Danny was nodding, writing.

"Talk with everyone. Get some additional detectives from Frankie. You're the lead. And can you please ask your uncle again if he had seen anything at all. I want a statement from him," Fletcher pressed.

Danny looked up at him. Fletcher thought he saw fear for a split second. After lightly nodding, Danny looked back down. He seemed a little embarrassed. Fletcher just continued.

"Also, we need to not just ask what they may or may not have seen or heard, but also if they knew the victims and what their relationship was with them. And any kind of relationship. Got that?"

"Yeah, yes, got it!"

"Good, now let me know your thoughts on all of this or what you know," Fletcher said. The detective didn't respond.

Danny looked up from his writing. For a short moment, Fletcher saw a tinge of what he thought was fear again.

Chapter 131 ~

MELANIE JUST SAT FOR A MOMENT. She let the initial page of the website sink in. To her, anyone who spent this amount of time and effort on a website planned every detail for a reason. For someone like Eddy, that means something. She knew the best approach to find out why would be to go very slowly.

"'FHC,' Fellowship of Hope and Change" she whispered repeatedly.

She sighed and clicked on the center to enter. She noticed there was no warning about age or content.

She was already familiar with the layout from seeing it before. This time, she took her time, looking rather than navigating.

She got to the sign-up section. It read:

JOIN NOW!! HELP CHANGE YOUR WORLD!! EARN CASH AT THE SAME TIME!!

She noticed that it said "your," not "the" world. Interesting, she thought. Nice touch to make it personal to teens.

The money part didn't really surprise her. Most young kids could use cash. What better way than to change your personal world at the same time. They were probably rebelling against their parents anyway. Now you can get money doing it. Another great touch, she mused.

"Well, here goes," she said with a deep breath.

She clicked on it. Immediately another page loaded. It

started by stating that all information remains confidential. Your e-mail and mailing addresses were only used to send "Your Free Literature and Notifications of Events!"

She started filling out the membership form. Name, address, e-mail, cell...

She stopped there. She noticed it didn't ask for a home number. She continued.

Age ... she stopped again.

She saw it didn't ask her exact age, only a range.

☑ – 9

10 – 14

15 – 20

21 – 30

31 – 40

41 – 50

51 – over

She saw immediately the age group 10 – 14.

"Well, my boy, that's an MO if I ever saw one!" she whispered to herself.

She clicked on the radial button next to it. She also leaned over, turning on her printer. Gotta print all of this, too, she reminded herself.

Other information wasn't required, but was optional, like Special Interests, Political Party or Affiliation, Willing to Travel, Willing to Hold Meetings in Your Area, etc.

She filled out things as if she was a teenager.

Then another thing caught her attention. At the bottom, it asked about family information. It was required. She had a thought.

She went up and clicked the age group 21–30. She then scrolled back down and smiled. The family information wasn't required anymore. She tested each age group. Only the 10–14 group forced the family information. For all other age groups, it was optional.

"Interesting," she said.

She re-clicked 10–14 and then went down to the family information.

Parent's Name.

Family Status (Poor, Middle, Rich were the choices).

Names of Brothers.

Names of Sisters.

Age of Brothers.

Age of Sisters.

"Poor, Middle, Rich?" she repeated. "Yes, of course, a young teenager would know those phrasings rather than actual income."

She looked back again.

"Names and Ages?" she whispered as if she found gold.

She sat back and took a deep breath.

"Now, my Eddy dear, why would you want that information ... *except...*"

Chapter 132 ~

SHE FILLED OUT FALSE INFORMATION about herself and her fake family. She had a brother and a sister. She was Rich. She then clicked on Submit For Approval and Acceptance. She sat back. It quickly processed and returned with a big centered popup, which read:

"CONGRATULATIONS, YOU HAVE BEEN ACCEPTED! YOU WILL SOON RECEIVE INFORMATION TO HELP YOU GET STARTED AND MAKE LOTS OF MONEY!"

That was it. Nothing more. Just a note about acceptance.

She leaned forward, looking around for something to click on. The only thing was a "close" X. She did that. The website returned to its home page and the "FHC" logo again.

"Well, well," she hummed. "All very interesting."

She wondered why it didn't proceed to have her do anything else. She clicked around more. It was all the same she had seen before.

She sat back again, sighing.

Maybe she was wrong about this. Maybe it was just an innocent site that actually had a noble purpose. Maybe Eddy was just a freak kid who actually wanted to help change the world. Maybe it was some kind of pyramid scheme to make money for the members. It would then accelerate the volume of money up to Eddy.

She sighed again, sipping her wine.

Chapter 133 ~

DANNY SEEMED TO STOP AND THINK for a moment. Anything that Fletcher had thought he saw was gone. He wondered if it really was ever there. Maybe he was just nervous about naked women too close to him. He felt bad for taking him there.

"Any thoughts about this case?" Fletcher repeated.

"Yes, I do have some, in fact," Danny definitively replied.

"Okay, shoot."

Fletcher sat back a little and slowly sipped his drink.

"Well, first of all, it's all pretty sick if you ask me."

Fletcher just nodded.

"And I'm very concerned about the missing kids. And now another one and no leads at all. None at all."

Fletcher believed him for some reason, confirming more that he was just an innocent and not involved with Brandon.

"Why do you think there are no leads or contact?"

"I don't know. Maybe it's a sexual thing. Maybe. God forbid they're being molested even as we speak. Then there would be no contact because there's no reason. They have what they want."

"Interesting thought," Fletcher added, though he knew that was already one of the theories with Merrie and his type.

"And I think," Danny continued, "that we're not doing enough."

"What do you mean?" Fletcher asked, now leaning forward a little.

"Well, you got these missing kids and their scared-to-death parents, and it just seems like we're constantly helpless."

"Well, so far we are. This maniac is really good. No trail, no leads, no clues. Just the passages left."

"Yeah, those things!"

Fletcher noted his disgust.

"Yeah, those things," he repeated Danny.

"Well, I think that the rich sometimes deserve things."

Fletcher paused.

Why the hell would he say that, he quickly thought. He unknowingly cocked his head, leaning forward more.

"Well, yes, the rich seem to be targeted. But do you think they deserve *this*? And children?"

"Well, no, I don't think anyone deserves this. But I do think the rich sometimes bring this stuff on themselves."

Right then for a moment, Fletcher thought of Eddy and his website.

"Maybe. Maybe they do and don't even know it," he played along.

"Yeah, yeah, I agree. I know people who agree, too."

"I'm sure you do." He wondered about the "CHF" discussion groups.

Fletcher took a breath, making a mental note to follow up with Frankie again on this guy, and anything on those groups.

He took another sip of his drink and felt his cell buzz. He looked down at the caller ID and breathed a sigh of relief. It wasn't Rosalyn.

"Excuse me a sec."

"Yep," Danny replied. He looked on blankly.

"Hey, Frankie, what's up?"

He listened a second and then started shaking his head.

"No! No way!" he exclaimed.

That caught Danny's attention.

"We're moving. We'll meet you there!"

Danny instinctively pushed back his chair.

"Let's go," Fletcher said, downing his drink. He tossed a five for a tip.

He glanced at the naked girl on the dance stage. He was sorry he couldn't stay.

Danny was up and ready.

"Follow me," Fletcher said, turned, and left.

Danny was right on his heels.

Chapter 134 ~

FLETCHER PEELED OUT OF THE parking lot with Danny right behind him. He had forgotten to tell Danny where they were going and why. He was about to call Frankie to get Danny's cell or hook him up through the police radio, but instead found himself dialing Melanie's home number.

He pressed the accelerator and noticed in his rearview mirror that Danny kept up with him.

"C'mon man, put it on!" he whispered firmly.

Finally, Danny put on his siren, attaching his light on the roof.

"Good."

Fletcher didn't want to be stopped by a cop at this point. He also wanted to get there before the crime unit showed up at the scene.

"Hey!" he heard on the line.

"Hey, babe, how's it going?" he started with.

"Got stuff for you and Frankie from little Eddy's site."

"I got stuff, too," he interrupted her.

She was silent on the other side waiting.

"They found a boy."

"Oh, my! No," she whispered.

"Yeah, I know."

"Is he?"

"Yes."

"Oh, my!"

"Yeah."

"Where you at?"

Her voice sounded concerned.

"I'm on my way there. Frankie's there and asked me to come."

"Where, can I ask?"

"Yeah, they found him in an alley downtown, ya know, one of those small side streets. It's Chancellor, right in the middle of it, right in the middle. Change in MO this time. Someone almost ran him over. It's all cordoned off now."

She heard a little distress in his voice.

"You okay?"

"Yeah, I guess. Really not in the mood for this again."

"I know. Want me there?"

"No. I think I know what I'll find. It's more important you think about that site and if this smart kid is really involved."

"Well, I did. It's like everything else, may be and may not be. But there's enough to follow up. I'm hoping for some clues from it."

"Oh, good, hold that thought. I'll come by afterwards, okay?"

Again, the sound of concern.

"Yeah, sure. Be careful, okay?"

"I will be. And Frankie's there. I hope no one else is so I can view it all pristine. There's gotta be something this time. Shit's going to hit the fan so bad ... so bad. We gotta get this psycho now."

"I know. Tell Frankie I'm thinking about him."

"Thanks, babe. Do whatever you can. Think everything you can. I'll be over. We'll find a way."

"I know. Love you."

Fletcher paused at that. Then he continued.

"Love you, too."

He hung up and pressed the accelerator.

Chapter 135 ~

MELANIE HUNG UP THE PHONE. She sat back in her chair at the computer. She stared at the screen and the logo for a long time.

She got up to make a drink. She found vodka, pouring it halfway into a tall glass of ice. Then she found iced tea and topped it off. She took a long sip.

She took it back to her computer. First, she went to a news site. The top story was their case. It covered the whole page. A picture of Frankie talking with detectives was the main photo. The headline right on the picture said:

"Philadelphia Innocence Murdered Crime Spree Out of Control."

She almost clicked on it but already knew what it would say. She wished it would just all be over. Then she could wake up from this dream and no children were hurt or missing. She felt her insides turning again. She held back the growing tears.

She sighed. She took two long drinks and went to check her mail.

To her surprise, there was an e-mail titled "Our Family." It was from "FHC."

She stared at it. Her heart started beating fast.

Taking a deep breath and another sip, she double-clicked on it. It opened up before her.

She read it slowly and carefully.

It first was a thank you for becoming a member. It also

reiterated back her information, asking to make sure it was correct.

There was a link to confirm.

She clicked on the link. It took her back to the site. It was a page for confirmation of information.

There was a button to click and confirm. She clicked it.

It then asked for a reconfirmation.

She did so.

It then went back to the home page and the logo.

"Damned pain-in-the-ass logo. FHC! FHC! Pissing me off now!" she muttered. She took a long drink. She almost slammed down the glass.

Closing the window, she went back to her mail.

Again, she stared at the screen.

Another e-mail from the site had appeared.

"Now that was fast," she whispered.

The subject line said: New Member Opportunity!

Her heart was now pounding. She shifted in her chair.

Clicking on it, it opened with a stunning animation of the logo again with a smiling play face.

The whole message was in color. There were fancy borders. The background had faces of people. It looked almost like a stadium full of fans. Most appeared to be teens.

There were boxes of text following. She didn't read them yet. She wanted to take in the whole effect. It was an elaborate display for an e-mail. It was extremely attractive.

"Man, Eddy, you do mean business, don't you?"

She ran her mouse over all the animations, colors, and pictures. Nothing was an embedded link.

"Nothing here to go anywhere," she whispered.

She sat back for a moment. She looked up at the ceiling. An

idea started to go through her head.

"What if..." she started to say. She then decided to hold that thought for a moment.

She was dying to read the text but wanted to be in the right frame of mind. She stood and stretched. She needed to get into character. She had to step away for a moment.

Melanie walked around the room. She came back. She took a sip of her drink and set it down. She walked around one more time, stopping in the corner of the room.

She bowed her head and closed her eyes. She blocked all thoughts from her mind except the images she had as a young girl.

School.

Friends.

Homework.

Mom yelling.

Teachers.

Boyfriends.

Getting in trouble.

Parties.

She kept up the images until she was feeling it all back again, as if it were today, this moment.

She walked slowly back to the desk. She sat down. She took a deep breath. Closing her eyes one more time, she saw all her friends with her. They were all laughing and joking around.

She then opened her eyes.

She read the text and gasped.

Chapter 136 ~

FLETCHER QUICKLY MADE IT BACK into Center City, continuing down 15th Street and passed City Hall. He turned down Chestnut. He immediately saw the lights from the police cruisers.

"Shit!" he muttered. He pulled up behind one that was parked at the corner of Chestnut and 13th Street. Chancellor was just down the block.

Danny had pulled in behind him, siren still on.

Fletcher got out and turned towards Danny, who saw his look and turned off his siren. He suddenly had a quick thought. He flipped his phone open and made the call.

"Stein here. Aw, Fletcher."

He didn't like him calling him by his first name, but he let it go.

"Yeah, just wanted to call you and let you know about—"

"You mean the little boy?"

"Yeah, how'd you—"

"I'm already here," Josh cut him off.

Fletcher didn't like how fast he had found out but didn't have time to ask. He just wanted to talk with him afterwards.

"Hang out after all is said and done, and let's talk," Fletcher said, not giving an option.

"Sure thing and I just wanted to—"

Fletcher hung up on him and then proceeded through the crowd down the short block. He was immediately stopped by an officer.

"Hold it there, bud!"

The officer looked burly, ready for a fight.

"Frankie wants to see me," Fletcher pressed.

"Frankie, eh? And who the hell are you?"

"He's with me," Danny said from behind him, moving forward.

"Oh, okay, sorry detective."

The officer moved and went back guarding his spot.

"Thanks," Fletcher said.

"No problem," Danny replied. He held his arm out for Fletcher to go ahead of him.

He turned the corner and stopped cold. Danny almost ran into his back.

"Aw, shit," was all Fletcher could mutter.

"Man," he heard behind him.

In the middle of the street, the little boy lay naked. It looked as if he was placed there carefully, and not just dropped.

Fletcher could see no movement. He took a deep breath, starting towards the body.

He saw Frankie nearby with another detective. There was a covering, also nearby. He knew that Frankie hadn't covered the body for both Fletcher and the crime investigation unit to have the scene as is.

He walked slowly up. Frankie saw him. The heat of the day was dissipating, but with this scene, Fletcher started sweating profusely.

He looked at the poor little boy and the fact that he was carefully placed in the exact center of the street. It brought back instantaneous images of the naked girl in the middle of that small room, on that lone bed. His heart dropped.

It was obvious to him that the killer or killers were

seriously playing with their minds. It was also obvious that they had no human feelings at all. They couldn't, Fletcher thought, as an unfamiliar rage was being fearlessly ignited in him.

"Hey, Fletch," Frankie softly said, as he came near.

Fletcher had stopped at the foot of the boy and was just staring down.

"Frankie," he quietly acknowledged him.

"Melanie's not—"

"No," he immediately interrupted him.

"Good. Well, it's all yours. A passing driver had almost run him over. This street pretty much has no traffic, so not sure how long he was here. ME and Crime Unit on the way. Be careful."

"Thanks," Fletcher whispered solemnly.

Frankie walked away shaking his head, hoping Fletcher could find some clue or anything. Frankie motioned the other detective to follow.

"Danny, do me a favor," Fletcher asked, "while I'm looking around, can you make sure no one comes into this scene?"

He turned to look at him. Danny was nodding. Fletcher was shocked to see tears coming down his cheeks. He made another mental note. He turned back to the boy in the street.

He took a very long, deep breath.

Chapter 137 ~

SHE TOOK ANOTHER DEEP SIP of her drink and then decided to down it. She reread the text, just to be sure. She was shaking her head unknowingly as she did. She wished she could talk right now with Fletcher about this. But she knew he was engrossed in a more gruesome situation.

She began to read the text out loud.

"Welcome to your new family! We would like to say hi to your brothers and sisters, too! They are also part of the young people of our world who can make a difference and have fun!"

"A very important thing now is for you to meet one of your new family members. They will give you neat stuff and can answer all your questions! We're sure you have some!"

"We like to also meet and speak with your brothers or sisters, so they can also hear and learn and join, too, as you have! We want them to have fun & make lots of money with you."

"So, pick one of them. It's your choice!"

"Because we are a family now, when you and your brother or sister meet our family member, it's our own little secret. Or you won't be able to make any money."

"You can keep a secret now, can't you? And tell them to keep it our little secret. You'll surprise your parents later with all the money you make! They'll be so proud of you!"

"So don't forget to keep this a secret!"

"Great! This will be so much fun together!"

"When can you meet? Just click reply—k?"

That was the end of the text. She assumed the kid would now reply with a time. She also knew if the kid clicked REPLY, they were hooked. Then Eddy and crew could work it out how they wished.

She was still weighing whether it was innocent or criminal. Still no absolute proof or any proof, she thought, remembering Eddy and they were just children. She did assume though that if they *were* involved, they would definitely have escape points all along the way.

Nevertheless, she was still convinced it was them somehow. She just couldn't understand why they would do such things. She also didn't understand why they hadn't turned the site off, as eventually, someone like her would investigate. She also wondered why they had even welcomed them to go see the site. Again, innocent?

Maybe it was just part of the game. Maybe they felt they would know if a sting operation was to occur from some kind of leak, like his father or someone in the department. Lots of balls, she thought, to play such a high-risk game. Of course, it could still be nothing. But when she saw Eddy in her mind, she knew this is exactly what he would do, if he were the one.

She decided not to click REPLY, just yet. She wanted to think it through.

She suddenly had a great idea on how to get to Eddy. She sat back in her chair, thought for a moment, and then pulled out a pad of paper.

She started writing frantically.

Chapter 138 ~

SHE FINISHED HER NOTES. She sat back, thinking it through. After another moment, she looked at the clock. Seeing it was not too late, she picked up her phone. She dialed the number from memory.

"Hello?" she heard on the other side.

"Hi, it's me," she replied.

"Mel! Hey! How are you?"

"I'm fine, Sis, I guess," she replied again.

"Uh, oh. What's the problem," she heard her sister say, with the beginning of alarm in her voice.

"Listen, Dana, I need your help, well, I need both your help and Kelly and Kimberly." She heard her own tentativeness in her voice.

"That's fine, but what's going on?"

She briefly paused. She knew this was the moment she had dreaded a minute before calling.

"Well, I've gotten involved with this guy, a wonderful man. He's a PI and used to be a cop—"

"Are you in any trouble?" Dana interrupted.

"No, no, not me, and not him either. But he's very close with the Philly Chief of Police and is helping—"

"What? With those horrid things happening to children? Oh, honey, you should stay away."

"Dana. Dana! Stop, please, for a moment, okay?"

She heard a pause on the other side. She knew her older

sister well enough to give her a moment.

"Tell me."

Melanie went into everything that had happened since she had met Fletcher. She told her of their fast-growing relationship, too. Dana was glad to hear about that. She finished with the chase and the recent church incident. She left out the fact that the little boy had been found. She didn't feel a need for that just yet, as it wasn't public.

"Mel. That's all insane, you know."

"Yes, but I'm involved. I'm actually helping with the case as an unbiased assistant to Fletcher. It's been approved by the DA, too."

"The DA? Huh."

She knew that kind of surprised her. But she needed her sister to at least accept her role, not just as a mystery writer, but also as a real contributor to solving the case.

And that's where she went next.

She described Eddy's desire to help by using them as insiders. She expressed their concern about it and the possible leak.

She didn't tell her that she believed it most likely was Eddy and his crew. There was still doubt. The possibility still existed it was Father Brandon as Fletcher suspected. And there was no way she could let her sister know Frankie's investigation of peds! She also knew some of her doubt about Eddy came from her own motherly instincts: how could children do something like this?

"Sure, I understand it all. I hope with you and with everyone, you'll solve this terrible thing."

"Yes, believe me, me too. And it's good you're far out there where you live and not being affected by this."

"Absolutely! Just promise you'll be careful."

"But—"

"But what?" Dana interrupted again.

Melanie took a deep breath and began.

Chapter 139 ~

FLETCHER LEANED DOWN TO THE BODY. The child was lying on his side, in the fetal position. The little boy's eyes were closed. There appeared to be no visible marks on his white skin, which shined somehow in the streetlights. He knew what he was looking for, but didn't want to disturb the body. He walked around carefully. At times, laying flat on the ground, he tried to look under the body.

He looked up at Danny. He hadn't moved and was just staring down at what Fletcher was doing. He looked past him and saw the police barriers. The night crowd was starting to pile up heavily behind it.

He spied more, seeing him. Josh was right up against the barrier looking on. He could see sadness in his young face.

He hoped they were far enough away to block any detailed view.

He motioned over to Frankie, who came over.

"Maybe move that barrier back around the corner and block any further view until we can—"

"Yeah, you're right, got it."

Frankie immediately walked away and was on his radio.

Fletcher saw the barriers moved. He felt a little better at what he was doing. Josh was arguing, but they moved him, too. Fletcher thought, I'll get to you soon enough, kid.

He turned back to the young boy. Suddenly, the innocence on his face struck him. He now actually saw a little boy who was alive not long ago. His heart swelled.

"Fletch, baby, get on with it," he whispered to himself.

He kept looking. There was nothing.

He motioned Danny over. Danny saw it but didn't move.

He made a pressing urgent face at him.

All of a sudden, Danny seemed to snap out of his dreamy daze and immediately transformed into Mr. Detective. He came right over.

"Yes," he replied.

"Check this whole area for anything that looks like a Bible passage. And put your gloves on. Give me a pair."

Danny obeyed. He started looking carefully around the street and the sidewalks, everything from trashcans to a gated fence area.

Frankie saw them, put on his gloves, and did the same. He already knew what to look for.

Chapter 140 ~

DANA LISTENED TO MELANIE without interruption. There was dead silence on the other end after Melanie finished. Melanie sat back with the phone held to her ear. She knew her older sister well enough to wait for her.

Finally, Dana spoke.

"You're serious."

"I'm serious. More than you can imagine."

More silence.

"Are you sure you can—"

"Sis, yes, I'll be right there and have immediate access to the police."

She didn't tell her that she wasn't going to inform anyone, at all, but she had not lied. She would have immediate access to the police when she wanted it.

On her notes she was looking at, she had written something in bold letters. She had wildly circled many times:

"DO NOT TELL THE POLICE OR EDDY WILL KNOW!!"

After a pause, she heard her sister's surrendering voice.

"Oh, my, I cannot believe I'm going to let you do this."

"Do you want to think about—"

"No, no. It's okay. I just want to ask them."

"Absolutely, and they need to know. Just try not to be graphic."

"Yeah, sure. I'll call you back."

"Thanks, Sis."

"Yeah, sure."

And she hung up.

Melanie held the phone to her ear for a little and then hung it up.

She went and made another drink. She came back.

She sat still for a while, waiting for the phone to ring.

An hour passed.

Finally, it rang. She almost jumped when it did.

"Hello?"

"Hey, Mel." Fletcher answered.

"Oh, hi, sorry, thought it was someone else."

"Who else?"

She could hear bustling in the background.

"Oh, just my sister, she was calling me back."

"Everything okay?"

"Yea, yeah, you know, sis talk."

"Actually, I don't, but that's fine. Just wanted to let you know I'll be here a bit. Did you still want me to stop over afterwards?"

"Um, actually, I'm a little bleary-eyed from looking at the computer. Can we meet up tomorrow? I think I'm going to go to bed soon."

"I can be of help—"

"Aw, shush!" she interrupted him. She felt a nice warmness at his proposition.

"I'll call you in the morning."

"That would be great! I can then go over what I've found."

"Is it good?"

"Actually, not really. It's just the same old crap we saw before," she calmly lied.

"I see. Let's regroup over coffee?" he offered.

"Yep, that sounds good."

"Bye, babe. Love you."

"Love you, too. Be careful."

"With all these cops around?"

They both hung up. She took a long drink again. It was the first time she had lied to him. Nevertheless, she couldn't afford any leak, at all. She also knew he would either want to stop her or be part of it.

She sighed and continued to wait.

After another fifteen minutes, she unwittingly started to doze off.

When the phone rang, she jumped right out of her chair.

Chapter 141 ~

JOSH KNEW HE JUST HAD to see what they were doing. He quickly ran down Walnut Street. He remembered a little alley that was only a walkway. He crept down it. In all the hurry, he hoped the police wouldn't have thought of it.

He was right and inched his way to the corner. Having his back up against the brick wall, he sidestepped along to where his face was right up at the bend.

"Okay, be careful, dufus," he quietly said to himself.

He took a breath, quickly glanced around the bend, and hid again.

"Good, no cops," he whispered so lightly it was more of a gasp. He felt his knees start to shake a little. He decided a better approach.

He knelt down, crouching further, until he was at knee level. He glanced around the brick bend again. Perfect, he thought. No one would see him. If they looked over, they may miss he was down here.

He had a perfect view of the small street. He was exactly opposite from where the barrier had been.

"Now, what are you three going to do?"

Chapter 142 ~

FLETCHER HUNG UP HIS CELL. He stared at it. She sounded a little weird, he thought. He brushed it off as her being tired and worn out after everything she'd been through. He figured, by now, she probably wanted out of it all.

He turned back to the boy. Then out of the corner of his eye, he saw Frankie coming over to him.

"Hey, Fletch," he said. "You okay?"

"Uh, yeah, yeah," he replied, still looking at the boy.

"It's gotta be here somewhere," Frankie said, as he looked around the street again.

"Yeah, I know. And the problem is that I think I know where it might just be."

He didn't take his stare away from the little boy.

Frankie looked quizzically around. He then followed Fletcher's eyes to the boy.

He grimaced. Fletcher didn't notice. He just stared down at the naked boy.

"No way," Frankie whispered.

"Yeah, way," was all he heard back.

"Fucking Ein-fucking-stein mutherfucker!" spewed out of Frankie's mouth.

"Yeah," was all Frankie heard again.

At that point, they heard rustling near the barriers. Both turned. Carl Gardner and his Crime Unit crew had arrived. They all stopped when they saw the scene. Gardner motioned to them all to wait. He came over to Frankie and Fletcher.

"Gentlemen. Pretty gruesome."

"Yo Carl," Frankie whispered. "Pretty bad."

Fletcher looked up, nodding.

"Find anything? Passages?"

Fletcher and Frankie looked at each other and then at Gardner.

"Carl, it's inside. Look down here."

Gardner leaned down, following Fletcher's pointing.

"Fucking damn," he whispered. He was a small stocky man with a hardened personality. But Fletcher noticed his shock at the sight.

"Carl, we need to see this now. I really would like to just—"

Gardner put his hand up for Fletcher to pause. He rubbed his chin, glancing around. He seemed to be making a decision. Frankie leaned over and whispered something to him. Fletcher just waited with his glove on. Gardner finally nodded. "Together," was all he said.

They both leaned down with Fletcher.

"Well, you ready?" Frankie asked Fletcher softly.

"Yeah."

"Okay, buddy. We'll help."

"Yeah."

They looked at each other. Both shook their heads in disgust.

Fletcher smiled a small smile of bravery. Frankie did the same.

As he was about to proceed, Fletcher had a quick thought.

"Frankie, tell Danny to leave."

"Oh, yeah."

He yelled over to Danny and they waited for him to

disappear. They were now alone with the poor little boy. Josh held his breath, looking on wondering.

"Here goes," Fletcher whispered to himself. He leaned down. Frankie turned the body. Gardner carefully moved the boy's legs.

Chapter 143 ~

"HEY, SIS," DANA CALMLY SAID on the other line. Melanie heard her voice and knew the decision. Melanie was so torn by it. Using her two nieces as bait for these maniacs cut right through her, especially when she would be the only one watching after them. At the same time, in her heart, she knew she had to do something to stop this, stop it now, and get the children back.

If not, her heart would just break. It all flooded back, knowing this time it was her beautiful, young nieces.

She decided to ensure her cell phone was charged. She also had change in case she had to use a public phone, though she knew there were very few around.

She just needed to make sure she could call Fletcher and the police, once she fools them and they trip over her trap.

And she couldn't take the chance that any leak could occur. At this point, she was positive that there was a major leak, either from Eddy's father, the DA, or from somewhere else. But it was there. And maybe Danny was in cahoots with Father Brandon. Catching Brandon in anything would just be an additional treat, she smiled.

She so wanted to tell Fletcher. But he might inadvertently say something that could be used to blow the whole deal, and even worse, cause harm to her family.

She took a deep breath.

"Hey, Sis," she replied.

"Okay, we're a go. They actually think this is exciting. I

can't stop them from feeling like that, without getting into gory details, which may then scare them. I can't believe I'm saying this about my own children!"

"That's fine. They'll be safe and watched the whole time. They just have to play up to whoever meets them, and then, we can immediately call the police—"

"Wait a minute! You mean the police won't be there or following or whatever?!"

She sounded very alarmed.

"Sis, I'm sorry but no. I will have them ready to immediately come to the rescue—"

"Who? Just you? What if they get you, too, or even worse, somehow hurt you and—"

"I can handle myself!"

She was getting a little annoyed at her big sister's protectiveness of her. The kids, fine. Her?

I'm fine, she thought.

"I'm going with you!"

"No, you're not!"

"Yes, I am or the deal's off!"

"Arghh!" was all she could muster.

"Mel, honestly, we're a team and it *is* my girls."

She sounded all of a sudden calmer and it took its effect on Melanie. Plus, her sister being divorced when the girls were very young made her very strong and independent.

"Okay, okay! You're in, but neither you, nor Kim or Kelly, can say anything to anyone. That's soooo important! You must promise."

"Sure, sure. So when do we start?"

"Promise!"

"I promise and so do they. Geez!"

There now was an adventurous tone to her sister's voice. Melanie began to think that maybe this wasn't a good idea, after all. She immediately brushed that aside in her mind.

"Tomorrow."

"*Tomorrow?*"

"Tomorrow. Sunday, yes."

"Fuck."

"Yeah, fuck."

Chapter 144 ~

FRANKIE JUST KNELT THERE IN THE streetlight, watching and shaking his head. He knew this wasn't easy for Fletcher, but it had to be done. He felt for his friend, placing a hand on his shoulder. Fletcher looked over.

"We gotta catch this son-of-a-bitch, ya know," he said with a stern face that Frankie immediately read.

"We will, we will," Frankie softly replied. "Go ahead."

"Saxtan, we will. Now get that out now," Gardner firmly whispered.

Fletcher turned back to the body. With his gloved hand and fingers, he spread the boy's buttocks. Gardner helped as a surgeon would.

"Awww," he muttered.

Frankie turned away. "Do it or I will," Gardner pressed.

He slipped his two fingers around the paper that was showing and pulled it out.

"Fuck!" he whispered.

Frankie turned back and looked at it.

It was wrapped in what looked like plastic wrap. Fletcher motioned Frankie. Frankie knew he meant get an investigation bag. Before he could, Gardner had one out.

He opened it and nodded to Fletcher to do it. Fletcher carefully removed the plastic wrap, placing the plastic wrap into the bag.

He then unfolded the paper, which was obviously from a Bible. He just looked at it. Elijah the Prophet, from Kings, from the Old Testament.

"Go ahead," Frankie said, meaning to read it out loud.

Fletcher looked over at him and then back at it. He started to read it aloud in the dark street.

"After that he put the pieces of wood in order and cut the young bull in pieces and placed it upon the pieces of wood."

"What the hell does that mean?" Frankie asked, after staring at Fletcher for a moment.

"I don't know. I just don't know."

And with that, Fletcher slumped back into a sitting position, in the middle of the street, with Frankie and the streetlights looking down at him. He handed the passage to Gardner.

He felt like crying.

Chapter 145 ~

"WHY TOMORROW?" DANA ASKED.

Melanie knew it had to be tomorrow, to do it while Eddy and his friends were still cocky and feeling invincible. She just knew Eddy wanted to show they could do it again, right under the cops' noses.

Plus, it was Sunday. They'd be out of school, and that would make it even more palatable and attractive. And their e-mail was prompting her now, too.

"Because I want to get to them when they're cocky and also as soon as possible," she replied. She also knew she couldn't tell her about the poor little boy Fletcher was dealing with at that very moment.

"Plus, it's Sunday and easier for kids to be free," she added.

"I see. What do we do next?"

All of a sudden, Melanie was glad Dana was going with her.

"Be ready tomorrow morning. I'll call you."

"Yep, and I should prompt them with what?"

"Um, let me think about that. I think Kelly should play the part of the one who joined their movement and is bringing her sister as instructed. So Kimberly needs to be inquisitive if she can."

Dana laughed.

"What?" Melanie asked with a smile beginning on her face from her sister's laughter.

"Kim will want Kelly's role!"

They both started to laugh. Melanie felt a little better that they were past the shock stage of her proposal.

"Well, I used Kelly's name when I signed up—only her first name. I made the last name Mitchell. But if Kim is better and you think so, then she must answer to Kelly. Know what I mean?"

Dana laughed again.

"Yeah, yeah, I'll handle them. Count on Kelly to be Kelly!"

"Yep, Sis," Melanie answered.

"Fine, I'll talk to you in the morning."

"Oh, and instruct them not to tell anyone nor gossip about it. That could end up being very dangerous. Please press this to them, being young girls. Know what I mean?"

"Oh, yeah, not to worry. I'll handle that part."

"Great, Sis and thanks. I'm sure many thanks from the other kids and their parents, too."

"No problem. It'll be fun."

"Yep, thanks."

They both hung up. Melanie wondered at the "fun" comment, whether it was a defense mechanism or she was really getting a little too adventurous.

Well, she thought, at this point, it didn't matter anymore. She was determined to catch Eddy or prove him out of it. And if not him, then end this whole charade and go right after Father Brandon, or Merrie and his types.

She turned back to the computer and re-opened the e-mail. She read it once more. She took a quick sip of her drink.

She then clicked REPLY.

Chapter 146 ~

FLETCHER TOOK OUT HIS POCKET notebook. He quickly wrote down the passage while Gardner held it for him. They all looked down at the little boy and then at each other.

"Almost ready?" Frankie said.

"Yeah, I really, really need a drink. I'm going to the closest bar."

"Yeah, let's go and review the passage. Carl?" Frankie asked.

"If you've checked the area to your satisfaction, I'm good. We'll take it from here."

"Thanks Carl," Frankie said. "Let me know if you find anything more or anything we missed." Gardner nodded to both of them. He glanced at the little boy again, grimaced, and went to his team.

Frankie moved to Danny, said a couple things, and returned to Fletcher. They walked around the corner. Fletcher saw the barriers still holding back the onlookers. He couldn't see Josh. Everyone staring and pointing at them started to annoy him. After glancing up and down the street, he figured Josh had left to write his story. He thought to call him, but really just wanted a drink.

They continued up the street and approached a small pub.

"This cool with you?" Fletcher asked.

"Yeah, sure—" Frankie's cell rang. He stopped in midsentence to answer it.

"Hello?"

He started to slowly step away as he listened to the caller. "Okay, yes."

More listening.

"Yes, yes, I will. I know! Yes, yes."

More listening. Fletcher was instinctively following him.

"Okay, okay. Yes. Okay. Will be there. Yes, him, too."

Fletcher's ears perked up.

"Yes. I know. Goodbye."

He flipped the phone shut. Fletcher was looking at him, waiting.

Frankie walked away, rolling his eyes. He proceeded to open the door to the bar.

Fletcher started following him. Frankie suddenly stopped at the entrance. He turned back. Fletcher almost walked into him.

"How thick is your skin?" he asked Fletcher.

"What for? Actually, I don't care. I just want a drink and a shot and another drink and a shot. You know, normal stuff after seeing little dead boys lying naked in the middle of city side streets."

The door person looked like he was going to crawl into the corner at Fletcher's tone.

"We're in the DA's office at 9:00 a.m. tomorrow morning."

"Press?" Fletcher asked.

"*Oh, yeah.* It's going to be a skinning. From Mike's inside sources, it's hitting the papers fast. It's not good. This time Stuart has teamed up with the other parents. They will be protesting, big time, tomorrow, right outside Mike's. Press is already setting up there. It's going to be bad, really bad."

Fletcher pushed him through the door, following him in. When inside, Frankie turned to Fletcher.

"Guess maybe the perp's finally getting the fame he wants."

"Well, it's not finally. It's just beginning."

"Yeah, wait till the fame they get after we get *them*."

Fletcher smiled at that, but then his mind went to Father Brandon and Elijah's Wrath.

Chapter 147 ~

THE REPLY E-MAIL OPENED. Melanie took a moment to get her thoughts together. She grabbed her pad again. She wanted to write it first on paper. She then decided just to type it in, being careful not to accidentally click SEND until she reviewed and printed it.

"Okay, Eddy, here I come!" she said, with more determination than she ever felt before. It was her family now. She was not only going to protect them, but also to catch this son-of-a-bitch, red-handed.

She began to type.

hi i can meet u tomorow k i can get my sistr to k? were going to the mall in the morning wanna meet there at springfild Kel ☺

She thought it was perfect. It had just enough misspellings and no caps. In addition, the smiley face was good, too, for a teen.

"Okay, let's first print," she said. She touched the printer button.

After it printed, she took a deep breath.

"Here goes!"

She clicked SEND. It disappeared. She got her "Send Successful" message.

She didn't know what to do next. Should she wait up? Should she go to bed and wait until tomorrow? Maybe set her alarm for later that night?

She decided just to sit a while, drink her drink, and let her mind wander. She still needed a break from it all and knew it. But this wasn't the time.

She slumped in her chair. She closed her eyes. Maybe just a little rest, she thought.

She jumped up when her phone rang. She looked at the clock.

"Oh, my, I fell asleep."

It was Fletcher's cell number on the caller ID. She was about to pick it up when she turned and looked at her computer screen.

"Oh, my," she whispered. "Sorry, Fletcher, babe, you gotta wait!"

She clicked on the new e-mail. She began reading it.

Fletcher's call went to her voice mail. She stopped reading for a moment to listen while he left a message.

"Hey babe, it's me. Didn't want to wake you but I have to go to the DA's office with Frankie first thing in the morning—in fact at nine o'clock. Shit's hitting the fan. I wanted to know if you wanted to come along. We found another passage and your help would be great. Anyway, call my cell when you get this. Love you."

He hung up.

She stared at the phone, thinking how much she wanted to be with him. She definitely wanted to go to the DA's. She really wanted to see the passage. But she knew what she had started had to continue.

She also decided not to call him back. She would pretend, even in the morning, that she never got the message.

She turned back to the screen and resumed reading.

hi kelly! tomorrow is perfect. where at the mall and what time?
your new friends and family, marcy & stacy ☺

"Beautiful!" was all she could say. She noted the returned smiley face, too.

She glanced at the clock. Good, she thought, not too late to write back, especially for young teenage girls. She thought again. She clicked REPLY.

hi marcy & stacy nice to meet u c u we'l be @ the front ☺

She clicked SEND and watched it go. She liked how she didn't make it totally clear, as that's probably how a very young girl would. They will just have to find them.

This time she decided to wait for the reply. She expected it to be soon.

After about ten minutes, it came.

k! cya! ☺ *send a pic so we know k?*

"Fascinating," Melanie whispered to herself. "That would be easy enough."

She searched through the pictures on her computer. She had saved many family shots with her digital camera. She found a recent one of Kelly that looked cute.

She replied again. This time only with the picture embedded in the mail, no text. She didn't expect any reply. After about fifteen minutes, she decided to go to sleep.

She finished her drink. As she got up, she looked directly into the computer screen.

She smiled a wry smile.

"Eddy, my boy, you're mine."

Chapter 148 ~

JOSH WATCHED THEM WALK in the opposite direction. He was about to run after them, when he saw him. He stood up. Yes, there was a silhouette, down the alley, right in front of him. He froze a second. He wasn't sure what the person's intentions were. Knowing he couldn't be seen, he decided to wait and watch.

His patience paid off. The silhouette slowly emerged, peering down the street where the boy lay.

Josh couldn't believe what he saw. It was a scraggly old man in soiled clothing. The combination of styles didn't match. He could picture bugs running all through them.

The man was hunched over. His wild, white hair shone in the streetlight. His unshaven face was so lined and streaked, Josh took a small step backwards.

The man saw his movement. He froze in a crouched position, reminding Josh of a cornered, frightened animal. His wide-eyed stare held on Josh. In an instant, he scampered back down the alley.

His first thought was to run after him. He wanted to know why he was there, watching. He took one last glance at the dark, empty alley. Looking back down the street, Josh decided to run around the path he had come. He stayed clear of the poor little boy. A commotion of cops, the press, and the coroner were now surrounding the area.

When he got back to where the barrier was, he saw Frankie and Fletcher disappear into a corner pub. He slowly walked up to it. He paused. He then jumped up the steps into the dark room.

They were at the bar. Frankie instinctively turned. That caused Fletcher to do so, too.

"Ah, look who has reappeared," Fletcher said. Josh caught the distaste in his tone. Frankie just leaned on the bar looking at him.

"Sorry, guys, but there was this old guy who——"

"Old guy? Where?" Frankie perked up.

Josh told them everything. Frankie just kept shaking his head. When he was finished, Frankie was on his cell commanding a search to find Merrie.

"May be nothing, Frankie," Fletcher said when Frankie was finished.

"I know but this isn't his turf. A little strange he's hiding right nearby. I don't like it," he frowned. "If the bastard has nothing to do with this, at least maybe he saw something."

"Yeah," was all Fletcher could think to say.

"Okay, young man, tell us what you know or think," Frankie pressed.

Josh went through the full history of Elijah's Wrath. He had done more research. There were a few missing gaps, but he firmly believed that child slavery exists today. It continued from the long line of bishops through centuries of their secret sect. Their coffers were brimming over all the time, even in times of economic hardships. They even created the false fear of witches and blamed them during the terrible "burning time." It was all for money and power through fear just like in ancient Israel. It's been behind a veil of supreme secrecy, until today.

Frankie and Fletcher just stared at him. Finally, Frankie spoke up.

"Have you ever heard of The Order of Faith, Hope, and Charity? It's a Catholic sect. Acronym is 'FHC.'"

"No, sorry, I don't know the name. But it could very well be that sect or evolved to that. I can research it."

"Melanie tried and nothing," Fletcher added.

"I can try. I have other resources," Josh offered.

"You do that and A-SAP. Here's my cell number. You have Fletcher's, right?"

"Yes, will do."

"Have you ever heard of 'CHF?'" Fletcher posed.

Josh looked quickly down and up again. "No, never did," he lied. "That's 'FHC' backwards. What's up?" He composed himself.

Fletcher easily caught his reaction. "You sure? It's important."

"Yes, absolutely," he lied again.

Fletcher could tell the young reporter wasn't going to give anything up. He looked at Frankie and then back at Josh.

"Ok, I find out you do, you're fucked. Now, we want your help."

"Huh? My help?"

"We want a headline for tomorrow or as soon as possible."

"Oh, I don't know. I'm not that high up," Josh replied. At the same time, he thought of Martino and his claimed ability with his Editor. Either way, he didn't care. He may get a headline and front-page story!

"We'll take care of that, just write our article and get it done, okay?"

"Why, can I ask?"

"So, for the first time, we may be able to take the initiative away from this psycho."

Chapter 149 ~

STUART MARTINO SAT IN THE DARKNESS. His heart was black. He couldn't find any feeling for any reason. His wife was in deep depression and hiding, his girls were gone, and all hope was dying. Nothing in the world mattered to him anymore, except one thing.

The only sound came from the police scanners. They were humming constant static and barely audible talk between officers and stations. He wasn't listening anyway.

As the tear rolled down his cheek, he leaned forward. Using the tiny key that had been on his desk since the first day his girls were abducted, he slipped it into the keyhole of the bottom drawer.

As he slowly opened it, his loss deepened. Never in his life, with everything he had, did he ever feel such emptiness in his chest. The never-ending despair engulfed him as the haze of memories faded into nothingness.

He pulled the large silver revolver out. After checking the rounds, he placed the .44 magnum on his desk, never taking his hand off it.

He closed his eyes. The darkness remained.

He sat alone, caressing the only friend he had.

Chapter 150 ~

SUNDAY MORNING WAS BRILLIANTLY sunny. Melanie woke up with a slight headache, remembering how much vodka she had downed. She smiled though, knowing that this was the day, her day to win. She sat up in bed, looking down at her naked body. She ran her fingernails up her thighs, up her tummy, tingling her skin.

She continued up over her breasts and then lifted one arm. She ran her nails lightly up and down it, and then the other arm.

Somehow, this helped wake her up. Plus she just loved it. She sat to the side of the bed and stretched long and hard, bending her body to the right and then to the left.

"Ahhh," she said each time.

Then she jumped up, hurrying downstairs to make some quick instant coffee. On her way, she stopped at her computer.

"Any news, my little Eddy?" she said to the screen.

She moved the mouse. The screensaver disappeared and she could see her mailbox.

Nothing. No reply.

She frowned, but also knew it was fine. They would be there; that she knew. She continued downstairs and started boiling water.

She glanced at the clock. It was 9:15 a.m. She knew she could call her sister. She picked up the phone, pressing in her number.

It rang and rang and then went to voice mail. She frowned again, hoping this day wasn't going to be one of disappointments. She heard the beep.

"Hey Sis! Good morning! Call me back—"

She heard a loud click and knew her sister picked up the line.

"Hey!" she heard and also a little hard breathing, as if she had run to the phone. Good, the day may be positive after all.

"Hey!" Melanie replied back. "Everything okay and cool?"

"Yep, let's do it! The girls are all excited. They keep talking about being in a real-life police drama, like all those reality shows. But this one is a real reality show they keep saying to each other. They were up before dawn, too!"

Melanie heard more excitement in her sister's voice than she really wanted to hear. She didn't want to spoil the moment and discourage either her or her daughters. But somehow she felt a need to level it out a little with the real reality.

"Well, good for them," she replied with a smile. "Let's meet first, over here. We can go over the details and all the possible dangers, okay?"

She planted that. She also wanted the meeting at her place not to make it so "homey" for them. It also would help place some of the realities in their heads. She didn't want them to go off doing something careless and getting them all into deep shit.

"Yeah, that's fine. What should they wear?"

"Whatever they would normally wear when going to the mall. If it's revealing, then let it be. It's gotta look normal to them."

"What about me?" Dana asked.

"You what?"

"Me to wear?"

Melanie rolled her eyes.

"Whatever you would normally wear on a hot summer

day."

"Cool! What time should we be over?"

The excitement and anticipation in Dana's voice was beginning to worry Melanie. It was also annoying her. She almost wished she had a picture of one of the dead victims to show her, but knew that would end it all, right then and there.

"Be over around 10:30 a.m. Don't be late. We have much to go over."

She tried to sound firm.

"Great! I'll see you then. Hey, girls…"

Melanie heard her trail off as her sister hung up. She said a small prayer, hoping they would all be fine. She pushed the picture of dead girls out of her head.

Chapter 151 ~

FLETCHER WOKE UP EARLY. It was still a little before sunrise. He lay in bed staring at the ceiling, letting his mind wander. He saw the little boy lying naked in quiet death in the street. He thought of the girl lying on the cot, entire young body exposed, dead. Then Eddy's grinning face appeared, then his young cronies, then Father Brandon's nasty pompousness, then Merrie's horrid stench, then his friend Frankie, and then Melanie's eyes and smile. He tried to smile back but couldn't.

He got up and got ready. He made a cup of instant coffee and dialed Melanie's number. He waited as it rang.

After the fourth ring, he began to wonder. She never took that long to answer. He thought either she wasn't up yet or she was in the shower.

He waited. It went to voice mail.

"Hey, girl! Good morning! Just wanted to know if you're coming with me to the DA's. I could really use you there. Well, call my cell. I'm leaving right now. Gotta be there at 9:00."

He hung up his phone and looked down at it. He didn't know why, but he felt strange. The conversation from last night came back to him.

Nothing about any of this was really weird. It was more of a feeling than anything. He wondered if it was just that his feelings for her were increasing more and more. Maybe this was how it went, when becoming great friends and now possibly falling in love.

He took a deep breath, letting it out slowly.

"Still bothering me," he muttered as he walked out of the house.

He looked up at the dawning sky, hoping the day would go well. He knew Frankie was under unbelievable pressure. Soon everything was going to fall hard on his friend. Time was just running out. Any more kidnappings or murders, without anything to go after, would cost everything to both the DA and to the Chief of Police.

Not just the parents, but the public and the press will no longer accept no results. The police appear completely powerless. As he drove down to the highway, he thought about how helpless they really were.

This game was so tight. It had become a full cat-and-mouse play with the cat in total control. He believed the cat was laughing at its ability to keep the police away, fooling them at every point.

And for the life of him, he thought, he couldn't figure out the motive. Why would anyone, even a person like Eddy, want to do this? Or that pompous priest? He could understand Merrie, though. And where the fuck were the kids that were missing? Were they dead? In some shack? Were they together? Were they being molested or even tortured?

The vision of them being sold into child slavery entered his mind. But how and to who? And did it really exist in this country? Or were they kind of "exported out" to the Mid-East or to some random country?

He actually could believe extremely rich and wealthy people wanting to have young slaves. There have been stories. If it followed the mode of the Romans, they would be *total slaves*—even sexually. They would have to submit to anything and everything, never returning home.

He cringed. As he turned sharply onto the on-ramp, he hoped that this just wasn't true. He didn't like the thought at all. If so, they would never find them. Maybe that's the whole idea.

And he could imagine how much a clean, young girl or boy would go for on such a market. But then why kill the other one each time? Unless, it was truly like Josh mentioned about Elijah's Wrath. The rebellious ones and undesirables were simply just killed and left by the wayside.

He shook his head, wondering how such things could exist.

Chapter 152 ~

MELANIE WAS WAITING PATIENTLY. She was on her third cup of coffee and began to feel it. She got up, dumping out the rest of her cup. She filled a tall glass of water and drank it down. She didn't need to be hyper. She was already very antsy. She was also wondering if she was out of her mind.

At exactly 10:30 a.m., they showed up. She saw her sister's red minivan pull up in front. After a moment, the two girls jumped out, followed by Dana.

She gasped at what the girls were wearing. Yes, it was very warm out but this was unbelievable.

Both were almost identical except for the color schemes.

Kelly had on a tiny light blue tube top. Her modest breasts filled it with small rounded firmness. Kimberly had on a flimsy red halter that showed most of her tummy. Both had on very low hip-hugger jeans that revealed a lot of young skin.

When they got closer, she saw hoop earrings on both. She could see more makeup than was necessary, especially around their eyes.

Dana was dressed with a tied blouse, also exposing her tummy. She also had on hip-huggers, but not as low as her daughters'.

Melanie felt like the mom. She had on a t-shirt tucked into jeans.

It looked like they were going to the beach or some amusement park. She opened the screen door for them. The two girls bounced up onto her porch.

"Hi, Aunt Mel!" they both exclaimed with beaming smiles.

"Hi, girls," she dryly said back, but with a smile.

"Hey, Sis!" Dana also exclaimed as she came up the porch steps.

"Hey!" Melanie replied, with a little more excitement. It'd been a little while since she last saw her sister.

They immediately hugged.

"So good to see you!" Melanie said, releasing her.

"You, too!"

"Just wish it wasn't something like this but—"

"That's totally okay," Dana interrupted her. "We're looking forward to helping catch them. Honestly!"

Melanie wasn't feeling the exact same excitement, except for the intense desire to catch them, too.

"Let's get started. Need to prep the girls. Also, I'll follow you as you drop them off. Then you come over to where I parked and, without being noticed, get in my car. And then we'll watch and wait."

"Yep, sounds good!" she replied. She followed Melanie into the house.

The girls were sitting very closely together. They were chatting very fast about girl stuff when they came into the room. Seeing them, they looked up and became silent.

Melanie pulled up a kitchen chair. She sat right next to them. Dana just stood by listening.

Melanie saw the excitement in their young eyes. She also caught a little apprehension, too. Good, she thought, now that the time has come, they're getting a little nervous. She just hoped they didn't want to back out at this point.

"Okay, girls, here's the scoop. First, do you both have your cell phones? Are they fully charged, like I asked?"

They both nodded, pulling them out to show her.

"Good, keep them on but on vibrate only. Can you keep it on your bodies to feel it?"

They both nodded. Melanie noted the silence and felt better.

"Okay, Dana, you?"

"Yep, and charged."

"Great, we all have each other's number. Let me give you two more."

They all opened their phones. Each tapped in Fletcher's and Frankie's numbers. She explained each and that they were only to call them if in an extreme emergency.

They looked at her, intently listening.

"Now, these two girls, Marcy and Stacy, are a little older than you. They may look a little older than that, too. I'm not sure how they will be dressed but the last time I saw them, it was strange. I'm assuming though that they will dress more like you are to make you feel comfortable. Understand?"

They nodded in unison and so did Dana.

"Kelly, you're the one who initially joined what they will call 'their family' or 'our family.' Remember, they consider you now in their family. And remember this: you wish to help change the bad world to good and make money doing it, right?"

Kelly nodded and just looked at her.

Melanie looked back to make sure she really understood. She felt she did.

"So, show excitement about it all. And Kim, you just listen and appear to want to know more. Pretend Kelly did tell you some things. You both looked at the site, right?"

"Yes."

"Yes, Aunt Mel."

"Good, so you know the information or at least the gist of it all, right?"

"Yes."

"Yes."

"Now, here's the important thing. They will probably want you to go with them somewhere. If they're the ones, they will most likely tell you a lie. Remember that this all may be innocent. But either way, you are to act like it was any other stranger asking you. You want to know where, because of your parents, etc. They will have some canned answer. You should protest a little more. Then look at each other like getting approval from each other. Then agree and go with them, okay?"

They both looked at her with a little fear.

"Girls, all will be fine. Your mom and I will be nearby, watching the whole time. We will follow you. We need to see where they are taking you and why. This is very important. We have no other option. When we find out why, and if it's enough to indict them, I will call the police to come in. It may also be nothing but a valid kid's club. They may just be feeling you out for the first time, too. But I think it's going to be more."

They just stared at her.

"Now, if at any point you feel in danger, just secretly press SEND on your phone. It will call mine and I'll know, okay? I'll immediately call the police."

They nodded again.

"Remember, we'll be right behind you the whole time."

She looked at them and then up at Dana. Dana's expression was one of extreme concern now. Melanie was glad for that.

The only thing she didn't know was what they would do that would indict them. Would it be prior to any harm coming to her nieces? She had to be alert for whatever was out of the ordinary, constantly alert.

"Now, Kelly, call my number."

She did and Melanie answered.

"Now, hang up. Kim, now you."

She did the same.

"So, now if you just press SEND, it will call mine. Do not answer any calls, unless it's me or your mom, okay?"

They nodded again.

"Ready?"

They nodded again.

Melanie stood up. The girls followed.

"Now get over here!" she said with a big smile and open arms.

They both ran over, tightly embracing her. She did in return. Dana came over and put her arms around them all.

They stood there for a long while. All let the very warm moment together sink in.

Melanie took a deep breath, and with that, they all released. She saw tears in Dana's eyes. She saw apprehension in the girls' faces.

"It'll all be fine and over with soon. You may have helped save other kid's lives. I'm very proud of you!"

They both weakly smiled.

"Be and feel natural. Breathe now," Melanie softly said with another big smile. She then made a weird, funny face at them.

They both smiled broadly at that.

"Let's go," she said.

They picked up their purses, following her out the door. Melanie closed it but left it unlocked. She had left a note on the kitchen counter for Fletcher. It explained everything and who they were meeting, just in case something went terribly wrong.

They got in their cars. As they drove off, Melanie looked at her home. She hoped she'd see it again.

Chapter 153 ~

FLETCHER WAS ALMOST AT the Center City exit. He called Melanie again, but still no answer. He wanted to speak with her. Damn it, he thought. He turned onto the off-ramp, speeding up to beat a car coming down the other lane. He almost cut the car off the road. He knew he could have easily waited. It was Sunday. Few were on the road this early. His action was completely unnecessary.

The other driver veered a little, giving him the finger. Normally, Fletcher would have responded similarly or worse. He just ignored it, driving past him.

He turned off Broad Street. The other driver continued down the road. He said a quick "sorry" to him.

When he got close to the station, the rally of people this early surprised him. There were protest signs around a little stand. Someone had a microphone. There were four news vans. Their big antennas were raised to full height. Not very normal for a summer Sunday morning, he thought.

"Shit," he said, under his breath. He pulled past them and went around back. It appeared a little safer to enter through the back door.

He parked and got out. He could still hear the PA system around front. The speaker was blasting the police and the DA.

He listened for a bit and then looked at his watch. He had five minutes, so he listened more.

The speaker was now beginning to chant. The crowd followed.

"We want justice! Justice now! We want justice! Justice now!"

And it went on and on. Fletcher decided to go in at that point.

He went to Frankie's office. Frankie was just walking out of his door. He looked pissed.

"Hey," he said as he walked past Fletcher.

Fletcher could only turn and follow him.

He knew where they were headed. He kept up with Frankie, who was almost in a trot. He had never seen Frankie look so determined.

When they got to the DA's office, Frankie just entered, which surprised Fletcher. He followed right in.

Only Mike was inside. He was standing behind his desk with his arms folded, just staring out the door. His intense stare didn't flicker at all upon their arrival. He looked like a wax figure.

Frankie placed his folders on the side table.

"Good morning, gentlemen," Mike stated, with no emotion at all.

"Good morning, Mike," Frankie answered similarly.

"Good morning," was all Fletcher could say. Fletcher just stood there. The tension was so high, he was afraid even to breathe.

After a brief pause, all that changed.

"WHAT THE FUCK IS GOING ON?" Mike bellowed. "And close that goddamned door!"

Fletcher almost jumped out of his shoes from the heart attack he thought he was having. He closed the door and came back.

"Mike, listen——" Frankie wanted to get a jump on the

conversation.

"No! You listen! And go outside and listen! You know who that main speaker is?"

"Yes, I do," Frankie said, meekly now.

Fletcher didn't know and wanted to.

"And you? Do you know who that maniac is yelling out there?"

He shook his head no.

"IT'S FUCKING STUART MARTINO!"

Frankie looked at Fletcher. He saw the recognition and surprise. The situation was quickly deteriorating. One of the wealthiest persons was again on a public stage in front of the police department. He had done it before. Mike had asked him for patience. This time had to be worse. After days passed with no leads, he must be completely crazed now and blasting the city, his friend the DA, the Chief of Police, and the whole department.

"Oh," came naturally out of Fletcher's mouth. He was immediately sorry it did.

"Oh? *OH*? Is that all you can say?"

Fletcher knew better than to say anything at that point. Mike suddenly appeared to him as a mafia hit-man with his hair slicked back.

"JESUS FUCKING CHRIST! The press is eating this shit up! And the other three parents are there, too—including the newest victim's parents and their whole friggin' family!"

They just stood there.

"Okay, sit down now, both of you!"

They hesitated for a moment, out of fear, and then realized they had better sit down as instructed.

Mike slammed his desk with his fist. He then sat down

behind it. He just stared at them, continually back and forth from Frankie to Fletcher.

They saw he took a long, deep breath and then released it. Then his face seemed to calm a little.

"Now listen, boys. This has got to stop and stop now! I'm going to get royally fried today, not only out there, but in the papers, too. I have set up an impromptu press conference at eleven o'clock to try to quell some of this. But I have nothing to say that I haven't said before! Help me, please. This psychotic fuck is winning at everything he does. You're losing. We need other options and *fast*."

Frankie quickly glanced at Fletcher and then looked back at Mike.

"Mike, we're doing everything we can. We have staked out everywhere possible with our people and the State Police, too. He or they are always a step ahead. We think there's a leak somewhere."

"A leak? A leak? Holy shit, that's all the press needs now."

"Yes, but we think there is one," Fletcher spoke up calmly.

"Where? Who?" Mike instantaneously replied.

They looked at each other and then back at Mike.

Fletcher knew Frankie wasn't going to say Mike, or possibly Mike. That would indict his own son. If he brought up that maybe Danny was talking with Father Brandon, Mike would clamp down on possibly an innocent person. Fletcher still held the priest in very high suspicion. He didn't know what else to do or say. So, he waited for Frankie. Sorry, friend, he thought.

Frankie sat quietly for a moment. He then spoke up.

"We think it may be other kids doing this."

"What? Kids? Why would you think this?"

Fletcher realized he slightly changed the subject. Mike

didn't catch it. Nice move, friend.

"Well, it's because how they know the area and what other kids would do, or where they would go, and how they can be attracted in."

"Attracted in? You mean they go willingly?"

"We think so, Mike. It's the only thing that can explain no signs of struggle, and how easy it is for them to just disappear with no trace. They somehow get conned in and then, when they get their confidence, they take care of them."

"Take care of them? Is that how you are putting it?"

"Sorry, you know what I mean," Frankie answered back, with a little flip in his voice. It was obvious he was now getting annoyed with Mike.

You go, girl! Fletcher thought.

"Sure, yeah, I know," Mike replied, sounding defeated.

Frankie looked at Fletcher quickly and pulled out the morning *Philadelphia Times*. He assumed Mike hadn't seen it yet. Fletcher nodded.

"Mike, we did do another thing that we're hoping will put this perp on the run and get him to start making mistakes—"

"Yeah," Fletcher interjected, "he's always been one step ahead of us and worse, always leading us along. With this, we hope his guard will go down and make a wrong move."

"Okay, okay, what the hell is it?" Mike harshly asked, but with a genuine look of interest.

Fletcher nodded again to Frankie who handed Mike the paper.

"NEW CLUES IN CHILD MURDER CASES
POLICE CLOSE TO APPREHENDING SUSPECTS"

Mike appeared to read the headline forever. He finally handed it back silently. Fletcher saw his slight nodding meant approval. Before he could ask him what he thought, his phone buzzed. He knew he had to look down at it.

"hey sexy! I read the paper! good for you! congrats! would love to talk about it! need your loving bad! call me. your waiting wench, R! :)"

Chapter 154 ~

MIKE JUST SILENTLY STARED AT THEM for a moment. Fletcher could see he was processing this information. Mike was probably trying to find a way to get it into his press conference, without making himself look like a fool or it backfire on him.

"Good. The paper idea is good. I can work with that. It buys us a little break, but not long. So, then we're looking for some random kids doing this. Do you have some idea of who they may be?"

Mike's tone was now sounding more agreeable. He was willing to work together, rather than blasting them with 155mm howitzers at point blank range. At least that's how Fletcher felt, each time.

"Well, we have some leads. We're following them up right now," Frankie replied.

Fletcher knew Frankie was skirting the real issue. They didn't want to be there if it came out that one of their prime suspects was, in fact, Mike's very son; *and* that Mike may be the actual, unwitting leak.

"What leads?" Mike asked back.

"We have some kids who said they might have seen other kids they didn't know around with some of the victims. It was days prior to the crimes and we're trying to track them down. We're doing everything to find out who they are and speak with them."

Fletcher knew Frankie was fully lying and his heart went out to him. It reminded him why he was glad he was permanently off the Force.

"Let me know when you do. I'll figure out something to say today."

"Okay," was all Frankie said.

"And keep me in the fucking loop, constantly. My line is always open. You better keep me apprised, before I get caught with my pants down again. Got it?!"

"Yes, Mike, no problem," Frankie replied.

Fletcher nodded.

Mike looked at both of them.

"Go!" he said softly but firmly.

They got up to leave. Before they were out the door, Mike spoke up again.

"I want these fucks' heads on a silver goddamned platter, delivered to me directly! And find that leak. Now!"

"Yes, Mike, absolutely!" Frankie replied, as sincerely as he could, which Fletcher didn't buy.

"Oh, by the way," Mike finished in a calmer tone, "good job on the story idea."

"Thanks, Mike," Frankie said and then walked out, wondering how the kid had gotten the story on the front-page so fast. It usually took Frankie's contact longer to get through the paper's bureaucracy.

Fletcher followed. He could only imagine what Mike's face would look like when his son's head was on that silver goddamned platter.

Chapter 155 ~

THE FIGURE SAT ON THE FLOOR and bowed its head. Time to shut it down, it thought. It so didn't want to and was desperately trying to find a way not to. As it thought, it scraped its fingernails across the wooden floor making little lines each time.

"Shut down, keep up, shut down, keep up," it kept repeating, with a venom that caused saliva to form and drip from the sides of its curled-up mouth.

Finally, as if something cracked inside, it pulled out a black cell phone and stared at it for a very long time.

In a rage of despair, it flipped it open and pressed "New Text." After hitting the caps lock, it typed each letter with such ire that spittle came out of its mouth as it spoke each word.

"TIME TO STOP! YOU HAD ENOUGH! NO MORE! DO NOT ARGUE! JUST STOP AND STOP NOW!"

Without a second thought, it pressed SEND. It watched the screen confirm the delivery and then threw the phone against the wall. It broke a little, falling to the floor.

It glared at it with intense anger. It spit at it. Then with apparent calm, it stood right over it for a moment. The mind exploded with complete fury. It stomped on it over and over again, until there was nothing left but broken black pieces of what used to be a cell phone.

Chapter 156 ~

"WELL, FRANKIE, LOOKS LIKE WE'RE really in the pit of Hell now," he said, with a weak grin.

"Yeah, and I'm supposed to be some kind of Ein-fucking-stein!" Frankie laughed a nervous laugh.

"We'll win this, somehow," Fletcher smiled back.

"Yeah, if things would just start going our way, for once. By the way, we can't find Merrie. He's gone, disappeared, vanished."

"How hard is it—"

"We've never had a problem locating him. Never."

"Not good."

"Nope."

They had made it back to Frankie's office. They started going over what they had and what they should do next.

They laid out all of the scenarios and events, posting everything all around the room. They made lists of any possible clues and ideas, no matter how random, with the hope something would click and fall into place. They discussed the interrogations. It was all the same material. But they hoped something would stand out. Something.

Fletcher loved working as a team with Frankie. Frankie was extremely precise and to the point. Nothing passed him by without extraordinary scrutiny.

They decided to go at it with no one else to avoid any further possibility of an internal leak. For all they knew, it may not be Mike.

Around 11:30 a.m., Fletcher took a break and called Melanie at home. With everything going on, he hadn't had a chance. He also was a little more than concerned she had not called him back from the message he had left earlier that morning.

It rang and rang. When it went to voice mail, he hung up without any message.

He then pressed SEND, this time with her cell number.

It rang and rang again and then also went to voice mail.

He shook his head, leaving a message.

"Mel, hope all is okay. Not sure if you saw my call this morning. The world's blowing up. Need to talk with you. Call my cell, okay?"

He hung up. He hoped his tone would do the trick, even though he felt extremely uncomfortable speaking like that to her.

He decided he would explain later, when she called. He hoped it would be right back, too.

He was getting very, very worried.

Chapter 157 ~

MELANIE FELT THE VIBRATION. She heard it ring, too. She picked up her cell and looked at the number. It was Fletcher. She pressed Quiet. She put it back in its holster and drove on.

"Sorry, honey, but gotta do this first. Hope all works out on your end," she said to the road.

Dana was a good driver when being followed. Just enough distance. Melanie was glad.

In the distance, Melanie could see the signs for the mall. Her heart started to race. Her fingers felt funny.

She told herself to be calm. She had to stay alert. She noticed Dana slow down a little. She hoped her sister wasn't getting cold feet.

They stopped at the light at the entrance. As they waited, Melanie's hands started to sweat. Her heart jumped at the green light.

Not many cars were in the parking lot. It was Sunday. The stores had just opened. She figured it was the workers and early-birds.

They went down a short ramp. At that point, Melanie started to peel back. She didn't want to look together. She saw Dana make the hard turn to the front of the mall. Melanie continued straight, weaving around the lot a couple times. She parked in a side spot but had a perfect view of the mall front.

She turned her car off. She kept all the windows open. Even though the morning was steamy, she wanted to be able to hear.

From her vantage, she saw Dana stop at the main mall entrance. She said some things to her two daughters. It looked like normal parental instructions. She gave them both a kiss. The two girls exited from the sliding back door of the minivan.

They waved to their mom, watching her pull away.

Melanie looked at her watch. It was 11:50 a.m. She hoped the girls knew the time, too. Hopefully Dana had reminded them.

The girls stood there talking to each other. Then suddenly they disappeared into the mall.

Melanie had not expected that. She thought they knew just to wait outside. Maybe they thought they had ten minutes to spare. Were they doing some shopping, since they were there? She knew the thought was absurd.

Dana called. Melanie told her where she was. She watched Dana drive in a wide exit pattern and then down past her. She went around the back bend. She could still see the minivan. But from where Dana had parked, it could not be seen from the main mall entrance.

"Good girl," Melanie said.

Dana got out. She nonchalantly walked towards Melanie's car. Dana made sure she was in the outside perimeter. Cars parked in various spots mostly blocked her. She had also donned a sun hat.

She made it to the car and got in.

"Where are the girls?" Dana immediately asked with alarm.

"They went into the mall. I'm sure they're fine. Just wait."

They both waited impatiently, hoping the girls knew enough to come out by 12:00. Melanie just couldn't wait. She pressed SEND to Kelly's number. It began to ring. She hoped they would get a signal in the mall.

"Hello?" Kelly answered.

"Where are you?"

She knew she sounded a little alarmed.

"Oh, we're okay, Kimberly needed to pee."

Melanie held back the upcoming laugh. Her smile caught Dana's attention. Dana made a motion to her to let her know.

Melanie ignored her for a second. She held up her hand nicely.

"Just hurry and get back out front."

"Yes, we will. Are you nearby?"

"Yes, I can see you clearly. Remember what we talked about, okay?"

"Yep, we're ready!"

"Good. Be careful and be excited, too. I'm with you."

Kelly hung up. So did Melanie.

"It's okay Sis, Kim had to pee."

Dana started to laugh.

It sounded very nervous to Melanie.

They finally reappeared. They stood out in the sunshine. The only thought that passed through Melanie's mind was that they looked like two prime pieces of young female meat.

After a couple of minutes, she saw two girls come out of the mall. She recognized them.

Marcy and Stacy approached Kelly and Kimberly.

"God help us," she whispered.

Chapter 158 ~

FLETCHER CONTINUED WORKING WITH Frankie, but his mind was on Melanie. Something just wasn't right. He couldn't see why she would not have come with him. No matter what, she always loved being in the thick of things. He couldn't see her passing this up.

Fletcher didn't realize he was just staring into space when Frankie was talking to him.

"Hey, you, over there!" Frankie joked.

Fletcher didn't hear him.

"Fletch-ER!"

"Um, oh, sorry," he said, as he snapped out of his daydream.

"You okay?" he asked. "Pressure too much?"

"No, no. I'm just thinking about Mel and where she is."

"Something wrong?"

"I don't know. It's just weird. She's not acting like herself. I left messages and no reply. Nothing."

"Maybe her cell is dead," he said as he fished through some folders.

"I left a message at the house, too."

Frankie glanced over at his friend.

Fletcher continued.

"I just wish I knew where she was and what she was doing."

"Sounds like you're in love," Frankie posed back, with a smile. Something snapped inside him at the same time.

Fletcher didn't know what to say. He then watched his

friend's face twist with anger.

"Ya know something, my friend," Frankie started and paused. He then immediately continued, not wishing him to speak. All he could feel was his own deep feelings, desire, and affection for her. "You deserve her just leaving you. Period."

"What? Why would—"

"If you have to ask, you're clueless!"

Fletcher hadn't seen Frankie this pissed in a long time.

"And I'll tell you another thing. Mel is a gem, a beautiful gem. Yeah you treat her nice, but sooner or later you're gonna have to give up the girls. I mean, what is up with you and Rosalyn? How can you do her and do that to such a wonderful girl like Mel? I just don't get it. Is it ego? Boredom? If I were in your shoes and had Melanie like you do, and you know she really loves you, I would be so dedicated to her. No other girl could ever get to me. Aw, forget it," Frankie finished. He looked down shaking his head.

The revelation hit Fletcher hard. He suddenly realized his friend was right. A gush of emotion for both his friend and Melanie rose up so fast in him, he was speechless. He got up and walked over to him. With his hand on his shoulder, he said, "Thanks my friend. I needed that."

Frankie looked up and smiled. Fletcher saw glassiness in his eyes and thanked him again.

"So, you think she's fine then?" he asked Frankie, controlling his emotion.

"Don't worry, I'm sure she is. Probably just working out some things for the case or something."

Fletcher looked at Frankie with a blank look.

"That's actually what I'm afraid of."

Chapter 159 ~

THE FOUR GIRLS SEEMED TO BE talking fine. They looked like just another group of girls at the mall. Marcy and Stacy were both dressed as Melanie had expected: extremely close to the way Kelly and Kimberly were dressed. She and Dana looked on.

Marcy then pointed somewhere away from the mall. Melanie saw Kelly smile and nod her head. Stacy then said something to Kimberly, who smiled and nodded, too.

Then Marcy waved to someplace in the parking lot. After a moment, a car pulled up.

Melanie started her car, putting it into gear. She was glad she had pulled forward, facing out of the spot.

For a moment, Kelly was saying something to Marcy. It appeared to be a little protesting. She was doing as instructed. Marcy was smiling and saying something. She then put her hand on Kelly's shoulder, as a friend would, making a point. Kelly was nodding the whole time. She then smiled as if in approval. Good, thought Melanie.

They watched as the girls got in the back with Stacy. Marcy jumped into the front seat.

Melanie looked over at Dana, who had a sincere look of terror in her eyes.

"It's fine. It's broad daylight," Melanie said putting on her own hat. It was a Phillies baseball cap. She started to pull out, reminding herself it could all be nothing.

The other car started to slowly pull away. Melanie did her best to follow without being noticed.

"I hope they'll be okay," Dana said softly.

"Don't worry, they will be. We're on it. Remember, we're a team, Sis," she said, turning and smiling at her apparently very nervous sister.

"Yes, yes, we are," Dana stuttered.

Melanie stayed cautiously with them. When they turned, she saw it was Stanley driving. Great, she thought, we have the full fucking echelon. She frowned and followed them.

They turned onto the pike, heading towards I-476. They then turned onto the south on-ramp. Melanie followed. She sped up a little to keep up with the traffic on the highway.

Once on the highway, they stayed on it until it approached its end. They had to go north or south on I-95. Either way, they could end up traveling very far. I-95 went from Maine to Florida. Melanie hoped they would stay very local.

They proceeded south. Melanie followed.

After a couple of miles, they turned onto an exit lane. It was apparent where they were going.

"Marcus Hook," Melanie muttered.

"And the refineries?" Dana followed with alarm in her voice.

"Yeah, probably. But why?"

"I don't know! But don't you dare lose them!"

"I won't! I won't!"

They followed them into a rundown residential area. Many of the row houses were boarded up or just empty shells of former homes. They passed vacant warehouses and small refinery-type structures. High wire fences surrounded most of them.

"A war zone," whispered Melanie.

Her heart had been speeding since they exited the highway.

Now she really began to feel a fear growing deep inside her. Was this really a smart thing to do? She did her best not to show it; especially not having it sound in her voice. She just wished her heart would stop pounding.

She tried to control her breathing.

"We're okay," she finally said. "We're still very local."

"For what?"

"For the police to arrive," she whispered firmly.

Chapter 160 ~

FRANKIE FINALLY HAD ENOUGH of Fletcher's preoccupation. With a smile, he told him to call her or he would. Fletcher looked at him and smiled back.

"It's just so not *her*, ya know," he said.

"Yeah, I do know. Call her back again. You're becoming useless until you know everything is fine."

"Yeah, I guess."

"And maybe it's your own insecurity. To be honest my friend, I've never seen you like this before with a lady. And I'm not sure if you're just being a little possessive," Frankie said, putting his pen down. He sipped his cold coffee.

"Well, maybe, and you're right—somewhat," he said giving Frankie a curt look with a grin. "But there's also a feeling of something. I'm beginning to think the closer you become to someone, the more you can feel the things about that someone. Know what I mean?"

Frankie nodded knowingly. He sipped again, putting down the cup with a grimace. He spit onto his own floor.

"This stuff really sucks!"

Fletcher laughed and continued.

"Just feeling like she's up to something. And worse, she's not letting me know—and that's bothering the shit out of me."

"Then *call her!*"

Fletcher laughed again.

"Fine, I will."

He called. It rang and rang and then went to voice mail.

"Hey babe, call me. Want to know all is okay. Please call back. Thanks."

He looked over at Frankie for approval.

"Lame, dude. Lame."

Fletcher gave him the finger.

Chapter 161 ~

MELANIE TRIED TO STAY FAR ENOUGH back without losing them. At the same time, she was getting nervous that there weren't many cars in this area. They were standing out too much. It didn't matter anymore because she wasn't going to lose them. Not in the middle of nowhere with her two nieces in the back seat with that Stacy maniac.

She glanced at Dana. She had the look of how Melanie felt.

"Maybe this wasn't a good idea," Dana pressed.

"No, it was, I'm sure," Melanie replied, not believing her own words.

The car made a left turn. It went down another deserted street. Rusty old cans, papers, and boxes were strewn everywhere. There were more old, abandoned warehouses. Melanie kept her distance.

The car made another left turn. Melanie was forced to follow. She knew something was happening.

Then the car made another left turn, stopping in front of a big gray warehouse. There were some cars parked in the parking lot, beyond a closed fence. Melanie drove right by them and didn't look. She then made a right turn and was finally out of view.

"What are you doing?" Dana exclaimed.

"Shush!"

She quickly made two more rights. She inched up to the corner until they could see the car. Everyone was still inside. Melanie sighed a little in relief.

"What next?" her sister asked.

"Wait. Just wait a moment."

Melanie's heart was still pounding. She started to breathe slowly to stop her heart palpitations. Her arms felt weak. Her fingers were sweaty and cold.

They watched as they saw Marcy turn and talk to the two girls in the back seat. Melanie saw one of the girls raise her hand as if saying "no." Then she saw Stanley turn.

He was motioning to the warehouse and then back to the girls. He looked like he was getting angry. He turned back, facing forward, raising his arms as someone would in disgust.

Marcy was still saying something. Then all of a sudden, Stanley flew out of the car. He stormed to the back door and threw it open. Melanie saw Stacy pushing the girls out. The girls starting to fight, flailing their arms.

"OH, MY GOD! OH, MY GOD!" was all Melanie could hear from Dana.

She reacted instantly and floored the pedal. The car leaped forward. She turned the wheel so hard the car lifted for a moment on just two tires.

"OH, GOD!" she heard Dana scream but she couldn't look at her.

The car banged back down. They both hit the roof hard. Stanley looked up in total shock. Melanie could see the girls all of a sudden staring out the back window. Marcy was yelling something.

Kelly and Kimberly were wide-eyed, watching their aunt flying towards them. Right at that, Stacy pushed the two girls out. They weren't expecting it. They fell out onto the ground on top of each other.

Melanie saw faces of pain on her nieces.

Stanley looked at them on the ground and then back at Melanie. He looked at Marcy, who was now wildly screaming. He hesitated for a second and then jumped back into the driver's seat. The car wheeled out spewing gray smoke from the back tires. The back door slammed closed from the severe forward motion.

The two girls were lying on the ground. Melanie had to slam the breaks not to run them over. She pulled hard to the side, coming to a screeching halt. Dana's head almost hit the windshield. She fell back against her seat hard. For a moment, she stared gaping out the window that had almost crushed her head.

A white cloud of gravel rose from Melanie's sliding car. Dana jumped out, running around to her two girls.

Melanie was frantically writing down their license plate number. She then jumped out, too.

The girls were just beginning to sit up and then hugged each other. Dana knelt, widely hugging them both.

Melanie stood above them. She breathed the biggest sigh of relief she thought she ever had in her life.

The two girls looked up at her. She saw their fear, but also saw something else. With tears coming down, Kelly smiled at her.

The smile was a smile of victory.

Chapter 162 ~

"YOU GIRLS OKAY?" MELANIE asked, leaning down to them. She saw that they were physically unharmed except for bloody scrapes on their arms and hands.

Dana looked more upset than they did.

"We're okay, Aunt Mel," Kelly said, looking up.

"What happened?" Melanie asked, touching her on the shoulder.

"It was funny," Kelly replied, "we were all talking about the family and the things they did and wanted to do and all and they asked us what we thought and all. And the whole time, I kept watching where they were going and then I didn't recognize anything and started to get nervous and it didn't seem like the place they had said, which was like a big nice house place where others like us were and we were going to a party and going to have fun and make money and all. Then they stopped and wanted us to get out, and I said no and Kim did, too. And then they started to yell and push and all, and I yelled back and said no way I'm going. And then that freaky guy in the front turned and said he was going to kill one of us and sell the other, like all the other kids they did, and we would never see our parents again, and no one would tell them. He said the police and no one would ever know. We were never going home, like the other kids. And then Kim screamed and that girl up front yelled at her and said they were going to smash us, unless we got out now. And then they saw you come around and they got scared and all. And then next thing I knew, we were pushed out and fell, and here we are."

Kelly was out of breath. Melanie smiled at her, leaned down, and kissed her on the cheek. Then she kissed Kimberly, who was nodding the whole time.

"Girls, you did great!" Melanie said, standing back up. "Just relax for a moment in my car, okay?"

"Yes, Aunt Mel, thanks!" they both said. The girls got up slowly and walked to her car, followed by Dana.

Melanie grabbed Dana's arm.

"Hey, just sit in there with them and keep them calm. They did great and we have their testimony against Eddy and his people. I just want to look at this place for a moment."

Dana nodded. She weakly smiled and walked away.

Melanie watched her go. She looked back at the warehouse. There were a couple of windows that looked dirty and smeared. But they were too high for her to peer in. Plus, she had to get through the tall fence.

She glanced around and saw some metal barrels nearby behind the fence. She looked back at her car. Everyone was in it now. She turned back to the fence and looked up. It was high but not too high to scale.

She placed the toe of her sneaker into one hole, starting to climb.

"Mel! What are you doing?" called out Dana.

"No problem. I've got to see what's in here. Just wait there."

Dana fell silent. She watched her, with the girls.

Melanie climbed to the top. She made it over and carefully climbed down. Close to the bottom, she slipped and fell to the ground. The fence ripped a long slit into her jeans. She checked and it missed cutting deep into her skin. But it left a long scrape that was beginning to lightly bleed.

She got up and shrugged back at Dana to keep her sister calm and quiet. She even put her finger to her mouth for silence. They all nodded.

She just hoped that Eddy's cohorts hadn't had a chance yet to warn whoever may be inside.

She walked slowly over to the building wall under the two windows. She looked at the barrels, hoping nothing was in them so she could move them. She grabbed on and rocked one. It was empty. She tried the other. It too was empty. She smiled and turned back to Dana and gave a thumbs-up. Dana did the same. Melanie still saw fear in her sister's eyes.

She rocked one over, placing it under the first window. After rocking the other over, she tried to lift it up on top. It was too awkward. She glanced back at Dana. Her sister had her hand covering her mouth.

Melanie tried again, lifting it from the bottom this time. She was able to get it slightly onto the other barrel, rocking it into place. She stepped back, taking a breath. Rust and dirt mixed with sweat, covering her.

She carefully climbed the barrels. At the top, she knelt cautiously. The sun's searing rays were burning her back. She tried to keep her face forward towards the building. Her forehead and cheeks were warming up fast from the reflecting heat. After a moment, she raised herself slowly. She reached the bottom of the window.

It was very smeary. She tried to use her fingers to make a small hole of clearness. She still couldn't see in. She tried to pull her shirt up to use it, but couldn't do it without falling from the little space on the barrel.

She looked back, shrugging. She flipped her cap off. Pulling her shirt over her head, she knelt there with just her white bra on. She realized how silly she looked and turned back to the car. She saw Kelly and Kimberly smiling and laughing. A smile even appeared on Dana's face. Melanie smiled and gave them a "shoo" motion with her hand.

She used the end of the shirt with some spit to clear a better hole. It worked fine. She turned and gave another thumbs-up. She saw the girls clap in applause. She had to smile at that. She slowly rose up to eye-level at the bottom of the window.

She peered in and gasped.

She quickly knelt back down, pulling out her cell.

Chapter 163 ~

JOSH TURNED THE SCANNER UP. He adjusted the treble on his stereo to eliminate as much hiss and noise as possible. He was able to hone in on the talking with just a couple more adjustments. Sitting back, he congratulated himself on the idea of feeding the scanner's signal through his sound system.

Josh listened intently. He picked up some information of what was going on. But it was fragmented. He knew Frankie and Fletcher wouldn't give him too much information on any leads, even though he did a lot of convincing to get Martino to help him with the headline they wanted.

He didn't care either way. His story had been fabricated. He still wanted a real headline. Josh swore he was going to get it somehow, someway.

After a long while, he decided to take a break.

He turned to the sound system. With the digital hard drive he had rigged up to his digital recorder, he turned it on and pressed RECORD.

The little red light blinked. It then turned to solid, indicating to him the system was functioning correctly. With the amount of storage he had, he could record for a very long time while away.

He vowed he wasn't going to miss anything.

Not now.

Chapter 164 ~

FLETCHER FELT HIS PHONE VIBRATE. At the same time, he heard it. He had the sound on maximum. Frankie heard it and turned to him. He waited for him to answer it. Fletcher pulled it out and saw it was Melanie on the caller ID screen.

"Hello?" he answered.

"Hey! Sorry I didn't call you back."

She balanced herself on the barrel. The sun was burning her.

"Oh, so you knew I called, huh?"

Fletcher knew he sounded flip. Frankie gave him a look and a motion to calm down. Fletcher nodded with a fleeting smile.

"Yes, yes, no time for that. Tell Frankie to go get Eddy or at least lock him down!" she firmly whispered.

"What?"

Frankie looked up at him.

"Do it. Then get over here before they leave and pack up or something!"

"Where are you?" he said frantically.

Frankie jumped up.

"I'm in Marcus Hook, and—"

"Marcus Hook?"

"*Marcus Hook?*" Frankie whispered loudly to himself.

Fletcher nodded back at him.

"Just go and get going. I'll give you directions on your way, okay? Hurry! Gotta go! Call you right back."

She hung up.

Fletcher still had the phone next to his ear. Then he just looked at it. He flipped it closed and turned to Frankie.

"Gotta go. She found something and must have proof on Eddy or somebody. She said to go get him or lock him down."

"I just can't do that without—"

"I strongly suggest you do and now. Gotta go!"

He got up and was halfway out the door when Frankie called back to him.

"You trust her that much?"

"Yes, I do!"

Chapter 165 ~

AFTER FLETCHER LEFT, FRANKIE was sorry he hadn't sent a detective with him. Too late, he thought. He called Danny, telling him to get ready to go with him. Danny asked where. Frankie held back from informing him. He just let him know he was coming with him in his car. Then he quickly tried to think what to tell Mike, or not to tell him anything. He made his decision.

"Hi, Mike?" he said when he heard the phone pick up.

"Yeah, what's up?"

He sounded stressed. Frankie didn't care.

"Mike, we have an issue with your son, Eddy, and we need to get over there A-SAP!"

"What? Eddy? What are you talking about?"

He sounded alarmed and angry at the same time. Frankie again didn't care.

"He may have information about the kids possibly doing this. We just got a lead. I just wanted to let you know that me and Danny are heading over there."

"This better be good, Frankie. I'm holding you personally responsible—period. You got it!"

Frankie rolled his eyes.

"Yeah, Mike, that's fine. Gotta go. See you there."

"On my way in a minute. Wait for me there."

Frankie hung up, ignoring Mike's last comment.

Danny walked in.

"Ready?"

"Yeah, boss," Danny replied. "Where to?"

"The Parker residence. You're coming with me."

Danny looked at him, and then glanced away. Frankie thought it was somewhat strange, but he was too much in a rush to take more notice.

Danny followed him out, right on his heels.

Frankie immediately was on his cell calling Fletcher.

Chapter 166 ~

FLETCHER WAS CURSING EVERY curse word he knew. Traffic was jammed everywhere for a Sunday due to activities in town. He was trying to get out of the city and onto I-95. He had to get to the river and the Penn's Landing area to reach it. This was the time he wished he was still a cop to have a blaring siren.

"Get out of my way," he kept yelling, knowing it was to no avail.

His concern for his girl was making him crazy. More so, he was angry. He tried calling her back. For some reason she had not answered his call a minute ago. He desperately hoped that she was not in any trouble.

He heard it ring and then pick up.

"Hello, babe," he heard. He sighed.

"Hey! What's going on?" he pressed. He knew he sounded a little too loud, but it was only from yelling at cars.

"Don't get mad at me, okay?" she sheepishly asked.

"Mad? Why would I get—what did you do?"

"First, where are you?"

"Stuck in traffic on Vine Street, but it's clearing. Oh, I see, it's one of those goddamned roving construction road crews. Too much going on in the city. Be there in a bit. Marcus Hook?"

"Yeah, take I-95 and get off there. Will you be able to remember?"

"Yeah, yeah, give it to me from off the exit."

Melanie proceeded to give him the best directions she could. She told him please to call when he got close.

"Hurry!" she said. She was about to hang up.

"Wait. Wait! What the hell are you doing in Marcus Hook?" he demanded.

"Setting a trap—"

"A trap?!"

"Yeah, just listen—I can't talk loud—hold a second."

He waited and then heard things that just weren't good. In the background, he heard someone else coming through her phone.

"Hey, you, what da' f'ck are you doin' on d'ose? D'is is private property! Get da' f'ck down from d'ere now!"

"Honey, gotta call you back—"

"Mel! What's going on?"

"Call back…"

She hung up.

"Fuck!" he stammered.

He saw an opening between cars. It was clear ahead. He found the exact moment to weave through the two cars. As he passed by the road crew and their trucks, he slammed the accelerator to the floor.

He saw the exit sign for I-95 South. He quickly pulled over to the exit lane and flew off the road down the on-ramp.

He came right up to a slower moving car on the ramp. He almost hit it. He ended up right on its tail. The driver continued his slow pace, not noticing Fletcher's car. Fletcher didn't want to be rude but he had to get around him. He pulled onto the little shoulder, hitting the gas again. His car flew right by the old man, who just looked over with a shocked stare.

Fletcher felt it necessary to wave. The driver just gaped at him as he quickly disappeared behind Fletcher. He merged onto I-95, increasing his speed to almost ninety miles per hour. He had no choice but to continue to weave wildly in and out of traffic.

He picked up his cell and called Frankie.

"Yo!"

"Hey, Frankie, you there yet?"

"Yep, just arrived. Mike's coming, too."

"Mike? Oh boy, how are you explaining—"

"I don't care. If Melanie's right and Eddy is the one, he ain't getting away. I just hope he wasn't notified yet or anything."

"Well, you got a good jump I think. Gotta get his buddies, too."

"Yeah, on that already. We're going to each home and well, not to worry."

"Good. Hopefully Mike doesn't go bananas and make hasty decisions. It is his boy."

"No worry. No worry at all. If he's innocent, I'll take the heat. Where are you?"

Frankie sounded so confident. Fletcher knew that tone from him. Frankie was on the hunt. He had something to go on. Fletcher knew that was what his friend was best at and hungered for.

"I'm on I-95 heading south now. I'm speeding like a fiend. Can you put out a call to all Philly cops to ignore me or escort me or whatever?"

"Yeah, yeah, consider it done. I'll also contact the locals and State-ies, too."

"You read my fuuuuuuuucking mind! WHOA!" he screamed, as he swerved around a tractor-trailer that almost came into his lane. He had approached at such a high speed that the semi driver hadn't expected him to get there so fast.

"You okay?"

"Yeah, damn it! Just trying to kill myself." He laughed a small laugh.

"Just be careful. Not good to kill yourself or anybody else. I'll get an escort on you A-SAP. Where you at right now?"

"The Point Bridge."

"Right. A cop will pick you up at the airport area. I'll get a State-ie to get on 95, right now, ahead of you. The trooper will be in the area close to Marcus Hook."

"Listen, listen, I got some directions," he interrupted him. He told him what Melanie had said.

"Got it. I'll pass on to the State-ies. They should get there fast, and probably before you."

"Great!"

"Good luck!"

"You, too, my friend. You, too."

He tried to call Melanie back.

Chapter 167 ~

JOSH COULDN'T BELIEVE WHAT he was hearing. He immediately turned up the volume. He was about to head out, when the information coming in caught his ear. He said a thank you prayer.

He kept the Record on. He wanted the ability to rerun it in case anything was too garbled.

"Wow," he whispered. He tried to follow what was happening. "This is way too good. Way too good."

Suddenly there was just static, right in the middle of orders spewing out from the station.

"Damn it!" he softly cried as he grabbed the scanner's big tuning knob. Josh tried to focus it back. "I'm missing it, damn it! Piece of shit!"

He pushed back his chair and stood over all the equipment. He told himself to calm down.

Like a thief intent on getting the safe open, he carefully and slowly turned the knob a little to the left and a little to the right. An immediate and wide grin came as the signal grabbed. He adjusted the treble again.

"Good, finally!" he sighed. After listening a little, all he could say was, "Oh, my GOD!"

Chapter 168 ~

MELANIE KEPT SHIFTING ON the metal barrel. She was constantly trying to keep her balance. The man below her was obviously a foreigner from his deep accent. She got all her courage up. She then leered down at him.

"Listen you little fuck-head!" she yelled down at him, still trying to keep her balance by pressing against the wall.

He froze, staring at her. He then glanced back at the door he had come out of. She glanced there, too. Two other men, who also looked foreign to her, had walked out. They saw her glare at them, too. One held a large pistol close to his side.

"I'm a Police Officer. In about a minute, there will be a swarm of cops and detectives here, including the fucking State Police!" she bellowed. Her eyes were on the gun as her heart started pounding.

The first man's eyes opened at that. He immediately looked back at the other two. All of a sudden, a very large man came through the door between them. He had a cell phone up to his ear. He was speaking another language quickly into it and then pointed at her. The man with the pistol stepped further out and raised the gun directly at her.

The language didn't matter at that point. She was looking right down the cold blackness of a gun barrel, pointed right at her face! She felt a warm wetness between her legs, which started all by itself.

She froze, imagining the bullet coming at her in her mind's eye. She realized now exactly what it felt like for people who knew they were about to be shot. She would bleed and die right then and there. She couldn't breathe. She couldn't breathe!

The big man quickly stepped back into the building. No one moved. She tried and tried, but couldn't find her breath. She began to feel faint. The gun! The gun was going to be fired! She kept thinking, oh, my God, I'm going to die! No!

Suddenly, the big man burst back out. Two of the men just looked at him, waiting. But the one with the gun just stood calmly still. Her face was directly in his sights. She then saw the big man nod. Her body was frozen in terror. Everything started to black out. She knew she was going to be shot and fall, fall off right there! And then in the distance she heard it. Could it be true? A siren? Yes, she thought, yes, yes!

The big man turned towards it. He listened. It was faint, but it was there. Then it sounded like it was getting a little louder, closer. Oh, please, she thought, please God, please!

The big man became frantic. He barked orders, pointing in the direction of the siren. They all immediately went back through the door, except the man with the gun pointed at her. He smiled the most evil smile she ever saw. She watched him whisper "bang," never taking his eyes off her. His tongue slowly wet his lips. Lowering the gun, he blew her a kiss that made her shiver with fear. He slowly walked back inside, slamming the metal door.

She had no breath at all. All of a sudden, all the adrenalin in her burst through her system. She started to sob uncontrollably. Her breathing became so fast, she felt the fainting coming on. She tried to grab the rough wall with her open palms. They slipped and grated and ripped her skin.

"Oh, my god! Oh, my god! Calm down! Calm down!" she screamed at herself.

Finally, her breathing caught up. She turned and looked at her sister. Dana had her face in her hands and was obviously wildly crying. The girls were screaming something.

Melanie regained her composure. Shaking her head a little, she was calm again, at least as much as she could muster.

She stared at the slammed door and assumed they locked it. She then leaned up, slowly peering back in. She saw a flurry of activity. Then she realized what they were doing. They were quickly gathering things up and packing everything away.

"Shit!" she exclaimed out loud.

Melanie watched helplessly as they were taking all the equipment. She saw them pushing everything through a large opening with a garage-type, drop-down door. She then realized there must be a truck back there that they were loading. All looked preplanned.

She ducked down, opening her phone. She called Fletcher back. But it rang before she could. It was him.

"Mel! You okay?"

He sounded so frantic, her heart went out.

"Yes, yes, fine, no problem. They're getting away, Fletcher. They're all getting away!"

"Who is? Who is getting away?"

"The fucking foreigners!"

"What?"

"Just get here!"

"On my way with the police. But still about five minutes!"

"But I hear a siren coming."

"Good! That's gotta be the State Police! Frankie called them, so hang in there!"

"Oh, please hurry!"

"Will do, and you're fine, right?"

"Yes, and so's Dana and the girls."

She immediately knew that was a mistake. It just slipped out.

"Dana? Girls? What Dana and girls?! Oh, no, you didn't!"

"Yes, I did. And we got them. But we have to get the evidence. They're moving too fast. We gotta get it!"

"We're coming!"

"Wait! Wait! Don't hang up. I forgot something!"

"What? What is it?"

"The other three, they drove away!" she pressed.

"Who? What three?"

She felt so bad for him that he didn't know what was going on and that she had hid it from him.

"Those damned kids of Eddy's! What's their names? Stanley, Stacy, and that other one … yeah, Marcy!"

"So, you put her girls in danger to—"

"Yes, yes, but they spilled their guts."

"Is everyone okay?"

"Yes, yes, stop asking me that!"

Now she was getting annoyed. She needed action, not questions.

"Okay, where did they go?"

"I don't know. They sped away."

She described the car, giving him the license plate number. He repeated it a couple of times to memorize it.

"Got it. Let me go. I'll call it in to Frankie."

"Great! Get those little fucks!"

"Fucks?" he said with surprise.

"Yeah, those fucking fucks! They tried to hurt my girls."

"Will do, will do."

"Good, and hurry and we can stop them—"

"On my way! Driving very fast with an escort."

"Thanks! Love you!"

"Ya know, I'm gonna kick your cute little ass!"

He smiled when he said that.

"Yeah, well, I may deserve that, but we also need to find those missing kids, too. And we must now!"

"Yes, and we will."

"I know. I know we will." She felt great about that.

"Okay, stay safe and keep them all safe. Will be there in a minute."

"Will do."

She turned, looked out, and saw the flashing lights of the Trooper's cruiser off in the distance.

"Thanks," she said with a smile.

"Love you, too."

"Me, too."

"And by the way."

"What?"

"I'm proud of you."

She smiled.

Chapter 169 ~

AFTER LOOKING ONE MORE TIME into the little hole she made in the window, Melanie decided she had seen enough. She decided to get down and maybe try that door. She just had to take the risk of that man with the gun not being there. Bracing herself, she quickly jumped down. She felt her ankle twist.

"Damn!" she shrieked, looking over at her car. The girls and her sister were watching her intently. She climbed back over the fence. This time it was a lot easier for some reason. She went over to the car.

Dana had the window halfway open. The car was running now with the air conditioning on. Melanie felt the cold air come rushing out on her.

"Hey, you guys still okay? How are you girls?" she asked, peering into the back seat.

"We're fine, Aunt Melanie!" Kimberly answered.

"Yeah! Fine," Kelly repeated. "You're like a secret agent! So cool!"

Melanie smiled a weak smile and shook her head. These two girls have more balls than most men she knew, she thought.

"Fletcher is on his way with the police, like I had said," she mentioned, looking at Dana with a smile.

Dana smiled back. It was nice to see her a lot more relaxed.

"Are you sure those men aren't going to come out and get us or do something to us?" Dana asked. She still had the window only halfway down.

"Yes, I'm sure. They're bugging out, packing up

everything. I'm hoping the State-ie and Fletcher get here before they're totally gone."

"Oh, I guess we'll just have to wait here for them."

"Yes, we have to. Your brave little girls are prime witnesses, as so are you and me. But mostly them."

"Yes, I know. I'm so glad it all worked out."

Melanie knew that this part had worked out fine. But there still was a lot more to it all that her sister just didn't know, nor did she need to know. Melanie just nodded.

"I'll be right back," she said firmly.

"Now where are you going?"

"To check out that door."

"Ya know, you're not 007! That man had a gun and was going to shoot you!"

"I know. I just have to, okay?"

"Yeah, sure, Mel. Like I could stop you," Dana muttered.

Melanie turned back, giving her sister a dirty look. Then she smiled.

Dana smiled back, watching her go.

She scaled the fence again. The image of a female spider-woman flashed into her head. She smiled.

She climbed down easily. After glancing back at the car, she went over to the door. She crept up to it. About a foot away, she just listened. She could hear a lot of noise and rumblings. She figured they were still packing and moving.

She leaned forward a little. She touched the large rusty handle. As light as she could, she started to pull it down. It moved easily. As she was doing it, a loud bang inside froze her. Her heart jumped.

She waited with her hand on the handle, listening. Nothing. She heard nothing at all.

All of a sudden, a large motor started. She instantly knew what it was. She pulled the handle all the way down, opening the door, hoping no one had remained to stop or hurt her.

There was no one in the warehouse. Everything was gone. Amazing, she thought. This was planned in case of being found out. Very coldly efficient, she mused.

The big garage-type door was closed. She realized that was what the loud bang was. Immediately, she turned back outside and ran down the side of the building. As she turned the corner, she saw a big white truck speeding down the street.

"Damn it!" she exclaimed. She hadn't gotten the license. She made a mental note of the truck, its direction, and the men she'd seen. She especially remembered her would-be-killer and his menacing smile.

She picked up her shirt, ran back towards the car, and climbed the fence again. At the top of the fence, she saw another police cruiser in the far distance with its lights on. She was beginning to hear its siren, too. She then saw Fletcher's car behind it. Her heart leaped.

She literally jumped down from the top and her ankle bent even more. That was damned stupid, she thought.

"Oh, well, what the fuck," was all she could muster.

She tried to stand. The pain hurt a lot but she got up. The first Trooper suddenly came around the corner, screeching to a halt with all lights flashing. She stopped as he swung his door open, pulling his gun.

"No, no, it's not me!" she cried with her hands up, holding her shirt.

"Please stay where you are!"

Another gun barrel pointing at me, she thought! A giggle was beginning to creep up which she knew wouldn't help her case.

"They're getting away! A white truck!" she screamed as she pointed in the direction they fled. She was wildly trying to control the giggle.

His face froze. He was obviously calculating everything. After looking at the car with the girls in it, he turned back to her.

"What's your name?"

"Melanie, Melanie Sanders!"

"Who sent me?"

"Frankie! Frankie Oswald!"

He pointed the gun upward. "Which way?"

She pointed, quickly giving him a description. He told her to stay put and that more help was coming right away. He jumped back in his cruiser. He sped off right in front of her, nearly sideswiping her.

"Somebody is going to kill me today," she whispered with a nervous laugh. She then thought of Fletcher.

She waited, smiling.

Chapter 170 ~

IT FELT LIKE FOREVER TO FLETCHER in the car. He called Melanie. She guided them to where they were. He passed the escort so it would follow him. He waved to the officers and they nodded. He floored it past the littered streets and the old warehouses. He then made the final turn and saw his girl standing there next to her car. He could see people inside the car and assumed it was her sister and nieces.

Even at that point, he still couldn't believe Melanie had gotten them involved. Even with the danger of it all, he was still proud of her being able to at least get this far.

He also hoped Frankie was able to get Eddy's friends. He wondered how far it actually went. Just them? The priest? Would the girls have been sold into bondage? Or was it more widespread? Still there was no answer as to why the hell they were doing this. And where were the other children? His mind kept going back to child slavery. He knew it still had to exist. Where would they be now? How can they get them back?

He pulled up in front of her car. He came to a screaming halt, only a foot from it. Dana looked shocked as if he was going to smash into her. The police cruiser pulled past them and went behind
the car.

He looked out. He couldn't believe what he saw. Jumping out, Fletcher ran over to her and stopped dead in his tracks. He looked over at the two officers who had gotten out. They were also staring.

"Hi, honey," she said whimsically, leaning on one leg with a smile, as if he just came home from work.

She expected a reaction, but nothing. He just stared at her.

"What the hell is wrong with you? Do I get a hug?"

He couldn't say anything. He just held out his hand to her, pointing to her body.

Melanie looked down and just started bursting out laughing.

She must have looked so funny in her white, and now filthy, sweaty bra. Her full waist was showing, dirty with grease and sweat. Her jeans were torn from top to bottom with dried blood from the long scrape on her exposed leg. Wildly messed up hair was hanging in her face.

He started to smile, followed by snickers.

"Funny, huh?" she asked, posing with her hand on her hip.

"Hilarious, babe. Hilarious!"

He then walked up and gave her the hug of her life.

Chapter 171 ~

DANA WATCHED THEM AND SMILED. The girls laughed and clapped. They started gossiping to each other about him and her. Dana turned around, shushing them. Then after a second, they all started giggling. They froze when one of the officers came over and looked in.

"Just checking to see everyone is okay," he said through the window. He smiled. They did again, too.

"Yeah, you all okay?" Fletcher leaned over asking.

They all said yes. He gave the two girls a thumbs up. They both melted.

"Just hang out here with the Officer," he said. Fletcher then turned back to Melanie. She was putting her shirt back on.

"Kind of liked it the other way," he softly said.

"Later, big boy! Let's check this place out," she replied, tucking in her shirt.

"Did the State-ie—"

"He went after the truck."

"Truck?"

"They got away in a big white truck with everything!"

"Damn," he said. He motioned to the other officer to follow.

The three of them went to the fence. The big gate was chained. The officer went back to his patrol car, opened the trunk, and pulled out a long crow bar.

When he came back, Fletcher and Melanie moved aside. He slipped it in between the chain and the gate. He pulled so hard, Melanie gasped at how the lock broke right off.

He pulled the chain through and opened the gate. They walked up to the door. The officer pulled his gun. After everything else that had happened, it again scared Melanie.

Fletcher motioned him first. The officer pulled down the handle. He slowly opened the door. It creaked a little. He peered in. Then he opened it fully, cautiously entering.

After a moment, he came back out.

"All clear," he said. He motioned for them to enter. He followed behind them, still with his gun pulled and pointed upward. Melanie glanced behind her. She saw it and quickly followed Fletcher inside. The officer was right behind her.

When they got inside, they walked towards the middle of the vast warehouse. The booming echo of their footsteps on the metal flooring was deafening. It all seemed like a movie to Melanie.

There was a little sawdust scattered on the floor. Some of it looked stained with blood, but it could have been dye or paint, Melanie thought. She pointed it out to Fletcher, who nodded.

"We'll check that out. Nothing else is here," Fletcher quietly said against the echoing.

"Oh, there sure was stuff here, all kinds of equipment. But it was hard for me to see through that little hole in that smeared window up there."

"That's where you were?" Fletcher asked with a surprise sound in his voice as he looked up and pointed.

"Yep. That's why I look like this."

She smiled. He just shook his head and continued to look around.

There were other doors and rooms on the far end. The officer started slowly walking towards them.

"Hold a sec," Fletcher said to him. The officer stopped and waited. Fletcher walked over. He saw something. It was a small pile of trash in the corner where one of the room's walls jutted out.

He took out his pen, leaned down, and fished through it. Most of the trash appeared to be brown paper for packing or stuffing crates. He was about to get up when something in the little pile caught his eye. It wasn't brown but more tan in color.

"What's this?" he muttered. "Do you have a plastic glove?" he asked the officer.

"Yeah, be right back."

"Thanks."

Melanie leaned over his shoulder and looked. He could smell her sweat and perfume together. She didn't see his smile.

He had fished it out onto the floor. She thought she saw dried blood on it.

"Looks like a label for boxes or something," she said.

"Yeah, or a piece of some kind of poster or something. See there's a symbol or something—wait a sec," he whispered.

The officer came back, giving them both gloves. They put them on. Fletcher picked it up, holding it up to the light.

"Shit!" he said.

"Damn, is that what I think it is?" she whispered right next to him.

"Yes, I do believe so. Now what would they need this for, here?"

"I don't know. Let's go ask Eddy," she said and smiled.

He saw her smile. She was becoming the cat now in the game.

"Okay, then. Still could be Brandon, too," he replied. "Just want to check out these rooms."

He motioned to the officer, asking him to go first. The officer did. All were clear except for some more scattered shipping material. Did they transport the children out in crates? Fletcher envisioned them in the dank, dark hulls of ships. A chill went through him.

He made sure they got some of the colored sawdust, putting it into a crime scene plastic bag.

After they left, Fletcher called Frankie.

"Yeah, you got him? Cool!" he said. While still listening, he turned to Melanie so she could hear him. "Oh, good, they tracked down the other three and they are being held at the station. Let's go."

She nodded in approval.

"On our way," Fletcher said. He hung up and turned to the officers. "I need someone to stand guard here and someone to escort these ladies to the station."

He had pointed to Dana and the girls. Dana smiled. The officers were immediately on it.

The two girls couldn't stop gossiping about everything: that cute Fletcher, how their aunt seemed to melt with him, how big the policemen looked, what had happened since just a day before, what will happen next, and that they were actually going to a police station. They were important people now and maybe heroines. They couldn't wait to tell the kids in school. Especially what all the boys will think! The other girls will be so jealous! They hugged each other and started to laugh. Dana could only shake her head. She made a mental note to give Melanie shit for creating two little monsters for her to handle. She smiled at that, feeling enormous love for them all.

She saw Fletcher turn to Melanie.

"You, my little 007, you come with me," he playfully

pretended to sound like her superior.

"Yes, Master," she sexily said, slightly bowing.

"Good. We have more for you to do, but that will be later tonight."

Slightly cocking her head, she teasingly glared at him. A coy smile then crept on her face.

"We'll see who's the master then, my big slave boy."

He smacked her butt. She jumped with a playful yelp.

They embraced in a hard kiss.

Chapter 172 ~

FLETCHER TUCKED THE PIECE OF PAPER into a plastic bag. They quietly left the building and got in the car. Melanie looked back as they drove away. All of a sudden, tears streamed down her face.

Fletcher looked over, saw them and smiled. He didn't say a word. He knew it was all the dark feelings being released. He saw that some of it was happiness, too. His heart went out to her.

They drove at a moderate speed. He just didn't feel like rushing this time. That monster could just sit there and wait, and stew, and wonder, for all he cared.

He thought about how that little egotist put his love into harm's way, and her family, too. Fletcher thought of the horror of what Eddy had been doing. There was no doubt that they were going to ream him to find out where the other kids were. He wondered if this was all still part of some game. He wondered if Brandon was involved. He shut that out, for now.

They drove on and on up I-95 in silence. Both were content. Each was thinking the same thing after a while. It was the need to be together that night, with a glass of wine, lying together.

When they got back in town, they both perked up. They were preparing themselves for the confrontation with Eddy.

Fletcher broke the silence.

"You ready for this?" he asked tentatively.

"Are you kidding?"

"Just thought I'd ask," he said, facing forward with a smile.

She looked at him like he was ridiculous.

In her mind, it was important not only to get the information out of Eddy, but also to let him know how everything he had done was so horrid.

Just so horrid, she thought.

(Ancient Israel)

Chapter 173 ~

THE GRIN ON MARIUS' FAT FACE told Daiafar everything. Still, in all his dreams, he couldn't believe his eyes. He was frozen there on that bench with his mouth open in horror.

He watched as his pride and joy, his young son and daughter, were dragged naked into the room, chained like animals, ready for auction.

"How could this be? How could this be?" was all that ran through his mind. Absolute dread grew in his heart.

As if in a tunnel, the echoing of Marius' laughter, followed by all the men in the room, became more and more real in his ears. In a blinding moment, he was back from the dream. He started to rise to defend and release his beloved children.

As his hood fell back, they recognized their own father. Utter terror showed in their eyes as they thought their own father was going to bid on them, and not save them. They tried to hide their nudity.

He saw and recognized their thoughts. As he tried to speak, hot liquid filled his throat. In a drowning gurgle, he realized that his throat had just been cut. His eyes bulged in pain and shock. Marius had betrayed him. He knew that Caiaphas would succeed him as High Priest and must have plotted against him for both position
and profit.

Through all the laughter, he stumbled forward. He tried desperately to cup the blood gushing from the wide wound in his neck. He fell down right at his own children's bare dirty feet. He tried to look up at them and explain, but the sudden pain of the sword thrust in his back made all feeling escape. And in a final moment of life, he knew the betrayal and that nothing of his wealth and power could save him. He also knew the loves of his life were now young slaves like all the parent's children he had so profited from.

He died in the silence of total loss.

Chapter 174 ~

FLETCHER PARKED HIS CAR. They walked, once again, back to Mike's home. They immediately saw the officer out front. He saw them, letting them pass. Fletcher felt it strange now to be let in, without having to be formally buzzed in. He let Melanie lead the way. He followed.

Melanie felt the place had lost its charm. Passing through the foyer again, they saw an officer in front of the living room area. He ignored them as they walked past him into the room. She gasped. Morgue, she thought. It's an icy morgue in here, a funeral without flowers.

Eddy was serenely sitting in one of the plush chairs. His father was standing by his side. Danny was across the room, apparently standing guard. Frankie was sitting on another plush chair, directly facing Eddy. He turned when Fletcher and Melanie entered.

"Will someone tell me what all this shit is about?" Mike bellowed.

"Just hold a sec, Mike," Frankie calmly said, putting his hand up. At this point, they both knew he had the power of the mayor and Mike was temporarily powerless.

"Hey, guys," Frankie said.

"Hi," Melanie replied, walking over to him.

"Hey, man," Fletcher also replied and stood behind her, wondering where Rosalyn was.

"Melanie, you look like—" Frankie started.

"Oh, shush!" she interrupted him with a cute smile, which he warmly returned. He then turned back to Eddy. His smile disappeared.

A calm moment of silence fell. For an eerie minute, everyone appeared as frozen wax statues to Melanie. She felt like she was losing her breath, until she caught Eddy's eye. He grinned and winked at her. She sighed in disgust, turning her look from him.

Fletcher whispered in Frankie's ear about the truck. Frankie just shook his head. He turned and whispered back that the Trooper hadn't found it. The search was still on. But it didn't look promising without a license number.

"Well?" Mike pressed, getting impatient with them whispering.

Melanie looked at him. She then glared back at Eddy. She just couldn't hold herself back.

"Listen, you. Your psychotic buddies have made the mistake of telling my two nieces everything about kidnapping and killing those other children, and that they were going to do the same to them. They also were in the process of kidnapping them, which was witnessed by both me and my sister Dana."

"Crap, just crap," Mike said. "It's obviously a plot. They're all family. Of course, they would say that!"

"Hold, hold, please," Frankie firmly said.

"And," Fletcher said, pointing at Eddy, "we will confiscate and dissect your computers for evidence. *And*, we caught all your workers at your warehouse."

He left out that they got away and that there was nothing there except what he had in his pocket.

All of a sudden, Rosalyn appeared at the entrance to the room. She had no expression on her face. She wore a long, red silken dress. Fletcher noticed her slim figure showing through.

Melanie saw she was fixated on Eddy. As everyone turned, she started slowly to walk in, in complete silence, never taking her gaze off Eddy. Melanie turned back. Eddy was looking right at his mom. A slow crafty smile crept onto his face.

Rosalyn stopped. Her aura captured the room. Her eyes glassed over, as if dead. The moment froze again. Everyone just seemed to be waiting for something. Suddenly, she silently lifted her arm towards Eddy. She held her open palm out, as if for him to answer.

Melanie saw Eddy's small smile grow and grow. She turned back. Rosalyn was already out the entrance and disappeared. The strange spell was broken. It appeared everyone sighed. Except Eddy.

Mike shook his head. His normally slicked back hair was now disheveled from his hand running through it. Melanie could see his face beginning to get red.

"That doesn't tie my son to any of this," Mike continued, as if his wife had never been there. "It must be those other kids by themselves!" he heatedly proposed to all of them,

"What about this?" Fletcher said, pulling out the plastic bag. "I'm sure we'll find out that this red stuff is blood. And if you hold it up to the light from behind, see?"

He held it up. They all looked except Danny.

Mike's face changed. He looked back at Eddy. Eddy sat calmly, smiling at him. Melanie saw it was a smile of acknowledgement. Mike looked back at the paper.

"It's your fucking logo," Mike turned back to Eddy. "Can you explain this?"

"You mean my website logo," he smugly answered.

"I mean yours!"

"Well, it may be a little different," he replied with a big

smile. Fletcher noticed his flip tone. It began to dawn on him that Eddy was playing around, once again. He wanted them to figure it all out. Fletcher still wondered why Father Brandon had it, too.

"Look, it obviously says 'FHC' and your logo: Fellowship of Hope and Change," Fletcher interjected. "And the blood, too. See?"

"I see and I know."

"So, you admit it all?" Frankie pushed.

"You're not getting it, are you? Are you all blind?" Eddy said again, with that smile that so disturbed Melanie.

"What? What aren't we getting?" Mike started to yell.

"Calm down!" Frankie yelled back, halfway looking at him.

Silence fell. Mike looked so frayed; Melanie thought he might just fall over with a heart attack.

"Okay, Eddy, what is it?" Melanie finally calmly asked.

"Oh, you look nice, ya know," he whispered.

"Fuck you," she replied.

"Whoa! Okay. When? Now?" he quickly answered back, whimsically.

She just stared at his arrogant pudgy face and his perfect bowl haircut. She wanted so badly to give him the finger, but decided not to.

Fletcher looked at her to see if she was okay. She turned from Eddy, looking back at Fletcher

"Argh!" was all she could say.

Fletcher lightly shook his head. She saw something flicker in his eyes.

"Everybody, wait a sec," Fletcher said. A thought came to mind. He whispered something in Frankie's ear. Frankie looked at him and then nodded.

With a plastic glove on and placing a piece of paper under it, he started to brush away some of the dried blood. Melanie leaned over and whispered what he asked Frankie. He told her he wanted permission to do what he was doing to evidence. He wanted, just a little, to see what he had thought were words under the logo.

He didn't have to take much off.

Frankie saw his face distort and then Melanie's, too. Her hand went up to her mouth, covering it. Both their eyes were wide with shock. Their mouths were agape.

Eddy just sat back, smiling.

Frankie looked at him and then back at them.

"I'm gonna get sick," Melanie cried, running out of the room.

Chapter 175 ~

FRANKIE WASN'T ONE TO JUST WAIT to see, especially in the tense situation that confronted him. He saw Fletcher not moving at all. He was just staring at the paper. He issued an "ahem," but it didn't faze Fletcher. Finally, Frankie smacked Fletcher's leg from where he was sitting.

Fletcher said not a word, but turned the paper to Frankie so he could read it. Frankie started to cough violently.

Fletcher looked over at Eddy, who sat relaxed and still smiling.

"What the hell is it?" Mike demanded.

"No, no!" Frankie eventually said between coughs. "Wait. Sorry, Mike." He held up his hand at Mike.

"Huh? Wait for what?" It was obvious to Fletcher that he was at his wit's end and would soon blow.

Fletcher really didn't care. He continued to gaze at Eddy. Frankie looked up at him. He followed Fletcher's eyes to Eddy, who blankly stared back as if in deep thought. All of a sudden, his eyes glowed. The corners of his mouth curled into a grin that sent a shiver down Fletcher's spine.

"Ya know," Eddy quipped in the most taunting tone Fletcher had ever heard, "they're still there."

Frankie looked up at Fletcher, who hadn't taken his gaze off Eddy. Were some of those workers still there, Frankie thought, hiding somewhere for some reason. His thoughts were quickly cut off by Mike.

"Um, hello!" cried Mike again. "What the fuck is on that

paper! I demand to know and *now!*" He started walking towards Fletcher.

"Wait!" commanded Frankie. "You just stay right there."

Mike froze in step. He ran his hand through his hair again.

"Should we?" Frankie calmly asked up at Fletcher, who was still glaring at Eddy.

"Yes," Fletcher immediately replied, so there was no doubt about his intentions. He was still staring at Eddy. "I think we should go now."

"Yes," Frankie said, standing up. "Danny, cuff him," he ordered, pointing to Eddy, who pompously stood up, obediently like a schoolboy. That itself troubled Fletcher.

"Where are we going?" demanded Mike again. "This is my son!"

"Yes, it is and he is under arrest. Read him his rights and let's go," Frankie said with absolute authority. He completely ignored Mike.

"I'll let Gardner know. Let's go," Frankie said after Danny had Eddy.

"Thanks, honey, oooh! Nice and tight!" Eddy said to Danny, with a smile. Danny's expression also troubled Fletcher. He just felt there was so much more to all of this. Father Brandon came back into his mind.

They proceeded to follow Fletcher out. Mike stood there alone. He grunted and then followed.

Melanie was outside. It was apparent to Fletcher that she had vomited. She was completely pale, holding a tissue to her mouth while tears streamed down her cheeks. She looked at him with pleading eyes.

"You okay?" Fletcher stopped and asked.

"Yes, and I know where you're going, and I'm coming,

too."

Fletcher didn't say anything. He continued walking out of the building. At the door, he instinctively turned around. To his surprise, there was Rosalyn standing there, now in a summery, flowered mini-dress, with high heels that tied crisscrossed all the way up to her knees. She had a glass of red wine in her hands. It suddenly looked like blood to him. She slowly ran her hand over one of her sculptured, bare thighs. She was slightly leaning against the wall in the hall. He thought he saw a small smile or grin. She was still mesmerizing. He shook his head, trying to break the oncoming trance he felt. It was as if she had no care that her son was just arrested. Fletcher left without a word.

Outside, Frankie, Fletcher, Danny, and Eddy got into Frankie's undercover car. Melanie took Fletcher's keys and opened his car to follow. Mike stood there motionless, staring at Frankie.

"If you want to come, go with her," was all he said as he closed his door. He started his car and pulled away.

Melanie unlocked the doors. Mike paused a moment and then jumped in. She started the car, pulling away just as quickly.

It was apparent Mike wanted to know where they were going. She just kept shaking her head.

Finally, he spoke.

"Where?" he calmly and quietly asked.

She knew where they had to go. It sickened her. She didn't know what to say or if she actually wanted to say anything. She took a very long, deep breath, smelling the vomit still. It began to make her queasy again.

She glanced into the rearview mirror. She thought she saw someone she knew in the car behind her. The overwhelming feeling of nausea made her look down a moment to stop it. Then she remembered Mike.

He remained quiet and waited and hoped.

She decided to tell him.

"Back to the scene."

Chapter 176 ~

THE RIDE WAS QUIET AND QUICK. Fletcher listened as Frankie calmly talked into his radio, informing where he was going and that he had a suspect. And that they were returning to the scene.

When they got there, Fletcher had an urge to turn and look at Eddy's reaction. He did. Eddy gave him a smile that to Fletcher could only come from a deranged, cruel person. The boy who was a man, he thought.

He turned back. When Frankie parked, he got out, looking for Melanie. She was a good follower, he saw. She pulled up right behind them. Everyone got out.

Mike looked subdued. Melanie figured he knew better not to say or demand anything from Frankie anymore. It was now all police business.

"Bring him in," Frankie said to Danny, who obeyed.

They walked past the cop guarding the place. Melanie saw yellow police tape everywhere. She left her Phillies cap where she had tossed it earlier. She would get it later.

When they got inside, the echoes started again from their steps on the metal floor. It was even more eerie now to Melanie. She felt a chilling shiver run down her spine and all the hairs on the back of her neck stand up.

They stopped in the middle of the massive warehouse.

"Now, where!" Frankie demanded.

Eddy smiled a defiant leer back at him as he swung his hair back. It immediately fell forward back into place. He turned his back slightly towards Frankie in an obvious motion of intent.

Frankie looked at Fletcher who lightly shrugged.

"Okay, uncuff him," Frankie said.

Danny did, putting the cuffs back in his belt. He remained right next to Eddy.

"Hum dee dum," Eddy mused as he slowly and playfully walked around. He appeared almost like a teen Sherlock Holmes to Fletcher.

"Well?!" Frankie ordered.

Eddy smiled. Then unexpectedly, he sat down on the metal floor, crossing his legs. He said no more.

Frankie looked at Fletcher who shook his head. Fletcher looked at Melanie who also shook her head questioningly. He saw her close her eyes, as if figuring out a secret. She opened them and turned to Eddy. He was still sitting on the floor, but this time he smiled at her. He then cocked his head, in what appeared to Fletcher as acknowledgement.

Fletcher gave Melanie a look. She leaned over, whispering to him. He took a deep breath and started to walk around, stomping his feet. Frankie watched him and knew.

He soon stopped in one spot, doing it a couple more times to be sure. He looked over at everyone. His stomach tightened. Melanie just looked away.

He brushed away the sawdust. There was a tiny square cut in the floor, barely noticeable. He took out a car key and popped it off. Under it was a ring to pull on.

He took a deep breath, looking at Frankie who nodded.
He pulled hard. A rectangular piece of the metal floor opened. He looked, gasped, and threw the door fully open. It clanged heavily as it fell backwards. The echoing was deafening.

Frankie walked over and covered his mouth. He felt the

intense cold.

Inside, they saw children, all frozen, and in long rows with tags on them. To their unbelievable horror, some had missing limbs that looked like they were neatly and cleanly severed. Some had slices of their bodies and abdomens missing. In neat little frozen piles, they saw wrapped meat, like steak and chicken from a supermarket, with a small 'FHC' on each of them, and some with labels noting: "Prime Stock," "Freshness Guaranteed," and "Young and Tender."

Both Frankie and Fletcher immediately felt sick to their stomachs as sudden heaving rose in their throats. But they just couldn't look away.

Mike walked slowly over, peering in. He wheezed as he stared and then finally turned, throwing up violently. He forced himself to stop. In a quick motion, he grabbed the paper from Fletcher's hand, which Fletcher had taken out when they had walked in. He read it, turned completely pale, and threw up again. It read below the "FHC" logo:

"*Fine Human Cuisine*"

Eddy sat smiling.

All of a sudden, Melanie heard a thunderous bang. In through the door came a man, appearing wildly crazed, standing with his feet wide apart. In his hand, she saw a very large gleaming silver gun. In a motion faster than she could believe, he was upon them, legs spread in firing position. He pointed the gun, first at each of them and then at Eddy, sitting on the floor, still smiling and unmoving.

It was Stuart Martino.

Chapter 177 ~

THROUGH THE DOOR BEHIND HIM was the officer with his hand on his arm. She saw it was heavily bleeding. He was leaning against the wall in a lot of pain. His blood was falling to the metal floor. It was obvious that Stuart had shot him. He had gone completely mad. And now it looked like he was going to shoot Eddy.

"Martino! Stop! Stop! Don't do it!" cried Frankie. He immediately started to pull his gun.

Stuart instinctively spun around. He fired and hit Frankie in the chest right below his shoulder. Frankie wheeled for a moment and then fell to the hard metal floor. It was all happening so fast. Melanie saw he was still breathing.

Stuart turned back to Eddy with the gun.

"You bastard! You dirty fucking bastard! You killed my daughter! I want to know where my other daughter is! Then, I'm going to blow your fucking head off!"

Melanie saw he was completely consumed in a wild, uncontrolled frenzy. Martino's sanity was gone. And she knew he meant what he said. She couldn't breathe. Time seemed to stand still. All she could think was that he must have been constantly listening to some police radio or signal. All the time, he was waiting for this moment when the killer was found. He must have been that person she had recognized in the car behind her. He had secretly tailed her the whole time. She had no idea how else he could have gotten here so fast. But here he was. And now Frankie and an officer were shot and possibly dying, right there in front of her. Blood was everywhere.

Eddy just sat quietly watching the man and the gun pointed at him.

"WHERE'S MY DAUGHTER!!" Stuart bellowed. It echoed wildly.

"In the freezer," Eddy quietly said. "Where else would she be? We're not done cutting her slender, sweet pieces. Very tasty, I might add."

He said it so nonchalantly, it sounded normal to Melanie.

"What? Where?!" Stuart demanded, looking even more crazed. His hair was pointing in all directions. His eyes were so wide, Melanie thought they were going to burst.

"In the freezer, you dumb, dense idiot," Eddy replied, this time pointing to the opening in the floor.

Stuart inched over. He peered in. His eyes widened. His mouth opened. His eyes glazed. He looked like he was going to teeter over. Still reeling, he turned his huge gun back to Eddy. Melanie saw Fletcher edge towards him. Stuart pulled the hammer back. She heard it lock into place. The insane movie wouldn't stop.

Eddy smiled.

"Ya know something, Stu-ey baby," he started, "you did see your daughter before."

Stuart looked at him. He hesitated.

"Um, remember our little cocktail party you rudely crashed?" Eddy continued. Melanie saw glee in his eyes. She watched Stuart barely nod in his frozen state. "Well, she was just a wonder there! Everybody loved her! She was today's special! Remember? It was exquisite Muf-Shal-Hen, I must say! And served so wonderfully on those tiny little wooden sticks! Like stated in one of our little Elijah passages!" he smiled and turned, glancing at Fletcher. "Mmmm-mmmm-*mmmm*!" he finished, smacking his lips.

Melanie felt it coming up again. She saw Fletcher starting to cough. And then she realized that they all must have eaten it! Even Frankie, in his pain, grimaced. She knew he knew, too.

She turned to Stuart. She saw the recognition in his own eyes that he had eaten his own daughter, her cooked flesh. He looked like he was passing out and falling. Then he found an element of composure. He turned the gun back towards Eddy. She heard a loud blast. She saw him reeling backwards from being shot. Blood was pouring profusely out of his upper abdomen.

In the corner of her eye, she saw Danny with his gun pointing at Stuart. He had shot him. Martino started to fall. He pointed his gun at Eddy and fired. Another loud reverberating blast and Stuart fell hard to the floor.

Everything appeared in slow motion to her. She turned. She saw he had missed Eddy wildly. Then she saw blood gushing out of Danny's neck where Stuart had accidentally hit him. He immediately fell to the floor, in front of Eddy. Eddy never moved. He was just watching. He looked down at Danny and smiled.

"Hey, honey, sorry, not today lover. Looks like not ever anymore, either." He kissed his own fingers and placed them on Danny's cheek.

Melanie immediately knew who the leak was. She turned again. Fletcher was kneeling next to Frankie. His palms were pressing against his wound to stop the bleeding. It was Danny, after all. And in the horror of it all, she saw they were lovers. Danny was doing a boy. She started to feel faint.

Eddy looked up at her, smiling.

"Yes, we were lovers," he admitted with a tone like it really didn't matter, "but I must say, he was just okay. Small cock, ya know. Sorry, baby. I guess Uncle Brandon was of no help. You still loved a little boy's cock!" he said, with a sneer back to Danny. She saw he heard him. He then closed his eyes. She saw he died. Eddy, in a motion that was so fast, picked up Danny's gun, examining it like it was a toy.

"You son of a bitch!" she immediately heard. Mike had Stuart's gun. He walked right next to her, pointing it at Eddy. She didn't know what to do. Then she saw Eddy point Danny's gun at him, too. In a whirlwind, she watched father and son ready to kill each other.

"Ya know, father dear, you have become so boorish!" Eddy said, imitating a British accent. "Mother dear really thought it was time to eliminate you, but I kept telling her, no, wait, he's still useful."

Mike's face turned ashen. Eddy continued as they both pointed guns at each other.

"Ya see, she was just okay with your poor sex, and honey baby, you picked a good one! She especially likes to be licked all over. You just never attended to her. So, I guess it fell on me to pick up the man of the house duties!"

Melanie quickly looked back at Eddy. Her eyes widened as she realized he was having sex with his mother and she had wanted it, too. Melanie's mind started to haze over.

"Well, mom and I, well, we were wonderful mates. And I gotta tell ya, really good business partners! Using those cocktail parties to taste-test our products was just a *wonderful idea* of hers. No one had ever thought of it before, not even in France. And it was great hearing your guests' reviews!" he exclaimed, smacking his lips again. Suddenly, Eddy went into a ranting rampage.

"You stupid fucks think you're rich! We sell so much meat. They pay anything, anything for it! You have no idea what wealth is! Our clientele, our world-wide *billionaire clientele*," he said with great pleasure and pride as he lifted his chin up, "pay millions for quality young flesh, *and* prepared just to each one's liking! We are excellent at meeting all tastes. And ya know, all very well packaged and tasting just like chicken!" He giggled a strange gurgling sound.

"Trimmed and all. And to top it off, we supply exceptional recipes. We were almost done with our first cookbook, 'til fuck-heads here interrupted it all!" She saw his face lose its smile, turning grotesquely angry. For a moment she thought, strange for a boy.

"Oh, it was truly entertaining, especially killing the others and dropping them off at really bizarre places. Well, *that* was my awesome idea. Gotta take credit. It was such an amusing, little game. Did you have fun playing? I did! Got the wonderful idea from my love," as he petted Danny's bloodstained hair, "and his stupid uncle with his dumb secret 'FHC' order. Ya know, after learning about that Elijah's Wrath stuff, it was so easy to do the same thing, just so easy ... actually a blast! They all deserved it anyway!" He smiled, waving the gun at each of them, as if he was taking shots.

"Mommy kept telling me that it was too dangerous and to stop. But I knew you fucks would never figure it out. It doesn't matter. She always said the rich-fucks will always get what they want anyway. We just milked their gluttony and simply took it to the next step *and*," he giggled again, "*fed them their own children*. It was so easy, while they satisfied their insatiable lusts and pride." He wildly laughed, quickly pointing the gun right at

Fletcher. "And how many goddamn passages do you idiots need! It's goddamn *prophecy!*" he cried out. Now his young eyes were wide with rage.

He quickly pointed the gun back at his father. She saw Mike had become immobile. Eddy calmed a bit. He pointed his gun again at each person and back again at Mike. Everyone was frozen in complete disbelief at what he was saying. He continued his wild tirade and
gun-waving.

"It was soooo much fun, as we forced those rich kids to drink our special drink! Oh, they cried so much when the other just fell over dead. We laughed. And little did they know they were meant for something even more special. See, no ransoms because they were never coming back!" He laughed such another gurgling laugh that Melanie saw the monster he really was.

"Well, mommy dearest finally forced us to go back to *one at a time,* and to stop giving away good meat. How boring! So, actually, the last little boys were our last pair, until we saw your lovely girls! Yum! I just couldn't resist! But I guess my love, my lovely sexy mommy, was right. Good for her. And at least *she* got away. Don't you think this is such a wonderful biz she had started? And all around the world, too! Hope it keeps going well for her!" He looked down a second in contemplation. "Wasn't it all just so great! Fuck 'em all!" he finished, smiling again.

He stopped. He just sat there serenely, a little out of breath and snickering like a hyena.

Melanie was wide-eyed. She reeled at the wild animal he appeared to be all of a sudden. And then she thought, the mom! It was the quiet, timid mom Rosalyn who was the brains! Eddy was just playing her game. She looked at Fletcher. She immediately saw he realized, too. She then heard Mike.

"You dirty little horrid monster!" he blurted out with spit spewing from his mouth.

She saw he was about to pull the trigger. Something in her snapped. She moved in front of him. With all her force, she pushed up his outstretched arm. The gun went off, hitting the ceiling. She instantaneously heard another shot. She knew it was Eddy firing back. Then she felt the stun, and then the pain.

Chapter 178 ~

IN A THOUSAND MOVIES, SHE ALWAYS wondered what it was like to be shot. Looking into Mike's eyes, she realized he knew what had happened. The pain grew and grew inside. She looked down and saw blood coming out of the side of her body below her breast. She barely was able to pull back from him and then saw the blood on Mike's chest. His look was not about her, but about being shot himself with the bullet passing through her and into him.

She felt herself falling as she tried to hold herself up, clawing at him. She fell to the floor. Looking up she saw that Mike had placed his hand over his wound, pointed the gun back at Eddy, and fired. He then fell straight backwards, hitting the floor hard. She saw he wasn't moving.

Then she felt herself losing consciousness.

Chapter 179 ~

FLETCHER'S EYES WERE WIDE. For an instant, he forgot about Frankie. He watched with grief and horror as he saw his love being shot, while she tried to protect the criminal. As in slow motion, he watched her fall to the floor, bleeding from her back and front. She wasn't moving anymore.

It was as if time stopped. All seemed quiet and tranquil.

He stood up.

He then reached down and picked up Frankie's gun, which was lying next to his body. He looked into Frankie's eyes. In that brief moment, they were sitting at the bar, having a drink together, laughing. Frankie's eyes shone back at him. He saw a slight nod from him, but it wouldn't have mattered anyway.

He stood up again. He quietly walked over to Eddy, who had been pushed back from Mike's bullet. It had slammed into the center of his chest. The gun was a foot from his outstretched hand having been knocked out from the shocking blast. Blood was pouring out of his wound.

Fletcher stood over him calmly. Eddy's lips were trying to move.

"La ... Lair ... of the De ... Devil! You're a ... lucky guy ... ya know," he barely was able to say as blood ran from the side of his mouth. His eyes became glassy and then he smiled a cracked smile. "I bet she tastes ... real good, too!"

The world seemed to end. He turned, seeing Melanie motionless, lying face down in a pool of blood.

He turned back to Eddy, firing the whole clip into him.

"Enjoy the Lair of the Devil, you son-of-a-bitch," seethed from him.

The gun fell from his side. All of a sudden, everything came back to life. He quickly shook his head and went over to Melanie.

He turned first to Frankie who had now placed his own palm against his wound. It was still bleeding. Frankie nodded for him to go to Melanie, and that he was alright.

"I'll help," he heard, turning to see Josh suddenly next to Frankie. Fletcher realized that he must have been at the door the whole time, watching the grotesque scene. He smiled at Josh. Josh weakly smiled back and then turned to help Fletcher's friend.

Fletcher turned Melanie over carefully. He saw that the bullet's trajectory was upward, because Eddy was sitting, and had entered her left lower back and had exited right below her left breast. There was blood flowing everywhere. As he turned her onto both his bent legs, she coughed up blood. Her eyes opened and looked up at him. He saw her pain and then in her eyes, he saw her love.

"Lo ... lo ... love you," she said, between coughs of blood.

"Hold on, love. Hold on," he said and then tore his shirt, jamming it under her shirt on both sides. She coughed again and more blood came out. He was really scared.

"Yo ... you okay?" she muttered.

"Yes, yes, I'm fine, stop talking," he said leaning down. He kissed her cheek. She was able to make a small smile and her eyes closed.

Fletcher turned to the young face that had been watching him.

"Guess you'll finally get that headline you always wanted."

Chapter 180 ~

THE FIGURE STOOD IN THE MIDDLE of the dark room and sighed. It was over. It knew it. Maybe something could be salvaged. Maybe.

But the only real thing it could think was "escape." It took one last look around its black hideaway, its lovely dark solitude of quietness.

The broken chair still lay where it had been left. The cell phone remained broken, on the floor near the wall. Otherwise, the room was still void of anything else.

In one last moment of pride, the Figure leaned back its head and stared at the dark ceiling and whispered, "It was fun while it lasted, fun while it lasted, fun while it lasted."

Slowly leaning its head back down, the tresses fell against its face.

It took a long last sip of the dark red wine and staring at the glass, it threw it against the door.

Swinging its short summer dress in a last moment of defiance, Rosalyn threw open the door. The brilliant light poured in. She smiled and spit on the floor. Walking out into the corridor, she grabbed her bags and strolled out of the house, as if nothing had ever happened.

She knew she'd never come back.

Chapter 181 ~

HE LISTENED INTENTLY. The earpiece pressed firmly against the side of his head. He nodded and then smiled. He knew it was the best he was going to get. And for right now, until everything dissipates into the lost memories of the public and press, he was satisfied he had done his job.

As he listened, the thought and image of the Vatican became crystal clear in his mind's eye. A small grin formed on his mouth.

"And once again, if I may say, a most wonderful performance against a world of odds. You are to be congratulated, Lucifer."

His grin became a smile.

"Thank you, Gabriel. I will do as you say and be assured, there will be no other leaks or associations to us. Hopefully soon we can continue with our sacred order."

"Yes, without doubt, we will. I will expect a call in six months with a complete status."

"Yes, Gabriel."

"Again, we are all very grateful. Fine work."

"Thank you, Gabriel. Goodbye."

"Goodbye, Lucifer."

Chapter 182 ~

FRANKIE PULLED UP IN FRONT of Fletcher's home. Fletcher heard a double honk. He downed his coffee. He looked in the mirror one last time. He wanted to look good for this. After everything, it was the least he could do. He just couldn't shake his sadness.

"Coming," he muttered to himself.

He opened the screen door. He saw Frankie's car. He closed the door and went down the steps. He opened the passenger door and got in. Frankie's arm was still in a sling. Fletcher could tell it was still very painful.

"Hey," Frankie said.

"Hi," was all Fletcher said.

"You okay?"

"Yeah, just drive on."

"Sure." Frankie said as he put the car in gear.

Fletcher spoke again, still staring forward as they drove on.

"How are you, my friend?"

"I'm fine. Thanks. Hurts like hell, but honestly, I'm fine."

They drove on in silence. They got out in silence and walked up the steps through the doors.

"What room again?"

"Room 202," Fletcher answered, sounding annoyed again.

"Oh, yeah."

Taking the elevator to the second floor, they went down past the nurses' station. They turned one corner. Frankie once more was speaking out each room number they passed, which again annoyed Fletcher. But then he smiled.

They went into Room 202 after Frankie announced it more dramatically than all the others.

Fletcher walked in and smiled. She was slightly sitting up today. The bed was raised a little more than the day before. She smiled back. There was a tray of untouched food. She tried to push away. Fletcher ran over and did it for her.

"So, how's our hero?" Frankie asked with a wide smile.

Melanie made a playful dirty look. She rebuffed him in a quiet and still weak tone.

"Heroine," she corrected him. They all laughed.

She looked at Fletcher, smiling. He leaned over and kissed her lips. She attempted to kiss back but winced in pain from trying to lean upward.

"So?" she finally asked.

They looked at each other. Fletcher nodded to Frankie.

"Well, we finally caught her. She had attempted to transfer what amounted to about five hundred million dollars. The Feds and Interpol had set up a continuous surveillance web. She finally fell right into it. She was brilliant though and had waited patiently."

"She then tried to leave the country. She almost got away. We actually had to stop the plane on the runway, believe it or not. And then, for passenger safety, we went to the plane on the runway, not waiting for it to return. Who knows what she would have done and—"

Fletcher picked it up from there.

"When we got to the plane, we looked up. There she was in one of the oval windows in First Class, looking down at us. She had exactly the same smug smile that Eddy had at the warehouse."

Frankie nodded and finished.

"We took her away. She didn't resist. Unbelievable she was smiling the whole time. It seems like this is very, very big business, too, as horrid as it is. The feds found hundreds of leads now that it has been uncovered. They found that truck, too. So, they got her and with Interpol, are tracking down many other cells. The ultra affluent of the world, the ones beyond rich, the untouchables, seem to enjoy this as a rare and very expensive delicacy. The demand is unbelievable. They'll pay anything. And they pay for the intense secrecy, too. Yes, for actual human flesh, especially young flesh."

Melanie cringed. She nodded for him to continue.

"Well, our beauty Rosalyn, we found out had actually been a high-priced hooker as a very young girl. This was well before marrying Mike. He knew she was doing some kind of business. He was glad she kept herself busy with all his late nights. She is so much younger than he is and he always said she got bored easily."

"He thought the whole thing was some kind of specialty meats from around the world. And since she was an independent thinker, he encouraged the business, never knowing what it really was. That's why he protected her and Eddy all the time. He felt bad for her."

"She on the other hand, outside of the perversion of making love to her own son, despised the rich and everything about them. They had been her clientele as a high-priced call-girl since she was young. She learned the meat-trade from a wealthy foreign friend who adored her. Then she went to studying. She learned a lot about the global appetite for young *meat* and the price being paid."

"Guess where else she got information from? Yep, the

friggin' Internet. There are secret sites with hidden, encrypted messages. Then she realized how much money she could make. She gave up whoring for what to her was a more elite profession. After making millions, with the world demand growing more and more, she decided to marry Mike to monitor the police locally. It was all planned."

"Her *wonderful* son loved her idea of doing taste-tests with the parents they got the meat from. They just fed it back to them. This was the ultimate revenge she was looking for. She loved doing it, just loved it: psychological revenge while making millions from it. Her clients also said that her selections were most exquisite. Her beauty added to her ability to become one of the world's richest meat-traders."

"She had stayed away from the local scene until she married Mike. She felt she needed inside protection this close to home. Even though she became crazy from her young years of being used as a prostitute, she had an absolutely brilliant mind to incorporate revenge and her new business."

"It also worked for Eddy because we believe he had many gripes with school friends. He was constantly teased. He wanted revenge, too. But most of their product, if I may, came from around the country, using their website and regional partners. They needed to recruit certain others to help them, like those foreigners you saw. Eddy added in crazed, mentally ill kids like Stacy, Marcy, and Stanley to help him."

"Oh, by the way, it wasn't just kids. They had a whole line of adult meats, too. You could get, and pay for anything, from age ten through age forty. Of course, the younger, the more expensive. And don't get sick about this, but the part of the body also mattered. Disgusting, but unbelievably profitable. I'm beginning to think now why there are so many missing people on milk cartons and all. These people were never coming back and would never, ever be found. Ever."

Melanie just stared at him. It had been a while now. They had held back telling her everything until she was strong enough for the doctors to allow it. Frankie continued.

"And the killings were solely Eddy's idea, as he admitted. Outside of intense revenge, part of it was to fool his father and the police with his game. He must have gotten bored after making and having so much money. It was the game more than the money with him. Proving his superior intelligence and feeding his ego led him to use prophecy. He wanted to see if anyone was as smart as he. When the heat got hot, mommy shut him down."

"And, as he said, he had gotten the idea from Father Brandon, through Danny. He had asked Danny to find out from his uncle anything from the Bible that dealt with missing children. That's why our Father was so hesitant to disclose anything to us. He realized the connection he had inadvertently supplied from his knowledge of Elijah's Wrath."

"To be sacrilegious, Eddy created his own 'FHC,' mimicking 'The Order of Faith, Hope, and Charity.' It also delighted him to have made up something that was the same letters as Brandon's and his mom's sick trademark. He manipulated it to his designs to feed his mother's business needs, and at the same time for his own personal revenge. He figured he'd never get caught because we would just think it was the priests anyway, as his mom kept pressing you with, Fletch."

"And his placement of the passages we think an expression of complete violation of the victims. Eddy was just so filled with hate. He followed right in his mother's footsteps against the wealthy."

"And if you," he nodded at Melanie, "hadn't done your own little sting right at that time, we probably never would have caught them. Since as he admitted, they were stopping the random killings and all the game clues—until your nieces."

Melanie weakly smiled, shaking her head.

"And Mike?" she asked, tentatively.

"Sorry," Fletcher replied, "dead. So's Stuart and Danny, and of course, Eddy." He glanced at Frankie who nodded, knowing what Fletcher had done.

"So, what was—"

"Danny's real role?" Fletcher interrupted her. Frankie continued.

"It appears that outside of being gay, which we knew, he had befriended Eddy. Or should I say the other way around. And Danny found he had an appetite for young boys, which Eddy obviously took advantage of and promoted for his own purposes, since he had no morals anyway. A la, our leak," he said with completeness in his voice.

"And I apologized to Father Brandon, even though I didn't want to," Fletcher noted with a small smile, "because his only role was actually helping his nephew deal with what he was doing, which was doing young boys. Danny had a huge guilt complex about it, but couldn't stop. Our Father was there to hear his confessions, which Danny kept doing even though he didn't stop with Eddy. Our secretive Father was just trying to get Danny to stop and distance himself from Eddy's game."

"Wow," was all Melanie could quietly muster. "What about the slavery and—"

"Our Father Brandon is free right now," answered Frankie, with a distasteful look, "but an FBI investigation is starting as we speak and maybe they'll find something."

"Maybe?" she whispered.

"Yeah, maybe," Fletcher continued, "because from what the FBI knows about their prior dealings with the Vatican, the Church is very good at covering up and waiting until things calm down."

"And the final puzzle piece," Fletcher finished, "was the 'CHF' discussion groups Danny belonged to. We believe Eddy created it for Danny, getting tired of hearing his guilt. Our little friend Josh, when he originally came into town, joined every social club and discussion group he could find on the Internet. He said he was told to do this by one of his professors as a great way to learn inside scoops and stories. Well, he met Danny and used Danny for his own gathering of police information. Pretty shrewd kid."

"And of course, we still can't find our friend Merrie. We think he's hiding from all the publicity and is scared to death. Hopefully, he's scared enough to never touch a child again."

Melanie just shook her head at the thought.

"Tom, is fine, too," Frankie followed.

Melanie looked at him questioningly.

"Oh, sorry, the cop shot by Stuart. He'll be fine. And, of course, thanks for asking, I'm fine, too!"

He made a face at her. She started to laugh and then cringed in pain. He heard her mutter, "You dick!" They all laughed.

"Well, I gotta go. I'll be back for ya," Frankie started to say.

"Hold a sec, I'll go with you. She needs to rest," Fletcher said.

"By the way," Frankie cockily said, pointing his finger at Fletcher.

"Um, yes?" Fletcher replied with the same tone.

"Told you the mom was wicked!"

Fletcher remembered that's what Frankie had said at the cocktail party, a party he keeps trying to forget.

"Um, told *you* she was a whore!"

"You did say that at that party, didn't you? And you——"

Fletcher gave him a look not to continue.

They both chuckled, until Melanie grunted at her two playful boys. She knew about the relationship and didn't want Fletcher to know she knew. It could come in handy later, she thought with a smile.

"I'll be outside, okay?" Frankie said.

"Yep, thanks," Fletcher smiled.

"Oh, wait, I almost forgot," Frankie turned back. He pulled out the folded *Times* from behind his sling. With a flip of his free hand, he proudly opened the front-page to her. He saw her smile the smile that always melted him. She silently mouthed the headline:

"CHILDREN MURDER CASE SOLVED BY
THE TRIUMVIRATE OF CRIME SOLVING"

She smiled at the picture of the three of them below the heading. She smiled wider at the writer of the article, Josh Stein. Frankie leaned over and kissed her on the cheek.

"You did great, our wonderful heroine," he softly whispered.

She whispered something back, causing a bigger smile on Frankie's face. He then left. Melanie turned to Fletcher.

"Well?" he asked.

A weak but big grin crept onto her face.

"Well?" he pressed again with his own growing smile.

"I told him we are the Triumvirate and I loved him and will always be his girlfriend forever."

He heard the pride in her voice. He knew it was her beautiful way with his dear friend. He also knew that it was her original naiveté, coupled with her incredible intelligence and independence, which had helped solve this one. He loved her for it.

"Yes, I guess we are, aren't we. Like the three musketeers, eh?" he replied in a joking tone.

Giving him a cute glance, she paused and then said with a small corner-of-the-mouth grin, "Ya know, I did figure it out."

"I know you did," he said, still smiling.

"No, not that. I figured out Muf-Shal-Hen," she grinned wider. She pulled out the little recipe card, showing it to him. She then crossed her arms with an air of superiority. She winced at the pain. Fletcher rolled his eyes. He then opened his hand at her indicating to proceed.

"Rearranging the letters, it spells 'Human Flesh!'"

"Oh, my god! You *definitely* got too much time on your hands, my little chef. Just don't get any ideas with those recipes!"

She so wanted to smack him but just stuck her tongue out, like a little girl.

Coyly imitating Frankie's tone, she cocked her head in defiance. "Well, had you, Mr. Ein-fucking-stein, figured it out, you never would have eaten it."

"Um, can we forget that? Like forever!"

"Sure hon, anything for you," she sweetly whispered.

"Glad to have you back, my love," he said bowing deep, never taking his eyes off of her. She remembered he had done this at the church.

"Glad to be back," she replied weakly, dipping her head a little. And then, slowly glancing up, her eyes met his. They said everything. Frankie had been right all along.

They gazed at each other for a long time. He felt his heart swell up from the emotion and tears he saw in her eyes.

"I so love you, Mel."

"I love you … always," she slowly replied. Her blue eyes sparkled.

He leaned down and placing the softest kiss on her lips, the world began again for them.

THE END